WICKED LOVE

THE SINGLE DAD PLAYBOOK
BOOK 4

WILLOW ASTER

All rights reserved.
No part of this book may be reproduced in any form or by any electronic or mechanical means, including information storage and retrieval systems, without written permission from the author, except for the use of brief quotations in a book review.

Willow Aster
www.willowaster.com

Copyright © 2025 by Willow Aster
ISBN-13: 978-1-964527-04-8

Cover by Emily Wittig Designs
Photo: Aisha Lee
Map by Kess Fennell
Editing by Christine Estevez

Silver Hills

- The Fairy Hut
- Luminary Coffeehouse
- Rose & Thorn
- Jupiter Lane
- Aurora's
- Twinkle Tales
- Wiggles & Whimsy
- Pixie Pop-Up Market
- The Enchanted Florist
- Starlight Cafe
- Serendipity
- Pet Galaxy

NOTE TO READERS

A list of content warnings are on the next page, so skip that page if you'd rather not see them.

Hi! I'm glad you're here. Thanks for picking up this book.

If you're new to my books or to this series, I'm especially excited for you to meet the characters in *thi*s book. Becca, the hero's little girl, has Down Syndrome, and because the level of function across all aspects of life for individuals with Down Syndrome is varied, there are many ways I could have portrayed her, especially regarding her level of communication. Please know that I tried to give the utmost care to research properly to make the story as authentic as possible. Beyond the friends in my life who have Down Syndrome, I also had a sensitivity reader who is an occupational therapist, and any mistakes I made are mine and not theirs.

And, last but not least, it is the honor of my lifetime that Lily D. Moore agreed to read the part of Becca in the audiobook. Thank you so very much, Lily!

XO,
 Willow

CONTENT WARNINGS

The content warnings for *Wicked Love* are sexual content, profanity, and death of a parent.

CHAPTER ONE

OUR STORY

BOWIE

I follow my daughter into the house, feeling like I'm letting her down with each step. She's tearing through the kitchen with her new present in her hands, rushing to showcase it in her bedroom.

"Look, Dad," she calls.

I follow her up the stairs, stopping when I reach her room. She turns to see if I'm there and when she beams up at me, I smile back and move closer to her.

"Look, Daddy, I put it with my favorites," Becca says.

She places the "present"—a picture frame of a woman and a young girl next to the others. This one has a woman with long blonde hair, and the young girl's hair is like Becca's, light brown. We can only see them from the back. They're walking by a lake with lots of fall leaves on the ground. All the other pictures have young girls with light brown hair, but the women's looks vary. The common thread is that all the pictures look like a loving mom with her daughter.

I sit on the oversized chair where we read books together, and she tucks her head in the crook of my arm as she shows me her framed pictures. There are pictures of us together and one of Becca with my parents, but the dozen or so frames of moms and daughters are her "collection," and she refuses to replace the stock photos.

"Where is my mom?" she asks quietly, almost to herself.

"I don't know, sweetheart."

It kills me every time she asks, which is often. Once her mom, Adriane, decided to leave, she made a clean break. I don't get check-in calls or updates on what she's doing with her life, she just disappeared.

She taps the picture. "This looks like Poppy and me."

I press the bridge of my nose between my fingers. Ever since Becca met Poppy Keane at our local bookstore, Twinkle Tales, a couple weeks ago, she hasn't stopped talking about her. Poppy didn't help matters by suggesting Becca come to Briar Hill where she works as an adaptive recreation coach. Since Becca has Down Syndrome, I'm already familiar with Briar Hill. They have an excellent reputation for all they do for kids with disabilities, but I'm hesitant to take my daughter, even knowing she'd love the activities they offer. Because of Poppy Keane.

Even though it's fairly typical of kids with Down Syndrome to accept and be friendly with new people, it still concerns me how quickly she attached to Poppy.

The frame with a lookalike Poppy and Becca is just another case in point.

She looks up at me. "We see Poppy again?"

I'm saved by my phone buzzing. I wave it. "This is Weston. I need to answer this. Can you be ready to leave for his house in five minutes?"

"Set the timer!" She hurries to hand me the timer we keep in her room, and I set it for five minutes. I hand it back to her as I answer the phone.

"Hey," I say to Weston, giving Becca a thumbs up. "Everything okay?"

"Will you guys be hungry? We haven't eaten yet, so I was going to order some takeout."

"Becca and I ate at Starlight Cafe just a little while ago, but go ahead. We can come later if you want."

"No, come on over. We'll just do leftovers for us then since you've already eaten."

"Yeah, man, we're good. We'll be over there shortly."

I hang up and Becca holds up the timer.

"It's time," she says. "Time to see my pretty dress again."

It's wedding season for my best friends, who also happen to be my teammates.

"Tell me our story…about our framily," Becca says on the drive over.

She loves our friends with a passion and loves to hear me talk about everyone. We call them framily around our house. I'm fortunate to have friends who have welcomed us into their lives. We're closer to them than our biological relatives.

It's both sweet and heartbreaking that my girl craves family more than anything.

I take a deep breath, about to use most of my words for the day. I'm the quiet one in our friend group and everywhere else, but there's very little quiet time when Becca and I are together. She likes to discuss all the things.

"Okay, here's the rundown," I begin, same as I always do. "As you know…" I glance back at her and she's looking at me with her bright eyes. She has the sweetest smile. "I'm a linebacker for the Colorado Mustangs, and Weston Shaw is our quarterback."

"I love Weston, and Sadie is the *best*," she says.

"Yes, they're great. Weston and Sadie are getting married in a couple of weeks, and Caleb is two years old and adorable."

"Yes, he is," she says emphatically.

"Our tight end, Rhodes Archer, just got married a couple of days ago and is on his honeymoon right now."

"Oh, I love Rhodes! And Elle is the *best*."

I chuckle. "I think you could tell our story better than I could. His son Levi is four and also one of the cutest kids I've ever seen."

"Levi is cute," she agrees. "He has curly hair. He opens doors for me."

"Levi's a little gentleman, isn't he? And even Henley Ward, our wide receiver—well, *former* wide receiver now, after a serious ACL injury—is engaged now."

"I sad Henley's hurt," she says. "I love him and Tru is the *best*."

I laugh again. She thinks all the women are the best. She's not wrong; they are incredible people.

"Henley and his ex-wife Bree have three daughters, Cassidy, Audrey, and Gracie, that we love dearly."

"So dearly," she adds.

If I don't say that every time, she's sure to add it.

"They're fourteen, ten, and seven," I say.

"I nine soon," she says.

The girls dote on Becca, and Caleb and Levi adore her too. She's treated like a princess every time she enters the room and I fucking love it.

"That's right. All of you are growing up too fast."

"And you bonded…" she starts then pauses for me to continue.

"The guys and I originally bonded over football and the fact that we were all dads raising our kids by ourselves, but we can't exactly call ourselves the *Single* Dad Players anymore now that some of the guys are getting married."

"Dad, you not married," she says, her lips puckering out.

"No, I'm not. We meet on the regular to talk about all things kids, life, football…and lately, a helluva lot about the women in *their* lives." I emphasize *their* because I need her to understand that there will not be a woman in my life.

Her smile is long gone now, and I focus on the road in front of me to avoid her scowl.

"You need a woman to talk about a helluva lot…on the reg'lar."

I clear my throat and charge forward, trying both not to laugh and to distract her from the topic of women.

"We have a book that we write in all the time, The Single Dad Playbook, where we exchange advice and stories when we're not together in person."

"And Penn too!" she says.

"I haven't forgotten Penn Hudson, our running back. He isn't a dad, but even he has developed a fatherly bond with Sam, a kid that he mentors. It started through a tutoring program, but Sam has become like family to all of us by now, right?"

"Right. Sam is eleven and so pretty," she breathes. "But Penn is the prettiest."

I roll my eyes and she sees it in the rearview mirror. Her loud laugh fills the car.

"Neither one of them are *that* pretty," I grumble.

"You call Penn pretty boy, Dad!" she argues.

"Oh yeah, that's right."

She leans back in her seat, satisfied.

Besides me, Penn is the only other single one at this point.

He sees a lot more action than I do though.

I'll be living and dying on the single dad hill.

"You're pretty too, Dad," she adds.

"Thanks, Tater Tot."

She giggles. She loves it when I call her that.

From the backseat, I hear, "I love you, Dad."

"I love you too, Tater Tot."

Damn near melts my heart every time, and she says Dad a lot, so basically, I'm mush whenever my daughter's around. Have been since day one.

She's the only one capable of eliciting that in me. She proves I *am* human after all, I guess.

"I call you Daddy too," she says.

"Yes, my literal girl, and I love when you call me Daddy just as much."

When we pull into Weston's driveway, Becca claps when she sees Henley and Penn's cars.

"Our friends are here," she says happily. "Look, Daddy!"

I smile over at her. "Yep. And you, Cassidy, Audrey, and Gracie are going to be the prettiest flower girls who ever lived."

"We are pretty a lot," she says. "Levi and Caleb too."

I know she's thinking about Rhodes' and Elle's wedding now.

"You were *beautiful*, but you always are. I wasn't in any weddings as a kid. Do you like being in all these weddings?" I ask.

"I like it lots." Her lisp is extra pronounced when she's excited and she's practically bouncing in her seat. "Sadie says we blow bubbles, but we wait until they say *I do*." She holds out her hands and bounces them with *I do*.

"That'll be fun."

We get out and walk to the door. I let Becca ring the doorbell.

Henley opens the door, holding Caleb. Caleb loves all of us, but "Unca Hen" is his favorite.

"Unca Bowie!" Caleb says happily.

I hold my fist up and he bumps it with his.

"Hey, you two, how's it going?" Henley asks.

"Great," Becca says. "Right, Dad?"

"Right." I nod, smiling at her when she looks back at me.

"Excellent." Henley grins and tilts his head to the side. "The girls just went into the family room, Becca. They're waiting on you to try on the dresses."

"I try on my dress now," she says, rushing off to the family room. She's moving so fast, she nearly collides with Weston. "Oh! Sorry, Weston! I want to be a princess."

He laughs and holds his hands out toward the family room. "Right this way, Princess Becca."

He walks with her the rest of the way, and Penn sticks his head out of the living room as Henley and I walk back with Caleb.

"There you are. Dude, preparing you now. Sadie's not giving up on this date business. Have you found a date for the wedding yet?" Penn puts his hand on my shoulder and squeezes.

"Not happening," I say.

Weston walks in then. "What's not happening?" he asks.

"A date for your wedding," I say.

"Oh man." He laughs. "Sadie really thinks you need to bring a date."

"Even if it wouldn't be fun for me?" I ask.

He grins. "She seems to think we could make it fun."

"I don't know where she's getting her information," I grumble. "I don't have a date and I don't plan on finding one between now and then. Your wedding is just around the corner."

"Man, it can't come soon enough for me," he says, grinning. "I can't wait to marry that woman."

"I can't wait for you to marry her either…so you can get off our backs about a date," Penn says. "Women get weird around weddings. It's more of a time to get acquainted with a stranger in a hidden nook in the church rather than be all formal and make things seem more serious than they are..."

"Gross," Henley says, laughing.

"I'm kidding. I'm not that bad," Penn says. "Unless she's really beautiful…"

I roll my eyes.

When the girls come out later, they're hyper from getting the final measurements on their dresses. As they're making popcorn, Sadie corners me.

"So…" she starts.

I shake my head.

She pouts. "But I want you to have someone to dance with."

"I'll dance with whoever wants to dance…but I don't

want to have to try to make awkward conversation during dinner. I want to actually enjoy your wedding."

Her face breaks out into a smile. "As long as you're dancing, I'm good." She hugs me and then goes off to help the girls.

Weston smirks at me and I swipe my hand down my face.

"She's really hard to say no to," I admit.

"Don't I know it." He looks at Sadie with such reverent love in his eyes, it makes my heart ache.

I was in love once.

I don't intend on making that mistake again.

CHAPTER TWO

I'D READ THAT

POPPY

I walk into The Fairy Hut thinking I'll get a quick drink and an appetizer. I normally don't dine alone, but in Silver Hills, it doesn't feel as daunting as it did in Denver. I've lived here for several months, but I'm only just now getting settled. My job is between here and Denver, and moving to the Silver Hills side of work has been a breath of fresh air. I spent a lot of time with my parents over the holidays, trying to talk them into making the move to Silver Hills too. I love this little town so much.

I hear laughter and then my name being called and turn to see Elle Benton…actually it's Archer now, I think. And in the book world, she's known as Zoey Archer. She's a new author that I love. The funny thing is that I met her at the adorable bookstore, Twinkle Tales, before I knew she was an author, and then I saw her at a signing there a month later, where we hit it off even more.

"Poppy. Hi. Come join us." She waves me over.

When I get closer, I see that Elle's with a table full of women that I also met at Twinkle Tales and really liked—Sadie, Tru, and the owner, Calista. They look like they've been here for a while. The table is full of food and the waiter brings them another round of drinks. I walk to the table somewhat shyly but excited to see all of them. The two times I've talked to them, they all seemed like great humans.

"Hey, how's everyone doing?" I say, when I reach the table.

"We're *great*," Sadie says ecstatically. "How are you?"

"I'm great too." I laugh at how dramatically Sadie puts her hands on her chest with wide eyes when I say that I'm great.

"Yep, I've had some *dranks*," she says, laughing.

"We all have," Calista says, her smile wide.

"Here, pull up a chair," Elle says.

They make room for me and I sit at the round table between Elle and Tru.

"We were just talking about book ideas for Zoey," Tru says, winking at me. "She's shooting us down for a male/male romance based on Penn and Bowie."

My eyes widen at the mention of Bowie. I can't fight back a laugh.

"Well, I would certainly read that," I say.

"So would I!" Elle says, laughing. "I'm just getting my feet wet with writing romance and creating a brand and all that. I'm not sure I'm capable of a MM yet…not that I don't love reading it." She takes a drink and sets it down carefully when she starts laughing again. "They *have* been talking about what I would write if I based a romance on them. Oh my God." She can't stop laughing with the rest of us. "I wonder what they'd think if I put them together. Oh, girls, this might be too good to resist."

We all crack up. The waiter comes by to get my drink order and as soon as he leaves, Sadie talks about how we could throw a party celebrating their love.

"It's too good," Tru says. "Please do it, Elle. If you don't do it, someone has to. There's got to be fan fiction somewhere out there with this already. Two hotties from the Mustangs who can't get enough of each other?" She snorts and nearly chokes on her mocktail.

"What is his story anyway?" I ask. "I mean, what is *their* story?"

"Ah," Elle looks at me knowingly, "I can guess which one *you're* more interested in based on the little interaction I saw at the signing."

My cheeks heat.

"Bowie is such a good guy," she continues. "One of the best people I know. Very stoic, very serious." Her voice dips low when she says *stoic* and *serious*. "But when it comes to his daughter Becca, he lights up like the morning sun. He would do *anything* for that girl or his friends. And we happen to be the happy recipients of that since he loves our men." Elle smiles warmly at me. "He needs a good woman."

My body feels feverish just thinking about Bowie Fox. That man has been hard to get out of my head after we talked at Twinkle Tales. It wasn't as if he said anything profound or that he showed any interest in me whatsoever; in fact, he was possibly annoyed by my mere presence. But just being near the guy made me tongue-tied. He's entirely too good-looking for me to maintain any sense. He looks like a Viking god, stern and towering, with broad shoulders and chin-length blond hair that waves away from his face. It's the kind of hair you just want to get lost in.

I sigh and look around, hoping these women can't tell where my thoughts have derailed.

Unlike her dad, Bowie's daughter, Becca, was not annoyed by me at all. We hit it off in a big way, with her inviting me over to dinner and everything. She's a dreamy little girl. Bowie shut that down fast. I'd really hoped he would bring her to Briar Hill though, so I could spend more time with her. In just the little time I was around her, I could tell she'd love to be part of all the activities we do over there.

"Did you guys know there's a social media account called BHOTD?" Sadie looks around at each of us. When we shake our heads, she says, "It stands for Bowie's Hair of the Day."

That makes us laugh all over again. I'm laughing just as hard and I'm only having a mocktail. The name and description got me—Love Potion #1. It's delicious—pink, with raspberries and watermelon. But it's the company of these women and talking about Bowie Fox that has me feeling almost giddy.

"He does have amazing hair," I say quietly. And the prettiest brown eyes I've ever seen…with full, perfect lips…

"Yes, he does," Calista interrupts my spiral into all things Bowie. "All those men are fine as hell. Javi better be glad I met him first!"

I feel eyes on me and turn to see Sadie watching me thoughtfully. She grins, tapping her chin.

"You never came to one of our girl nights. We invited you, remember? After meeting you at Twinkle Tales."

"I know! I'm sorry. I really wanted to. Work was crazy there for a while and then the holidays got so hectic."

"It's okay. You'll have to come to the next one. We got distracted too between holidays and the end of the season. And Elle just got married."

"You did? That's awesome. Congratulations."

"Thank you." Elle smiles. "We put it together quickly, but we've been close forever, so we thought, why wait?"

"I love that."

"It was the prettiest wedding," Sadie says. "And we'll get together more often now that the season is over. In the meantime, you should come to my wedding…"

"What?" I say, shock lacing my voice.

"Yes, I'd love to have you! I can just tell you're good people. There will be plenty of food and it's going to be such a fun night…lots of dancing." She clasps her hands together. "Please, say yes. I would love to have you there."

"That's amazing. So thoughtful of you!"

"Oh, you'll be perfect," she says. "You'll fit right in with everyone. It's not a big affair. Don't get me wrong…with the team and all their plus ones, it'll be plenty of people, but still feel intimate." She leans in and looks so pretty, her cheeks rosy and her eyes lit up with excitement.

I'm the only one with blonde hair in this group. They're all gorgeous and each has a distinct look and various eye colors, but they all have long, dark hair. Calista has dreadlocks right now, so it looks even longer than the other times I've seen her. They're dressed really well too…makes me wish I'd stopped by the house to change out of the athletic wear I live in at work. I'll have to get a new dress if I plan on going to this wedding. I can't believe she's inviting me to her wedding! I'm a huge Mustangs fan and I think I'm in shock that these women are so welcoming.

"We're going to be taking over the Landmark Mountain Ski Lodge & Resort and we'd love to have you. It's coming up soon, February 28th."

"I'll be there," I say, already knowing that my schedule is clear.

"Wonderful. Type your address in my phone so I can send you an invite. I cannot wait."

"Neither can I. Wow. Thank you."

Tru and Elle look at Sadie and her smile grows. She hands me her phone and I put my address in before handing it back.

I can't help but think I'm missing something, but I'm just so honored she's asked me to be there, I don't even question it. I've wanted to make new friends in Silver Hills and it looks like I'm getting my wish.

Sadie leans in. "Make sure you save a dance for Bowie."

Oh my. For a second I'd forgotten about Bowie. My cheeks heat again.

"I'm not so sure he'll want to dance with me. He didn't seem very…into me."

"He'll dance with you," Elle says, bumping my shoulder with hers. "He holds everything close to his chest, but I think you intrigued him."

I make a face, laughing. "You must have seen something I didn't then."

"We need to get one drink in Bowie—he rarely ever drinks, but when he does, some of that gruff exterior falls off of him," Tru says.

Sadie points at her, nodding. "You're not wrong. Oh, this is going to be so fun."

My eyes narrow. "You're not trying to set us up, are you?"

"Who me?" Her eyes widen comically. "Poppy, I am going to let the love in the air work its magic. Don't you worry about a thing."

I call my sister when I get home. Marley's twenty-four, three years younger than me, and we're really close. She got married last year and she and Eric live in California now. I hate that I can't just drive over to her house to see her.

"You're not going to believe this," I say before we've even said hello.

"Spill it!" she says.

"I've been invited to Sadie Chapman and Weston Shaw's wedding."

"No *way*."

We have followed the Mustangs forever and were very invested when Sadie popped into Weston's life. I hated how the press treated her. The way she dressed was criticized so harshly, and she has stepped it up a lot in the fashion department, but I always thought she was so beautiful, no matter what she wore.

"I ran into them—she was with the same group I met at Twinkle Tales—Tru, Calista, and Elle…oh my God, I can't believe I'm hanging out with Zoey Archer! She's actually the one who called me over to the table. They're all so nice."

"The cheekbones on Elle Benton…legendary." Marley sighs. "What are you going to wear?"

"That's why I'm calling…I mean, we both know I would've called either way because…I so rarely have news."

"Your life needed this excitement. Although you did meet Bowie Freaking Fox last month, so…maybe your life is looking up. Who knew that moving to a small town would increase your social life by like, a thousand?"

"My life wasn't *that* sad," I argue.

"It was pretty sad. All you did in Denver was work and go to Mom and Dad's. All you do now is work too, but you're venturing out. I like it. I approve."

"Well, now that I feel completely pathetic…tell me what to wear."

"Yeah, you have nothing in your closet that will work. You're going to need to start shopping immediately. When is this thing?"

"The 28th."

"Oh my God. We're going to need a miracle."

"This conversation is not adding to my excitement in any way."

"Aw. I'm sorry. I'm so excited for you! But yeah, you can't go in yoga pants, no matter how hot you look in them."

"You do know how to compliment me…I wasn't so sure there for a minute."

"Of course I know how to compliment you. You're stunning and your looks are only outshined by your younger, more beautiful, and only *slightly* shorter sister."

As obnoxious as she is, I laugh at her and she tsks.

"We both know it's true. Okay, your boobs are better than mine as well, but I'm hoping once I get pregnant, I'll reach D status."

"I agree, you're the prettier one. And I'd take your B cups any day."

"Yeah, that's what all you double-D people say, but let me tell you, the Bs aren't very exciting."

"Well, Eric seems to think they are."

"Yes, he does." I can hear the smile in her voice and it makes me smile. "Okay, here's what we're going to do. I'm going to look online and you're going to go to Denver the first chance you get. I think you should go with something black or blue…with your hair and eyes, that will be stunning."

"You're gonna make me wear a dress, aren't you?"

"I know you probably haven't worn one since my wedding last year, but yes, Poppy, you *have* to wear a dress."

I sigh. "Okay. Send me pics of anything you find that can come in a hurry, and I'll go shopping tomorrow after work."

"FaceTime me from the dressing room."

"Will do."

"Oh, and Poppy? You're going to look so hot, it will bring Bowie Fox to his knees."

I laugh, unable to see how that could ever come true. I should have never told my sister about how outrageously good-looking Bowie Fox was in person.

"I swear it on my life, sis. If that man isn't knocked sideways by your beauty, there's something wrong with him."

CHAPTER THREE

TO FLIRT OR NOT TO FLIRT

BOWIE

I'm always restless right after football season ends. It takes me a while to adjust to not playing, not moving as much. I work out faithfully, but it's still not the same as the adrenaline rush when we're out on the field.

Fortunately, the McGregors keep us in order. They've been here since Becca was six months old. They live in the cottage on our property, and Mrs. McGregor takes care of Becca. She worked as an occupational therapist for years and is great with Becca. She drops her off at school and picks her up when I'm not able to. And Mr. McGregor takes care of my property. We live on Silver Hills Lake, the same lake that the guys live on, and when Mr. McGregor is done for the day, I often see him fishing off of our lake. They've been a godsend.

Becca needs routine and consistency. She has a lot of energy. When she was a baby, Becca traveled with me, along with a nanny. My coaches have made an exception with me as far as that goes. It's rare for a player to travel with his family. But since Becca started school, she's stayed home and it's been better for her. She doesn't like it when I travel, but she's gotten used to it.

The McGregors are in their early sixties but look about fifty and have an energy that matches Becca's. Hopefully they'll be around for a long time.

My parents live in Denver, and I can't say that they've ever been much help.

My friends and their kids help as much, if not more, than those I've hired. It seems like they have a sense for when I need a break and Weston and Sadie will ask if Becca can come over, or Henley and Tru will take Becca on an outing with the girls. Becca and I went glamping with Rhodes and Elle before he and Elle were even dating, and Penn and Sam come over often to swim in our indoor pool with Becca, which wears her out in the best way.

Becca and I walk into Luminary Coffeehouse early Saturday morning, and the first customers I see are Marv and Walter. They're even grumblier than me and didn't appreciate that we didn't win the Super Bowl this year.

"Mr. Fox," Walter growls. "Not much of a fox, if you ask me. Not very quick on his feet this year."

I don't think he cares that he said that loud enough for

everyone to hear. He and Marv always have a complaint to lodge. It doesn't matter that the Mustangs won three Super Bowls in a row. This year, we were on a losing streak. We only turned it around at the end of the season, but not enough to get us there.

"Hey, Marv. Hey, Walter," I say.

"Hey, Marv. Hey, Walter," Becca repeats after me.

"Good morning, Becca!" Walter says, smiling cheerfully.

"How are you doing this morning, Becca?" Marv asks.

"I doing good. How are you?" she asks.

"Can't complain," Marv says.

"Me either," Walter adds.

I snort. All these old men do is complain. I can't dislike them though—they always manage to pull out the sweetness for Becca. It's the *only* time I ever see them sweet.

We go to the counter and Clara's there, smiling. She owns the coffee shop and I'm not sure she ever goes home. She's great, dotes on the guys and me and all our kids. We have our meeting here regularly in a room in the back.

"This is a great way to start my Saturday morning," she says. "You guys are up bright and early. Just you two this morning?"

"Morning, Clara. Yeah, just us. We couldn't sleep this morning. I'm not sure why," I say, looking at Becca.

She grins up at me. "I not tired," she says happily. And then she gasps. "Poppy!"

Oh no.

I turn and see Poppy Keane grinning back at us. Her cheeks are rosy on this chilly morning and she's wearing a blue shirt, leggings, and a vest that all match her eyes perfectly.

"Good to see you both," she says.

"Poppy! I wanted to see you," Becca says.

She goes to hug Poppy and I put my hand on Becca's shoulder.

"We hardly know Poppy, Becca. Remember, we don't hug people we don't know well?"

"She my best friend!"

"You sure know how to make me feel good, Becca." Poppy holds up her hand. "High-five?"

I give Poppy a grateful look as Becca slaps her hand happily. It's important to me that I teach Becca boundaries, not just for the sake of other people, but for her own safety when I'm not with her.

"Do you guys come here often?" Poppy asks.

"Yes." Becca nods. "I'm happy you find us."

Poppy's smile grows and her eyes cut over to me quickly before she turns back to Becca. "I'm happy about that too. What a nice surprise," she says.

We step out of the way, and she places her order.

"Sit with us!" Becca says.

I try not to groan out loud. For some reason, Becca is all about this woman. She seems nice enough, but I'd hoped to spend time with my girl this morning, not a stranger.

"Well…sure, if that's okay with your dad." Poppy turns to look at me.

I pause and when I speak, it's not the warmest. "All right."

Poppy gives me a sharp look, her smile faltering somewhat, and I try to soften my next words.

"Sure. Join us."

We wait for our drinks and breakfast sandwiches, and when Clara hands them over, we go to Becca's favorite table. It's by the fireplace in the back.

"Elle says you flirt with my dad, but my dad says no, you did not."

Wow, Becca is getting really good at retaining what she hears. We've worked with various speech and language therapists and occupational therapists over the years who have widened Becca's communication skills, but she still surprises me with the leaps she's made. We didn't have enough help in the beginning and unfortunately some of the things the doctors said initially left me with little hope that she'd be as communicative as she is.

So while I'm proud of her right now, I also want to dig a hole and fall into it. I didn't think I was capable of being embarrassed, but I guess in front of a beautiful woman, it can happen.

Poppy's cheeks turn pinker than they already were, and her eyes fly to mine, wide.

"Um, I wasn't flirting," she says. "I was just being friendly."

"I like flirting," Becca says. "I flirt too."

"Not exactly," I say quietly.

"You flirt too, Daddy."

"No. No, I don't flirt."

Poppy laughs and takes a sip of her drink, fanning her face.

"Flirt with Poppy, Daddy."

"Flirting is when you pay extra attention to someone you have a crush on and like lots and lots," Poppy says. She puts her hands on her cheeks and looks at me, laughing. "So, no, your dad doesn't want to flirt with me." Under her breath she adds, "She's putting it all out there this morning."

"It's the way she rolls," I say.

"*Oh*, I crush on Sam and Penn," Becca says, looking at me.

I sigh. I'm so not ready for my daughter to like boys.

"Yeah, like that," I say, quietly.

Becca nods. "I flirt like Poppy does with my daddy," she says.

She puts her hands on her cheeks and looks at me, much the same way Poppy did, and my lips twitch from trying not to laugh.

Poppy laughs outright. "You don't miss anything, do you, Becca?"

So, was Poppy flirting with me? Shit. I have no idea.

We both avoid looking at each other.

"I miss Dad when he not here. When he play football, I miss him. When I not see you, I miss you, Poppy." Becca takes a long sip of her drink. "I miss my mom. She not here. I see her when I a baby, but I not…" She shakes her head.

God, she's going to tell our whole life story here in the coffee shop.

Poppy's eyes soften and she gives Becca a warm smile. "I missed you too. We hit it off right away, didn't we?"

"Yes. Best friends," Becca says.

Thankfully she jumps to another subject, but my joy is short-lived.

"You play lots of fun things at work," she says.

"Yes, I have," Poppy says. "We went ice skating this week, and on Monday, we're having a flag football game between all the kids and the staff."

"I love flag football," Becca says.

She looks at me and I know she's thrown off by the word flag with football.

Poppy smiles. "It's really fun."

Poppy is not doing me any favors in this conversation. If I had any hope of avoiding taking Becca to Briar Hill, it's shot out the window now.

"Flag football is what we've played at Friendsgiving, when the weather's not too bad," I tell Becca.

"Oh, I love that game," Becca says. "I good because I run fast."

"I remember that," Poppy says, laughing.

"I play flag football with Poppy," Becca says.

"We have plans after school, remember? Wedding stuff."

Becca gasps. "I a princess!"

Poppy's eyebrows lift. "That sounds way more fun than flag football."

"My dress. I am beautiful," Becca says proudly.

I need to get Becca out of here or she's going to be inviting her to the house next. I stand abruptly and both of them turn to look at me.

"We need to go. Have a good day." I nod curtly at Poppy and she looks confused as she stares up at me. "Come on, Becca."

"We stay here," Becca says, her brow furrowing at me.

She folds her arms and starts to pout.

This doesn't bode well for me and can only mean I'm in for a showdown.

I pick up our plates and walk them to the counter, careful to delegate the barely-there bread to the trash, and the plates to the cleaning bucket. I'll likely need both hands to help move Becca out of here.

When I turn back around, Poppy is quietly talking to Becca. I can't make out what she's saying, but I watch as Becca smiles at Poppy. I return to the table, grateful for whatever Poppy said to Becca to turn things around.

"We have to go, Becca," I repeat.

"I see you soon, Poppy," Becca says, leaning over to hug Poppy.

"That sounds great," Poppy says. "Enjoy your Saturday."

I nod at her and we walk away.

"We flirt, Daddy," Becca says.

"No, I don't think so."

"No, I don't think so," she repeats.

I wouldn't trade the whole world for my daughter, but she's more than most women can handle. Just one of the many reasons I don't bother dating. No one is more important to me than her.

CHAPTER FOUR

TRANSPORT ME

POPPY

I don't know why I've been so nervous about this wedding. I guess because these people are what I would consider celebrities...in my world, they are. But when I've talked to Sadie and everyone, they seem so down-to-earth. I'm sure I'll be fine.

It was crazy running into Bowie and Becca the other day. Bowie is so hard to read. He isn't rude, but he's not warm either. He's somewhat icy. And apparently, he and his friends are clued in on my attraction to him. I don't think I've flirted with him, but it's hard not to check him out when he's in the room. If I run into him, I'll attempt to play it chill and not give away how hot I think he is.

Oh God. I am so out of my element.

The wedding is in Landmark Mountain, an adorable town about an hour and a half away from Silver Hills. When Sadie called to make sure I knew she wasn't kidding about my invitation, she said, "Please come. I know Landmark Mountain isn't convenient, but we just love the town. Weston's sister lives there and you'll love her extended family so much. Weston's brother-in-law's family owns a lodge and we'll reserve a room for you after the wedding, so you don't have to drive back late that night."

"I have to work late that day, but I'll be at the wedding," I'd promised. "And the lodge sounds perfect."

"Yay, I'm so glad you're coming," she'd said, and at the time, I couldn't wait for this day, but now that it's happening, *I am so nervous*.

The drive to Landmark Mountain is beautiful. I'm running so short on time that I did my hair and makeup on a break at work and then I change into my dress in the lodge's bathroom. I'll worry about checking in later, the wedding is about to start.

I follow the flowers to a beautiful room with glass ceilings. It is magical. I'm ushered to a seat on the bride's side and transported into another world. Pink and white flowers are everywhere, white lights and candles creating a sepia-toned mood.

The ceremony is breathtaking and so touching. A little boy, I believe it's Rhodes' son, pulls Caleb down the aisle in a white wagon. It's the cutest thing I've ever seen. Becca looks so pretty in her princess dress, and she can't stop smiling as she walks down the aisle. Despite how beautiful Weston and Sadie look, it's hard to tear my eyes away from Bowie in his tux. Bowie, Rhodes, Penn, Henley, and another stunning man are all standing up with Weston, and Sadie has Elle, Tru, Calista, and another beautiful friend that I don't recognize. The couple I don't recognize stare at each other with such love, I think they must be the sister and brother-in-law of Weston's that Sadie mentioned.

Weddings can be hard as a single woman. I'm sure they're not difficult for everyone, and if I didn't want to get married myself, I guess they wouldn't be for me, but…they are. I long to have that connection with someone. To fall in love and have someone to share all my secrets with…to fall asleep in his arms at night and know that he'll be there the next morning and the next. I'm not big into dating apps, and with how busy I've been with my job, it's been hard to find time to date. I'm still busy with work, but now that I'm in Silver Hills, my evenings are freer. It's not like Silver Hills is overflowing with single men who want to date me though.

The one man I've met that I'd be interested in getting to know better is way out of my league…and completely uninterested in me.

When the wedding is over, I wander into the section designated for the reception and look for my table number. As soon as I find it, I walk to the table. No one else is there yet. I turn to look around and Bowie is standing there, staring at me.

The way he looks me over makes me think maybe he likes what he sees, until his eyes meet mine and he frowns.

"I'm surprised to see you here," he says.

"Yeah, I was so surprised to get an invite! I met Sadie at Twinkle Tales a couple of months ago and then reconnected at the signing…then ran into her again at The Fairy Hut and she was kind enough to extend an invitation." I run out of air and take a deep breath.

What is it about this man that makes me even more awkward than I already am?

"Hmm," he says.

"Hmm," I repeat.

He turns and walks away and I can't help but be hurt that the guy doesn't seem to like me very much. It's like I actually *bother* him. I'm not sure why…I'm a nice person.

Elle, Rhodes, and the little boy I noticed earlier walk up and then Henley and Tru. Both girls give me big hugs.

"It's so good to see you, Poppy. I'm so glad you made it," Elle says.

"Thank you. Me too," I say.

"I'm not sure if you've met Levi yet," Elle says.

"No, I haven't." I smile at Levi and he gives me a wide smile. The little boy is too cute for words.

"Levi, this is Poppy."

"Hi, Poppy!" he says.

"You did such a good job in the wedding," I tell him.

"I pulled that heavy wagon," he says proudly.

"You were amazing."

I look around to see if Bowie's still close by. I hope I didn't run him off. Maybe after all that talk about flirting, he thought I was hunting him down.

I don't spot him right away, but then I see him talking to Sadie and Weston and Sadie's laughing. Bowie doesn't look as happy and walks away. Wow, he's intense.

I'm introduced to Henley and then Penn when he walks up. Penn is all charm.

"You look lovely tonight," he says after the introductions are made.

"Thank you," I manage to get out.

These football players are even better looking in person than on TV. I feel a little starstruck in their presence. They're also all far more agreeable than Bowie Fox.

"Looks like we're sitting together," Elle says. "Where's Bowie?"

"I saw him for a second, but he left. I don't think he liked that I'm sitting here very much."

"Oh, you're here for Bowie?" Penn asks. "Damn."

I laugh. "No, I'm not here for Bowie. I was just invited by Sadie."

Penn nods, his grin deepening, and he and the guys exchange a look.

Rhodes chuckles. "We're really glad you're here, Poppy. Don't mind Bowie. Sometimes he's more bark than bite. But trust me, get him on the dance floor, and he won't be so grumpy."

"Ah, so that's the secret?" I ask, laughing.

We all sit down.

Sadie and Weston are at the next table with her parents and his parents. Little Caleb sits next to Weston.

"They are such a cute couple," I say.

"Aren't they?" Tru says.

"The wedding was beautiful. You all look gorgeous," I say.

"So do you," Elle says.

"Thank you." I smile at her and then see Bowie out of the corner of my eye. He's leaning over Becca. She's at a table with Henley's girls and a boy that looks about ten or eleven.

"Sam is feeling a little too cocky after his first kiss," Penn says. "Look at him over there trying to impress Cassidy."

We all look at the table where the girls are sitting.

"Sam is the boy sitting over there," Tru says, pointing to

the table. "Penn met him while tutoring and now we're all attached to him."

I want to ask more about Sam, but Bowie chooses that moment to come back to the table and all the air is sucked out of my lungs. He sits in the only open chair, which is next to me. He smells like pine and a Jolly Rancher, and when he sets an empty wrapper on the table, I understand why.

He's far more relaxed than he was when it was just me, easing into conversation quickly with the guys while I talk to Elle and Tru. We eat and I'm aware of every time Bowie's elbow or shoulder brushes against mine. The man is so tall and built. All of the players are, and even though I'm five nine, I feel *tiny* compared to Bowie.

Rhodes has brought me back a drink every time he goes to get one for Elle, and I haven't had a cocktail in so long. My inhibitions fade as I get more liquid courage. Weston and Sadie have their first dance and it's so beautiful, I almost cry. Then Weston dances with his mom and Sadie dances with her dad and I'm not the only one sniffling at the table.

"Are we ready to do this?" I hear Penn ask.

The next thing I know, all the guys are standing up and walking to the dance floor.

"Do you know what they've got planned?" Tru asks Elle.

"No idea," Elle says.

Weston leads Sadie to a chair on the edge of a dance floor and then walks out with the rest of the guys. They've all taken their jackets off and the sight of all five men strutting out to stand in the middle of the floor is a sight to behold. When "I'm a Slave 4 U" comes over the speaker, Elle and Tru crack up.

"Oh, God, this is gonna be so good," Tru says.

When they start moving, Elle whistles. "They are making me so proud right now." She laughs.

I can't speak because I'm too caught up in watching Bowie shake his hips and do pelvic thrusts that make my cheeks heat. He's good! They all are. But I'm shocked the ice man can let loose like this.

Weston ends up on his knees in front of Sadie, who is laughing her head off as she fans her face. The room erupts in applause and then everyone starts moving toward the dance floor.

"Ready to dance?" Tru asks.

"What? Now?" I ask. I enjoy dancing, but I don't feel like I'm especially great at it.

Tru laughs. "Yes, come on. It'll be fun."

I finish my drink and follow her and Elle, still pinching myself that I'm even here.

CHAPTER FIVE

THE EXCEPTION

BOWIE

It's been a fun-filled couple of days. Time with the guys is always like therapy, whether we talk about anything deep or not. I guess besides being out on the field, it's one of the only outlets I have. I know with them I can speak freely and not be judged, and it helps to know that I'm not alone in doing this dad thing.

Right before the ceremony, I pulled out The Single Dad

Playbook and set it on the table where we'd been getting ready, and wrote an entry.

> *The Single Dad Players are going down like*
> *gummies at a Lana Del Rey concert,*
> *and I am here for it.*
> *I like that our kids will witness healthy*
> *love and marriages…*
> *from someone besides me.*
> *So cheers to you, my brave brothers,*
> *for carrying this mantle.*
> *I salute you.*
> *~Bowie*

I'm not a cynic about love, despite my disastrous experience with it. I can appreciate that my friends are finding it and can be happy for them, while still not going within a ten-foot pole of it.

When I see that Poppy Keane is at Weston and Sadie's wedding, I think, *Well, Sadie got her way after all. She knew I wouldn't bring a date, so she found a way to deliver one to me.*

What I end up saying to Sadie is simply, "Really, Sadie? *Really?*"

She laughs her ass off and she can do that because it's her day, and she gets whatever the fuck she wants. I don't even begrudge her matchmaking busybodyness all that much, but it's not going to work.

After our initial interaction, I don't look Poppy's way again until after Mrs. McGregor takes Becca to the three-bedroom suite we're sharing and puts her to bed. Becca got to dance her heart out and was exhausted from all the wedding festivities.

Now, several drinks in, I'm watching Poppy out on the dance floor looking all kinds of sexy in the deep blue dress that matches her eyes perfectly, and I'm not so aggravated with Sadie.

There's just something about Poppy that I'm drawn to. I can't explain it.

Yes, she's beautiful. She's charming and quirky and kind.

She's incredibly sweet with my daughter, which softens me every time we see her.

But I've met beautiful, kind women before and I have not been moved.

What is it about her?

Tonight, for once, I don't feel like second-guessing it. So when we end up dancing in the same space on the dance floor and she grins up at me, I dance with her. Before I know it, the floor gets crowded and my hands are on her waist. Next thing I know…her arms are looped around my neck and we're staring at each other as we move in time.

I've been burned before. Goddamn, have I ever been burned.

But having a woman as beautiful as Poppy in my arms tonight…it makes me want to set all of that aside for a few hours and just enjoy this.

Neither one of us talks. We just move from one dance to the next like we were made to do this together.

Until the end of the night when the music stops and the few of us that are left help see Weston and Sadie out the door. They're staying at the lodge tonight, so there's no big fanfare, but there are hugs all around.

"Love you, man," Weston says.

"I love you too. It was a beautiful wedding. Let me know

if you need anything before you take off for your honeymoon."

"Thanks for everything. Sutton and Felicity are taking us to the airport tomorrow, so we should be set. You'll see us again at brunch though."

"Oh, that's right. See you then."

They walk out and the rest of us stand there blinking in the bright lights. The staff of the lodge are bustling to get things back in order now that it's clearing out.

"Great night," Rhodes says, putting his hand on my shoulder. "You guys looked flawless out there." He smiles at me and Poppy.

Poppy looks at me over Elle's shoulder as Elle hugs her goodbye.

Henley and Tru already left. Tru is pregnant and danced until she was too sleepy to keep going. Penn found a girl to make out with and probably took her upstairs.

And then it's just Poppy and me.

We walk to the lobby and Poppy shivers. If we'd been dancing, my arms would've been around her, but it feels weird now to step in and do that.

"That was fun," she says. "I don't know why I'm so surprised that you can dance like that. You're great out on the field, makes sense you'd be good at dancing too."

"You're good at it too," I say and then feel silly. I'm the worst at small talk.

She laughs. "I'm actually not good at it. You made it easy out there."

Now I really don't know what to say. She stops and I realize I've walked her to the reception desk.

"Thanks for dancing with me," she says softly. "I had thought earlier that you—"

When she doesn't say anything for a long pause, I blink. "That I what?"

"That you don't like me very much," she blurts out.

Her cheeks bloom and she looks like she wants to take it back, but I'm still surprised by her candor…and that she would assume I don't like her.

"I like you fine," I say.

She snorts and my head tilts as I study her.

"Such high praise," she says.

"It actually is coming from me," I finally say.

"Why is that?"

It takes me a few moments to answer and when I do, I try to say it as simply as possible.

"I don't do this," I say, pointing between the two of us.

"Do what, exactly?"

I sigh and look up around the lobby. The lodge is beautiful every day, but they've gone all out for this wedding. The flowers and lights are everywhere. When I look at Poppy again, she's still watching me tentatively. It was much easier to dance with her than it is to have this conversation.

She's so pretty it fucking hurts.

She looks radiant in the glow of the lights. Her long blonde hair nearly reaches her waist and shimmers with every turn of her head. Her eyes hold mischief and warmth, drawing people in effortlessly.

If she can draw me in, she can draw in anyone.

Her dress clings to her curves in all the right ways, the color making her blue eyes even more vivid. Her smile actually makes me want to smile back. It's natural, unforced, and lights up her whole face. She's not just pretty; if that were it, she wouldn't affect me like this. She's captivating, every part of her.

I shouldn't have gone near her.

I clear my throat and take a deep breath.

"I'm close to my friends and their girlfriends and kids, but otherwise…I don't…I'm not looking for..." My teeth clench and I shake my head. "Friends," I finish.

"Why is that?"

"Long story."

She stares at me for a long time and then nods.

"Okay," she says finally. "I'm glad that for at least one night, I was the exception."

She turns and moves toward the reception desk. She gives me one last look over her shoulder and lifts her hand, smiling before she turns and talks to the clerk.

I can't help but feel like I've blown it.

For at least one night, I was the exception…

Something in Poppy's tone makes me tune in and I take a step closer.

"But when I left my bag here before the wedding, you assured me I had a room," she says.

"I'm so sorry," the girl says, looking mortified. "We had a shift change and our usual staff wasn't here because they were attending the wedding. I'm afraid your room has been given to someone else when you didn't check in before ten o'clock this evening."

"I didn't know there was a time limit on checking in," Poppy says. She sounds near tears, but then her shoulders straighten. "It's okay. I'll drink some caffeine and head home." She lets out a long exhale and nods.

"I'm so sorry, ma'am."

"It's okay. I should've checked in earlier. Would you mind grabbing my bag, please?"

"I'd be happy to," the clerk says.

She walks back and when I step next to Poppy, she jumps.

"I didn't know you were still here," she says, wincing.

"I overheard what happened. I have a large suite. You're welcome to stay with us."

"I couldn't," she says, shaking her head.

"Why not?"

She presses her lips together and they shift to the side. "That's something friends would do."

"Well, then consider us friends for the night," I say, only half teasing.

She rolls her eyes before closing them, but she smiles, and when she opens her eyes, I see how exhausted she really is.

"Okay. I'm saying yes, but only because I'm sleepy. It's been a long week and an even longer day."

I nod. "Good. You shouldn't have to drive all the way back to Silver Hills tonight." I glance at my watch and wince. More like one thirty in the morning.

The clerk rolls Poppy's bag out and Poppy thanks her. I reach out and take the bag. Our walk to the elevator is quiet and when we step inside, she goes to the opposite wall and leans against it. The elevator dings and we step out, our footsteps quietly padding across the carpet. When I open the door to my suite, I hear Poppy's gasp and look down at her stunned face.

"This place has always been nice, but it was recently remodeled and it's next level."

"Gorgeous," she whispers.

I point to the couch. "I'll take the couch and you can go into that room there."

She frowns. "I'll take the couch."

"Absolutely not."

She makes a face. "You really want to try to fit on that couch? Good luck with that."

"If Becca wakes up and sees you sleeping out here, she's going to have questions for the rest of my lifetime."

"And if she wakes up and sees you sleeping out here, she won't?"

I pause. "Good point."

"Come on. We're adults and I'm so sleepy, I couldn't be naughty tonight even if I wanted to."

"Naughty?" I echo.

She smirks.

Part of me is disappointed that she wouldn't want to be naughty with me, but the rest of me relaxes.

"You're right. The bed is big. Stay on your side," I tell her.

She makes a derisive sound. "Get over yourself. You stay on your side."

I nod. This is better. I can tolerate her irritation with me far easier than the slightly swoony eyes she was giving me all night. Although that was a helluva lot of fun while it was happening.

I shut off my thoughts and stalk to the bedroom.

"What time does Becca get up?"

"Around seven usually, but she might sleep longer after the night she had."

"Okay, I'll be out of here before then. I can go to the gym or walk around town until I meet everyone for breakfast."

"Oh, you're going to that too?" Damn, she's getting tight with my friends in a short amount of time. Is there a fucking conspiracy to set me up with this woman?

She nods.

"You could also take your time and leave after we do.

Becca will get up and watch TV for a little bit and Mrs. McGregor will be up with her. She won't come in here and if she's asking for me, I'll go out there. No need to not sleep in."

"Okay. Thank you."

I hold out my hand, pointing out the bathroom and she goes in there with her bag and shuts the door. I put on the T-shirt and pajama pants I brought and wait for her to come out so I can use the restroom and brush my teeth. When almost ten minutes pass, I wonder if she's okay in there.

"Uh, Bowie?" she says.

"Yeah?"

"Can you turn out the light? I thought I was staying in a room by myself and didn't bring the right things."

"Uh, sure," I say.

I turn out the lights and yet I still catch a glimpse of her fitted, thin-strapped tank top, erect nipples, and pretty underwear when she walks out. Her legs are long and shapely, and my eyes wander back to her tits. She's fucking *beautiful*.

Nope. Can't do this. I hurry past her into the bathroom, as fast as I can with how hard I am, and brush my teeth as I try to think of everything but that woman getting in my bed right now.

But then I think of the last couple of women I've slept with. It's been so long that I'm not even positive about the timeframe. There was a friend from college who came through Silver Hills a couple of years ago. She'd been friends with Adriane and me and was sympathetic about how I'd been mercilessly dumped. We talked and commiserated over her recent breakup and ended up spending a night together.

This is why I don't do friends. Too many lines get crossed.

And then last year, I had too much to drink after we won

the Super Bowl and ended up in bed with that actress from the heist movie I really liked.

This is why I rarely drink. Too many lines, yada yada.

Tonight, I've gotten a little too close to the friend line *and* I've had alcohol.

Fucking hell.

CHAPTER SIX

BARRICADE

POPPY

While Bowie's been in the bathroom, I've arranged a row of pillows down the center to keep me on my side of the bed. However, when he slides into bed next to me, everything in me wakes up. I want to scoop those pillows off the bed and toss them across the room.

No, you're exhausted! I shout at myself. *Ignore the hot man in your bed and go to sleep, ma'am.*

"Thanks for sharing your room. I'm sorry you got more

than you bargained for with this night…and with a non-friend at that."

He chuckles and the sound skitters over my skin like pixie dust. The pillows between us shift slightly as he gets comfortable.

"Please don't take anything I say personally. I'm an ass. Especially when I don't have alcohol in my system…but yeah, even when I do, apparently."

"Oh, so alcohol makes you a little looser-lipped?" I giggle.

"You could say that."

"Probably why you danced with me as well, I take it?"

"Uh…that was probably more because you're beautiful and you looked fucking amazing in that blue dress. But yeah, we can thank the alcohol for the way I'm admitting any of that right now."

My skin heats and every part of me bristles with awareness of how close we are to each other right now.

"Wow," I say softly. "Thank you, alcohol."

He chuckles and because I've heard it so infrequently from him, I'm addicted to making that happen again.

"Good night, Poppy," he says.

His voice is huskier…and closer. We danced together all night, but this is the most talking we've done. It sure was fun, all of it. He made me feel beautiful and special and like I was capable of holding his attention the whole time. He didn't turn away to dance with anyone else even once.

The curtains are still open, so the room isn't pitch black, and we lie there like two wooden planks.

I force myself to turn onto my side, away from him. "Good night, Bowie."

It takes time, but his breathing evens out and I eventually fall asleep too. I dream I'm in California with Marley and then the dream morphs and I'm in a dark room with Bowie. We're wearing our wedding clothes and instead of staring at me as we dance, his lips meet mine. It's such a good kiss, it almost feels real, and I tell myself to stay in this dream for as long as possible.

When he hitches my leg over his thigh and pulses against me, I gasp and kiss him harder.

I hear a groan and my eyes fly open. Bowie and I are pressed against each other, hearts pounding hard, our lips a breath apart. The pillows are nowhere to be found. We've managed to work our way around them. Bowie's hand is on my waist, touching my bare skin under my tank top. With his other hand, he reaches up and pushes my hair back.

"I thought I was dreaming," I whisper.

"Me too."

I expect him to pull away, but instead he stares at me, his gaze heated. And then he leans in, and this time, I know I'm not dreaming when his lips touch mine. He tastes like peppermint, so we haven't been asleep for long. I gasp into his mouth, the zing of electricity that zaps between us taking my breath away for a second, and then I tug his head closer so I can taste more of him. He lets out a ragged groan and it fuels me. My hands explore the wide expanse of his back and I grip his biceps, eager to feel every inch of him. His hand slides down to my backside and he squeezes, tugging me tighter against him. I moan when I feel how hard and long he is. I can feel the heat radiating off of him through our layers. I want to rip his shirt off and shove the pajama pants down so I can feel him bare against me. When our lips finally break apart, he kisses down my neck and moves down to my breast, where his tongue traces over my hard peak over the tank top.

I tug his hair, loving that it's long enough for me to get a good grip. All those sites I've seen talking about Bowie Fox's hair can't even grasp how good it *feels*, and how insanely sexy his bedhead is. He looks up, his stare pinning me to the bed, and I'm a puddle.

It's been a really long time since I've had sex or even kissed someone, and I can't quite believe this is happening right now.

With Bowie Fox.

I shift, needing more, so much more, and he lowers his head, his nose sliding my shirt up as he places soft kisses on my stomach. I'm brazen and slide my tank over my head, and he groans his approval when he sees me. His mouth latches onto me, his hand pinching the tip on my other side, and I writhe against him.

"You feel so good," he says, his voice raspy.

"*You* do," I whisper.

"Can we do this the rest of the night?"

"Yes, please."

"Do you really want this?" he asks, looking up at me.

The view of him leaning over me is sinful.

"More than anything," I whisper.

He leans over and fumbles around with his dress pants, pulling out a condom.

"Rhodes gave me this as a joke earlier," he says.

"I'll be sure to thank him when I see him."

He grins and pulls down my underwear, looking at me reverently.

"Beautiful," he says, his breath skating over my center.

I shiver and he parts my legs before leaning down to flick his tongue over me. I whimper and it encourages him. His fingers spread me wide and then his large hands encase my hips as his tongue does magical things I never knew were possible.

It's like he can't get enough and I have never felt so good in all my life. I hold onto his hair and lose myself in the rush.

When I start fluttering against him, he groans and keeps going. I put the pillow over my mouth and cry out and when the waves slow down, he places a kiss between my legs and moves over me, hovering with his hands on either side of my face.

"I can't resist you," he says huskily.

He dips his head so his forehead touches mine.

I feel how hard he is between my legs now, but he's still wearing his pajama pants. My fingers move beneath the band and I slide them down.

"You want more?" he asks. "We don't have to—"

"I want more," I tell him.

My hands wrap around him, and I gasp at the feel of him. He's huge and fevered, so thick and long. I turn to liquid just touching him. My thumb slides over the tip of him and he shudders with a low groan.

"Poppy." It sounds like gravelly worship coming from his lips.

He pulls away to put on the condom and I wish it was brighter in here so I could see him better. What I can see in the dim light is enough to make me woozy with lust.

When he barely slides his tip in, we both gasp. He brushes my hair back with his fingers and looks at me intently, dipping in a little deeper.

"You're perfect," he says.

I'm so wet that his slide in is easier each time. Once he's all the way in, he pauses and his eyes squeeze shut. When they open again, he looks feral, but I feel safe and brazen and feral myself. He drags out of me slowly and back in, a few long glides that leave me weak.

I widen my legs and he sucks in a breath, pistoning into

me, hitting deeper and deeper. My breasts bounce and he leans back to look at them, his teeth stretching over his bottom lip as he thrusts. I hold onto his hips and meet his thrusts, gasping when he does an extra roll that hits me just right. He's so deep and the rhythm is so intense, it doesn't seem possible that I could already be this close, but I am.

My mouth parts and I can't stop the moan that comes out. He moves faster and my whole body stiffens as I clamp around him like a vise, squeezing the life out of him. He lets out a hoarse moan and pulses into me. His head burrows into my shoulder and I clutch his hair, holding him close as wave after wave goes through me.

Seriously the best thing I've ever felt.

There's a sound in the next room and he stiffens, his head lifting.

"I'm sorry," he says and pulls out, wincing as I reluctantly let him go.

He jumps out of bed, throwing the condom away, and hurriedly puts his pants on before rushing out of the room. I lay there, panting, still blissed out and in disbelief that it even happened.

After a few minutes, I wonder if I should make sure everything's okay.

Do I stay here letting my breasts air out in the breeze or put my tank top and panties back on?

What to do, what to do…

I hear his low voice in the next room and think I hear Becca's tearful voice and then it's quiet. I slide my tank over my head. When an hour passes and Bowie doesn't come back, I give in to sleep.

The click of the hotel door in the other room wakes me up hours later, and I sit up. I slept later than I'd intended and I hurriedly get ready, noticing that Bowie's things are gone. He managed to get ready in here without me hearing a thing.

I look around before I wheel my small bag out, half expecting a note or something and then I chide myself. Bowie doesn't seem like the note-leaving type. I'm unable to stop thinking about what happened in the night. The hungry way he kissed me, the way he felt inside me, the way his hands felt as he touched me…his mouth. The way his voice sounded when he said my name.

If I didn't still feel the slight rawness on my chin…and the other parts of my body that he kissed…from Bowie's stubble…the ache between my legs…I might not believe anything happened.

I shake myself and leave the room, heading downstairs to the restaurant in the lodge. There's a separate smaller room that I'm led to and it's full of the wedding party…and a few other guests I noticed last night, like Zac and Autumn Ledger and Summer and Liam Taylor—Marley will *die* when I tell her.

My face heats when I see Bowie at the end of the table.

He glances up and I smile. His expression is unreadable before he looks away and my heart wilts.

"Good morning, Poppy," Sadie calls. "I'm so happy you could make it."

"Sorry, I'm late. I overslept."

"It's okay. We just got here ourselves," she says.

I wave at Tru and Elle.

"Everyone, this is Poppy," Sadie says. "Poppy Keane. Isn't that a great name?"

A slew of hellos comes at me at once. Weston goes through the specific introductions, and I try not to stumble over my words when I meet the celebrities.

"Poppy!" Becca says. "Sit here!"

She pats the place next to her. It's across from Bowie and it looks like it's the only open seat available in the room. I make my way over there and sit down, hugging Becca when she reaches out for me.

"I sick last night," she says. "Daddy says bad food."

"I said your food probably made you feel bad when you did all that dancing, and it upset your stomach," Bowie says quietly.

His eyes meet mine and I wish I could say there's warmth there, but his face is wiped clean of expression. I also wish I could say it didn't hurt, but it does.

It hurts like *hell*.

How embarrassing that I tore my shirt off in front of him, so eager to let him do whatever he wanted. Never mind the fact that he kissed me like a man starving. That he said I was perfect and drove into me like I was all he'd ever wanted. It clearly didn't mean anything beyond a drunken fuck that he'd like to pretend never happened.

You hardly know the man, Poppy. Consider yourself lucky that you scratched that itch.

Now you can forget it ever happened.

Right.

I can still feel his mouth and hands on me. I can still feel everywhere he's been.

I focus on Becca. "I'm so sorry you were sick. How's your stomach feeling now?"

"I fine. I eat pancakes!"

"How about we go easy, Becca? Maybe some oatmeal or some toast and jelly?"

"Pancakes!" she insists.

I look down at my menu and smile. "What if we share? I get pancakes and you get oatmeal and we see how your belly feels. If your stomach feels good and not sick, I'll share the pancakes with you."

"We share?" she repeats. "Levi shares Bogey with me. Bogey is a dog," she says. "I love Bogey." She nods happily. "Dad, I share with Poppy. We share."

I smile at her and she pats my back. "Excellent."

"*Ex-cellent*," she repeats.

When I sneak another look at Bowie again, he's watching me. He looks down at his menu quickly.

"Sounds good," he says.

The ice man approves.

CHAPTER SEVEN

FOOL TOOL

BOWIE

I messed up royally last night. It didn't feel like it while it was happening. Fuck, everything about it felt right in the moment.

Poppy.

Everything about her is so…good. She's beautiful. She's fun and funny. She's kind. Dancing with her made me feel more alive than I've felt in years.

I knew better than to drink while being around her

because it broke down some of the walls I've worked so hard to keep up.

And the way she felt against me, the passion in her kisses…the way she looked, the sounds she made, all of it… well, despite how right it felt, it was a colossal mistake that should've never happened.

I wanted nothing more than to go back in there and sink into her heat again and again and again.

I adjust myself in my seat as I sneak looks at her across the table, where she's sitting next to Becca. They're laughing at the picture Poppy just drew on the kid's menu.

Why does she have to be so fucking cool?

Last night, I knew what a tool I'd been as soon as I had a little clarity. While Becca was sick, I sobered up and acknowledged the mess I'd made, having sex with Poppy. It felt fucking amazing, but *fuck*. Long after Becca had fallen back to sleep, I lay awake, cursing my poor choices and talking myself out of going back in there to continue what we'd started.

I couldn't go back to that room, that *bed*, or I would just sink deeper into the Poppy trap.

She noticed that I didn't return her smile when she came into the restaurant, and the way she ignores me now feels wrong, but this is the way it has to be. I can't afford to go down that rabbit hole. She's local, she's nice, she's becoming friends with all of my friends. Becca loves her. She's *here*, for Christ's sake, invited to the wedding of my friends after barely knowing them a minute.

She's not going anywhere…which means I cannot afford to get invested.

I feel like the world's largest asshole, but I'm actually saving her a world of hurt. No one needs my baggage.

Across from me, Ruby Landmark, Weston's sister Felicity's sister-in-law—try saying that fast—starts talking about her emus and I just pray to God Becca won't overhear her as she invites everyone over to visit. I've managed to avoid seeing the emus when we've come to Landmark Mountain. I'd much rather take Becca on the gondola to the top of the mountain or something else fun, but Becca loves animals. Problem is, she won't want to leave them.

Sure as heck, it catches Poppy's attention and she turns to look at Ruby.

"Did you just say emus?" she asks.

Kill me now. I bury my head in my hands.

"Emus?" Becca repeats.

"Yes, we have so many and they love visitors," Ruby says excitedly. "You guys are more than welcome to come over and visit."

"I come to your house," Becca says.

Poppy looks at me and the smile drops from her face. She turns back to Ruby.

"I can't turn that down," she says. "It's not every day that I get invited to come visit emus. Count me in."

The rest of the girls nod excitedly.

"I'm in too," Elle says.

"You're going to love them," Sadie says.

"Dad. We go see emus," Becca says.

"We probably need to head back to Silver Hills," I tell her.

"We see emus," Becca says, pounding her fist lightly on the table.

Now I don't just give Becca whatever she wants all the time, especially not when she has a meltdown over something. There are times I have to put my foot down. But today is not one of those days. Most of the people in this room know and love Becca, but I still don't want this to escalate during Weston and Sadie's celebratory weekend. We have time to take a little detour. We don't actually have to be back to Silver Hills for anything important. She'll love the freaking emus. It'll probably make her whole week.

Just because Poppy might be going doesn't mean anything.

Keep telling yourself that, I think.

And that's how I end up at Callum and Ruby Landmark's ranch after brunch. It's a beautiful piece of property with the mountains surrounding a stunning house and barn. As soon as we step out of the car, Becca starts laughing and I feel like a jerk for wanting to avoid this stop. A flop-eared goat and cow are the first to greet us, and then an emu comes running up like she's late to the party.

Becca squeals when the emu stops right in front of her, half-terrified and half-delighted.

Ruby comes running up behind the emu. "Dolly, slow your roll! Sorry for that in-your-face greeting. Dolly really loves company. She won't hurt you, I promise."

Becca holds her hand up to pet the emu and the goat sticks its head in the way. Becca cracks up.

"Daddy, he pet my hand!"

I laugh. "He sure did."

"That's Delphine and she loves to hog all the petting time. And this is Irene," she says, petting the cow.

Delphine and Irene realize there are more people arriving and go to greet them. Dolly stays near us, ducking her head.

"She likes you," Ruby tells Becca. She points at the other emus roaming the property. "They'll like you too, but they're not as friendly."

Out of the corner of my eye, I see Poppy getting the same star treatment from the cow and the goat. Her head falls back as she laughs, and Becca turns at the sound.

"Poppy, look! Dolly!" She points at the emu and Poppy's eyes widen.

"I've never seen an emu in real life. Wow. That is *wicked* cool," she says.

I snort and then frown, trying to play it off like that sound didn't come from me.

But it's too late. Poppy's eyes narrow as she looks at me.

"What was that?" she asks.

"Hmm, what?" I ask, turning to look behind me.

"Was that a scoff I heard coming from you?"

Her eyes are shining and I can't tell if she wants to laugh or knee me in the nuts.

"Not a scoff. I just haven't heard 'wicked' used that way in a long time," I say.

She lifts her shoulder, the tension in her face relaxing. "I grew up in Boston, what can I say? My parents still say it all the time, even though we've lived in Colorado for years now."

Becca runs off, chasing after Dolly as she runs around. It's too funny to not laugh.

"She loves animals, doesn't she?" Poppy says.

"She really does."

"Do you have any animals?"

"No," I say firmly.

"Too bad," she says, walking away. She looks back at me and takes a step toward me. "By the way, you don't have to make it weird about last night," she says under her breath.

"I didn't mean to make it weird," I admit. "Becca was sick in the night and then it just…" I lift both shoulders, suddenly at a loss for words.

Her expression is tense again, the walls back up. "Yeah. Got it," she says. "No worries. I'm not gonna…well, never mind."

She looks past me and smiles, and I turn to see Callum standing there. She walks away to join the girls. They laugh as Becca and Dolly run around the yard.

"Let me turn on the music," Ruby calls. "You'll get to see her dance, Becca." She turns on the music and it's hilarious watching Dolly zooming around the yard. Becca starts dancing too and laughs harder than I've ever seen her laugh. Despite the less-than-stellar way I just handled that conversation with Poppy, now I can't stop laughing.

"Hey, Callum," I say.

"Hey," he says. "Sorry, I interrupted a…moment there."

"Oh, you picked up on that."

"Hard to miss, he says, chuckling under his breath.

Callum is the second oldest in the Landmark family. And he's a good guy. They all are. I've been around him some from Weston's wedding activities, the bachelor party, etc. I like the guy. He might be the only person who typically has less to say than me. But he's talking now. Weston's brother-in-law, Sutton, says that Ruby brought all that out in Callum when he fell in love with her.

"You know, it's not the worst thing you can do to fall in love with a woman." He looks at me out of the corner of his eye.

"Yeah, so I keep hearing," I say, grumbling under my breath, "Not you too."

Callum laughs. "Yeah, I was opposed to the idea myself until Ruby pulled into town."

"Pulled in?" I ask.

He points at the RV across the yard. "Broke down in that thing right in front of my property. She was in a wedding dress. Kind of hard to miss."

Now I'm laughing and intrigued. "That's quite a story. How did you get her to marry you?"

"Well, she was stuck here for a few days. The part needed to repair it wasn't around for the old thing, which is nicer than a house inside, by the way. But it gave us time to get to know each other. She's the best thing that ever happened to me." He looks at Ruby, a small smile playing on his lips, the sorry sucker. "Love, I wouldn't knock it," he says in his gruff voice. "And the way that woman just looked at you, I see potential there."

I groan. "All you guys, once you get married, want to pass off love to everybody else. Some of us just aren't cut out for it."

Callum turns and gives me an assessing look. "We're all cut out for love, Bowie. Every single one of us. If you think you don't deserve it, it's probably because you deserve it more than anyone."

He tilts his head up and walks away, leaving me to think about that.

My phone buzzes and the timing is ironic after what I've just heard.

> MOM
>
> I'm worried about your dad. Can you come?

My mom is worried about my dad every other week, and that's not to say that I'm not. My dad has been an alcoholic from as far back as I can remember. My mother hoped leaving Austria when I was a kid would magically cure him of it, but vodka is his first and only love, always will be.

> I'm in Landmark Mountain right now. Is he in the hospital?

> MOM
>
> You know I can't get him to go to the hospital.

That lets me know the situation isn't too dire or she would've called an ambulance by now.

> The McGregors went back to Silver Hills already and I've given them the day off, but I'll see if Mrs. McGregor is able to watch Becca when we get home and come over.

It's not easy taking Becca to my parents' house. I don't like her being around the dysfunction, and my parents aren't exactly the loving grandparent types either. It's not a great feeling when you know your parents would rather not be around your child. They're not mean to Becca, they're just uncomfortable, and because they've made so little effort to become more comfortable with her, I choose to not put her in that situation as much as I can help it.

"You okay?" Henley comes over and stands by me.

"Yeah."

Rhodes is not far behind him, moving to my other side. "Fun having Poppy around, right?"

Rhodes has been pushing for me to pursue Poppy since the day I met her at Twinkle Tales. It's my bad luck that he was there when we first met because the guy does not let a matter drop.

"Can't say I love it," I say.

"Why the hell not? She's great," Rhodes says.

Just then, Becca takes Poppy's hands and they dance around the yard. My chest gets a weird pinch as I watch them.

"Don't start, okay?" I mutter.

Poppy and Becca stop dancing and Poppy fans her face despite the chill in the air. She turns and her eyes meet mine, and the elation in her eyes dims.

"Holy shit." Rhodes laughs. "What did you do?"

"You don't want to know." I sigh.

Penn and Weston walk over.

"Don't want to know what?" Penn asks.

Fuck me.

When I feel all their eyes on me, I throw my hands up. "We're not going there, okay? This is not a Single Dad Players meeting right now."

"Sounds like it should be," Rhodes says.

Henley's the one my eyes can't avoid. They all know me well, but Henley and Rhodes know me better than anyone.

"Next meeting, you're talking," Henley says, pointing at me.

CHAPTER EIGHT

BLINDED BY THE HAIR

POPPY

After having sex with Bowie Fox, it's hard to just block that out. But a few days after my fun weekend—and it really was fun despite (and because of) Bowie—I'm getting better. I refuse to let his cold brush-off bring me down.

If I keep telling myself that, maybe it'll work.

I told Marley about it on the way to work yesterday morning, and she was sufficiently outraged on my behalf. She also thought maybe I shouldn't be so quick to shut that door, but she didn't see the look in Bowie's eyes. We're not happening.

For the past two days, I've buried my head in work. Tonight, though, as I drive to Twinkle Tales to meet the girls, it's really hard to not dwell on where I went wrong with Bowie.

And why do I even care? Besides the fact that he's fun to dance with and knows how to work my body like no man has before him, I hardly know the man.

When I arrive, we all hug and take off our coats.

"All we're missing is Sadie." Tru sticks out her lower lip. "But I can't miss her too much because she's on her *honeymoon*," she sings.

"Yeah, I doubt she's thinking about us at all right now." Elle laughs.

"Come on back, ladies," Calista says, motioning for us to follow her to the table near the back.

The store has just closed and she has wine and a charcuterie board set up on the table.

"Thanks for meeting me here," Calista says, opening the bottle. "I know we could have gone somewhere more fun, but I'm so tired. I knew if I left, I would be too tempted to go home and I needed to see you guys to recap on the wedding festivities."

"Wasn't it beautiful?" Elle says.

"Just dreamy. I love Landmark Mountain," Tru says.

"Me *too*," I add. "I need to get over there more often. And I loved the Landmark family. They were all so great."

"Aren't they?" Tru says. "I love it every time Felicity or the rest of them come to see Sadie and always horn in on their visit." She laughs.

"We should insist Sadie invites us to all their family

events," Elle says, her smile wide as she picks up a piece of cheese.

"Agreed," Calista says. "Hey, are you feeling ready for this release?" she asks Elle.

"So ready. I just want the book to be out already. I'm exhausted with all the marketing. It was so much easier when I just put the book out with nobody knowing who I was." She shakes her head.

"Yeah, well, that day is long gone," Calista says, smirking. "And aren't you glad?"

"I am..." Elle's head tilts. "Although now, every time I write a sex scene, I'm imagining people from my dad's church reading it."

We all laugh.

"It'll give them something to try at home," I say.

That makes everyone crack up.

"How are you doing, Poppy? I'm so glad you came tonight," Tru says.

"Yes, I've been wanting to talk to you," Elle says, a mischievous twinkle in her eye. "I was detecting some vibes at the wedding between you and Mr. Bowie."

"Oh no." I laugh, fanning my face. "I don't even know where to start with that guy."

"Let's go back to his hair, please," Calista says. "I need to discuss."

She brings her laptop over so we can see it better, and pulls up BHOTD. We spend the next half hour laughing and swooning over the latest Bowie hair posts.

I don't tell her I've been keeping up with it on the daily ever since I first heard about it.

"The man bun, though," Tru says, sighing. "I love it when he wears it like that."

"I love it like this." Calista taps the picture of him with it down. It's chin-length and a perfect amount of wavy.

The way it was at the wedding.

"Yeah, so good," I say, thinking of how it felt under my fingers. "So soft."

Elle gives me a sharp look. "You say that like you know how it feels."

My face flames and they all stare at me, mouths open.

"Okay, spill," Tru says.

"Oh, you guys." I cover my feverish face.

"Are we coming on too strong?" Calista asks. "We have a way of doing that."

"No, I have a sister. You're fine," I say, laughing. "Uh, Bowie and I…we might have had a little moment…"

A little moment is highly downplaying it on my end, but whatever.

"A moment," Elle says, clasping her hands together. "I *knew* it."

"Mm-hmm, I think we all saw *lots* of moments on that dance floor," Calista says.

"It was so hot." Tru sighs. "Bowie rarely dances and I've *never* seen him dance like that. He couldn't take his eyes off of you!"

"What happened after the dance floor is what I want to know!" Calista says.

They cackle when I flush even brighter.

I hold my wine glass against my face and take a deep breath.

"Something…happened, but it doesn't even matter because he regretted it."

They all talk at once.

Calista clutches my arm. "No!"

"What?" Elle cries.

Tru leans in. "What do you *mean*?"

"Since I'd been running late to get there from work, I didn't get a chance to check in before the wedding, and we danced so long afterward, the room was taken by the time I tried." I pause and laugh when I see the rapt attention on their faces. "It's not going to be that exciting, you can relax."

"I am hanging on every word," Tru says.

"Me too," Elle says, laughing. "Please tell my romance-loving heart that you ended up in the same room with Bowie."

"It gets better…same bed."

Again, they come at me all at once.

"Get out!"

"No way!"

"*Oh my God*!"

"Yeah, and we chatted a little bit before we fell asleep. It was nice. I had a row of pillows between us and everything."

This makes them laugh.

"But somehow, in the middle of the night, we were on each other and it was so—" I drop off here, glazing over at the thought of everything that happened with Bowie.

"Tell me you are not leaving us hanging there!" Calista cries.

"Was it amazing?" Elle breathes.

"So amazing," I whisper. "But then Becca got sick and Bowie ran out of there…and never came back." I exhale. "And I could've gotten past that, but he could hardly look at me at brunch, so I got the hint. He's not interested. He'd had too much to drink, we were in the same bed and all worked up after dancing…it didn't mean anything."

To him, I almost add.

"Oh, I guarantee you, it meant something to him," Elle

says. "I've known that man for years now, and he doesn't just do this. I swear, he doesn't. He *likes* you."

I shake my head. "Even if he entertained the idea for a second, he was over it by morning. And it's Bowie Fox. He could have anyone he wanted. There are entire sites built around him, for crying out loud." I point to his page and we all look at the pictures of him with a variety of different hairstyles.

Calista's shoulders sag as she scrolls down, and we all gasp when we see a picture of his hair even longer than it is now. His helmet is in his hands and he's scowling from the sidelines.

"Holy Nordic god," Tru says.

"Actually, it's Austrian god," Elle says.

"Oh, that's right." Tru shakes her head. "I was blinded by the long blond hair."

Elle clears her throat and looks at me. "You are gorgeous, Poppy. I don't know what you're talking about…this whole *he could have anyone he wanted*. So can you! Are you interested in him?"

Tru and Calista jump in too, telling me I'm so pretty.

I laugh. "You guys are so good for my ego. Thank you. My sister is prettier."

They laugh but then realize I'm serious.

"Okay then, there are two models in your family because seriously, have you seen you?" Calista asks.

I close my eyes and press my lips to the side, trying not to laugh. "I have a healthy dose of self-confidence, but I'm more girl next door than a model!"

"Girl next door Bowie would like to *fuck*," Calista whispers the word *fuck* and we all crack up.

It sure seemed like he liked it. I sigh.

"I'm sorry to disappoint you guys, but there's not going to

be any of that going on, trust me. I got the message loud and clear from Bowie and he does not want—" I point at myself and wave it around my body. "Not happening."

"If Sadie were here, she'd know what to do," Tru says.

"Yes, we need Sadie on the job," Elle says. "In the meantime, I just decided I'm having a party at my place on Saturday night. Can you all be there?"

"I'm in," Calista says.

"I'll check with Henley, but I think we're clear." She rubs her stomach and makes a face. "Do you know I have never liked olives before now, but I just ate one and could eat every single one off this board!"

"Baby likes olives!" Elle cheers.

Calista holds the board up to Tru and Tru scoops off the olives. When she leaves a few, Calista gives her a look and she laughs, taking the rest.

"You're coming Saturday night, right, Poppy?" Elle says, giving me a pointed look.

"Uh, I think I can?"

"Good. And I'll tell my husband to get Bowie's head on straight before that night," Elle says.

"*Oh*," it's dawning on me now, "no, please don't say anything. I'd die if he knew I talked about this with you guys."

"Poppy, those boys do more talking than all of us combined," Elle says, laughing.

Tru nods, cracking up. "That's the truth. And if they haven't, I'm going to put a little bug in Henley's ear to subtly get Bowie to open up. The poor guy needs to let loose and live."

I think of the way Bowie's whole body tensed when he saw me Saturday morning and agree that he might need to loosen up and live…but I'm not going to force him to do that with me.

CHAPTER NINE

BOX IT UP

BOWIE

HENLEY

We still meeting today?

RHODES

Hell yeah!

WESTON

I'll miss you. But married life…guys! Highly recommend. 100/10

PENN

Miss you, brother. And I'm happy you're happy, but dude! Bowie and I are not joining the cult. How many times we gotta say it?

> For once...what Penn said.

WESTON

You will never kill my hope.

RHODES

What Weston said.

HENLEY

I wish Tru would marry me TODAY. Yesterday would've been better.

PENN

YOU GUYS ARE HOPELESS. I've gotta get off this thread right now because I'm gagging. It's too early for shouty caps, and I'll be late to Luminary if I don't. 😊

Luminary Coffeehouse is bustling. It always is on Saturday mornings, but today feels extra crowded. It's been a long week and I'm dragging. I've been sitting with my dad a lot, hanging out with Becca every minute that I'm home, and trying my best to wipe Poppy Keane from my thoughts. It's impossible and exhausting to even keep trying.

I wave at Clara and she motions that she'll be right back with my Americano. Becca is with Mrs. McGregor this morning. They were working on an art project as I was leaving and Becca didn't want to stop, so I'm meeting the guys alone.

I step into our room in the back—even Clara calls it our room now because, besides her, we're the only ones who use it. Henley is the first to arrive and he's nursing his drink, staring into space.

"You okay?" I ask.

"Hey. Yeah. Just tired. I had a meeting about the podcast that went late last night. It's fun, but damn, I already miss the days of just playing ball."

"We sure miss you out there."

He smiles and leans back in his seat. "Thanks, man. I have to admit, my body is thanking me for stopping when I did."

"No doubt," I'm saying, as Rhodes and Penn walk in.

"Two for one," Penn sings.

"How did we manage that?" Henley asks, doing the slap shake with them before I do.

"I had a quieter than normal Friday night," Penn says. "Not intentionally, but it was for the best. I had to pull a runner out of the club last night. There was a stage 5 clinger and it was not good." He shudders. "Sam saved the day by calling. I ended up taking him to Starlight Cafe and then home." He shrugs. "I felt like you old coots, going to bed by ten o'clock."

Rhodes smirks. "Going to bed by ten o'clock is my new favorite thing now that Elle is in there waiting for me." He taps the table. "Hey, you guys are all coming over tonight, right?"

Everyone chimes in with their yeses.

"I might put Becca to bed and then come over. I've been in Denver a lot this week and need to spend some time with her."

"How's your dad?" Henley asks.

"Not good. They admitted him yesterday. I'll be going over there in a little while." I make a face and try to move on. I don't enjoy talking about myself, but I *really* don't like talking about my family. "I'm looking forward to tonight. Should I bring anything?"

"Just yourself," Rhodes says. "Let us know if we can do anything, Bow."

"Will do."

Out of all the years I've known these guys, they've only been around my parents a few times, and those times were doozies. My dad was drunk and belligerent and cussed my mom and me out when we tried to usher him out of the room. It was in German, so no one but us knew the vile things he was saying, but I'm pretty sure everyone got the gist.

"Is your brother in town?" Rhodes asks.

My brother is another topic I avoid. We've been estranged for years and although I hate it, I've learned to live with it. Well, if shoving it to the recesses of my mind to avoid thinking about it is learning to live with it…

Yeah. I've got issues.

"No. He wants nothing to do with my dad, so I'll be surprised if he shows."

If the guys are surprised by this, they don't show it. They've learned not to push too much about my family and I'm grateful they don't push now.

"Well, I hope your dad will be okay," Henley says.

"Me too," Penn says. "The whole thing sucks."

I nod and am grateful when Clara knocks and steps inside the room, holding a tray of our drinks.

We all thank her and she hurries back out.

"Marv and Walter are on a tear this morning," she mutters.

"I'll handle them," Penn says. He walks out of the room and we look at each other.

"What's with that?" Rhodes asks.

Henley shrugs. "Last time we were in, I noticed that Penn seems to have a way with them."

"Interesting," Rhodes says. He turns to look at me and by the slow, mischievous grin that forms, I'm already nervous.

"What?"

"Oh, nothing. My wife just wanted me to encourage you to let loose tonight. Poppy will be there," he sings.

"Fuck. Why is she everywhere?" I swipe my hand down my face and lean back in my seat, feeling what little energy I had drain out of me.

"Why not?" Rhodes says, shrugging. "She's nice, she's funny…she's really great, Bowie. Honestly, she's like a ray of sunshine in your black-and-white life. I don't know why you're not all over that. She's clearly into you." He frowns. "And you seemed into her at the wedding. A little bit like a stick was up your butt the next day, but that's nothing new for you. Am I missing something?"

"Thanks a lot," I choke out.

Henley and Rhodes chuckle and Penn walks in, shaking his head.

"Those old bastards are trying to scare off the customers. Too crowded for them." He holds out his hand. "But I managed to talk them down."

"How'd you do that?" Rhodes asks.

"Gave them tickets to our first game."

"I thought they hated going to games," Henley says.

Penn shrugs. "They seemed happy about it. At least as happy as those guys ever get."

"We'll let you deal with them from now on." Henley laughs. "Clara will be happy about that."

Penn sits down. "What did I miss?"

"Rhodes is asking what he's missing about Poppy and Bowie because they were all about one another at the wedding and then this one was a distant motherfucker. I noticed that too, but you've been too busy this week with your dad to chat." Henley tilts his head up toward me. "We're waiting for the answer."

My dad being sick has been distracting in a lot of ways, but not nearly enough.

"It's a long story, and one I don't have time to go into," I say, standing up.

"What? You're leaving?" Rhodes frowns up at me. "Come on, man. Talk to us."

"If I want to make it to your house tonight, I need to go see my dad now and then get home to Becca."

"All right. But you're not off the hook. Text us," Penn says.

I lift my hand in a wave and don't say anything, and the motherfuckers notice.

Of course. They might be oblivious about a lot of shit like most men are, but when it comes to gossip, they're like a bunch of old biddies.

"Here, take the book with you," Rhodes says, handing me The Single Dad Playbook. "It'll give you something to read in the hospital."

When I get there, I open our book.

Being in love is making me a better dad.
Hell, I'm a better human for it.
I wake up every morning
and feel so grateful to be alive.
If this is what seeing everything
through rose-colored glasses is like,
I'm all for it.
~Henley

. . .

My jaw clenches and I look up at my dad in the hospital bed. Mom has a chair pulled up to the bed, and her chin is brushing her chest as she dozes. Every now and then, her head flies up and she relaxes when she sees that I'm here before nodding off again. I've tried to get her to go home for a while to rest, but she refuses.

Dad's bad off. His liver is failing, and his organs are shutting down.

I'm shutting down too, but I don't have the health reasons to blame.

Sam wants to know if he'll know when he's in love.
I said I think so, but what the hell do I know?
Will he know?
I'm beginning to think
I'll never know firsthand myself.
~Penn

I sigh, my whole body feeling heavy.

I look at the book again, the words swimming in front of me.

I think we're cured of Levi peeing on trees.
Now he's into streaking.
It was twenty degrees yesterday,
and by the time I opened the car door

to help him out of his booster,
he'd stripped down to his birthday suit.
I swear, this kid is going to be a dangerous teenager.
Hoping that he gets it all out of his system now.
That's how it works, right?
~Rhodes

This one makes me smile, but I still can't shake my mood. Being around my parents has that effect on me, but it's more than that.

Sleeping with Poppy affected me more than it should have. I have so much regret about so many things. I shouldn't have had alcohol. I've never struggled with an addiction like my father has, but it's enough that it lowered my inhibitions. I can't afford to make any mistakes. My daughter is counting on me, and I can't let her down. I'm the only parent she has.

I shouldn't have had sex with Poppy.

I shouldn't be such a cold motherfucker.

I pinch the bridge of my nose, feeling a headache coming on.

I'm there for a few hours and my dad sleeps the whole time. I run to get food for my mom and eat with her and then head home and hang out with Becca. We take a walk and she talks about the emus and cows and goats she met in Landmark Mountain.

"We get pet, Dad," she says for the umpteenth time.

And because I'm already ridden with guilt about the way my life is going and because ultimately, I cannot deny my girl anything for very long, I say yes. I love her so fucking much.

We go to Pet Galaxy and I try to talk her into a fish, but

wouldn't you know it…there's a fresh batch of dogs and cats up for adoption. I move toward the cats because I've heard they're easier to take care of, but Becca goes straight for a little grey-and-white dog. I cringe just looking at it. Hairless except for the mad scientist wisps of hair on its head, its body is spotted and its brown eyes are sheepish as it gazes up at us…with its tongue out. Does it have a single tooth? I'm not sure.

"Look, Dad!" Becca turns to me and sticks her tongue out.

I laugh and shake my head at the same time. "How about this one?" I point to the beautiful cat behind us.

She shakes her head. "No, him." She points at the hairless dog.

Fred and Jenny, longtime employees of Pet Galaxy, are both milling through the kennels and Fred lights up when he sees Becca stick her tongue out.

"You like Martha?" he says.

"Martha," I echo.

My nose curls up just looking at her. She is seriously the most pitiful dog I have ever seen.

Fred opens her kennel and lifts her out of there, holding her close enough for us to pet. I touch her skin and shudder.

Fred laughs. "It's different after you're used to a dog with hair or fur. But she's a sweetheart. And you don't have to worry about shedding!"

"We take him," Becca says.

"Martha is a girl. Would you rather have a boy dog?" I ask hopefully.

"We take Martha. Girls are better."

"Why don't we see if she likes us first," I say.

"I hold her," Becca says.

I look at Fred and he motions for us to follow him to the bench.

"She's not nippy at all?" I ask.

This will be the true test, how Martha responds to Becca.

"She's as docile as they come," Fred says. "Potty-trained, four years old. Her owner is Mary Nugent...did you ever meet her?"

I shake my head.

"She's only lived in town for about a year but is transferring back to California and her new apartment doesn't allow dogs."

Becca holds out her arms and Fred places Martha in her lap.

"Be still with her, okay? It's important to be calm around dogs we don't know," I remind her. "And even after we know them well," I add.

Even I have to admit that the dog nestles right into Becca, which delights her, but she does as I asked and remains calm. The dog looks up at me groggily and then her eyes close and she falls asleep.

"She's sleeping, Dad!" Becca whispers loudly. "We take her home for nap."

I chuckle and so does Fred.

"Looks like you've found the one," he says.

I text the guys after we get home with a carload of dog paraphernalia. I had no idea dog shit was so expensive.

> Sorry, I won't be able to make it tonight. Becca and I got a dog.

I send a couple of photos of Martha and the responses are immediate.

PENN

What the fuck is that?

RHODES

Are you sure that's a dog? Bring her over! We need to meet the newest member of the family…even though I'm a little scared of that thing. Bogey needs friends.

HENLEY

A Chinese Crested. Spectacular. I could not have imagined a better dog for you, my friend. 😄

> Her name is Martha and it's okay, get all the wisecracks out of your system now, because she doesn't need to hear that mess in person.

WESTON

I need to go on a honeymoon more often. You miss me so much you got a dog. You love me. You really love me.

PENN

I miss you, but hell no, I'm not buying a dog.

WESTON

Guess you don't love me enough.

RHODES

Get home and convince Bowie to go out with Poppy. He's got a dog, I think he's ready. And Bowie, get your ass over here tonight! A new dog is no excuse and you know it.

> Yawning. Have fun tonight. Peace out.

I turn my sound off and go play with Becca and Martha.

It's possible that I'm the king of compartmentalizing emotions, but I'm just doing the best I can.

Martha's head leans on my hand and I scratch her head softly. She gives me one long swipe of her tongue and I grimace but smile down at her.

"You're not so bad, are you?"

CHAPTER TEN

ONWARD AND UPWARD

POPPY

"Okay, let me see the outfit," Marley says, motioning for me to move back from the phone.

I set the phone on my bathroom vanity and step back.

She frowns and shakes her head.

"What?"

"You can do better," she says.

I sigh. "What if this is what I feel like wearing?" I pull

down my long-sleeve T-shirt over my jeans. "It's a good color on me, right?"

"You can do better," she repeats. "Do we want Bowie to see you and keep giving you the ice man stare or do we want his mouth to drop and him to not be able to keep his eyes off of you?"

"I want him to stare at me, but me to go like this." I wave my hand and then pretend like I'm shooing something away.

She laughs and rolls her eyes. "Okay, your boobs do look good in it, but turn around, let me see the view from the back." I turn and she yells, "Absolutely not."

"What's wrong with the back?"

"It's covering your tush and that thing is fine! No. Let me see something else. Something that shows off your assets. Come on, Poppy. This is not a work event."

"I wear joggers at work," I mumble.

"Which shows off your tush, I might add."

"Why are you saying tush?"

"Eric's mom is in the next room and you know how particular she is about language." She leans into the phone and whispers, "She doesn't like the word ass *or* butt, so it makes it challenging."

I laugh as I pull a few shirts out of the closet and bring them back to show her.

"Ooo, I like that floral. Let me see it on you."

"K, one sec. I wear a tank top under it—"

"No tank top. Let's see a little cleavage."

I level Marley with a look and she gives it right back.

I put it on, ready to argue my point when she sees how low it is.

"It's perfect," she cries. "Yes. But I think you should wear it with those black pants you bought recently. Your bubble tush will look perfect in those."

I laugh.

"The jeans are good too…but do the black."

"This outfit doesn't scream *here I am, take me*?"

"It screams *I am here to rock your world, but I'm so unavailable to you now, buddy*."

My eyebrows lift. "Okay, that is perfect."

She smiles smugly. "I've done my job."

"Okay, I've gotta go. I'm already a little late."

"Okay, love you. Text me tonight. Or better yet, tomorrow after you've had a wild night of passion."

I scrunch up my face. "I'm unavailable to him now, remember?"

"Oh. We meant that?"

I groan. "Yes! Yes, we meant that."

She sighs. "Damn. I was hoping Bowie would become my brother-in-law one day. After you chip away his icy reserves."

"Sorry to disappoint. Not happening."

"All right. Well, go make him suffer then."

I grin. "Now, you're talking."

When I pull into Rhodes' and Elle's driveway, I gasp. Wow. I haven't forgotten that I'm dealing with the rich and famous, but *wow.*

I knock and Elle opens the door.

"Hello! You look gorgeous. Come in, come in," she says.

"So do you!"

I'm glad now that I went with this outfit because Elle is wearing a short dress and looks stunning. She motions for me to follow her, and I gush over how beautiful the house is. She takes me back to the family room with high vaulted ceilings where everyone is hanging out. I say hello to everyone and hug the girls, scanning the room quickly, but there's no sign of Bowie. The tension in my body eases, but I'm disappointed at the same time.

Elle takes me to the kitchen and there's a massive taco bar set up.

"Bowie got a puppy today…actually, not a puppy. She's a little older, but he bailed." She looks at me apologetically. "Sorry."

"Oh no, don't apologize. I'm happy he's not here. I mean," I hold up my hand, "not happy, but yeah. Just…no, it doesn't matter," I stutter and laugh at myself.

She smiles like she knows exactly how I really feel and sighs. "Sadie is always able to pull off the matchmaking, but clearly I am not the best at making it happen."

"Nothing needs to happen," I say. "In fact, I don't want it to happen."

"Really? From what you said the other night, I could have sworn you were really into him."

"I was," I admit. "But he kind of wrecked it."

"Ah, not already! Give him another chance," she says, smiling.

"He wrecked it pretty bad."

"But he is such a good guy," she says. "He just needs to be shaken. When it comes to relationships, he's been so burned. He needs someone to shake him out of it."

"I don't doubt it. And I can be happy for him from afar when that happens."

"Ugh, so you think you guys won't even be friends?"

"I'm nice to everyone," I say. "But yeah, I don't know. He completely blew me off after a very intimate night. And I don't need that kind of person in my life."

"*Really*. I didn't know that it got that far. When you said something happened, I was thinking just a little…maybe a little kiss or something."

"No," I laugh, cringing. "But it's okay. I know that football players are different than real people. Sorry." I shake my head. "God, I'm putting my foot in my mouth all over the place tonight. I'm not insinuating Rhodes and Henley and Weston are or were any kind of—" I shake my head and she laughs.

"Don't worry. I know. And you're right—a lot of professional athletes are the biggest players. They have every opportunity to be. But that doesn't mean they're all like that."

"I know, and I'm not shaming Bowie for ghosting me after sex. It's just not for me. I am not normally a one-night stand kind of girl. That was actually the first time I'd ever done anything like that and I'm twenty-seven freaking years old."

She makes a sympathetic face. "I hear ya. I'm so sorry it went that way. The thing is, he's not that way either. Like, yes, I think that's happened occasionally, but I don't think he just goes around being a player...at least not from what I've heard him and the guys say. I'd say he is the *opposite* of a player."

I think about that. "Maybe it was just me then...that he regretted. And it's okay. Whatever happened...the whole thing turned me off of him. So I'm good. I don't need this in Silver Hills anyway. Like, I shouldn't have gotten involved with someone in this small town. I can stick to going out with guys who live in Denver, so I don't have to see them on a regular basis if it doesn't work out."

"This is going to be uncomfortable for you. I hate that."

I shake my head and add a dollop of sour cream on my taco. "No, I'll get over it. I'll be fine. I *am* fine."

And I am absolutely fine...until he walks into the party an hour and a half later. By that time, I've thoroughly relaxed and had the best time talking with all my new friends. It's like the air sucks out of the room when he walks in and looks right at me.

Marley was right. I do think the outfit helps. His eyes roam down my body, almost like he can't help himself. Maybe he didn't hate what we did after all. My ego wants to believe that anyway. But he doesn't come search me out either, so there's that. I meant it when I told Elle I was turned off…it'll just take frequent reminders to myself for a while when I see him. And I don't mind if he feels a little regret when he sees me. I don't mind that *at all*.

It gets awkward when we're all talking about how we're ready for the weather to get warmer.

"We need to have a pool party soon, Bowie," Penn says. "I'll bring a few palm trees…see if that makes it feel tropical."

"I'm game," Bowie says. "Let's do it."

"Bowie has an indoor pool, Poppy," Rhodes says, grinning at me. "You'll love it."

I open my mouth to say something, but nothing comes out. I glance at Bowie and he looks as awkward as I feel. Pretty sure Bowie didn't intend for me to be in on that invitation. When the conversation moves on, I go into the kitchen to get a glass of water. I hear something behind me and nearly spill the water when I see Bowie.

"Sorry," he says.

"No problem, just jumpy, I guess." I fill my glass a little more, pulling back once it's full.

"Uh, Poppy. Can I say something?"

I turn toward him and he looks painfully uncomfortable. "Of course."

"I don't normally drink."

Not what I was expecting him to say. I nod when he doesn't say anything else. "Okay."

"My dad is an alcoholic and I haven't struggled with addiction, but I usually avoid it anyway."

He takes a deep breath and runs his hand through his hair. His waves fall back into place and one thick strand lands against his cheek. He's so gorgeous.

"I also don't make it a habit of…sleeping around. Last weekend was…very out of character for me." He swallows hard.

I press my lips together and nod slightly. "It was very out of character for me too. I've…*never* done that actually. I mean, sex, yes, I've done that." I laugh nervously and his lips lift slightly. "But never when it's not…someone I'm…you know, going out with or whatever."

If a hole could come along right now and let me fall into it, I'd be so grateful.

"I didn't handle everything very well afterward," Bowie says.

"It was a little weird," I say, letting out a strangled laugh that is just awful. I feel like I'm in high school all over again, trying to be cool but failing miserably.

There's a painful silence.

I eventually clear my throat and forge ahead.

"How about we just forget it ever happened and move on?" I hold out a hand and he looks at it like it's a foreign object, but then he shakes it slowly. My skin burns from the contact. "Since we'll be running into each other around town and all."

He's quiet for a moment and his jaw clenches slightly. I kind of think I disgust him or something. Whatever I felt having sex with him, all the rainbows and butterflies and bliss…he did not feel the same.

"Okay," he says simply.

He lets go of my hand and leaves the room. It takes me a good ten minutes to work up my nerve to go back to the party, and when I do, he's gone.

CHAPTER ELEVEN

F-WORD

BOWIE

The past few weeks have been mind-numbing. I feel like I'm failing at life. The time I usually spend during the offseason doing fun things with Becca after school has been spent at the hospital with my dad and making sure my mom is okay. Becca isn't being ignored, it's not that. We're usually swimming and spending time hiking or playing in the snow, but it's few and far between. It's now fast food on the way to the hospital and taking a last-minute swim before bed. Eating differently and getting off of our routine is affecting both of us.

As much as I didn't want a pet, I'm eating my words now. Martha is a trouper. I don't know if it's because she's a rescue or what, but she just seems so grateful for any attention. She's actually made my job easier, occupying Becca while we're at the hospital and at home too, when I have things to catch up on. Becca's obsessed with her and Martha goes everywhere we do. People have a physical reaction to the pup and I find myself defensive of the little thing now that I've gotten to know her.

Our time is consumed by my parents and I wish I dealt with all of that better. It's hard to think kindly toward a father who hasn't been kind to me. There are a lot of mixed feelings that come with that and I *suck* at dealing with feelings.

I've been in a constant foul mood, really, since the wedding. Okay, since sleeping with Poppy. I regret blowing her off and I don't deal well with that either.

I call my brother Tobias and he finally answers.

"What's up?" he says.

"Hey, I'm glad you answered. Things aren't looking good with Dad. He's rarely awake anymore."

"Yeah?"

I wait, expecting him to say more, but when he doesn't, I sigh.

"Look, Tobias, this isn't easy for me either. But he's our dad, and at the very least, Mom needs us."

"Mom has never needed us. She's always put him before everyone and everything, especially you and me."

"That may be true, but her family's on the other side of the world and we're at least close enough to remind her to eat and whatnot."

His exhale is loud in the phone. "I'm sorry you're left to

deal with it alone. I just don't think I can do this. I can't afford the time away from work right now. What good does it do if I just end up resenting both of them more?"

"Okay," I say, conceding. "As long as you don't regret not seeing him later. I don't think he's got long."

"I wish I could say I would regret things with Dad. Maybe I will. But all I regret right now is that he hasn't been a better fucking father."

"That's fair," I say. "I feel mostly the same, honestly. I guess I feel the need to try, but that doesn't mean you have to. He certainly doesn't deserve it from either one of us."

"You've got that right. We both have the physical and mental scars to prove it. Look, you're a bigger man than I am, Bowie. We've always known that. Since you were a kid. You've been the star child."

"Don't say that, Tobias. Come on."

He laughs, but it rings hollow.

"I love you, Tobias." I rarely ever say it, so I think it catches him off guard. It does me too, honestly, but sitting at my father's bedside with too much time to think might be messing with my head more than I realized.

"I love you too, little brother. I'm sorry," he says.

"Don't be. If anyone gets it, it's me."

"I would be there for you more than anyone else. Except I'd have to see Mom and Dad if I did that." He laughs again and this time I do too.

"I don't need to see you all the time to know you love me," I tell him.

I wish my daughter could know her uncle better, but that's not something I want to guilt him into doing. Just another reason I appreciate the bond I have with the guys on the team. They've been the family we needed.

"I've done a sorry job of showing it, but thanks for saying

that anyway. All right, motherfucker. Go be the awesome person you are. I'll keep being the scoundrel. Maybe I'll show up there one of these days."

"I won't hold my breath," I grumble, but it doesn't have any bite. "Talk to you later."

"Bye, Bow."

I hang up and stare out the window. Martha skitters over to her water bowl and takes a long drink and then looks over at me. I chuckle when I see the pink bow Becca's put in her hair. When Sadie got back from her honeymoon and met Martha, she had a little bag of dog goodies for us the next time we saw her.

"Hi, Dad," Becca says when she walks into the room.

"Hi, Tater Tot."

"We see Poppy today."

This is how she begins most days, and every day, I think of an excuse for why we can't. Today, though, I pause before going straight to no and gradually nod.

"Okay," I say.

"Okay!" She claps. "We take Martha."

"I'll have to call the facility and see if Martha is allowed. If they say yes, we'll take her. If they say no, she'll stay home."

Becca looks sad for a second, but then she looks around the room. I laugh when she picks up my phone and brings it to me.

Someone named Janice answers and when I tell her my name, she has a momentary freak-out. She gives me the schedule for the day and assures me that it's fine to bring Martha as long as she's well-trained. When I hang up, I smile at my daughter.

"Okay, we can take Martha."

"Yay!" Becca does a little dance that she learned from Cassidy and Audrey. "Dance, Dad."

I chuckle and do a little hip shake, which thrills Becca.

Next, she goes over and carefully picks up Martha. She's really great with her and Fred was right about Martha, she's been angelic with Becca. The first few days we had her, I watched like a hawk and told Becca over and over how to approach the dog, how to pick her up, how to leave her alone while she's eating…but Martha is so easy, I'm not sure it matters.

"We'll go for a little while and when it's time to go, I want you to not give me any fuss," I tell Becca. "We'll have fun and be happy, and then we'll leave and be happy."

I'll repeat this again on the drive over and when we get there.

"No fuss, I be happy," Becca repeats. "Let's go, Daddy."

I groan and pump my fist in fake excitement. This is probably a huge mistake, but I'm in it now.

When we arrive at Briar Hill, Becca speed-walks into the building. It's only then that I consider Poppy might not even be here today. Maybe the fun activities will be distracting enough that Becca won't mind. Who am I kidding? She'll totally mind.

Janice is thrilled to see us when we walk in the door. It makes me question whether this was a good idea, seeing her level of excitement. But then she seems to get ahold of herself and calms down, walking us through our options.

"I was wondering if we could speak to a Poppy Keane," I say.

She looks surprised and a little disappointed. "Oh, sure, yes. Poppy is with a group right now, but if you'd like, I can show you around the building, and by the time we get done, Poppy should be available."

"Great," I say.

She walks us through Briar Hill and it's an impressive building. A lot of kids are here and they look happy as they do various activities. It's encouraging to see that the kids are well supervised. Many of the staff are stepping in to help them participate in activities that might be difficult for them elsewhere. I try to stay in the background and not be a distraction, because several of the directors, when they see me, seem to go into shock.

Becca wants to try volleyball and flag football. She's also interested in swimming, even though I remind her that she can swim in our pool any time. My girl has had swimming lessons since she was little, so she's a great swimmer, but it is never quite enough. She would live in the pool if she could.

We come to the end of the tour and are rounding the corner, back to where we started, when Poppy walks through the doorway. She comes to a standstill when she sees me and then looks at Becca, her face breaking into an excited smile.

"Becca, hi!" she says.

"Poppy!" Becca yells.

I don't even bother to remind her about inside voices because they won't be surprised by her loudness here and she's too excited to see Poppy to hold back. She stops in front of Poppy and stares up at her.

"Ooo, ice lashes," she says, pointing a little too closely at Poppy's eyes.

Poppy's head tilts back, and I step closer to make sure Becca doesn't accidentally poke Poppy in the eye. From here I can see that Poppy has white on her eyelashes instead of black mascara. The look is different, but it works on her. I think *anything* works on her.

"Ice lashes," Poppy repeats, looking puzzled. She lifts her fingers to her eyelashes and freezes. "Oh no, did I not put on my mascara again? Ugh," she groans. "This is the primer to make my lashes healthy, and I keep forgetting that it's not the last step because it feels like mascara."

"Pretty," Becca says adoringly. "Ice lashes," she repeats in awe.

Poppy laughs. "Well, I'm afraid I won't have ice lashes for much longer, but I love that name for it. I'm going to get my mascara and fix this. But—oh my God!" she says, suddenly noticing Martha on the leash behind me.

Martha chooses this moment to move forward and sit down at my feet.

"Who is this?" Poppy says, eyes wide. She bites her lip and gives me a funny look.

"This is Martha, our new dog," I say.

"Wow, she is something," Poppy says.

"She so pretty," Becca gushes.

"I love her hair bow. I've never seen a dog like her," Poppy says, trying to say all nice things when I can tell she really wants to laugh.

Somehow Poppy doesn't make me as annoyed as everyone else who has made fun of Martha. But I don't question that right now.

"I'm so excited you're here, Becca," she says. "Did Janice show you around?"

"Yes," Becca says. "I love it."

"Excellent. We'll have to see what you love the most around here. I'm going to be working with volleyball today. Would you like to try that?"

"Yes," Becca says emphatically.

Poppy laughs. "Perfect. Let's go. We're about to start." She turns and looks at me over her shoulder. "If you'd like to leave Becca here, you can. I can keep her busy for a few hours. I heard about your dad," she adds. "I'm sorry he's not doing well."

"Thank you," I say. My mouth parts and I'm uncertain about what to do. I surprise myself by saying, "It would actually be great if I didn't have to take Becca to the hospital today. I had planned on staying, but if you're sure she'd be okay here, I can come pick her up whenever you say."

"That would be fine. I could also drop her off at your house if that would be more convenient for you." She holds up her hand and shakes her head. "Forget I said that, I was thinking we were the *f*-word," she mouths the last part.

I frown, trying to get what she's saying.

She holds up her hand around her mouth and whispers, "Friends."

I chuckle despite how awkward this is. "We started over, remember?" I say, somewhat grumpily. "But you don't have to go to that trouble, really, I'll come back for her."

"It's no trouble at all. Let me help. I'm sure you can use the time."

I nod finally. "You know what? I could. My mom needs me to run a few errands for her. It would help a lot."

"Consider it done," she says.

"Thank you."

"I'll just need you to sign a few things with Janice before you go. And I believe you know how to reach me. Here, I'll give you another card if you tossed the other one."

I smirk. "No, I still have your card."

She lifts her eyebrows. "Okay, cool. Well, I'll text when I'm on my way or just let me know when it's a good time to bring her back. We'll think of tons of fun things to do until then."

"Thank you, Poppy."

"You're welcome, Bowie."

We share a long look. I repeat the plan to Becca and tell her bye, but she is already walking away.

"I see how it is," I say. "Hey, my girl, hug me before you go."

Becca giggles and turns back to hug me. Poppy's smiling as she watches us, and then Martha and I watch them walk away.

CHAPTER TWELVE

FILLING THE GAPS

POPPY

I lead Becca into the gym, where the kids are already warming up. We walk over to Angela, who's tossing the volleyball back and forth in her hands.

"Becca, this is Angela. She's one of the coaches here. Angela, this is Becca. She's joining us today."

"Hi, Becca," Angela says. "I'm glad you're here."

"Hi," Becca says, shyer than she is with me.

"Do you like volleyball?" Angela asks.

"I like..." Becca nods.

She looks at me then, uncertain. I give her a reassuring smile and hold up my hands for Angela to pass the ball. She tosses it and Becca laughs when I catch it.

"Would you like to play with the team right now, or would you rather watch this time and I'll show you a few tips?"

Becca nods.

"Watch this time?" I check.

"Watch," she says.

"Okay, how about we give this ball back to Angela and I'll get one for us to practice with." I toss the ball to Angela and she waves at us before jogging off to start the game.

I grab another ball and take Becca to the side. When the game starts, I point out the server and then show her how to hold her hands to make a serve like that. Demonstrating a few times, I eventually hand her the ball and she tries. She yelps when the ball goes flying, but it's a good serve.

"Excellent, Becca. You've already learned the hardest part."

She beams. "I like bollyball."

I grin at her pronunciation. "Bollyball would've been a better name for it, wouldn't it? I like volleyball too."

"You are fun," she says. "Daddy is sad."

I falter, pausing from showing her another way to hit the ball. Maybe I didn't hear her right. "Sad? Or fun?"

She nods. "My daddy always sad." She reaches out and taps near my eye. "He sad right there."

I swallow. I think she's saying that he has sad eyes. Or is she saying he's been crying? Either way, if I'm right, this is breaking my heart right now.

"Is he sad about his dad being sick?"

She shrugs. "He sad because I have no mommy."

Oh. My heart pinches and I step closer to her without even realizing it until our shoes touch.

"I sad too because I have no mommy, but I have Daddy."

"And he's a great daddy, isn't he?"

"He's a great daddy," she repeats, laughing. She leans in. "My pictures are nice. You come see my pictures."

I tilt my head. "Maybe you could bring one of your pictures the next time you come here."

She frowns and shakes her head. "Too big," she says, holding her hands out to her sides as far as they'll go. "I have this many."

"Oh, lots of pictures!" I laugh.

She looks so pleased that it warms my heart. Her personality is pure sunshine. If Bowie is as sad as Becca says he is, and for as little as I know Bowie, I believe his daughter is completely right, then I'm so glad he has her in his life to inject some joy.

We join the next game and Becca picks it up quickly. There are a few ways I can tell that Bowie has worked with her a lot. Besides her obvious love for being active, Becca has surprising endurance to stay engaged in the game. I can also see an advanced level of sportsmanship with how well she handles it when she doesn't make the best plays.

When the game is over, I introduce her to a few of the other kids and casually observe her interactions, the way I do with all of the kids who come through here. Angela turns on the music as we're wrapping up the session. It's a slow song so we can stretch, and I stand in front of the kids, going through each move as Angela walks around and makes sure no one is doing anything too strenuous. At the very end, we shake out our hands and take deep, cleansing breaths, and then smile at each other.

"Have a wonderful day," I say. "I'll see you next time."

"See you next time," some of them chant back.

When the kids start clearing out, Becca comes and stands next to me.

It's technically my last class of the day, but I want to give Bowie plenty of time.

"Would you like to see my office and maybe color for a while?"

"Yes!" she says excitedly.

We go to my office and Becca studies everything in the room like it's a science project. She's endearing as she sticks her face close to every book, looking them over. She brightens when she sees a picture of me and my sister, tapping it.

"Who that?" she asks.

"That's my sister, Marley."

And then when she sees the picture of me with my parents and Marley, she stares at it for a long time. Eventually she points at it and says, "Your mommy."

I nod, a lump forming in my throat. She's breaking my heart about her mom. I can't help but wonder what happened to hers. Where is she? Why isn't she part of her life? My mind jumps to the worst scenarios. Unfortunately, I see way too many marriages break up between parents of kids with disabilities. I wish that weren't the case, but it is, and it's understandable in many ways with all the pressures and challenges it brings into your life that you didn't see coming. But it kills me nonetheless.

Growing up, our neighbors, the O'Haras, had a daughter my age who had Down Syndrome. I adored Kara and she adored me. We had more classes together when she was younger, but we still ate lunch together throughout high school and hung out after school. She died in a car accident when we were seventeen and I still miss her. But between complications with the different surgeries she had, and the financial struggles it put on them, the O'Hara's marriage didn't last. I think seeing what they went through *and* what Kara went through shaped what I wanted to do with my life.

I can't remember if it was an interview with Mr. Rogers or in his documentary *Won't You Be My Neighbor?*, but he talks about his mom in such a beautiful way that it's stuck with me. When he was a boy and saw scary things in the news, his mom would say, "*Look for the helpers.*" I've tried to apply that to my job and be a helper. So often, the marginalized are ignored. In a way, it's my calling to see a need in these families' lives when they have a child with disabilities and to do what I can to help.

But I'm not exaggerating when I say that I get so much more out of it than they do. The kids I have the honor of working with at Briar Hill have become my favorite people on earth. Simply put, they fill my life with joy.

I get a text from Bowie an hour later.

> **BOWIE**
> I didn't mean to be this long. I can stop by and pick Becca up. Or you're welcome to bring her to Silver Hills if that's easier, given the time.

> I'm happy to bring her home. We'll be about thirty minutes.

> **BOWIE**
> Thank you. See you then.

He sends his address in the next text, and Becca and I leave within five minutes. Becca chats all the way, excited for me to see her room and pictures and pool and yard...and more of Martha.

I smile the entire drive. It's doubtful that Bowie will even invite me inside and I don't want to disappoint Becca, but I'd rather not be in his space either.

"I'm sorry, Becca. I can't stay," I tell her. "Your house sounds wonderful, but I need to go home and do some work."

I'm not certain she hears me or if she's choosing to ignore what I've said, but I don't try to repeat it.

Bowie lives in a gated community on the lake that Rhodes and Elle also live on, and he's already cleared my name with the guy at the gate, but unlike them, there aren't any guards once I reach Bowie's house. He seems to stay under the radar more than some of the other players. With the exception of the BHOTD posts about him, I don't see a lot of press on him. It must be the intimidating presence he has that lets people know he's off-limits. I'm glad for his sake that he has that privacy with Becca.

"Beautiful house," I say as we pull down the long driveway.

The house is surrounded by trees, and the lake and mountains are the perfect backdrop for the dark blue house with a turret.

"Yes," Becca says.

I park and we get out of the car. The front door opens before Becca reaches it, and Bowie stands there holding Martha, yet still looking formidable. I lift my hand to wave.

"It was fun, Becca. I hope you can come see me again at Briar Hill!"

I back away and she grabs my hand and tugs.

"Come see," she says.

"I was telling Becca I should be going," I tell Bowie. "Have a good night."

"Please stay with me," Becca says. She looks at me and I have a hard time resisting. "See my pictures."

"Becca, if Poppy needs to go, you should let her go."

"See my mommy pictures," she says, starting to cry.

I look at Bowie helplessly and am surprised to see the look of devastation cross his face. It makes me hesitate.

"I can stay for a few minutes if that's helpful," I tell him quietly. "I don't want to override what you're saying in any way, but I can stay long enough to see what she wants to show me."

He gives a terse nod. "Thank you. That's nice of you."

To Becca he says, "Poppy can stay for a few minutes, but let's not fuss when it's time for her to go, okay, Becca?"

Becca sniffs. "Okay. Come on, Poppy." She holds out her hand and I take it, and she hurries us through the house.

Now that I'm inside, I want to take my time and look at their house. It's not as massive as Elle's, but it's still larger than I'm used to. The decorating is more modern than I like, but it's beautiful and clean. The kitchen has open cabinetry, where there are minimal dishes, and there are unique materials used for the walls and flooring; however, Becca is pulling me forward too fast for me to see what it is exactly.

The house is long and when we reach one side, I can see that the turret is full of windows and leads to the pool. The pool is both indoor and outdoor, with a glass solarium on the indoor part and a place to swim through to the outdoor. It's the most spectacular pool I've ever seen.

"That is wicked stellar," I say, exactly the way my granddad would say it, stellar sounding more like stella.

I hear Bowie snort behind me and turn around. He's looking down and trying to hide the smile on his face. When he feels my eyes on him, he lifts his head and the half-smile is still there.

"What do you have against the word wicked?" I ask.

"Nothing." His face is pure innocence now, but I think of

what the hair sites would be saying about him if they were witnessing this. His hair is like the poster child of dream hair. One wave is perfectly outlining his face and just lightly curves against his chin…which makes me stare at his neck. A memory of gliding my tongue across his neck and the gasp it elicited from him comes back in vivid color.

I must stare at him too long because his head tilts.

"Do I have toothpaste in my hair or something?" he asks.

"No, I was just thinking it should be illegal for a man to have hair as pretty as yours. I bet you don't even appreciate it."

His face crinkles up into a frown, but I think he's trying not to laugh. There's more than a hint of amusement in his eyes and it emboldens me.

I lift my hand up and drop it, unable to form a coherent thought. "BHOTD," I mutter.

"Pardon me?"

I wave him off and Becca whisks me away, leading me down the hall. I hear Bowie on our heels and since he doesn't stop us, I keep going. Becca opens her door and her room is pretty. She has white walls and a pink bedspread.

"I love pink," she says happily.

There are three stuffed animals on her bed and I'm about to comment on them, when I notice the pictures. I'm *beyond* curious about Becca's mom and what she looks like. On one side of the room, picture frames line her desk and several shelves. I look at them closer and am surprised to see that they're mostly the pictures that come with a frame when you buy it, not personal pictures at all. Besides a couple pictures with Bowie and maybe Bowie's parents, each picture has a different woman and a girl. She holds up one where the woman has long blonde hair and points at it.

"You and me," she says.

The full impact of what she's saying hits me hard. This little girl craves—if not a mother's love, at the least, a woman's presence in her life so deeply that she's built this imaginary world where it's true.

I smile at her, trying to swallow down the lump in my throat. My eyes meet Bowie's and the heartache in them is staggering. I turn away, blinking away tears and clear my throat.

"I have an idea," I say. I pull my phone out of my pocket and hand it to Bowie. "Would you take our picture?"

He's surprised at first and it takes him a moment to snap out of it, but he does.

"Sure," he says finally. "Where would you like it?"

"Let's do one in here and one where all those windows were…near the pool. I liked the light in there."

"Me too," Becca says, clapping her hands.

I put my arm around her shoulder and she smiles up at me. I smile back, my heart splitting wide open for this little girl who loves so freely. Bowie takes a few shots and then nods.

"These are nice."

"I see," Becca says.

Her grin splits wide open when she sees the pictures. I peer over her shoulder.

"I approve. Delightful," I say, remembering how much she liked that word the first time we met.

"De-lightful," she repeats.

"Should we take some by the pool too?" I ask.

"Yes!" she yells.

She runs out of the room and I follow.

"Thank you," I hear Bowie say behind me.

"Are you kidding? Your daughter is a rock star."

CHAPTER THIRTEEN
DRAMA QUEENS

BOWIE

It's nice to have an excuse to look at Poppy. I don't like the way my heart thunders in my chest around her—I've become so accustomed to turning off my feelings that sometimes I forget I have one. This time, said heart is probably in a state because my daughter just once again broke it with the pictures, but there's a good chance it's also because Poppy is in our home.

She's perfect with Becca.

It hurts how perfect she is with her.

Scratch that. If I had a heart, it would hurt. But it's proving me wrong right now, pounding complicated rhythms in my chest as I try not to be obvious with my staring.

Poppy's hair is luminous in the solarium. With all the windows and light bouncing off the white gleaming walls and the blue water, she radiates even brighter. There's a dull roar humming through my body, and I feel like Becca, grasping for reasons to make this woman stay longer.

My body doesn't forget the way she felt. Every single nerve ending in my body is drawn to connect to hers again. To latch on like a magnet and not let go.

But that's just because, as uninterested in sex as I like to pretend I am with my friends, my body actually does crave physical contact. Desperately. If not for the fact that I jack off at least once a day, I would've blown my load in Poppy a helluva lot quicker than what happened. As it was, it took every possible resource in my brainpower to hang on as long as I did. Now that I've had a taste of her, everything in me craves more.

And not just anyone, specifically *her*.

That's what's so troubling.

It in no way scratched the itch.

I take a few pictures and Becca studies each one in delight. Poppy adds her approval too.

"These are great. If you text them to me, I will print them and have them ready the next time we see each other," she tells Becca.

"I see you tomorrow," Becca nods. Her excitement is off the charts.

Poppy laughs. "If you come to Briar Hill again, yes!" She wrinkles her nose when she looks at me. "I'm not sure if that's what you had planned for your Saturday, but I *will* be working tomorrow." Her eyes widen like she's just thought of something, and I brace myself because she looks so fucking cute. "I don't suppose you'd feel like helping with flag football tomorrow."

"Oh. Not what I was expecting," I say. I'm not sure what I was expecting since my head was envisioning her in my bed.

Her cheeks flush and I wonder if she can tell what I was thinking.

"You don't have to. It was just a thought. We only do this every other week and I'm not always there, but I agreed to work this weekend. We'd love to have you. It's nonstop entertainment." Her eyes twinkle.

"Yes," Becca says. My girl has already decided we're going.

"Nonstop entertainment, huh? You make it sound like I'm capable of fun."

Her grin deepens and it's an even better look on her. "I didn't say that…"

My lips twitch. "Hmm. Well, in that case, I guess I should come and prove you wrong."

She lifts her shoulders. "I mean, I don't want you to hurt yourself by smiling, but your face probably *could* use the break from your perma-scowl."

I bite the inside of my cheek while she laughs.

Becca looks at me. "Dad, smile!" she demands.

I bare my teeth at my daughter and she cackles. That makes me smile. I roll my eyes when Poppy nudges Becca, saying, "You got one out of him! I'm impressed."

Becca looks at her proudly.

"Should I see if I can round any other players up? Make a day of it?" I ask.

Poppy's eyes go huge. "You think anyone else would be interested?"

I get a little jealous by how excited that makes her. "Maybe."

"It'd be amazing, but really, we'll be happy for even one extra player."

"I'll see what I can do."

Becca gets distracted cooing at Martha and I walk Poppy to the door.

"Thanks again for your time with Becca today. And here…just now. There's nothing you could've done to excite her any more than taking pictures together."

"It was fun. She's so great, Bowie." She worries her bottom lip and pauses by the door, turning back to look at me. "You don't have to tell me, but…is her mom involved in her life?"

I shake my head. "No, not at all."

Her brow furrows and her hand presses against her heart. "That…I'm sorry. That's really…well, I don't even know what to say. She doesn't stay in touch at all?"

"No."

I'd normally leave it at that, so I don't know why I keep going now.

"She thought she was up for all of it, a baby, my career, marriage, but everything became more involved than we expected. My career blew up, Becca had to have surgeries right away. She didn't want it after all. Any of it."

The expression on her face is exactly why I don't talk about it, not seriously anyway. The guys know about Adriane, and when I say anything now, it's flippant comments and jokes. I don't like seeing the pity on anyone's face when it comes to me. I saw that enough as a kid when they realized the kid who was an athletic maniac also had a raging alcoholic for a father. Like maybe they suddenly understood why I was so driven to succeed.

What they didn't know was that it had nothing to do with any drive I had for excellence. Not then anyway. My dad's family was wealthy and even as a kid, we always had famous people come to the house. He liked to collect celebrities, as if they were trophies. But then I gained notoriety when I beat an Olympic swimmer at a swim meet. He was there to blow up a charity function and I stole the show. And I kept doing it for several years, even after we moved to the US, swimmers from all over the world coming to swim with me, or we'd travel to various competitions. I beat every single one. I became my dad's trophy and it was both necessary and torturous. I only wanted to keep my dad on the road with me to keep him away from my mom and brother. He couldn't afford to let any bruises show on me since I was swimming all the time, but when we were home, my mom and brother weren't safe from his fists.

Eventually, I was sick of being his show pony and turned my focus on the sport I loved most, football.

"That's such a heavy responsibility you're carrying alone, Bowie," she says.

I swallow hard, still stuck in the past. But what she's said registers, and for some reason, it doesn't hit me completely wrong like it would coming from most people I don't know well. Maybe because it's said with such understanding and compassion.

"Loving Becca is the easiest thing I have ever done," I say finally.

And it is. Even on our hardest days, when she's struggling with her temper and having a meltdown, I have always loved being with her most. It doesn't mean life is easy. Some of her health struggles have nearly taken me out, and I hate to see her going through any kind of hardship more than anything…

but the heavy responsibility I carried was as a child. As a man, I've earned my stripes.

And doing it alone suits me fine. I have help when I need it.

She smiles. "And you love her so well," she says. "That little girl worships the ground you walk on."

"Seems like she worships the ground you walk on right about now," I say, my lips lifting.

Her laugh bounces around my house and injects it with warmth. "I'm just the new, shiny thing." She waves me off. "It'll pass."

I tilt my head, narrowing my eyes. "Becca doesn't really work that way. Once she's in, she's all in."

She laughs. "I love that about her." She frowns suddenly and points at me. "Hey, wait a minute. Is that…are you smiling?"

"Shut up," I mutter, grinning down at the floor.

I hear a gasp and groan.

"Dad! Say sorry," Becca says, coming up behind me with Martha.

"Sorry I said shut up," I tell Poppy. I let out a long-suffering sigh and it just makes Poppy laugh.

"The games will begin at ten in the morning."

"We'll be there."

She nods. "Excellent. See you then."

"Excellent." Becca nods just like Poppy and my face actually feels weird from smiling as much as I have.

She leaves and I loathe admitting it, but…I kind of miss having her here.

I pick up my phone and text the guys.

> I'm taking Becca to Briar Hill tomorrow at ten and agreed to play flag football with them. Anyone else in?

HENLEY

I'll be there in spirit. My leg's not up for it and we're taking the girls to Boulder this weekend. Wait a second. Isn't this where Poppy works???

WESTON

Dang. I'd love to get in on the next one. We have plans with Sadie's family.

RHODES

Let me see if I can pull it off. I think maybe I can.

PENN

Hell to the yeah. Is it okay if I bring Sam?

> Absolutely. Just give him a heads-up first about Briar Hill in case he doesn't know already. It won't be the fast-moving pace he might be used to keeping with flag football.

I don't have any concerns about Sam at Briar Hill. He's fantastic with Becca, as evidenced by the massive crush she has on him. But it's helpful to be prepared before being around kids with a large range of different disabilities.

PENN

Will do. But have you seen the kid lately? He'll be eleven before too long, so maybe it's puberty? I don't remember being so slow at his age. I'm not sure he's capable of hurrying to do anything.

WESTON

LOL. He hightailed it out of the house when Rhodes stuck an ice cube down his shirt the last time we were all together.

RHODES

He swapped out my water for Sprite and filled my bowl of chili with El Yucateco habanero sauce. That shit only takes a little bit to spice things up and I think he just dumped it in the bowl.

HENLEY

😂 I wondered why you were chasing him.

RHODES

Yeah, don't feel sorry for him. He was just fine.

PENN

I thought he was gonna pee his pants waiting for you to try the chili. 😂 I'm glad I was around to witness that.

RHODES

Where is the loyalty? Bowie? You gonna let them talk this shit with me?

> I think I might have it all on video.

I chuckle to myself and then wait for the onslaught of texts.

They don't disappoint.

RHODES

No fucking way. Where's the fuckin' respect?

> **PENN**
>
> I just choked on my burrito. I'm glad I didn't have El Yucateco on it because some came up my nose.
>
> **WESTON**
>
> You guys should take this bit on the road. So fucking funny.
>
> **RHODES**
>
> I'm not even trying to be funny!
>
> **PENN**
>
> I wasn't either, and hot damn, my nose burns like the bowels of Lucifer.
>
> **HENLEY**
>
> It's like a front-row seat to SNL when someone really good is on and even the cast can't stop laughing…but free!

These guys. I swear. My chest and head feel lighter just from this crazy thread.

> **RHODES**
>
> Okay, I checked and I can be there for a little while. It'll feel good to do something active outside of the gym.
>
>> Okay, thanks. Becca will love seeing you guys there.
>
> **HENLEY**
>
> Hey, wait! You never answered my question. POPPY?
>
>> She works there, yes.

HENLEY
And?

And she'll love seeing you there too.

WESTON
And you know this…how?

God, you're a bunch of nosy birds.

WESTON
And this surprises you…why?

RHODES
Sounds like we're needing a little update.

When I don't say anything, Penn jumps in.

PENN
Waiting…

There's not really a story to tell. I took Becca to Briar Hill today. She hung out there with Poppy and Poppy brought her home. She mentioned flag football tomorrow because, you know Becca, she wanted to go back. Poppy distracted her by inviting her to play flag football, and before I knew it, I was invited too.

RHODES
I think that's the most words I've ever heard you say at one time. What are you not saying is what I want to know right now!

PENN
She invited you because she wants IN YOUR PANTS.

She's already been in my pants and tolerated me acting like a bastard afterward.

I keep that little nugget to myself or I'll never get any sleep tonight.

> **WESTON**
>
> Don't scare Bowie off, pretty boy.

> **PENN**
>
> Ugh. I thought you guys had stopped calling me that and I was happy about that fact. I'd say I'm more rugged than pretty, wouldn't you?

> **HENLEY**
>
> The fact that you're discussing it makes the nickname still work for you, pretty boy. That and your pretty black hair. 😌

> **PENN**
>
> FUCK ME SIDEWAYS! I've had something to talk about this whole time. I can't believe I almost let you guys sidetrack me!!! This is news. I only wish we were together right now to see your faces. Our man of mystery, Bowie Fox, has entire blogs, Instagram/Tiktok accounts, you name it… based on his HAIR. It's called BHOTD. Can you fucking believe it? 😂 I hereby bequeath the pretty boy title to you, Bow.

> What?

I open my browser. I can't even remember the last time I checked social media. BHOTD. Is that the same thing Poppy said earlier? I didn't know what the hell she was saying. I watch in shock as Bowie's Hair of the Day pops up in small letters under BHOTD. The fuck? Article after article pops up, but I click on a video before reading anything. It's nothing but music and photo after photo of me and my hair. People really pay attention to this shit? I click another and it's dozens of shots of me with a man bun. Another has me running my hands through my hair countless times.

> **HENLEY**
> Oh, this is rich. LOL

> **RHODES**
> Elle is saying she's known for a while! We're having our first married fight that she kept this news from me.

> **WESTON**
> I can't breathe. This is too good.

> Where do people come up with this shit?

> **PENN**
> From your pretty head, that's where.

I groan and toss my phone on the island, shaking my head. My phone buzzes for the next ten minutes, but I ignore it, and *that* makes me laugh harder than anything because I know those drama queens will go crazy if I ignore them.

CHAPTER FOURTEEN

TIN MAN

POPPY

The sun shines brightly over the field, the small crowd forming already lively with excitement and they don't even know what I know…that Bowie Fox will be here and possibly some of his NFL teammates. The parents of these kids are the best, so supportive and grateful for the outlet Briar Hill provides for their loved ones. We have some who aren't as involved, but they're not out here on a chilly Saturday morning.

My adrenaline skyrockets when I see Bowie striding toward the field, his hair looking like perfection as it blows in the breeze. Does the guy ever have a bad hair day? And oh my God, Becca is between Penn and Sam, and on the other side of him is Rhodes. I can't believe they came, and even better, they're all wearing Mustangs jerseys. The wow factor is off the charts. Becca's wearing a Bowie jersey and Sam is wearing Penn's.

The admiration I have for these players quadruples.

"Poppy!" Becca yells.

I hug her when she gets closer. "Hi, guys! I'm so excited you're here!"

"Hey, Poppy," Rhodes says. "This'll be fun."

"This is Sam Miller," Penn says, putting his hand on the boy's shoulder. "Sam, this is Poppy Keane."

"Hi, Sam. It's nice to finally meet you. Thanks so much for coming." I smile at the boy. He's adorable with a mop top of thick black hair.

"Nice to meet you too," he says, grinning. He glances over at Penn and Penn bumps his knuckles like he's approving something.

Bowie tilts his chin up at me. He has a way of looking at me like he's trying to sort out an equation or figure out a puzzle, and today is no different. I want to yell that I'm not that hard to figure out, but I kind of like his eyes on me.

"Weston and Henley wanted to be here too, but they had other commitments," Bowie says formally.

I sigh inwardly. I thought after our last interaction, it'd be a little easier between us, but we're back to being stiff with each other.

"Well, I'm thrilled that I have you guys. Thanks again. I'll introduce you to everyone and then let's play!"

After the introductions are made, rules are repeated, and

teams are assigned, we get started. Bowie adjusts his jersey and grins as he high-fives the group of kids on his team. I'm happy to see that he's not formal with them at all. Nope, that's only reserved for me. And then he puts his hair back in a man bun with easy precision, and I feel like I might slowly die right here, right now. Didn't know I had a thing for man buns, but on Bowie, I *so do*.

When I finally tear my eyes away from Bowie, I notice Rhodes smirking at Bowie from across the field.

"Don't get too comfortable," he calls. "We're gonna show you how it's done."

"You mean Sam and Davey are gonna show us how it's done," Bowie shoots back, making Davey on Rhodes' team jump up and down.

I laugh. "Oh, so we're already trash-talking?" I'm on Bowie's team and he looks at me over his shoulder, looking smug.

"We've got this," he says, winking at Daphne next to me.

I die.

"Penn, keep it fair," Rhodes says to Penn.

Penn is going to be the ref for this first game and he blows his whistle dramatically, making all of the kids jump and laugh.

"I can maybe ignore calls in exchange for pizza," Penn says.

Becca moves next to me.

"What are we gonna do with these guys?" I ask her.

"Play," she says.

I laugh and high-five her.

As we get into place, I pass Bowie. "Try to keep up," I tell him, tightening my ponytail.

"I'll try," he says, flashing a grin that nearly makes me trip.

The game begins and it's a combo of skill and chaos as we dart around the field. The cheering from the sidelines is double what it usually is. We are giving them a show and Bowie and Rhodes play their roles perfectly, throwing exaggerated fake-outs and dramatic dives that have the kids staring at them in shock and then roaring with laughter.

Becca gets the ball and runs with it…in the wrong direction at first, but we get her turned back around and she makes the first touchdown. Everyone, including the kids on the other team, huddle around her to cheer. Bowie runs over and lifts her in the air, and everyone cheers louder. It's so cute and funny that I swear my heart is going to explode.

At one point, I shock myself by intercepting a pass from Rhodes and take off down the field, but then, somehow, I trip and go flying. Bowie's hands grip my waist and I'm lifted and turned so when I fall, I have a nice body to land on instead of the hard field. I stare down at Bowie, breathless. He's looking up at me, dazed. I put my hands on his cheeks and hair.

"Are you okay?" I ask, panicking that I have just injured a professional football player in what was supposed to be a low-key game of flag football.

"Just fine," he says.

"Oh, okay, good," I say, still staring down at him. "I would hate to be the reason the star linebacker of the Mustangs is injured."

Having all his hard ridges hitting me in all the right spots is not a hardship.

"Are you okay?" he asks, and I think he's trying not to smile.

"Oh, yeah, I'm fine," I say, playing with his hair between my fingers. "It's even softer than what they say."

He stares at me for a few beats. "So you know about the blogs too…"

I grin. "I do."

He lets out a little growl and I crack up. His lips lift a tiny bit and it thrills me.

"Should we keep playing?" he asks.

My cheeks break out into a fiery heat. I clamber to get off of him, but for some reason, I'm dizzy and can hardly manage it. He lifts me up, standing at the same time, and sets me on solid ground.

"Thank you," I say weakly.

He nods and I jump when Penn blows the whistle. Bowie chuckles and I turn and jog away like I meant to do all of that.

Somehow, despite my sudden clumsiness playing around Bowie, we win the game. The other team wins the next, and on the third, I sit out to take pictures of everyone. I get some great ones—the kids all laughing after the game, one of Becca celebrating with Bowie that I love, and a funny one of Penn pretending to throw a penalty flag.

After the game, the guys sign autographs and once it clears out, I thank them again.

"And signing autographs at the end…you guys went above and beyond," I say. I'm so touched by how great they were with the kids. "Can I take you out to thank you? Starlight Cafe? Serendipity?"

"I could use a burger from Starlight Cafe," Rhodes says. "But you aren't paying." He smirks.

Elle nestles into his side. She showed up during the second game, cheering on the sidelines, and then played in the last game. "Mmm, that sounds so good."

"We're in," Penn says.

Bowie nods.

"Great." I think I've smiled nonstop today. "I'll meet you over there!"

Rhodes, Elle, Penn, and Sam are at the table when I get there, and Bowie and Becca walk in right behind me. I end up between Bowie and Becca, and as we're eating, various people from town come and talk to the guys.

"Is it always like this?" I ask Elle.

"It happens more during the offseason…and it's more the tourists than locals around here," she whispers.

I'm impressed with how gracious Bowie, Rhodes, and Penn are with each person. It must get exhausting to always be *on*.

When we finally have a moment to ourselves, we talk about how fun the day was.

"It's obvious all the kids absolutely adore you, Poppy," Elle says.

"Aw. Really? I mean, I adore all of them, so I'm glad if they love me back," I say, laughing. My cheeks are warm from the praise.

"It's great what you're doing," Bowie says quietly, and my cheeks get even hotter. "I regret not bringing Becca there sooner. We've gone to a lot of places over the years, some excellent, some not so much, but we hadn't gotten to Briar Hill yet. We'll be back, for sure."

I couldn't wipe the beam off my face if I tried.

As we say bye in the parking lot a little later, I put my hand on Bowie's arm without meaning to.

"Sorry," I say, dropping my hand. "I just…I have a little something for Becca in my car."

"You don't need to apologize," he says.

"I just…I wasn't trying to grab you."

His lips pucker as he gives me an amused look. "Now or out on the field?" His voice remains even despite his teasing.

I groan. "You grabbed me out there!"

"So you wouldn't hurt yourself."

"It was a much better landing," I say softly.

His eyes glitter with something, I wish I knew what. He's so damn hard to read.

"Hold on one sec, Becca," I say, holding up my hand. I turn to my car and get the bag out of the backseat.

When I hand it to her, she laughs.

"I love presents," she says.

Bowie smiles a real smile now. There's no mystery to him when he looks at his daughter. He is an open book when it comes to her, and I adore that about him.

Becca flings the tissue paper out of the bag and Bowie and I scramble to catch it before it flies everywhere. She takes the picture out and stares at it, a huge smile on her face.

"Me and you," she says happily. She holds the picture of the two of us from the other day up to Bowie. "Look, Dad. Me and Poppy."

"It sure is," he says, his eyes meeting mine. "Thank you."

I smile and nod slightly.

"That was…really wonderful of you," he adds.

I stare up at him, surprised by his rare vulnerability.

Becca lightens the moment by waving the frame in front of us again. "I love me and Poppy. I put it on my shelf."

I get choked up and fortunately, I don't think Bowie sees because Becca throws her arms around me and we hug it out. When we pull apart, I look at Bowie again and his expression has gone completely soft and melty. He swallows hard and gives me a closed smile. It wouldn't seem like much coming from anyone else, but from him, it feels like maybe I've cracked through just a tiny bit of his armor.

CHAPTER FIFTEEN

SMALL MERCIES

BOWIE

I inhale the aroma of coffee before I even push through the door of Luminary Coffeehouse, ready for my coffee fix. I haven't slept enough the past week and a half. Things have escalated with my dad…he's hanging on, but it's not looking good. Seeing him so close to the end is bringing up memories I thought I'd buried, things I needed to forget.

And then there's Poppy. It doesn't help that I've seen her almost every afternoon, dropping Becca off at Briar Hill.

We've established a routine now, where I drop her off and she brings Becca home in the evening. Those few minutes at the door, chatting about the day, have become a bright spot.

Damn it, I don't want to think about Poppy Keane.

Music blasts through the speakers and I wince at the sound. Patrons are scattered around mismatched tables, and normally they'd be chatting or looking at their phones, but not today. Every eye is on me as I walk inside.

Clara stands behind the counter, her usual wide grin stretched across her face.

"Morning, Bowie!" she calls, buzzing with more energy than is reasonable for this hour. "You're just in time."

"For what?" I clear my throat to get some of the gravel out.

Clara's grin is mischievous and I get a bad feeling. "Dance-off."

I stop mid-step, brows scrunching up. "Dance-off?"

"You heard me," she says, hands on her hips. "No coffee for you boys today until you dance. It's my new policy."

A groan rises from the corner table where the resident grumps, Walter and Marv, sit at their usual table…without coffee.

"This is ridiculous," Marv mutters, crossing his arms.

"Back in my day, we just handed over a nickel and got our coffee," Walter scowls. "No wiggling involved."

I pinch the bridge of my nose. "It's too early for this."

"It's never too early for joy," Clara chirps.

Henley walks in and Clara points at him.

"Dance for your coffee, Henley."

He does a little shimmy and she beams, handing him the solar latte that already has his name on it in decorative letters. The patrons cheer for him. What fresh torture is this?

"That's how it's done," Clara says, nodding at me.

Weston and Penn walk in together and pause when they see me standing there like a lump.

"Hey, man," Weston says. He hugs me.

"Welcome back," I say.

"Thanks." He grins. He motions for me to go ahead. "You got your coffee yet?"

"Gotta dance for it," I grumble.

"Come again?"

"You heard him right," Clara says. "Dancing for the coffee. I'm ready for spring and the weather isn't cooperating. This is the next best thing."

Penn grins. "You got it, Clara." He does an elaborate break-dancing spin I have no idea how the hell he pulls off, but he does and the place erupts in cheers.

Weston laughs. "Show-off." He takes off his jacket and does a boy band move, which makes everyone go crazy.

Rhodes walks in to the cheers and thinks it's for him. He struts his shit without even being asked and Clara hands him the coffee, which earns more cheers.

"Your turn, Bowie," Clara says.

Marv gets tired of waiting and cuts in front of me, doing the Cleopatra and Walter folds his arms over his chest, but walks over, shaking his ass slightly.

"I coulda broken my hip," Marv says, pointing at Clara.

"But you didn't," Clara sasses back.

I tilt my head back and groan, but even I am smiling by now. Clara lifts her eyebrows at me, waiting.

"Fine, but it's not gonna be pretty." I go robot with it and the place goes wild.

"You're good!" Clara cries.

"Don't quit your day job," Walter says.

"You're lucky I love you, Clara," I tell her.

"I love you too, Bowie Fox. And you'll be back," she

says, grinning as she hands me the coffee. "I can't wait to see what you do next time."

"So cheeky," I grumble.

She just laughs.

"Next time, try jazz hands," Marv says.

I raise my cup in a mock toast and head back to our room. The noise barely quietens when we close the door and Weston laughs.

"Clara's feeling good today," he says.

"So are you, by the looks of that tan. You trying to compete with me?" Rhodes asks, holding his arm up to Weston's.

"A week more in paradise and maybe I could've gotten there," Weston tells Rhodes.

"You look good," Henley says. "Rested even. How was your honeymoon?"

"It was heaven. Beaches, spectacular sunsets, drinks with tiny umbrellas, all with Sadie. What's not to love?"

"Tiny umbrellas," Henley repeats, nodding sagely. "The key to any successful relationship."

"Isn't marriage the best?" Rhodes asks.

"You apparently think so," I say, pointing at his face. "You're fucking glowing, man."

Rhodes beams and slaps his cheek a couple times. "Damn right, I am."

"Speaking of…when are you guys getting married, Henley?" Penn asks.

"I don't know…you guys have got me thinking," Henley says, somewhat cryptically. He looks at me. "What about you? When are you gonna ask Poppy out? I heard that I missed some hot tension out on the field at Briar Hill. I'd like to hear in your words how she landed on top of you for ten minutes."

Everyone laughs but me…I snort.

"It wasn't ten minutes," I say, shaking my head.

"But you do admit she was on top of you?" Penn, the shit-stirrer, says.

"Yeah, I broke her fall so she wouldn't get hurt."

All four sets of eyes look back at me with derpy grins.

I groan and swipe my hand down my face. "It was nothing."

"Well, when are you going to make it something?" Rhodes asks. "You've gotta see how she lights up every time she's around you. I thought I was going to have to cover some kids' eyes out there on the field."

"Shut up." I laugh.

My ears feel hot and I'm glad for the hair coverage.

"Time to man up," Rhodes says, smirking.

"I'd normally be all about keeping you single so I'm not alone," Penn says, leaning his forearms on the table, "but I'd like to see you get some. We don't want you having old man problems with the prostate." He points his thumb toward the door. "You ever need the fear put in you properly…get stuck talking to Marv and Walter about that issue." He tilts his head down, his wide eyes staying pinned on mine. "You can't unhear it."

"My prostate is fine. *God*. You guys are too much." I pinch the bridge of my nose and barely hold back the laugh that's trying to come out. "You think I've got time for a date right now?"

Remorse crosses their faces and I'd feel guilty for it if they weren't such nosy bastards all the fucking time. They've actually been saints while my dad's been in the hospital. Weston's the only one who hasn't been to the hospital yet, but he's called often, even while he was still on his honeymoon.

"How is your dad today?" Weston asks.

"Seems about the same. I'm heading over there after this."

"I'm so sorry, man," he says. "Can I bring food over to the hospital later?"

"You don't have to do that. You've barely been home. Catch your breath. We're good." I smile when he squeezes my shoulder.

"I want to," he says. "I'll text this afternoon and if you're not still there, I'll take something for your mom."

"You guys are too good to me."

"You're good to us too," Henley says. "You know that I have you to thank for pulling me out of my depressed state after the accident."

My eyes narrow. "Pretty sure that was Tru and your girls who did that...and the rest of these guys."

"No, you literally pulled me out of bed first…and then it was everyone." We all laugh with him.

The conversation shifts to Elle's book release party coming up and then Weston's honeymoon again, but my mind circles back to Poppy. The way it does way too often these days. She's invading my thoughts without me even consciously letting her.

When we leave, I brace myself, but Clara doesn't make us dance our way out the door. I have a feeling her new policy isn't going anywhere though.

CHAPTER SIXTEEN

THE GOOD AND THE BAD

POPPY

I take my dress off of the hanger and slide it over my head, then bend my head forward and shake my waves out. When I flip my hair back, I look at the results in the mirror. Marley approved of this dress that I ordered online. It's a lightweight black sweater dress with flowers embroidered along the hem, and I absolutely love it. She'd approve of the hair too, but I don't have time to call her and show her. I'll make sure to take a picture before the night is over.

I wonder if Bowie will be at Twinkle Tales tonight to celebrate Elle's book release. When I dropped Becca off at his house last night, he'd opened the door wearing a gray T-shirt and jeans. His hair looked like he'd just run his hands through it, and his expression was its usual stoic mask, but there was that flicker of softness in his eyes and a smile when he saw Becca. It shifted to me too, but that was probably just a holdover from seeing Becca…as much as I wanted to think he was glad to see me.

And I feel ridiculous for even feeling that way because I'm not going down that dead end. I'm not. *I'm really not.*

But seeing him more often…he's softening me too, slowly wearing those defenses down.

Twinkle Tales is packed to capacity. Fans are buzzing with excitement, clutching copies of Zoey Archer's latest book. Elle was only able to remain incognito for a relatively short time, but the word is fully out now that the romance author we all adore is Rhodes Archer's wife. He's standing near the back like a proud peacock. And Bowie and Becca are standing right next to him, Bowie looking exhausted. I falter when I see the shadows under his eyes.

At the front of the room, Henley adjusts his headphones and taps his mic. "Welcome, everyone, to a very special episode of *Huddle with Henley*," he announces with a grin. "I'm Henley Ward, and I'm happy to say that Zoey Archer," he emphasizes her name and I'm sure he has to think hard to not say Elle, "is a dear friend of mine and an extremely talented author. Tonight, we're swapping touchdowns for tropes, and football plays for foreplay—"

The crowd erupts in laughter and Elle buries her face in her hands.

"Did I get that right?" Henley asks the crowd, focusing on Tru.

She nods, cracking up, as the rest of the women yell an emphatic *yes*.

"She's got plenty of research material, Henley," Rhodes calls out, winking at Elle.

The crowd loves that, of course.

"It's going to be a long night," Elle jokes in her mic, and everyone laughs even harder.

Henley clears his throat, trying to maintain some semblance of professionalism. "As I was saying, Zoey's book, *Chasing Sunrise,* is already breaking pre-sale records. And lucky for you all, we're here to dive into her writing process, inspiration, and maybe a little tea about her next book."

We all clap and cheer as Henley turns to Elle with a grin. "So, E—er, Zoey—what's the most common misconception people have about writing romance?"

Elle relaxes slightly, tucking her hair behind her ear. She looks gorgeous tonight in a pink dress that perfectly matches her new cover. "Probably that it's easy. People who don't read romance assume you just throw in some love scenes, add a little fluff, and call it a day, but creating characters with depth and chemistry…getting that banter feeling right…it takes some work."

"Speaking of chemistry," Henley says. "Let's talk about those spicy scenes."

He glances at Tru again and I giggle. She must have schooled him on the romance lingo because he is nailing it.

Before Elle can answer, Penn—who's sitting in the front row—whips out a notebook and a pair of glasses that make him look like Clark Kent. He clicks a pen and poises it over his notebook.

Elle starts laughing. "Penn…what are you doing?"

"Taking notes," he says, throwing up his hand. "This is crucial information."

"For what exactly?" Henley asks, leaning closer to the mic.

"Future endeavors," Penn replies, earning another round of laughter.

Henley smirks. "Well, you're all in luck tonight. Zoey's books are a masterclass in the art of seduction. And from what I can tell from the questions sent in, everyone really wants to know…" He turns to face Elle, who starts fanning her face. "When you write those scenes, do you picture—"

"She pictures her husband and don't anyone forget it," Rhodes says.

The room roars with laughter and Henley leans into it. "Ladies and gentlemen, this episode of *Huddle with Henley* is brought to you by the phrase, *too much information*."

"He's not wrong," Elle adds, wiping the corners of her eyes as she tries to pull it together.

The Q&A continues, and my stomach hurts from laughing. Every now and then, I feel eyes on me and look over to find Bowie watching me. He's laughed a lot tonight too and looks better than I thought. Maybe the lighthearted evening has been exactly what he needed.

As the Q&A comes to a close, Calista explains how the signing process will begin. I see sudden movement out of the corner of my eye and watch as Bowie tries to quietly answer his phone. He takes Becca by the hand and they walk out of the bookstore quickly.

Later, when I'm home and in bed, heart full from such a fun night, I get a text in the group thread with the girls.

TRU

It was such a fun night. I hate it so much that it ended this way for Bowie. He looked like he was finally letting loose for the first time in so long too.

ELLE

It's so sad. I know…it was wonderful to see him laughing. He needed that and then, bam.

Oh no. I get a sick feeling.

What happened?

TRU

I'm so sorry, Poppy! I was going to text you separately to let you know about Bowie's dad. He passed away tonight.

Oh no.

I stare at the ceiling and then pull up Bowie's number.

I heard about your dad. I don't even know what to say except that I'm so sorry for this loss, Bowie.

He doesn't answer right away. But when he writes back, it's simple.

BOWIE

Thank you, Poppy.

For some reason, those words, along with him saying my name, unmoors me. I shed tears for Bowie and Becca. I've picked up on an underlying tension that Bowie carries about his family, especially his dad, and I hate that he has to carry all the feelings that this brings. It's a different kind of sadness when you lose someone you should be close to but have unresolved issues with…it makes me so grateful that I have a close relationship with my dad and my grandparents. If it wasn't so late, I'd call them right now. I'll go see them after work tomorrow. We normally see each other every other week now that I'm in Silver Hills, but now that they're all getting older, I should make more of an effort to see them every week.

> Please let me know if I can do anything. Pickups and drop-offs with Becca, hanging out with her, running errands, food, anything.

BOWIE

That's really kind. I just might take you up on that.

I want to keep texting him, but I leave it at that.

CHAPTER SEVENTEEN

THE SHADOWS

BOWIE

The cemetery is peaceful, quiet except for the rustle of wind through the trees. I feel stiff as I stand near the casket, my hands clenched at my sides. We had the funeral at Elle's dad's church, and now he says a few words at the gravesite. I like Doug Benton, but what he's saying barely registers as I stare at the polished wood of the casket.

Throughout the funeral, I heard Dad's friends and some of his family members talk about a man I didn't recognize. I know some of them saw the sides of him I knew, and I wonder if they've already slipped into that way of talking about the deceased that isn't quite true. Where we immortalize them and make them sound better than they ever were.

Or maybe they truly didn't know the monster he could be.

Tobias steps into place, late. I catch his eye and we share a flicker of understanding without saying a word. He knows the truth. My mom does too, but I don't think she'll ever admit it.

Mom stands between us, her face mottled from crying. She dabs at her eyes with a handkerchief and shakes her head now and then when the grief seemingly overtakes her.

When the service ends, I stay behind, thanking people for coming. My guys stay with me and I invite them to the house later. Becca and I will be going to my parents' house immediately following this, and normally that would be enough peopling for me, but I think maybe I'll need the easy camaraderie that we have with each other by then. Probably desperately so.

Poppy walks over to us and looks up at me. Becca is by her side because as soon as the service was over, she bolted for her.

"It was a beautiful service," Poppy says.

"Thank you for coming."

She nods and looks like she wants to say more, but instead, she turns and hugs Becca. They say something quietly and do a little handshake the two of them have started doing lately. It's nothing too complicated, but it's cute. Just another thing to endear me to Poppy...like I needed another thing.

When everyone leaves, I'm still there standing, feeling drained but unable to move. I don't know why. I don't have any final words to say. I haven't been able to say anything, sitting next to him in the hospital room, and I can't now. I think the opportunity died when he chose the bottle over his family. When he shook me until my teeth rattled. The first time he gave me a black eye.

Yeah, there's nothing really left to say.

"Bowie."

My mom's voice pulls me from my thoughts. She stands a few feet away. Her hair is pulled back in a taut bun and she looks tired. Tobias lingers by the cars. I thought he'd left.

I straighten. "Hey."

"I wanted to thank you," she says. "For everything. It was a nice funeral."

I nod. "It was."

Her lips press into a thin line. "He wasn't easy to love."

"No, he wasn't." My voice sounds flat.

"But he was your father and now he's gone." She sighs, wrapping her arms around herself.

She says it so simply, like the past can just be buried along with the man. I bite back my frustration. Now isn't the time to voice my bitterness.

"I've been thinking about what's next. For me," she says.

I nod slightly, waiting.

She turns to face me. "I'm moving in with you and Becca," she says firmly.

It takes a second for those words to sink in. "What?" I say, startled.

"I can't live alone. And I don't want to go back to Austria. Not yet, anyway."

"Mom, that's…not exactly something we've talked about."

"We're talking now," she says, pinning me with her stare. "I've already made arrangements to sell the house. It's too big for me and it's time for a change."

I rub the back of my neck, trying to process this. She's always been difficult in her own way—demanding, sharp-tongued, and unyielding—but as she said about my dad, she's still my mother. I can't exactly refuse her outright when my dad isn't even in the ground yet.

"Becca's got her routines, her space...it might be a tough adjustment for all of us."

"I'm not expecting a palace, Bowie, although your place is a palace compared to mine."

It'll be too big for you too, I want to tell her. *But too small for us with you there.*

"I just need a place to stay while I figure things out. I want to be a better grandmother...to help you more than I have."

I sigh, glancing at Tobias, who walks up and leans against a tree. I'm not sure how much of this he's heard.

"Okay," I say finally. "While you figure out what's next."

"Of course," she says.

Her tone makes me doubt her sincerity, but I guess now's not the time to bring that up either. My head is reeling a little bit.

She moves toward her car and Tobias moves into step beside me as I walk to mine.

"Did I hear that right?" he asks.

"I guess so," I mutter.

"Better you than me," he says.

I shoot him a look and he gives me a sheepish look. "Good luck, little brother." He hugs me and then is gone.

My dad might be gone, but things haven't gotten any less complicated.

The air inside my parents' house is heavy. In the day following my dad's death, I helped arrange all the flight details with my first cousin Amelie. She's one of the few family members I've kept in touch with over the years. My family and I left Austria when I was twelve, but before then, Amelie and I were always close as kids, and when I see her now, I hug her, grateful that it feels the same between us.

"Thanks for your help getting everyone here," she says.

"You did the hard part."

"Yeah, but you paid for it all," she says with a pointed look. She rubs my arm. "I hate the reason for this visit, but I'm so happy to see you."

"I'm happy to see you too. We'll have to get together more while you're here." I hug her again.

She nods and then we're interrupted by Amelie's mom, my aunt Anna. Everyone mills around the rooms, speaking in hushed tones, and it sounds like a low hum. Becca is uncharacteristically quiet, taking it all in. I introduce her to people as they come up, and she smiles shyly. So far, the only one she's really taken to is Amelie, which doesn't surprise me. She doesn't love meeting a ton of new people at once…she's like me that way.

When she sees Henley's girls, she perks up and runs off to join them.

I hear another aunt from Vienna attempting to explain Austrian funeral customs to one of Mom's friends from here. A second cousin has Weston cornered, asking questions about life in the NFL, but Weston can hardly get a word in to respond.

"Bowie."

I turn to see Henley, carrying two drinks. He hands one to me. "I thought you could use something stronger but figured you'd prefer Coke," he says.

I smile gratefully. "You figured right." I've provided thousands of dollars' worth of alcohol, but there's no way I'd feel right about drinking it here. It feels sort of hypocritical that I provided it, but my family would have been outraged if I hadn't.

"You okay?" Henley asks.

"I'm okay." I nod once.

Rhodes and Penn are in conversation across the room, Penn gesturing wildly.

"What do you think he's talking about?" Henley chuckles.

"Some girl he met last night? Or maybe the meal he ate. Either one would excite him."

We both laugh, but mine falls flat fast.

"Say the word and I'll get you out of here," Henley says.

"I'm probably required to be here until the end."

"Nah," he says, but he doesn't push.

The voices get louder and I flinch when someone drops a glass. The sound of glass breaking takes me back. My father's voice, slurred and angry, the crack of the glass shattering across the wall, the look in his eyes before he'd strike…

"I do need to get out of here," I say, pushing away from the window.

The walls feel like they're closing in.

Henley straightens. "Do you want us to bring Becca home in a while?"

"Yes, please. Anytime. I just…I need a minute to get it together. Tell the guys to move the party to my house. Bring the swimsuits…I'll be better once I'm home."

Henley leans in close. "You don't have to be better, you know. Your dad just died. It's okay to handle it however you need to."

"I can't be here," I say. "I need to go home."

"Do it. The guys and I will stay for a while and no one will even miss you if we get Rhodes and Penn entertaining them," he teases, and I'm grateful for it.

I find Becca and let her know that Henley will bring her home and make my escape. I'll text my cousin later and invite her over.

The tension in me eases just driving away. For years, I've worked so hard to get my dad's voice out of my head. It's like he sits on my shoulder, telling me how worthless I am. The way Adriane left didn't help. I thought she was in love with me and it turned out I was dispensable. As soon as life got hard, she was out.

There are only a few times when my head is completely clear...when I play football or when I'm with the guys. If I feel like I'm failing Becca in any way, I spiral.

When I pull into my driveway, I take the first deep breath that actually fills my lungs and it's even better when I step inside my house. Martha runs to greet me and looks around for Becca. When she sees it's just me, she rubs against my legs before curling up next to my feet. I lean my head against the wall and close my eyes.

Your dad can't hurt you anymore. Not with his hands or his words or his choices. His damage might be lasting, but you don't have to carry the weight of it anymore.

For the first time in years, I cry.

CHAPTER EIGHTEEN

SHOCKER

POPPY

I pull into the driveway, heart hammering harder than I'd like. I hadn't planned on coming tonight since Bowie didn't invite me himself, but the girls insisted that I come. I want to be here—I need to see for myself how Bowie and Becca are doing—but it'll be so embarrassing if he doesn't want me here.

Sadie opens the door when I knock and envelops me in a hug.

"I was hoping that was you," she says. "Everyone's back here."

She leads me to the solarium and I immediately find Bowie. He's standing by the pool, listening intently to the beautiful woman beside him. She's tall and elegant, her dark hair cascading over her shoulders and her perfect body encased in a red bikini. My chest tightens and I'm tempted to back out of here right now, but I'm trying to be a good friend, whether Bowie wants my friendship or not. Lately I've thought we might actually be forming a tentative friendship, but…now all the insecurities are flooding back.

I straighten my shoulders. Bowie is free to be with whoever he wants, and if that gorgeous woman is the one who can make him smile, today of all days, I have no right to be jealous about it. But it stings.

"Poppy!" Becca yells from the pool. "Come swim!"

"Hi!" I wave back and nod. "I will."

Sadie looks over at me and her eyes widen when she sees my face. "You okay?"

"Fine," I say, shaking my head and laughing slightly. "Just feeling a little weird being here…"

"Bowie wanted you to come," Sadie whispers.

"He did? Are you sure?"

"Positive! He told me and Tru to make sure you were invited." She follows my gaze. "Oh, have you met Amelie yet? She's Bowie's cousin from Austria. Isn't she gorgeous?"

"His cousin." I laugh as relief courses through me. *Get it together,* I tell myself. "No, I haven't met her yet, but yes, I was just thinking about how gorgeous she is."

Sadie gives me a knowing look and loops her arm through mine. "Let's go change." Under her breath she adds, "You're gorgeous too, by the way."

I roll my eyes. "Am I that obvious?"

Sadie presses her lips together. "The utter dismay when you thought Amelie might be into Bowie? Don't worry, I don't think he noticed."

"Because he doesn't care, you mean," I moan quietly and go into the bathroom that Sadie points out.

"Trust me, he very much cares where you're concerned," she says from the other side of the door.

I want to ask why she thinks that, but remind myself that I'm not interested in anything more than friendship with Bowie.

My eyes roll as I put on my swimsuit.

"Yeah, keep telling yourself that," I whisper to my reflection in the mirror.

Elle is standing by Sadie when I walk out of the bathroom and they both light up when they see me.

"Hot damn," Elle says. "You look smoking hot, Poppy."

My cheeks flush. "Thank you. It's the only bathing suit I own. Too much?"

My bikini is a unique purpley-navy material that sparkles…not obnoxiously so, but it's prettier than a solid color. At least I thought so when I bought it. It fits well and is flattering, but I feel a little self-conscious now.

"Not at all. You look amazing," Sadie says.

She slips into the bathroom to change and Elle undoes the zipper on her dress and steps out of it, already in her white bikini.

"Hello, you're the one who looks smoking hot," I tell her, laughing. "Miss Mustangs Cheerleader."

"Not a cheerleader anymore," Elle sings, laughing. Her eyes light up and I turn to see Tru in her bikini and her little baby bump. "Oh my God, I die," Elle says, rushing to Tru. "That is the cutest baby bump ever."

Tru rubs her stomach proudly. "I wasn't sure how I'd feel

about it, but I kinda love it now that I'm showing. Makes the morning sickness feel like it's productive instead of just a giant pain in my ass." She laughs.

"Is that getting any better?" Sadie asks, coming out of the bathroom.

"I still have my moments, but as long as I eat something salty before it gets too bad, I'm okay."

"I can't wait to meet this little one," Elle says, leaning her head on Tru's.

"Neither can I," Tru smiles and it's true what they say about pregnant women being radiant.

I pile my hair in a high, messy bun, and we walk back to the pool together. I feel Bowie's eyes on me before I even see him and turn to find him checking me out. His eyes are heated when they meet mine again. I swallow hard and wave, smiling slightly. He tilts his head up, acknowledging me in that way he has that's neither rude nor overly friendly. Coming from anyone else it wouldn't work, but with him, it just does.

I giggle when I see Martha sitting at the edge of the pool, on alert as she watches Becca swim. Becca spots me and calls me in and I step into the pool. The water is the perfect temperature and Becca swims over.

"You're such a good swimmer," I tell her.

She beams. "We race?"

"Sure." I laugh.

We do several laps, but as I turn to do another, I feel dizzy and frown.

"My head feels funny," I try to explain to Becca quickly. "I think I need a break."

"Okay," she says.

I climb out of the pool and a towel appears in front of me. I turn and see Bowie holding it out for me. His hair is pulled back and his chest glistens from being in the water too.

"Thank you."

"Thank you for coming tonight," he says, drying off his chest. I try to not be obvious with my staring.

"I almost didn't," I admit, then flush when his brow arches slightly.

"I'm glad you did. I needed this," he says, gesturing to the laughing and splashing in the pool behind us. "People I actually want to be around."

My face heats at the thought that he might want me around and I inwardly groan, telling myself to get a grip once again. I turn sharply to look at everyone again so he doesn't see me blushing, and that dizziness hits me again.

I reach out and grab his arm, trying to steady myself.

"Poppy? Are you okay?"

I nod, but dots line my vision and I blink. "I'm not feeling so well," I say.

"Oh." He leans in and then leads me to a chair. "You went pale all of a sudden. Have you eaten enough today?"

I make a face as I sit down and try to remember what I've eaten. "You know what? No. I haven't had much of an appetite today." My stomach churns and I swallow hard. "I… I better go." I stand up and rush back to the room where I changed.

I splash cold water over my face, and it helps, but not enough. I have a sudden urgency to get home. I don't necessarily think I'll throw up, but I'm not positive I won't…and I don't want to be here if I do.

Tru walks in and pauses when she sees me. "Bowie said you're not feeling well. He wanted me to check on you."

"No, I'm not." I scrunch up my nose and put my clothes

on over my swimsuit. "Can you let everyone know I'm heading home? I hate to leave, but ugh."

"Aw, yeah, I'll tell them. Get better. Let me know if you need anything. I can bring soup or something by tomorrow. Are you okay to drive home?"

"Yes. I'll be okay. Hopefully this will pass quickly."

I wave at her and go out the back door. When I get home, I strip and get under the covers. Exhaustion pulls at me, but as I nestle into my pillow, my stomach twists again. I groan, pressing a hand to my abdomen.

It must be my period. My cycles are so unpredictable, and occasionally, the cramps are awful. It's good that I got home before that starts.

I stare at the ceiling, thinking about Bowie and how sweet he was tonight. My heart clenches thinking about the way his eyes lingered on me when he first saw me. I should text him and let him know I'm—

Wait a minute.

I bolt upright in bed, my pulse pounding in my ears. I scramble for my phone on my nightstand, pulling up my calendar with trembling hands. My fingers hover over the dates as realization hits me with a heavy blow.

Even with unpredictable periods, I should have had my period by now.

"Oh my God, oh my *God,*" I groan.

How did I miss this? Between work, hanging out with Becca, loving my new friendships with the girls, and daydreaming about Bowie—*freaking Bowie Fox*—I hadn't even realized I was late.

My hands are shaking as I count the days again, just to be sure.

"Shit." I throw back the covers and throw on my sweats and a baggy sweatshirt.

It's ironic that the dizziness and funky stomach feel better now. All that feels weird is my heart hammering in my chest. The lights in Aurora's are harsh as I scan the shelves, grabbing two boxes of pregnancy tests, just to be sure. I avoid the cashier's eyes as I pay and hurry home.

Once I'm home and have aimed on the stick, I sit on the edge of the tub, clutching the instructions tightly in my hands as I wait for the result.

When the line appears, I stare at it, my breath catching between a gasp and a sob.

"Oh my God," I say again, the realization nearly taking me under.

I sink to the floor, clutching the test to my chest.

How in the world did this happen? Scratch that—I know exactly when and where…and technically, *how* this happened…but we used protection!

What am I going to *do*?

I bury my face in my knees and bawl.

And then I stand up, wipe my face and blow my nose, and crawl back into bed, pulling the covers to my chin as I blink in the dark.

I'm having Bowie Fox's baby.

CHAPTER NINETEEN

CHANGES

BOWIE

The boxes are piled high in my living room, mocking me. Stamped with my mom's loopy handwriting, I wonder how she had the time to get everything packed so quickly. She must have not been sleeping since the funeral. She sits perched on the couch with a cup of tea, overseeing the chaos with an air of calm that grates on my nerves.

The guys bustle around the house, carrying furniture

inside. Poor Martha skitters all over the place, trying to stay out of everyone's way.

"Do you really need all this? It's a temporary situation, remember?" I ask.

She frowns. "You don't want me to feel displaced, do you?"

"Of course not." My jaw grinds together and I walk out of the living room.

"Last box is in the truck," Henley announces, wiping sweat off his brow with his shirt. "But fair warning, it's labeled 'kitchen,' and I don't think there's a single thing in it that belongs in a kitchen."

"Antiques," I mutter, dragging a hand through my hair. "She can't let anything go."

"Not true!" Mom calls from the other room, sounding perkier than she's sounded in years. "I let your father go."

Rhodes shoots me a look. "Awkward," he mutters.

I pinch the bridge of my nose, feeling a headache coming on. The noise, the boxes, my mom's cheerful tone—it's all too much. I step outside to take a breather…and grab the last box.

I didn't expect my dad's death to hit me hard. I actually thought it might be a relief, if I'm honest with myself. He was abusive and a shadow I've spent my whole life trying to outrun, but now that he's gone, there's no closure. There were no final parting words to settle the wounds, no moment of warmth by his side in the hospital that softened any edges of our history.

And my mom thinking she can show up for me now…I'm not sure how to categorize these feelings. The normal things I do to lock things away are not working.

I set the box on the porch and lean against the railing. My mom steps out, pulling her sweater tighter.

"I know this isn't what you want," she says. "Me being here."

I don't respond.

She sighs and looks down at her hands. "I want to be a better mom," she says, her voice low but steady. "And you need someone to be all over you, meddling in your life. That's what moms do."

I let out a humorless laugh. "You? Meddling? That's a scary thought."

She reaches out and touches my arm. "I mean it, Bowie. I want to try. For you. For Becca."

My throat tightens and I nod, not trusting myself to speak.

"Now," she says briskly, patting my arm. "Go help your friends unpack the kitchen box. It has my collection of miniature giraffes. They will look so good in your kitchen."

I groan. My house is decorated sparsely on purpose.

She laughs. "Come on, your house could stand some brightening up."

For some reason, that makes me think of Poppy, and I pull out my phone. "I'll be there in a few minutes. I need to check on someone."

She goes inside and I text Poppy.

> I hope you're feeling better.

I wait outside a few minutes to see if I hear from her. She usually texts right back, but she doesn't this time, and when an hour passes and then two and I still haven't heard from her, I'm concerned.

I happen to be outside again when Elle pulls up and gets out of the car, holding huge containers of food. I jog over to take them from her.

"Hey," she says. "Thanks. I'll grab the rest." She turns back to the car and gets more food out.

"How much food did you bring?"

"Enough for an army…or you know, five huge football players with hearty appetites…and Tru's coming right behind me. She says she's hangry."

We both laugh.

"Have you heard from Poppy today, by any chance?" I ask.

Her eyes light up and she smirks. "Why, yes, I have."

My face must fall slightly because her smirk drops.

"What's wrong?" she asks.

"Oh…nothing. I just wondered if she was okay. She left in a hurry the other night, not feeling well, and hasn't answered my text today."

She frowns. "She must be busy or something. She texted in our thread this morning that she's feeling better."

"Good." I nod, feeling awkward as shit.

She bumps me with her elbow. "You *like* her."

I aim for nonchalance when I say, "Well, sure. She's nice. Everyone likes her."

Her eyes narrow on me and I shift uncomfortably. "No, you *like* her, like her. You should ask her out, Bowie. I bet she'd say yes."

I'm already shaking my head. "I don't need to complicate things."

"So you *do* like her."

I look at her dryly. "This food is heavy."

"Psssh. Like it weighs anything for you, Bowie Fox." She rolls her eyes and motions me forward with her head. "Go on. Let's eat. But this topic is not tabled."

"You and Rhodes actually share a brain, don't you."

She looks so pleased by that, I have to laugh.

"It's possible we do, but I'll never admit it to him," she says, laughing.

We eat and it helps so much having my friends here. The mood lightens considerably and my tension eases as the day goes on. I still don't want my mom living with us, but I don't have to work through it all today. Everyone stays late playing cards and just keeping us company, and I'm grateful.

Weston hands me The Single Dad Playbook before he leaves and I open it after everyone's gone.

We all have parts of our family in us,
but it doesn't define who we are.
It doesn't have to, anyway.
We have the choice to carry the good with us,
and the choice to not repeat any history
that doesn't serve us.
I'm proud of who we are as fathers.
Bowie, you are the most selfless dad I've ever known.
Rhodes, you are the funnest (and funniest)
dad I've ever known.
Weston, you are the coolest dad I've ever known.
Penn, even though you're not a dad yet,
I can see how great you'll be when the time comes
from the way you are with Sam and all of our kids.
But for now, you're the prettiest. ;)
I'm just extra proud of us right now
and needed to say it.
~Henley

It's weird that we're at the age where we're

going to start losing parents.
Not that it's going to happen right away,
but with Bowie's dad gone now, it's a reality check.
It reminds me to prioritize those
who are important to me:
Sadie, Caleb, my family, and you guys.
That's all I need right there.
~Weston

Sam has started talking more about the abuse
he's gone through at home,
the reasons he's in foster care.
I hate it, you guys.
I want to take him out of that situation
and make it all better
because his foster homes aren't always better either,
but I feel helpless.
I think I'm going to start trying to figure out
how to get custody of him myself.
Is that crazy?
I'm a single guy who doesn't have much consistency,
but I want to.
I have you guys to look up to and show me the way,
but you're not the ones
the court system will be evaluating.
I don't know…it's probably a horrible idea.
~Penn

I set the book down and open our text thread.

> I just read the last few entries in the playbook. I love you guys. I don't know what I would do…on a regular basis, not just right now…without you. But thank you for today. Thank you for all the days. And Penn…what you said about getting custody of Sam—you should do it. You love that kid and he loves you, and I have complete faith in you. All the shit we give you aside, you're a good man and you'll be an even better dad.

RHODES

Holy fuck, crying.

WESTON

^ Same.

HENLEY

That is perfectly said, Bow. And he's right, Penn. You've got this and we will support you every step of the way.

PENN

For once in my life, I'm speechless. Thank you, Bowie. Thanks, guys. 😭

And before I can talk myself out of it, I text Poppy.

> You're alive over there, right?

I see the dots and breathe easier. They disappear and then pop up again.

POPPY

Hey, sorry. Yes, I'm alive over here. Thanks.

Something is unsettling about her response. She doesn't sound like Poppy…which is dumb because it's not like we've texted a ton to begin with, but when we do, it's more animated, like she is.

I round the corner to the kitchen and see my mom pouring another cup of hot tea. She points at me.

"It's past your bedtime." When I don't say anything, she laughs. "I'm kidding. Lighten up, Maus," she says.

My lips lift at the nickname. "You haven't called me mouse in a while."

"You'll always be my maus," she says.

She opens her arms and I go over and hug her. I tower over her, so she has to rear back to look up at me. She gives my hair a tug.

"You need a haircut."

I lift my eyebrows.

"And I'm *not* kidding about that," she adds.

CHAPTER TWENTY

MOMAGER

POPPY

I've always been good at faking normal, while my insides are all topsy-turvy, I can remain cheerful and perky on the outside. Marley and my parents are usually the only ones who can tell when I'm not as sunshiny on the outside, so I've been avoiding them. And everyone.

I didn't mean to go quiet—it just happened.

After staring at that little plastic stick with its life-altering answer, my world has tilted on its axis. I put my phone on silent the next day, ignored the notifications, and beyond work, my only constant, I have mentally and physically covered my head…in bed. I'd stay there if I could.

Beyond that? Nothing feels fine.

By day four, the concerned texts start pouring in. Marley gets adamant.

> MARLEY
> Are you alive? Answer me, dammit.

> Sorry! Just crazy busy at work!

> MARLEY
> Call me when you get a minute. I miss your face.

> Will do. Love you. Xo

It isn't a total lie. I have been busy—mentally cataloging how every single thing in my life is about to change.

Bowie even texts again.

> BOWIE
> Still doing okay?

I've come up with every possible scenario of how to break the news.

Not today. Not now. Not yet.

> I should be asking you that question.

It's true. The guy just lost his dad and any tentative, shaky friendship we may or may not have started is now completely teetering when I bail on him in his time of need.

On the sixth day, I decide enough is enough. I book an

appointment with an OB-GYN, hoping the doctor will tell me I imagined the whole thing.

The doctor's office smells faintly of lavender and antiseptic. My nose stings with how strong it is and my stomach turns slightly. Nope. Not doing the nausea thing. I remember what Tru said about something salty and pull out the little bag of goldfish I keep on hand at Briar Hill. I chew a few and am surprised when my stomach settles.

Hmm, I guess it does work.

Ugh. I haven't imagined the whole thing.

My knee bounces nervously until my name is called. I follow the nurse into the exam room that's decorated with cheerful posters about prenatal care. I answer a few questions, tell her about the positive pregnancy tests and my unpredictable periods.

Dr. Talbot knocks on the door a few minutes later and walks in, energetic…how I normally try to be when I meet new people.

"Hi, I'm Dr. Talbot," she says, extending her hand with a grin.

"I'm Poppy," I say, trying to smile back. I still feel like crying, but fortunately, I don't burst into tears.

"Let's see what's going on, shall we?" Dr. Talbot says.

Within minutes, the ultrasound confirms what I already knew. Dr. Talbot's smile softens as she turns the monitor toward me.

"Well, there's your baby, Poppy. You're about nine weeks along."

Nine weeks. Two months. My breath catches.

"Wow," I whisper.

"It's a lot to take in," she says. "How are you feeling about all this?"

I laugh nervously. "Completely overwhelmed."

"That's fair. Pregnancy is no joke, but you're healthy, the baby looks good, and you've got some time to figure out things. At least until mid-November. Baby steps." She grins. "I'll want to see you back in a month. Blaire will help you set up your next appointment."

"Okay."

I leave the office clutching a folder of pamphlets and feeling like I've stepped into an alternate reality.

I stop by Luminary on the way home and then pause in front of the counter. Wait. I think I'm not supposed to have caffeine.

"Hi, Poppy!" Clara says. She lifts her eyebrows when I step out of the line. "You okay, honey?"

"I…good. Hi! Just need a sec."

I back up and bump into someone. Hands wrap around my biceps, steadying me. I look over my shoulder, and my mouth drops open. Bowie. What are the chances?

"Poppy?"

"Hello? It's me," I sing.

Yep, like Adele. Only without the beautiful voice. More like a wilting, sad seal.

He chuckles. "Hey, you."

"You look good." I sigh and again, he chuckles.

Why does my torture bring him joy? I know not.

"Uh, I mean. You always do, but you seem good…" I turn to face him and lower my head, rubbing my temples. "I'm sorry to fall off the face of the earth when you've needed friends more than ever."

"*Are* we friends?" He wrinkles his brow and my mouth falls.

"Are you…being playful?"

He puts his hand on his chest in mock outrage. "Me? Playful? Never."

I grin, all the while the words, *I'm having your baby,* pump through my chest, begging to come out. My smile drops and I laugh like a hyena. "Right. You? Never. Hahaha."

His eyes widen and I don't think I've ever seen him smile this big. It's still not normal people's big, but for him, it's big. Very big. And I'm stuck on big.

I shake my head, backing up. "Gotta run! You take care, okay? Okay?"

I turn and run out, with Clara saying, "She forgot to order!"

Fumbling with my phone when I get to the car, I call Marley and I feel terrible about this, but when she croaks out a hello, I breathe out a sigh of relief.

"Aw, you're sick?" I cry. Hypocrite, hypocrite.

"So sick."

"I'm so sorry. I'll call you later. Or call me when you feel better. I love you so much."

"I love you. Okay, I will."

We hang up and I glare at myself in the rearview mirror.

Over the next few days, I try to decide when—and how—to tell Bowie. Waiting until the twelve-week mark feels safer, but am I really going to be a bumbling idiot every time I see him until then? And what if it's just worse after he knows?

I decide to try to avoid him for the next three weeks, but he brings Becca to Briar Hill…and stays. What the hell? I would've been thrilled over this predicament a couple of weeks ago, but now it's sheer torture.

The kids love him. He comes and plays volleyball with us and then lingers afterward. I try to pick up the balls and keep dropping them, which has always been a problem of mine, but it's magnified with the way he's watching me. He helps me put them away.

"You okay?" he asks.

"Yeah. Fine. Totally fine!" I say, my voice way too high.

He raises an eyebrow but doesn't press.

"Are you okay?" I try to deflect.

"Besides my mom driving me crazy? Yes."

I wrinkle my nose. "No update on a new place?"

"Oh no. Paulina is making no effort to go anywhere. She's nesting." He swipes his hand over his face and I watch the beautiful curve of his bicep, his perfect veiny hands. I *love* a veiny hand.

I shake my head and clear my throat. "Nesting," I repeat.

"Putting her shit up everywhere. There must be thirty giraffes in the kitchen alone."

"No!" I gasp, laughing.

He lifts his hand to the back of his neck, and again with that bicep. Damn.

He leans against the wall and watches Becca talking to her friends, while I watch him. When he turns to look at me suddenly, I'm caught.

He looks sheepish and my cheeks flush. He totally caught me ogling him.

"You should come out with us tonight."

"I. What? Out…with you?" I repeat. "I mean, us." I sigh and give up.

I give up right the hell now.

"Uh, yeah. Becca and I are going out to eat tonight. We may or may not be avoiding going home."

"Oh! Dinner." I blink.

"We've got to eat, right?"

"Right." He's not asking me out, I remind myself. My heart is still doing embarrassing leaps inside. "Yeah…we've gotta eat. I'm in." I fling my arm out and knock over the whole rack of balls.

I scramble to catch them and Bowie helps me put them back in place. I hear his chuckle again and I should be pleased that I'm making a grieving man laugh, but I just want a hole to swallow me.

"Shall we do Rose & Thorn?" he asks.

"I've never been there."

"Oh, I think you'll like it."

"Should we meet there?" I ask.

He looks at his watch. "I would've picked you up, but it's getting late. Yeah, how about we meet there?"

He was going to pick me up? No, it's not a date. Right? We're going with Becca. Not a date.

"Sounds good," I say, keeping my arms to myself so I don't send anything else flying.

He gives me a tight smile and calls Becca over. They hang out for a few minutes while I go to my office. When I walk out, he lifts away from the wall and holds the door open for us.

Yep, having his baby, I think.

I've never felt completely sane, a point to which Marley has always wholeheartedly agreed with me, but now I'm *really* losing it.

Fortunately, Becca keeps the conversation going at the restaurant.

"Oma likes lots of things," she says. She holds her hands up to show me something tall. "Giraffes. And cups. And shoes."

I laugh and Bowie nods begrudgingly.

"It's true. She likes all those things…and then some," he adds.

"Dad and I…" Becca starts, looking at Bowie for help.

"We—" she shakes her head. "We not messy."

"We don't love as many things as Oma does, do we?" he says.

"We don't," she says.

"Can you talk her into storing some of her things…you know, have it ready to go for when she moves into her new place?" I suggest.

"If only she were agreeable to that," Bowie grumbles. "This morning, she decided five thirty was the perfect time to reorganize my kitchen. Do you know how disorienting it is to reach for a mug and find a bag of prunes instead?"

I snort. "Yikes."

"I had these nice glass containers that she's replaced with bright orange Tupperware."

"Wait, she's replaced them? What did she do with yours?"

He leans on his forearms and he looks so delicious, I gulp.

"She tried to send them to Goodwill. I found them in a box and had to unpack my own damn bowls."

My eyes widen.

"She's not trying to reorganize, she's trying to conquer. I thought she was moving in to grieve maybe, you know? But no, she's on a warpath. Every drawer, every cabinet—nothing is safe."

"Your house is already very organized," I say.

"Not anymore. It's never been so cluttered." He sags back in his chair.

"Maybe it's her way of trying to help?" I bite back a laugh.

"Oh, she's helping all right," he says darkly. "She's helping herself to my entire existence. She thinks I need to cut my hair and that my wardrobe lacks personality."

"Don't you dare cut your hair," I blurt out. "But she's not wrong about your wardrobe."

He looks down at his sweatshirt and folds his arms. "Athletic wear is timeless."

"Timelessly boring."

Total lie. He makes athletic wear look delicious.

"Well, tell me how you really feel," he says, his eyes narrowing on mine.

I laugh and his lips twitch. Our plates are set in front of us and when I go to take a bite of my burger, my nose flares. I set the burger down quickly and eat a nice, salty fry instead.

"It gets worse," he says. "She's started cooking dinner."

"That's nice, right?"

"No, Poppy, it's not nice."

Becca turns up her nose. "Yucky," she says.

Bowie and I laugh.

"Last night it was some kind of…casserole. She called it Austrian Comfort Delight. Ham and peas with noodles, which," he lifts a shoulder, "in theory shouldn't be a disaster necessarily, but…" He shudders. "So much salt."

I can't stop laughing now.

"You didn't like it either?" I ask Becca.

"Martha likes it," Becca says.

"Becca fed it to Martha under the table," Bowie says, cringing. "I discourage that, but we needed a quick fix and Martha was there."

I cover my mouth with my napkin as I crack up.

"She wants to adopt another dog, says Martha doesn't have enough life in her."

At that, I double over, clutching my stomach. "This is too good."

"She's a menace," he says with amusement.

"This is the most I've heard you talk ever," I say, trying to wipe off my wistful expression. I clear my throat and try to get serious. "Maybe she's just trying to make up for lost time," I say gently.

He looks down. "Yeah, maybe." Then he glances at my plate and frowns. "Is your burger not good?"

"Oh…I'm…it's…would you like a bite?" I hold up my plate and he stares at the whole burger still sitting there.

"Well, now I'm curious about why you're not eating it." He picks it up and takes a big bite. "Tastes great to me." He places it back on the plate.

"Take it. Please." I nudge the plate toward him.

"I can always eat," he says. He looks down at his plate. "I finished my steak," he says apologetically, "but there's still some salad. Want some of this?"

I look at it. I don't normally like avocado or Kalamata olives, but… it looks *unbelievably* good.

"You know what? I think I would like some of that," I say, grabbing his plate.

He looks surprised. "Oh, here you go." He moves things out of the way so I can get to it easier.

I take a cautious bite of olive and hum. "Why does that taste so good?" My next tentative bite is the avocado and once I start, I eat it all. "Delicious," I say in shock. "This is the best salad I've ever had."

It must be a fluke because I hate olives and avocado, but I'll take it…I'm not queasy at all.

Bowie gives me an amused smile. "I'm glad you enjoyed it. We should've traded sooner."

Conversation continues to flow and I try not to pinch myself that I'm at dinner with Becca and Bowie…because if I think about it too long, I could get hopeful. I could start imagining things…how it could be.

As we get ready to leave, Bowie says, "Hopefully I don't get home to a color-coded underwear drawer."

I laugh. "Well, you guys are always welcome to crash at my place." My face flames, and I try to reel it back. "Or, you know, create boundaries."

That earns another laugh. My heart is full from the smiles and laughs I've gotten from Bowie tonight.

"Right. Boundaries. Your place definitely sounds more fun."

It's a good thing we go outside in the dark then, so my swoony eyes and red cheeks don't show.

Oh my God, *I'm having his baby.*

CHAPTER TWENTY-ONE

MY MADNESS

BOWIE

I lean against the counter at Briar Hill, taking a drink from my water bottle and trying not to stare.

Poppy is across the room, her silky waves falling forward as she bends over her clipboard, and her yoga pants hug every curve in a way that infuriates me. Wisps of blonde hair get in her eyes and she blows them away, looking at ease in her element. Something tells me if she knew I was here, she wouldn't look so comfortable right now and that doesn't sit well with me.

Dinner the other night was…surprising. I hadn't expected to enjoy myself so much, but Poppy helped me make light of everything I'm dealing with at home. It helped to talk about my mom, and the way she teased me without hesitation—it was easy, normal…it was nice.

"Poppy!" Becca says, waving happily.

Poppy looks up and walks over. "Afternoon, you two. How was school today, Becca?"

"Delightful," Becca says, grinning.

I think she's pulled that word out every day since she first met Poppy.

Poppy gives her a huge grin and they do their cute handshake. "Excellent. I'm very happy to hear that. You ready to do something fun?"

"Ready!" Becca cheers.

"Okay, why don't you head to the gym and I'll be right there."

She looks at me now and her smile falters. Is it my imagination? Maybe she's worried that after our dinner the other night, I might get clingy or some shit like that…maybe she didn't have as much fun as I did and thinks she needs to let me down easy. I mean, does she realize it wasn't even a date? Right? Right.

"Bowie," she says simply.

"Poppy," I respond. When she doesn't say anything, I feel the need to fill the space, which is so unlike me, I don't even recognize myself. "You okay?"

"Of course," she says a little too brightly. "Why wouldn't I be?"

For some reason I don't buy it, but she turns and walks down the hallway before I can press further. She's moving too fast, her shoulders hunched as if she's trying to shrink into herself. Something is off. Without thinking, I follow her.

"Poppy," I call.

She doesn't stop, disappearing around the corner. My long strides catch up with her just as she pauses to flip through the clipboard, and before I can second-guess myself, I reach out and place a hand on her elbow.

She whirls around, colliding into my chest with an *oof*. The clipboard slips from her hands, clattering to the floor.

"Bowie?" she says, blinking up at me in surprise.

I mean to step back, to give her space, but she tilts her head, her blue eyes locking onto mine, and every rational thought flees.

A stray strand of hair falls across her cheek and I reach out and tuck it behind her ear. My fingers brush against her skin and her mouth parts as she stares up at me.

"Are you okay?" I ask, my voice quieter now, rough with something I don't want to name.

Her mouth parts wider, but no sound comes out. Her gaze drops to my lips then back to my eyes. The tension between us hums with electricity. My pulse pounds in my ears as I take a half step closer, my hand still lightly gripping her elbow.

"You don't…seem like yourself." I wince. "Did I do something to—"

"No. You're good. You're…great."

Her voice is so soft and so sweet, her full lips beckoning me closer. Without giving it a second thought, I lean in and kiss her.

The moment my lips meet hers, the world tilts and settles all at once. She melts into me, her hands sliding up to grip my shoulders as she kisses me back. I deepen the kiss, my free hand coming up to cup the side of her face, my thumb brushing her cheek. She tastes so good, *feels* so good. Heat spirals through me and steals the breath from my lungs until there's only this. Only her.

I angle my head, kissing her with a hunger that I've been too busy denying myself. For the life of me now, I can't understand why I ever held back. When I'm kissing her like this, I never want it to end. Our lips were made for this, that's all there is to it.

But she breaks away and we're both breathing hard, our foreheads touching.

Poppy tilts her head back, her eyes dazed. "What…was that?"

My thumb caresses her jaw as I swallow hard. My voice is hoarse when I finally speak.

"That…was long overdue."

I want to apologize for being cold after we had sex, apologize for bolting mentally whenever I'm around her, apologize for kissing her at work when I can't spend the next hour kissing her more.

But she takes another step back and her face is stricken. Shit. Not what I was expecting.

"I have to go," she says, her eyes getting glassy.

What is happening right now? Is she about to cry? My God, how did I misread the moment that much?

I step back too and nod. "Okay."

She blinks and nods. "Okay."

And then she turns and takes off in the opposite direction.

Becca and I pull into the driveway. She's chatting away about the game they played, and I'm distracted by the fact that Poppy was nowhere to be found when I went back to Briar

Hill. I'd planned to talk to her, maybe smooth things over after the kiss, or at least figure out if I've done something wrong…but she wasn't there.

My thoughts are interrupted when we step into the house.

"You can't possibly think it's appropriate to move my things," my mom's clipped tone echoes from the kitchen.

"I was simply trying to make room for Becca's plate," Mrs. McGregor says. "She likes to see—"

"Her plate doesn't need to be out," Mom argues.

I stop in the kitchen doorway, my shoulders tense. The sight before me is something out of a sitcom, but it's more like my nightmare: my mom, standing ramrod straight with her arms crossed, glaring daggers at Mrs. McGregor, who stands her ground with a broom in hand like she's ready to take flight.

"What's going on here?" I ask.

Both women turn toward me, speaking at once.

"She's trying to get rid of my things—"

"She's putting her things where Becca has—"

I hold up my hand and they pause. "Mom, Mrs. McGregor has been running this house and helping with Becca for a long time. She knows how things work here… what is helpful with Becca and how she functions best."

"I'm simply trying to make it homey, Bowie," my mom says, sniffing.

Mrs. McGregor raises an eyebrow. "Becca doesn't deal well with clutter," she says somewhat haughtily.

"These things mean a lot to me, and they add beauty to any room they're in," Mom argues. "They are *not* clutter."

"Mom," my voice edges toward warning, "Mrs. McGregor is invaluable. She's practically family. And I need her to stay happy if this house is going to function. And honestly, I'm not used to so much—" I wave my hands toward the various giraffes positioned around my kitchen.

"I'm only trying to help." My mom's voice softens slightly, but her posture is still rigid.

"You're not helping by steamrolling the one person who keeps everything together," I say. "You're here as my guest, and I need you to respect that."

Mom purses her lips but doesn't argue further. Mrs. McGregor shoots me a grateful look before turning back to the cabinet.

As the tension eases, I exhale and run a hand through my hair.

"I'll stay out of her way," my mom says, but she still sounds miffed. "But don't think I won't voice my opinions when necessary."

I smirk. "I would expect nothing less."

Mom retreats upstairs and I lean against the counter, feeling the weight of the day settling on my shoulders.

All the complicated dynamics in my life are colliding at once.

And as much as I hate to admit it, I'm not sure how much longer I can keep them all from imploding.

Because I'm a glutton for punishment today, I pick up my phone and text Poppy.

> I apologize for kissing you at work…that was not okay and I'm sorry for upsetting you.

She doesn't respond for a few minutes, but when she does, I run my hand through my hair, groaning. I should've kept my mouth shut.

POPPY

Not okay? You sure know how to destroy a girl's ego, Bowie.

> I didn't mean that. The kiss…for me…was perfect. 30/10.

POPPY

That's more like it. 😊

I let out a choked laugh.

> You're messing with me?

POPPY

I'm messing with you.

I grin at my phone and then remember the look on her face afterwards.

> So you're not upset at me for kissing you?

Again, she takes longer to respond than I'd like, but when she does, it's simple…

POPPY

No.

I wait, hoping she'll elaborate, but she doesn't and I decide to leave it at that.

Until Mrs. McGregor comes around the corner and sees me smiling at my phone. Her lips lift.

"It's nice to see you smiling," she says.

I smile at her. "I don't do enough of it, do I?"

"No, I'm afraid not. What has you smiling now?"

I hesitate and then just say it. "Poppy Keane."

"Ahh," her smile widens. "I like her. A lot." She leans in conspiratorially. "You know, I can watch Becca for a little while if you want to take Poppy out or…whatever." Her eyes twinkle. "Since Becca's been going to Briar Hill so much, I've missed spending time with her."

I consider it and then shake my head. "She probably doesn't want to see me tonight. I kind of…botched things up with her earlier."

Her brow lifts. "All the more reason to go see her."

I look at my phone again. "I would like to clear the air."

"Okay, well, let me know. I'll just go say hi to Becca."

"Thanks," I say, and she nods, walking down the hall.

I start typing and press send before I can talk myself out of it.

> Do you think we could talk?

POPPY
> Now?

> Yes. In person, preferably. So I don't find a way to be even more confusing than I already am.

POPPY
> LOL. You are pretty confusing.

> Noted. And I agree. I confuse myself. Mrs. McGregor said she could watch Becca for a little bit. We could get coffee or ice cream or…popcorn.

I shake my head. Popcorn? I'm clearly not cut out for human interaction.

POPPY

I can't say that I've ever been asked to get popcorn, but sure. I have popcorn here actually. Do you want to come over?

Yes.

POPPY

Oh! Okay. I didn't think you'd actually say yes.

You can take back the invitation.

POPPY

No, come over!

Now?

POPPY

Yes.

I walk to my room and brush my teeth, avoiding looking at myself in the mirror because I know if I do, I'll talk myself out of this. Then I go to Becca's room and see her and Mrs. McGregor reading a book together.

"I'm going to head out for a little bit, okay?"

"Okay," they both say.

I text my mom that I'm leaving too, but she doesn't answer. When I walk by her door, it's closed and I almost knock, but decide to leave it with the text.

Poppy's told me where she lives before, but this is my first time here. When I walk up to her condo, I smirk at the ceramic frog sitting in a rocking chair by her door. I knock twice and she opens the door, devastating me with her beauty.

Her hair is wet like she just got out of the shower, and

she's wearing a long-sleeved loose T-shirt over leggings. Her face is shining, clean of makeup, and she looks so beautiful it hurts.

I nearly turn and bolt right then, but she opens the door wider, and I step inside.

CHAPTER TWENTY-TWO

HEADS OR TAILS

POPPY

I pace around my tiny living room, hands wringing nervously as I wait. My phone sits on the coffee table, the earlier text thread with Bowie glowing faintly on the screen. He'll be here any minute. I don't even have time to text Marley to have a freak-out about Bowie Fox coming to my place. I have *so* much to talk to Marley about...

After our kiss—the mind-bending kiss we shared at Briar Hill—I've thought of nothing else. It was enough of a shocker to get my mind off of being pregnant for at least five seconds.

The knock at my door makes me jump out of my skin, but when I open it and see him standing there, looking imposing yet shy, I relax a little bit. His hair is slightly tousled and there's an intensity in his eyes that makes my stomach flip.

"Hey," he says, his voice low.

I let him inside and close the door behind him. For a moment, we stand there, awkwardly shifting as we stare at one another.

"Nice place," Bowie says, glancing around.

"Thanks. It's small," I say, fidgeting.

"It's cozy."

The way he says it makes me feel warm all over, and I bite my lip when my heart does an annoying pinball bounce around.

"Do you want something to drink?" I ask, walking toward the kitchen. "With your popcorn?"

"I'm good actually. I'm not really hungry."

I turn back and find him watching me, his lips curved up. His gaze is steady, but there's a softness that makes my breath hitch.

"I've been a wreck all day," I blurt out.

His eyes flare slightly. "Why?"

I laugh nervously. "I don't know. You're here. That kiss. Everything." I gesture vaguely, my hands flailing a little.

A small smile tugs at the corner of his mouth. "You're nervous?"

"Obviously."

"Don't be."

He crosses the space between us, his hand brushing mine. My pulse picks up as our eyes lock.

"Bowie…"

His hand reaches out and takes mine, and our fingers weave together. I sigh. This man. I can't make heads or tails of him, but most of the time, I sure like trying.

"Clearly, I suck at all of this," he says. "I say the wrong thing, do the wrong thing…at the wrong time."

"It's a good thing you're cute," I interject, and thankfully, it makes him laugh.

"You're the cute one," he says. "I…have felt bad about the way I handled everything after our night together." He makes a face. "And I know I made it even more confusing by kissing you…"

With his free hand, he pulls his hair back in his fist and I watch it fall back into place when he lets it go. I squeeze his hand and he swallows hard.

"It's just that, with you, I want—" He pauses and I try to wait patiently, but I'm dying here.

"You want?"

"I want…more. I can't stop thinking about you." He takes a step closer and my stomach does another flip.

Now. You should tell him now, I think.

"I can't stop thinking about you either," I say instead.

"I don't do relationships."

Things inside me halt. "I know, you've kind of made that clear."

"But you make me think I do…want to."

My mouth parts. "I do?"

He nods.

I step forward this time, and my chest brushes against his. He's still holding my hand and he pulls our hands up, leaning them against his chest. His other hand lands on my waist and I put mine on his, feeling the warmth of his body through his shirt. His muscles are taut. I have the fleeting thought that he's nervous, and everything about that warms me.

It would be a good time to tell him, but I'm enjoying this moment too much. And when he leans in and kisses me and it's just as electric as before, but slower, deeper… *sweeter*…I lose myself in him. He pulls me closer and I melt into him, wrapping my arms around his neck. Time blurs as we kiss and kiss, the urgent give-and-take building into an inferno.

He pulls away, our chests rising and falling.

"Do you think about that night?" he asks roughly, kissing his way down my neck.

"All the time." For more reasons than he realizes. I swallow back my guilt and focus on his touch.

"Me too," he says.

I arch into him when his hand cups over my breast and gasp when I feel how hard he is.

"Bowie," I whimper.

"I love how you say my name," he groans.

He did not talk when we were intimate that night and I have to say, the things he's putting out there tonight are making me a puddle.

"I came over to talk, I promise," he says.

"We can talk anytime…but this is more fun."

He grins and it's so seductive, I gulp.

"Agreed," he says.

I stand on my tiptoes and kiss him again and he picks me up, wrapping my legs around his waist. He walks to the couch and lays me on it, planking over me as he tries to read what I want.

I lean up and kiss his neck, my tongue barely sweeping over his skin, but he moans, a hungry sound. He tastes like the ocean on a winter day.

"We sort of go from zero to one hundred, don't we?" He laughs into my neck and I tug on his hair, squeezing it in my fist when he arches against me. We both groan at how good it feels.

"I don't know, we've been hanging around twenty or thirty for a bit...fifty earlier today...so not exactly zero."

I feel his smile against my skin and I can't stop smiling.

"Can I touch you?" he asks.

I nod and his hand slides under the band of my leggings, gliding over me at a leisurely pace, and the dazed concentration on his face is so hot.

"You like that?" he asks when I gasp.

"So much," I shudder.

"Me too," he says.

He pulls my leggings down so he can get better access and watches his fingers slide over my bud and then lower, inside. Every nerve in my body hums.

"You're beautiful," he says. "Have I told you that yet or just thought it?"

My mouth parts to answer him, but what he's doing with his fingers feels too good. He smiles like he knows, and his free hand goes under my backside and lifts me so I feel everything he's doing with his other hand even more.

"Bowie," I whisper, tugging his hair harder.

"Yeah?" His voice rasps.

"This feels...too good."

"Show me how good," he says, his eyes intent on mine.

He increases his tempo, the circles over me going faster, and I squeeze my eyes shut, coming with a cry. My whole body tenses and when I open my eyes, he's still watching me, his eyes heated with lust.

His fingers still and I lean up and kiss him, pulling his body flush with mine. I wrap my legs around his waist and he groans, arching into me.

I fumble between us and undo his pants, tugging them down.

"Are you sure?" he asks.

"Positive," I say.

He lifts off of me and pulls off my leggings the rest of the way, tossing them over his head. His eyes are bright and playful as he looks at me.

"How are you still dressed?" I ask, leaning up on my elbows.

He moves toward me to kiss me, and I duck, moving off of the couch. I look over my shoulder and he's standing there, staring at my backside.

"Come find me," I say.

The last thing I see before I race toward my bedroom is the hungry look on his face.

I smile when he stalks toward me and pulls my shirt off, tossing it back in his face.

He laughs and catches it and almost catches me, but I'm too fast. When I reach my bed, I climb on it and turn around to face him, sitting on my knees.

He points at my bra. "You forgot something."

"Not until you're nekkid."

"Nekkid, huh," he smirks.

He pulls his shirt off from the back with one swoop, and I sigh when I see the ripples of muscle, his abs, and that wide expanse of shoulders. The effect of him in my tiny bedroom is sending me into overdrive. When he looks at me, motioning that it's my turn, I point at his pants and he sighs, pretending to be put out. But he slides them down and I take in his thick thighs, and the heavy, long length he's dealing with. I gulp when he lowers his briefs and his cock snaps back on his stomach, hard as stone and oh, so exquisite.

When we had sex before, we were sleepy and it was dark and almost frantic, like we couldn't get to each other fast enough. Or maybe we didn't want to think about it too much just in case it put a stop to things.

This time I make sure to take it all in. Our gazes are exploratory, unrushed, and bold. When I undo my bra and let it drop, he stares at me for the longest time.

"Wow, Poppy," he finally says.

He reaches down and does a long glide of his fist over his cock and it undoes me. I lift my hand up and pinch my nipple between my fingers and his Adam's apple bobs. He advances toward me, hungrily, and I shift from my knees, still sitting up, but with my legs parted. His eyes flare and he curses under his breath.

"We're doing this," he says firmly.

"Thank God," I breathe.

Any lingering doubts I may have are silenced when he kisses me again, and we don't stop. He only pulls away long enough to put the condom on and to position himself at my entrance. I almost tell him we don't need the condom, but his lips are back on mine when he sinks inside me. And they're on mine when the rhythm between us intensifies and it's hard to tell where he ends and I begin. His kisses are punishing and beautiful, like worship and like fucking, and I feel drunk on him. We move urgently, our bodies wet with sweat by the time we're shuddering together.

"I'm waiting for you," he says against my mouth.

And just hearing those words makes me fall apart.

True to his word, he doesn't come until I'm clenching around him, and the ride is so perfect, so out-of-this-world, that I can't quite believe I'm not dreaming.

Later, as we lay tangled together in my bed, I trace lazy

circles on his chest. He hasn't bolted like before, hasn't pulled away at all.

His arm tightens around me, and for a moment, I believe that everything might just be okay. Better than okay…wonderful.

I want to stay right here for now, hoping that it's all going to fall into place.

CHAPTER TWENTY-THREE

SPIRALS

BOWIE

"I swear I didn't come over here to take you to bed," I tell her sheepishly.

I twist a strand of her hair around my finger and glide down the wave and then do it again. Her head is on my chest and I don't want to move. Everything feels too perfect. My body is sated. Her fingers are teasing me, her leg is hitched over my thigh, and we're still naked…I don't want this night to end.

She leans her chin on my chest and looks up at me, grinning.

"You won't find me complaining," she says.

"Me either," I say into her hair. She smells so good, like citrus and flowers.

From the other room, my phone interrupts the quiet, and I can tell by the alert that it's my mom. I groan.

"Do you need to check that?"

"Yeah, that's my mom. I should get home. She and Mrs. McGregor are trying to work out the kinks in the household."

Poppy stirs against me, tilting her face up to look at me. "A little more drama than you're used to?"

I nod. "Yeah. You can probably tell I don't love the drama. Unless it's Penn's." She laughs and I smile down at her. "Becca is with Mrs. McGregor, and they've done the bedtime routine countless times without me when I'm on the road. But I didn't prepare Becca for that tonight, so I should get back."

"I understand. I think it's commendable how hard you work to keep her routines. That's a challenging endeavor."

I lean down, catching her lips in a lingering kiss. Her hands land on my face and it warms everything inside me. I want nothing more than to lose myself in her again, but I force myself to pull back.

"Tonight was…" I trail off, searching for the right words. "Really nice."

She smiles before biting down on her lower lip and nodding. "It was."

I get out of bed reluctantly and get dressed. Poppy pulls her sweatshirt over her head and I make a face, bending down to kiss her temple. "It's a shame to cover that body up."

Her eyes are lit up when she looks at me, and I think that

she is the most beautiful woman I've ever seen. I feel like the darkest part of the night to her sun.

My thumb caresses her cheek and then I walk out of her room. She follows me to the door, her arms wrapping around herself as if bracing for the cold.

"I'll see you soon, probably tomorrow at Briar Hill," I say.

"Bowie," she says suddenly.

I pause, smirking. "Yeah?"

She hesitates, taking a deep breath. "I need to tell you something."

My heart skips a beat at the seriousness in her tone. "Okay."

Her eyes skate over my face and she reaches up, smoothing away the furrow in my brow.

"What is it?" I ask. My phone buzzes again and I wince.

She shakes her head, smiling. "It can wait. Sleep well."

My eyes narrow, but her smile deepens.

"Really," she says. "I'll see you…later."

I give her a lingering kiss, hating to leave her. "Later," I say, putting my hands in my pockets and walking out. I turn and look back at her. "Night, Poppy."

She leans against the doorway in nothing but her oversized sweatshirt and my mouth goes dry.

We smile at each other and I leave, a bit shaken up by all that just happened. And we didn't even have any popcorn.

I follow the sounds of Becca and Mrs. McGregor laughing in the kitchen. Mom's door is still closed.

"How's it going here?" I ask.

"Good," Becca says.

Mrs. McGregor nods. "It's been a good night. We had a little snack and Becca's had her shower."

"I'm glad. Thank you."

"I brush my teeth now," Becca says.

"Perfect. I'll be in there soon to tell you good night," I tell Becca.

"Night, you two," Mrs. McGregor says.

"Night," we both answer.

I turn off the lights and then head to Becca's room. She's looking at her mommy pictures, and the one of her and Poppy is front and center now. My mind starts racing. I try to shut it down, focus on nothing but Becca, but it's hard when she's focused on Poppy.

"I like Poppy," she says. "You like Poppy too."

Yes, I do.

"I wish Poppy was my mommy," she says.

Fuck me.

"She's a good friend, isn't she." I try to redirect.

"My best friend." Becca nods, as she crawls into bed.

I smile at Martha curled up next to Becca, wearing pajamas that match Becca's, thanks to Elle. I scratch her little head, laughing as the little hair she has on her head flies out in every direction. I'm happy I caved with Martha. She's growing on me.

I tuck Becca in and wish her sweet dreams before turning out the light.

Instead of going to bed, I go downstairs and work out.

I haven't slept with someone more than once since Adriane. I thought she was my everything…until she wasn't. And I know now that the only person in my life who's been my everything is Becca. Because I'd give up everyone and everything for my daughter.

Adriane and I were inseparable for years. She knew my dreams and it seemed like she was ready for it all…until she wasn't. She didn't really know what she wanted to do with her life, didn't have anything she was passionate about, and as it turned out, I think she just craved a simple life. I don't fault her for that. The level of my success was too much. She was like me—more comfortable being on the outside of things, out of the spotlight. Where we were so different was that I knew exactly what I wanted to do with my life. She didn't realize how my career would put everything we did in a fishbowl.

I blame myself for her leaving. But I don't think anything —even me walking away from football—would have changed her mind once she wanted to leave. When we found out she was pregnant, it was a brief respite of hope, like maybe I wasn't losing her, but in the end, she didn't want to be a mother either.

She didn't leave because of Becca, but she didn't stay for Becca either.

It's more complicated than that, but once Becca was born and I fell in love with that little girl, to me, nothing was more black and white: I loved Becca and would die for her.

For Adriane, it was one more thing that threw her off balance.

She left without looking back and left me to pick up the pieces alone.

As much as it hurt, I've worked through her not wanting me, but I'll never understand her not wanting Becca.

I run on the treadmill until I'm sopping wet and then head to the shower, standing in the steam as the water sluices over me.

Poppy isn't Adriane. It isn't right to compare them.

But it's almost impossible not to when Poppy is the first person who's made me think twice about my no-dating stance.

Poppy is genuine in a way that feels almost impossible.

Unlike Adriane, she knows exactly what she'd be getting into if we had a relationship. And she adores Becca.

It's the way that Becca adores Poppy that scares me the most.

Somehow, I did manage to sleep last night, but I wake up dragging. After I take Becca to school, I go to Luminary. The bell jingles over the door as I step inside and my jaw tightens when I spot Clara behind the counter, looking at me expectantly. The music is booming like it was the other day.

"Not again," I mumble.

"Morning, Bowie!" she calls, her grin huge. "Hope you're ready to boogie!"

"Clara," I say flatly, regretting my decision to come here.

"You know the drill," she says, pointing at the floor.

I sigh, scrubbing a hand over my face. The small crowd in the shop watches, some pulling out their phones to record me.

"It better be an extra-large drink," I tell Clara.

She nods happily. "Coming right up."

I start the Gangnam Style dance and as I'm doing the horseback rider, Penn appears out of nowhere and slides on the floor between my feet, pretending to be the horse. The shop erupts into cheers and applause and when Penn stands up, we do the shuffle steps together. When we're done, Penn holds his hand up, beaming, and I slap it, not beaming.

"That was awesome," Penn says, laughing.

"We shouldn't be encouraging this," I say dryly, giving Clara a look.

She just laughs at me, handing me a large Americano. "I knew you had it in you, Bowie Fox."

I grumble nonsense and then a tangle of long, blonde hair

catches my eye. Poppy's smile is huge until she sees that I've spotted her and she turns to the cart that Clara keeps with napkins and a variety of creamers. She fusses with the napkins and something about the way her shoulders hunch tells me she's had her own night of contemplation.

"Morning," I say, sliding into the seat closest to the cart.

She freezes then turns, clutching a handful of sugar packets like they're lifelines. "Oh! Hey!"

I raise an eyebrow. "You okay?"

"Fine! Totally fine," she says too quickly. She stuffs the packets back into the bowl with too much force.

Before I can press further, she startles at the bell jangling and knocks into the cart, sending stir sticks and napkins flying. One of the creamers turns over and glugs down the side of the cart. I stand instinctively to help, but Poppy is already in full panic mode, scrambling to clean up the milk and grabbing a fistful of stirrers.

"Why am I so clumsy?" she groans. "Like I don't have enough to worry about, and now—" she stops mid-sentence.

"Now what?"

She glances around, her face flushing as she sees all the attention she's getting. Clara comes over with a mop and Poppy tries to take it from her.

"Honey, don't worry about this at all. Happens at least once a day. I need someone to do a built-in here instead of this rickety old thing."

"I like this rickety old thing." Poppy sniffs.

Clara smiles.

But when I look at Poppy again, I'm shocked to see tears rolling down her face.

I lean in. "Poppy, what's got you so upset? It's really all right."

She exhales sharply and straightens, looking up at me. "I'm pregnant with your baby!" she says.

The coffee shop goes silent and I freeze, the words like stones pelting me nonstop.

"What?" I whisper.

She turns a shade of red I didn't think was possible. "Oh my God," she whispers, burying her face in her hands.

"Did I just hear that right?" Clara asks in delight.

"I didn't mean to just…blurt it out like that," Poppy says, looking panicked.

I stand there, my brain scrambling to catch up. The coffee shop is unnervingly quiet and it's then that I feel Penn's hand on my shoulder. It steadies me.

"Let's…talk outside," I say finally, my voice gruff.

Poppy nods quickly, ducking her head as she walks away. I look at Penn and he nods.

"You've got this," he says quietly.

When I step outside, Poppy is pacing on the side of Luminary…away from the windows. When she sees me, she stops and looks at me with uncertainty.

"How about we start over," I say. "What—?"

Tears are streaming down her face now and I have a sick feeling.

"I'm pregnant. I realized it the night of your dad's funeral…when I got sick at your house. And I've wanted to tell you ever since…I just didn't know how…I wanted to be further along so I could be sure I even was, but I went to the doctor and," she throws her hand in the air, "I definitely am. She said I'm due in November."

"You knew last night?" I say, feeling numb and bewildered and a little delayed in the whole processing of this. "Since the night of my dad's *funeral*?"

She steps forward, her face a torment. "Yes. I'm sorry, Bowie. I should've told you, I know."

I stare at her, the weight of her words settling over me. I feel like I'm drowning in this news. A baby.

"We used a condom," I say weakly.

"I know."

"I've always thought Rhodes was probably wrong about using a condom when Levi was conceived, but—" I close my eyes and press my fingers to the bridge of my nose, exhaling roughly.

"Things happen," she says.

"Things happen." My eyes open, and I try to focus on her. "I didn't plan on ever having another baby."

Pain flashes across her face and she nods, biting her lower lip. "I understand."

"No, I…I just…I need a minute or a million to process this."

She nods. "I get it, trust me."

CHAPTER TWENTY-FOUR

KUMQUAT

POPPY

After he's walked away, I bend over, trying to catch my breath, and then hurry to my car so no one sees me crying.

Why did I just blurt it out like that?

Why didn't I tell him the moment I found out about it?

I'm not sure it would've done any good, but the accusing look in his eyes when he said I'd known about it last night…

Last night.

I've been replaying those moments in my bed over and

over again. Our first time together was amazing, but last night was surreal. It far surpassed anything I've ever experienced, and I've practically been floating around all morning…until I saw him walk into Luminary, had a lust fit over him dancing, and realized I didn't know how to play it cool. Especially with the baby news hovering over me at all times.

He looked gutted. I don't know what I expected. Him to smile and say, *Poppy, this is exactly what I wanted?* No, I knew it would hit him hard. The guy just lost his father, not to mention raising Becca as a single parent. He needed more consideration with the news than it to be blurted out in a coffee shop for the whole town to hear.

The news will probably be everywhere by lunchtime.

I slam my fist on the steering wheel, my thoughts going a mile a minute. Bowie didn't say he didn't want the baby exactly…even though it's not what he had planned…but he didn't say he wanted it either.

My voice is shaky as I say the words aloud, "There's never been a doubt in my mind. I'm having this baby."

My stomach twists and I pull over past the shops on Jupiter Lane and call my sister. She answers and sounds a lot better than the last time we talked.

"Hey, I was gonna call you today," she says.

"You feeling better?" I ask and my voice cracks at the end.

"So much better. Poppy? Are you okay? What's going on?"

"I'm pregnant," I say, full-on crying now.

"Oh my God. Pregnant! From that night with Bowie?"

"Yes. And we had sex last night too, but I didn't tell him until today. And I botched it up royally."

"What did he say?" she asks breathlessly.

"He said he didn't plan on ever having another baby."

"Oof."

"I know. And then he said he just needed to process it and left." I can hardly get the words out now.

"A baby, Poppy! You've always wanted kids."

"But I'd hoped that when I had a baby, the father would be excited about it too."

I wipe at my face, frustrated that I'm taking it so hard. I knew Bowie wouldn't be ecstatic about this—it's the main reason I've put off telling him. His life is complicated and he's guarded...I have no idea where I stand with him, even after having sex with him a second time. But a part of me had hoped for a flicker of something—even if it was just acceptance.

All I saw was shock.

"What if he doesn't want this at all?" I ask. Just saying it out loud makes my heart hurt.

The thought of raising a baby with someone who doesn't want to be there, who might resent me...and the baby...it sounds truly awful.

"From what you've told me, Bowie is an incredible father. He'll come around. Give him time," Marley says. "Poppy, I'm so excited. I can't wait to meet my little niece or nephew." Her voice cracks and she's crying too. "You're gonna be the best mom."

"You think so?"

"I know so."

"Okay, I have to get to work, but thank you. I'm a mess and you've helped."

"I'm here...always, day or night. And I can be there in a heartbeat if you need me to be."

"I'll be okay. Let's save it for when the baby comes. You're coming for Easter too, right?"

"Yep, we'll be there. You're having a baby," she yells.

"I want to be as excited as you are," I say wistfully.

"You will be. You're just in shock still. Have you told Mom and Dad yet?"

"No!" I groan. "I will…soon. I want to wait just a little longer."

"Poppy, tell them. They'll be shocked, but they'll be happy for you."

"I know. I just…I wish…yeah, anyway. I love you. I'll talk to you later."

"Love you."

I drive the rest of the way to work and when I get out of the car, I wipe my face again.

Sorry, little one. I promise I won't always cry.

I'm distracted at work and distressed when there's no sign of Becca and Bowie in the afternoon. When I get home, I eat a grilled cheese sandwich because it's the only thing that sounds good, and I flop onto my couch, phone in hand. I scroll on Instagram…where I may or may not check out BHOTD…okay, I totally do and it's a good one. A slow-motion reel of Bowie on the sidelines at Clarity Field, throwing the ball. His hair flares out when the ball leaves his hands and it's a glorious sight.

I'm playing that over and over again…possibly obsessing about our child's hair possibilities…when my phone lights up with a text from the girls.

> ELLE
> OMG, you guys. It happened!
>
> SADIE
> You're pregnant!

> **TRU**
>
> Tell me we're pregnant at the same time!

> **CALISTA**
>
> WHAT! WE'RE HAVING A BABY?!!

My face heats and I know that if we were all in the room together, they'd see right through me and know that *I'm* pregnant at the same time as Tru.

> **ELLE**
>
> You guys. 😭 No, I am not pregnant. This feels like a letdown now. Lol Calista already knows because she keeps up with this stuff better than I do…Chasing Sunrise HIT THE NEW YORK TIMES LIST! 😭

> Elle! That's amazing. Congratulations!!

> **SADIE**
>
> AHHHH I'm so excited I can't take it, Zoey Archer!

> **TRU**
>
> Holy crap, Elle. That's huge. You're a literal literary goddess.

> **ELLE**
>
> Thanks, you guys. I'm an emotional mess.

> **CALISTA**
>
> I'm so proud. So, so proud.

> You deserved this so much. The book is incredible. I stayed up until 2 a.m. crying over chapter 18.

> **ELLE**
>
> Okay, but chapter 18 was supposed to make you cry. 😊
>
> **TRU**
>
> I almost threw the book across the room at the twist in chapter 12. My heart cannot take you, Ms. Zoey.
>
> **ELLE**
>
> Stop it, you're making me blush.
>
> **SADIE**
>
> Let's celebrate! Drinks at The Fairy Hut? They've got delicious mocktails that you can enjoy too, Tru.
>
> **TRU**
>
> Yes to celebrating at The Fairy Hut!
>
> I'm in!

Bowie must have asked Penn not to tell anyone yet. I'll just have to figure out a way to be subtle about ordering a mocktail myself.

> **ELLE**
>
> You guys are the best. I'd love to get together. Tomorrow night?

We all chime in that it works for us, and I find myself smiling for the first time since I talked to Bowie. I'm so happy for Elle, and celebrating with the girls is exactly what I need.

Marley has started a baby room ideas Pinterest board and has also been texting me her favorites. It's sweet and a fun distraction, though I still feel somewhat detached that this is really happening to me. I touch my stomach and look up the size of a fetus at this stage. A kumquat. Hmm. That doesn't tell me much. I see somewhere else that it's the size of an olive or grape.

Hmm. Olives sound good.

So crazy.

Later that night, as I slip under the covers, I'm back to that gnawing worry. I haven't heard from Bowie. Basking in the warm afterglow of being with him last night was very short-lived.

I glance at my phone one more time. I've willed it to light up with a message from him all day long, but the screen stays dark. The quiet of my room makes my thoughts louder.

He's processing, I tell myself, feeling hollow.

I curl onto my side, clutching my pillow. The sting of tears burns and I turn out the light, giving in to the uncertainty of my future.

Tomorrow I will wake up and not cry about this. It's not good for the baby. It's not good for me. But tonight I feel powerless to stop it.

CHAPTER TWENTY-FIVE

SOS

BOWIE

I push open the door to Luminary, the post-workout fog clinging to me as much as the news I'm still wrestling to process. I've hardly slept, every thought since Poppy's revelation reeling me under like quicksand.

Clara glances up from behind the counter, her usual mischievous grin fading when she sees my face. "Americano coming right up," she says, knowing I'm not up for dancing today. She slides it across the counter a minute later and when

I look at the cup, I stare up at her. She wrinkles up her nose. "I couldn't help myself."

The cup says Daddy with a star next to it.

"Thanks," I mutter, grabbing the cup and heading to the back room.

Henley, Weston, Penn, and Rhodes are already waiting, their expressions ranging from curiosity to full-blown concern.

"What's going on?" Rhodes asks, standing up and squeezing my shoulder and then pulling out a chair for me. "You never call meetings. This is…unsettling."

I sit down heavily, taking a long sip of coffee before setting the cup down.

"I'm scared," Penn says, only half-joking.

Henley squints at me, leaning in, and Weston gulps nervously.

"Poppy's pregnant."

Silence falls over the table.

And then it goes haywire, everyone talking at once.

"Wait, what?" Henley nearly knocks over his coffee.

"You've been having sex with Poppy?" Rhodes screeches.

"Poppy?" Weston asks, eyes wide.

"I'm shook," Penn says. "You didn't even tell us you two hooked up. Here we've thought you were suffering from the world's longest dry spell and you've gotten her pregnant?" He sounds deeply offended, but when I look at him, he gives me a small smirk.

Turns out I've not given Penn's acting skills enough credit.

I acknowledge him with a little chin up.

"More than once, clearly," Rhodes says, smirking.

"Twice, but guys, can we focus here?"

Henley reaches across the table and pounds me on the

back, his smile huge. "We're focusing. On the fact that you— Mr. I-have-no-time-for-relationships-Fox—have been sleeping with Poppy Keane."

"And now she's pregnant," Weston says, letting out a low whistle. "*Dude*."

I groan. "This was a mistake, telling you guys today."

"Oh no," Rhodes says, holding up a hand. "This is amazing. Like Christmas, but better. Keep going."

They all laugh. They freaking *laugh*.

I glare at them. "What do you want me to say? I'm at a loss. But Penn, thanks for keeping it a secret. I know that must have been killing you."

Penn collapses on the table. "I was dying!"

"Wait. How did he find out about it before us?" Rhodes asks, smirk completely gone now.

"I was there for the blurtouncement," Penn says.

They all look at him blankly, but I actually laugh. "She blurted it out here."

"It was epic," Penn says, laughing.

"I can't believe we didn't all hear about it by last night," Weston says.

"Clara must have made everyone swear to keep their mouths shut," Penn says.

"Okay," Henley says, waving a hand for silence. "Let's get serious. Tell us how you're feeling about this."

"I'm a wreck," I admit. "I haven't been able to think straight since she told me."

"I can't believe you didn't call this meeting yesterday," Rhodes says, annoyed.

I roll my head back to the ceiling and Henley clears his throat.

"You're upset," he says.

"I don't know. It's…a lot."

"Imagine what she's feeling," Weston says and then gives me a sheepish look when he sees my expression. He lifts a shoulder and I frown, guilt creeping into my chest. "How's she handling the news?"

"I…don't really know. We didn't talk for long. She told me here…I'm surprised you hadn't already heard the news actually. I'm not sure how many heard her say it, but Clara for sure did." I show them the cup and they all crack up.

"You should check on her," Rhodes says. "She's having your baby, man." He reaches out and holds onto my shoulder. "Do you have feelings for her?"

I swallow hard. "We had sex night before last again…I was sort of an asshole after the first time." I glance at Weston. "It was the night of your wedding."

He grins. "We should've all known after watching the two of you dance that night."

"Damn straight," Penn says, laughing.

"It was a big deal for you to have sex with her in the first place," Rhodes says knowingly. "And you don't do repeats. You *like* her."

"I like her," I say, head in hands. "Goddammit, I do." When I look up at them, they're all staring at me with pleased expressions and I shake my head. "All the more reason for me to not get involved with her."

"Holy hell, what are you saying?" Rhodes says, scowling.

"I can't go through that again," I say. "I can't do it to Becca."

"Poppy is not Adriane," Henley says. "Not even close. You've been closing yourself off for so long. I think this is the best news ever." He points at me. "Don't run from this, Bow. Talk to her. Don't leave her hanging. Let her know you're gonna be a great dad to that baby."

"And then take her to bed again and celebrate," Penn says, holding up a hand for me to high-five him.

When I don't, he looks around the table for another taker. Weston slaps it and then looks at me.

"For once, Penn's got a great idea."

"Hey!" Penn says, bopping Weston over the head.

"Maybe have a conversation first," Rhodes says. "See where she's standing with all this…and then take her to bed and celebrate."

"There will be no taking her to bed," I say firmly.

But even as I'm saying it, I'm imagining her hair spilling out over her pillow, her body on display for me, and I shift in my seat, hungry for her again.

I can't believe how much I like the woman.

How did I let this happen?

"Let us know how it goes," Weston says. "You'll go see her today?"

"I don't know. I feel like I need to have my head wrapped around it all a little better before I see her again."

"Get your head wrapped around it *together*," Weston says.

Rhodes points at him. "That. Exactly. Don't wait on this, Bowie. I love you like a brother, we all do, and we want your happiness as much as our own, so I'm telling you, do not fucking blow this. Poppy is incredible and the two of you together could be straight-up magic. Give her a chance."

"Rhodes is telling the truth," Henley says. "And since Tru is pregnant right now, I know firsthand how vulnerable this time can be, even when the circumstances are the best. Whether you know how you want to handle a romantic relationship with her or not, it's important that you have a good relationship for the sake of your child. But I'm rooting for the two of you." He winks, leaning back in his chair.

"Hold on a second…" Weston says, pulling The Single

Dad Playbook out of his bag. He flips it open, pointing to the page where I wrote that Becca has been asking for a sibling, and I groan.

"I can't even think about telling Becca yet," I say. "She won't be able to think of anything else until November."

"That's when Baby Fox is coming?" Henley says, beaming.

"You sly motherfucker," Penn says, shaking his head. "You've been holding this secret all this time and now you're Poppy's baby daddy." He throws his hands up. "This might just be the only way you'll let yourself get involved in a relationship."

They all laugh and Rhodes slaps Penn on the back.

"I think Penn might be right again," he says.

Penn tries to scowl, but he's too damn proud to have Rhodes' praise to pull it off.

"Let's not get ahead of ourselves," I say.

"You already did that when you got her pregnant." Rhodes laughs.

"I used a condom," I mutter.

"How you like me now?" Rhodes sings like the pigeon in *Storks*.

It's a line we've all sung from time to time, having watched way too many animated movies between us.

"How you like me now?" Penn echoes, giving me a smug look.

"You guys are useless," I grumble, putting my hand on the back of my neck.

"Tell me it was at least a phenomenal night…excuse me, two nights…with Poppy," Penn says.

"It was a phenomenal night…two nights," I say rotely.

But then my lips crack, breaking into a smile and they hoot like a room full of frat boys.

I hold up my hand. "Settle. We can safely say that I was overdue, so..."

The words feel cheap and ring false. I hate that I even said that. But they all look at me knowingly.

"Yeah, keep telling yourself that," Rhodes says, rolling his eyes.

"Poppy is special," I say quietly.

I can't help myself. I can't leave that last sentence hanging like it didn't mean anything to me that we had sex. It did mean something, both times…but night before last…that was groundbreaking for me.

For the past nine years, I haven't once come close to changing my mind about staying out of a relationship. But Poppy…she makes me want to consider it.

More than that…I think I'm already invested.

She's having my baby. I'm invested whether I want to be or not.

But the truth is…I want to be.

And that is seriously fucking with me.

CHAPTER TWENTY-SIX

WHY DON'T I INTRODUCE MYSELF?

POPPY

When I walk into The Fairy Hut, Tru waves and I head back. Everyone but Calista is there and she walks in behind me. I hug everyone and sit down, sliding the napkin onto my lap. Feeling eyes on me, I look up and Sadie, Tru, and Elle are all staring at me. They have these wide eyes and are so smiley, I laugh and then turn to look at Calista next to me. She squirms, giving me the same doe-eyed smile.

"What is it?" I ask.

"We know," Sadie bursts out and then clamps her hand over her mouth. "I'm so sorry, we were going to try to wait for you to tell us, but—"

"The guys can't hide anything," Elle says apologetically. "And then I went to Luminary today and everyone was talking about it there..."

My cheeks flame.

"You don't have to talk about it," Tru says, reaching out to lay her hand on mine. "But we're here for you, when and if you do want to talk about it."

"I made such an idiot of myself at Luminary," I say, groaning. "And it's not that I don't want to talk about it. I need to talk about it probably...I just know that it's awkward, given that you're all so close to Bowie."

They wait for me to go on and my cheeks get hotter. Fortunately, the waiter comes then and takes our order and the fact that I'm getting a mocktail is a non-issue.

"Did you know when you texted?" I ask, laughing. "I was dying when you said that about Elle being pregnant."

"No, we didn't know," Tru says, her eyes bright. "But I am *so excited* about it. We can raise little besties together!"

I press my hand to my heart, so moved that they're being so incredible about this. I'm so new to this friend group and I'm not even dating Bowie...they could've potentially been weird about the whole thing.

"Has Bowie talked to you yet?" Elle asks.

"No," I say, shaking my head. "I think I've thoroughly freaked him out."

"That man," Sadie sighs. "He'll do the right thing though, Poppy. Don't worry. He needs to get used to the idea, but he's going to be a great dad to that baby."

"That's what my sister said too. I haven't fully wrapped my head around it all, but I'll be fine doing it on my own, if that's what it comes down to. I'd rather my child have a dad who wants to be part of their life though." I lift a shoulder and feel the tears building behind my eyes. I glance at the ceiling and fan my face, trying not to cry.

"I love Bowie so much, but I could kill him for making you even question whether he's going to be there for you," Elle says.

"It's a lot to think about." I sniff. "And I haven't had much more time than he has, but a little…"

Sadie straightens and she's smiling over my shoulder. "Looks like he's had some time to think about it."

I turn and see Bowie walking toward the table. When Bowie Fox walks into a room, heads turn and voices hush. He seems oblivious to it all.

He reaches the table and stares at me as he says, "Hi, Poppy." He looks around at everyone and does the head-up tilt to them.

"Hi," I say when he looks at me again.

"Do you think we could talk?"

"I'm kind of in the middle of something right now," I say, nose in the air.

I hear a snort behind me from one of the girls, but I don't break. Bowie's had time to talk to me and he can wait until my night out with the girls is over.

He nods like that's perfectly acceptable. And damn right, it should be.

"Okay. I'll be right over there," he says, pointing to a booth in the back.

"I might be a while," I say, lifting a shoulder.

"I can wait."

I nod coolly and he turns and walks to the booth across the room. When I look at the girls, they burst out laughing.

"That was so badass," Calista says, cackling.

"I'm so *not* badass," I say, groaning. "It's just…he sort of left me hanging and that's fine. But I've been looking forward to seeing you guys all day and now that he's ready to chat, maybe I'm not." My voice sounds prim and it makes them laugh harder.

"Well, we can do this another night too," Sadie says.

"I want to celebrate Elle's book hitting the New York Times!" I say.

"The baby news is much more important," she says.

Our drinks come and we all lift our glasses.

"To hitting the lists and having babies!" Tru says.

We all laugh and repeat it, clinking our glasses together. Half an hour goes by at least, and it's not that I'm just trying to make Bowie wait…I really am enjoying myself. But I'm also nervous to talk to him.

"He can't take his eyes off of you," Calista says. "It seems like whatever he needed to think through has been *thought through*. Everything's going to be just fine."

I want to look so bad, but I don't. "You can tell that from looking at him?"

"Mm-hmm," she hums.

"Eeeeek," Tru squeals. She leans in. "This is right up there with when we found out Rhodes and Elle were finally sleeping together. We wanted it so bad for them," she looks at Sadie, who's nodding emphatically.

"*Yes*, so, so bad," Sadie gushes. "I have such a good feeling about this."

I make a face. "Just because I'm having his baby doesn't mean we're going to be together."

"Mm-hmm," Calista hums again and they laugh while I take a deep breath.

"I should probably see what he has to say. He'll need to get home to Becca soon."

"Go with grace," Tru says, grinning.

"We're here if you need backup. And to spy on you," Elle adds, making all of us laugh.

"Thanks, guys. Sorry to bail early on the party."

"Oh, we are living for this, don't you worry," Sadie says, giving me a cheesy grin.

Tru laughs and clinks Sadie's glass.

I laugh as I stand, but it drops when I walk toward Bowie. He surprises me by standing when I get near the table, and then he holds out his hand. I look at it, confused.

"Hi, I'm Bowie Fox." He tilts his head toward my hand and I lift it, shaking his weakly. "I was hoping maybe we could start over."

When I just stand there staring at him, my hand still in his, he gives it a slight shake.

"And you are?" he asks.

I give him an exasperated look, determined not to be swayed by his charm now. His charm is what got me in his bed in the first place. Well, that, and his boulder shoulders, perfect hair, and veiny hands.

"Poppy Keane," I say, lips puckered.

I refuse to smile when his teeth swipe over that plump lower lip that is capable of the most amazing things.

"Have a drink with me?" he asks. "I noticed you had a drink with your friends already, but did you try the Hop Away With Me?"

I snort and he grins, relieved. All the names in The Fairy Hut crack me up.

"No, I did not have the Hop Away With Me, I had the Top Shelfless Elf. What about you? What are you drinking?"

"I enjoy Tink's Mead occasionally, but…I heard you're having my baby, so I went with the You Slay, Fae…you know, for solidarity and encouragement." He grabs his mocktail from the table and lifts it.

I bite back my smile. "So…we can start over, but we're talking about the baby?"

He holds his hand toward the booth. "If you'll sit with me, we can talk about whatever you'd like. Get to know each other…better." He falters slightly and I sigh, pretending to be put out.

"I guess I could give you a few minutes of my time."

He grins and I sit down. He waits until I'm seated and then sits across from me.

"I'm sorry, Poppy. I'm sorry I went quiet on you and left you to deal with this alone." His voice is earnest and I swallow hard, my eyes filling…which I hate.

I don't want him to see me cry!

Panic floods his face when he notices, and he reaches out and touches my hand. Sparks fly like they do every time he touches me and I pull away, putting my hand in my lap.

He straightens and his eyes are sad as he looks at me.

"I've really blown all this, haven't I?" he says.

"We just met, remember?" I say, and his expression lightens just a little bit.

"Right. I have a daughter. Her name is Becca and she knows I'll be out past her bedtime, so I…have plenty of time to talk. If you're willing."

I sniff and wipe my face as the waiter comes over. Perfect timing.

When he walks away, I clear my throat. "You don't need to worry—I know that just because I'm pregnant…it doesn't mean we're going to be…anything." I wave my hand awkwardly. "I hope that you'll want to be involved in our child's life because I want that for them, but if you decide not to be, I'm going to be fine."

My jaw clamps and I give him a steely look.

He leans in. "Poppy, what I said about not planning on having any more kids...that doesn't mean I don't want to be involved in our child's life."

Hearing *him* say *our child* hits different. It makes my heart salsa its way out of my chest.

"I'm terrified. For so many reasons," he adds. "I have a fuck-ton of baggage. But I'm not going anywhere, I promise you that. I'm a bit screwed up, but I'm...dependable and loyal...and I'll be there for you. If you'll let me, I want to be at the doctor appointments...I hate that I've missed even one." He takes a deep breath and runs his hand through his hair.

I watch, entranced, as it falls back to his chin, and I wish I could be the skin that it touches. *Poppy! Stop lusting over this man and be firm.*

"And I know you're not assuming we're going to be a couple," he says.

Are his cheeks coloring slightly? It's a little hard to tell in The Fairy Hut with all the twinkle lights, but he looks nervous.

"But I like you, Poppy. More than I've liked anyone in... almost a decade. And I don't say that to pressure you in any way," he rushes, "but I've already proven that I can't resist you."

I laugh in disbelief. "That's the way you prove you can't resist me?"

He makes a face, swiping his hand down his jaw. "Trust me. It may not have been obvious, but I am so into you."

My face flames and I lift a shoulder, pretending to be oh-so-chill when inside, my heart is shimmying all over the place. "It seems like you're into me about twenty percent of the time."

He shakes his head and points at his face. "Resting dick face…it means nothing."

My lips twitch and I want to laugh, but I'm still trying to maintain my cool. "And your chilly demeanor?"

"Self-preservation."

"And your bolting when times are hard?"

"Something I will never do with you again, I swear it," he says.

I gulp. He looks like he means it. His gaze never wavers from mine and it's intense…sincere. I could get lost in this look.

"Whatever we end up being to each other, I like you, Poppy. I like the person you are. I like the way you are with Becca. I may not have shown it enough, but I think we can be great friends. But, I also like the way you feel, the way you kiss, the way your nose crinkles up when you laugh. I like that you're athletic but also clumsy. I like your cushiony upper lip and I'd like to park myself on your bottom lip."

My hands are trembling with the desire to touch him when he says that, but I don't.

"And despite being fucking terrified, I like that you're the one having my baby. Because even though I don't know you the way I hope to, I have a feeling that I can trust you. The list of people that I trust is quite small…and you've met every single one of them. They accepted you before I did because they're smart that way and their hearts are bigger, but…I trust you, and in my book, that means just about everything."

I have a lump in my throat when I reach out and touch his hand, squeezing it. "It means everything to me too. I want to trust you. You've made me nervous with the way you respond to me…after we had sex the first time and…when I told you I'm pregnant…but that all fades away when I see you with Becca and your friends. I'm…honored if you trust me too.

Despite the baggage, I hope you can be open about…everything. The pregnancy…any feelings you may or may not have for me, long-term…"

"It's hard for me to open up, but I'm willing to try. I want to try."

"Okay." I let out a shaky breath. "I like you too. A lot."

He weaves his fingers through mine and we stare at each other…until there's cheering across the room. We look over and the girls are cheering for us. Pretty soon, everyone else in the restaurant is looking our way and cheering too.

Bowie's shaking his head when I look back at him, but his smile is wide. He looks so much younger when he smiles like this.

"Well, this was a pretty great first meeting," I say.

He laughs. "Agreed. Do you think you'd like to go out with me again sometime?"

I lift a shoulder. "Sure," I say breezily.

"Tomorrow?" he asks. "And the next day?"

I pretend to be outraged. "A bit forward, don't you think?"

He laughs. "Thought it was worth a try."

"How about we see how tomorrow goes before we jump the gun. God," I say snottily. "I know you're into me, but seriously…" I hold my hand up.

He nods, his eyes tracking over my eyes, my mouth, and back to my eyes. I shiver with the heat in his expression.

"*So* into you. Thank you for hearing me out," he says.

I blink and press my lips together. I did not see my night going like this. We talk for a while longer, about Becca, about some of the kids at Briar Hill and ideas I have for new activities. It's light and easy and fun, and underneath all of it, a simmering chemistry pops off between us like bottle rockets.

The girls come over and hug both of us when they leave,

and Bowie walks me to my car when we finally decide to leave ourselves.

"This was really nice," he says.

"Yes, it was."

I don't know what to do now. Do we hug? Kiss? Shake hands again?

He steps forward and gives me a light kiss on the lips. Just long enough to say *hello, soft, cushy lips that feel like heaven,* and then steps back.

"I'll see you tomorrow," he says.

I hear the promise in his words. He opened up to me tonight, *finally*, and I believe he meant everything he said.

CHAPTER TWENTY-SEVEN

LITERARY LESSONS

BOWIE

I didn't expect to be this anxious, not over a date...even though it's been way too long since I've done this. But as I pull up to Poppy's place, my knuckles white on the steering wheel, I come face-to-face with the facts. I'm freaking nervous. I can't believe I'm doing this or that we're having a baby or that everything is about to change...

Whoa. I look at myself in the rearview mirror. One thing at a time.

I get out and knock on the door and Poppy opens it, looking hot as fuck in jeans and a soft-looking sweater, her long hair trailing over her breasts. My mouth goes dry.

"Hey," she says, stepping out.

"You look beautiful," I tell her.

"Oh." She looks surprised. "Thank you. So do you."

"Hmm," I grumble but grin.

"Handsome, whatever," she says, laughing.

We walk toward my car and I open the door for her.

"Very gentlemanly," she says.

"Trying something new."

She laughs, sliding into the seat. The sound eases something inside me. I'm not good at this—romance—but I can try. For her, I want to.

I drive to the end of Jupiter Lane and take a left, going into the mountains.

"Wow, it's beautiful up here," she says when we round the bend and see the lights of Silver Hills below. "I feel like I'm living in a storybook here…another little world. Don't you?"

"It is a pretty little town," I agree.

After the next bend, I pull into the parking lot of the Silver Hills Dinner Theatre. The lot is full and Poppy looks around, curious.

"I've wanted to come here but haven't had a chance to yet. Fun! What are we seeing?"

I stop the car and glance at her. "Pride and Prejudice."

Her eyes widen. "Did someone tell you that's one of my favorite stories?"

My eyebrows lift. "No."

"Have you ever read the book or seen the movie?"

I shake my head.

"Oh, you are in for a treat." She laughs. "Get ready to see a glimpse of yourself, Darcy."

I give her a perplexed look and get out of the car, moving around to the other side to open her door. She's more animated now and seems less nervous, but when I reach out and take her hand, she looks up at me and gulps.

"Is this okay?"

"Y-yes." She trips on something and I steady her.

"You sure?" I ask, chuckling.

She groans. "I hate my feet right now."

"I won't let you fall."

We step into the old theatre, the building lovingly maintained with creaky floors and velvet seats. The guys would give me such a hard time if they could see me right now. We look over the menu and place our orders and chat for a few minutes about how our days have been, when the lights dim. I pay close attention to Mr. Darcy, the proud, reserved asshole Poppy compared me to and give her a mock glare when he's being particularly rude.

I guess I can relate to a guy who doesn't like small talk.

About halfway through, Darcy makes his painfully awkward proposal and Elizabeth rejects him. The audience chuckles. I glance at Poppy, who's watching with her chin propped on her hand, her smile wide. When Darcy storms off, looking wounded and superior at the same time, Poppy side-eyes me, biting her lip to keep from laughing. I growl and she laughs out loud.

I spend the majority of the second half watching Poppy instead of the play. She's way more fun to watch.

Afterward, as we walk into the cool evening air, Poppy loops her arm through mine and I like that she made the first move to touch me.

"What did you think?" she asks.

"I don't know whether to be offended or amused that you compared me to Darcy. The guy's a bastard."

She giggles. "A little, yeah. He's broody, hard to read, doesn't like to make conversation just for the sake of it… sound familiar?"

"More like rude and standoffish."

She raises an eyebrow and when we reach the car, I move closer so that she's got her back against the door. I lean into her and hover over her mouth.

"You think I'm rude?"

"Not always."

I sputter. "I just don't dance for coffee unless I have to."

She snorts. "Right. Darcy would've never agreed to that." She stands on her tiptoes and kisses my cheek. "I guess you're not as bad as Darcy."

I give her a dry look. "High praise."

Her hands hook around my neck and she grins. "And way better hair," she whispers.

I decide then that I kind of love it when she teases me.

There's a sudden hush, as every distant sound and worry falls away, and our lips slowly, softly meet. It's featherlight and then deepens as our bodies melt into each other. I explore her sweet mouth, the lingering taste of strawberries from the dessert we shared, and kiss her until we're both breathless.

"I bet Darcy didn't kiss like that." I open her car door and she sinks onto the seat, looking up at me with glazed eyes.

"No, he did not," she says.

We talk about the play all the way to her house and then I walk her to her door. She hesitates and I don't want her to feel like she has to invite me in. I give her a chaste kiss.

"Thanks for a great night," I tell her.

"It was a lot of fun, Bowie," she says shyly.

When I get home, I text her.

> Darcy wouldn't have told Elizabeth that kissing her has become his favorite thing in life. What a dumbass.

POPPY

Is there something you'd like to say, Bowie?

I grin. I love it when she's sassy.

> Kissing you has become my favorite thing in life. I'd like to do a lot more of it. Please. If you're game.

POPPY

I'm game. 😊

> Night, Poppy.

POPPY

Night, Bowie.

The next day I call her during her lunch break.

"Hey!" she says, sounding surprised.

"Hey, you. How's your day going?"

"It's been a good one. How about yours?"

"Yeah, same here. Mrs. McGregor is bringing Becca to Briar Hill after school. I have a meeting with my agent."

"Oh, okay."

"But I wondered if you'd want to come over for dinner tonight."

"Well, look at you, two nights in a row. I might start to get ideas," she teases.

"I hope so," I say. My cheeks get hot when I talk to her.

It's the dumbest thing. I feel like a kid, trying to impress a girl...*the* girl. I put my hand on the back of my neck and smile down at the floor.

"I guess I could come over for dinner," she says.

"Anything I can do to make you certain?"

"Hmm. I like it when you say *please*."

"Please, Poppy Keane, will you please come to my house for dinner tonight?"

"I'd love to."

I laugh and she gasps.

"I just made Bowie Fox laugh...on the phone."

"Shut up," I mumble.

She laughs and I grin like a motherfucking cheesehead.

"What can I bring?"

"Just yourself."

"That I can do."

I'm in the kitchen talking to Mrs. McGregor about dinner, when Mom walks in.

"What's going on?" she asks suspiciously. "Why are you all dressed up?"

I look at my button-down shirt and frown. "Is it too much? Poppy's coming over for dinner."

"Oh!" She brightens up, clapping her hands. "What are we making?" she asks Mrs. McGregor.

"*I* was making my Bolognese," Mrs. McGregor says.

Mom sniffs, looking Mrs. McGregor over. "Your Bolognese?"

"Well, an old neighbor's recipe, but it's an authentic sauce."

I look at the ceiling and count to five. "Was it a mistake to try to have a date over here tonight?"

Both women look contrite.

"Absolutely not," Mrs. McGregor says.

"We'll work together and then get out of your way," Mom says, giving me a gentle nudge out the door. "Don't worry about a thing."

CHAPTER TWENTY-EIGHT

NUMBER ONE FAN

POPPY

When Bowie opens his door, I think three things:

He looks incredible.

He looks stressed.

What smells so good?

"Are you okay?" I ask.

He tugs me inside and my senses blink and then erupt as they seem to always do when he touches me.

"I almost called to see if I could take you out instead because—"

I hear it then. Raised voices spilling from the kitchen, both fiery.

"I'm telling you, you have to brown the meat first," Mrs. McGregor's Scottish brogue carries clear as a bell. "No shortcuts, just a proper sear!"

We walk back and peer in the doorway. Bowie's mom is lifting a ladle as if it's a royal scepter.

"No, you should always cook the mirepoix slowly first, then the meat goes in. That's the authentic way."

"And you're Italian?" Mrs. McGregor sniffs.

"And you are?" Bowie's mom counters.

"I've made Bolognese for many years. It's Bowie's favorite. I know what I'm doing," Mrs. McGregor says.

That seems to deflate his mom for a second and Bowie steps into the kitchen, looking back at me with an apologetic smile.

"Oh, you must be Poppy. I'm Paulina," Bowie's mom says. "I don't believe we've officially met."

"It's so nice to meet you," I tell her.

"You are gorgeous," she says warmly.

"Oh…thank you! You are too," I say sincerely. She really is. From the pictures I've seen, Bowie is tall and built like his dad was, but his features are similar to his mom's.

She hugs me and I glance at Bowie over her shoulder. He looks a little calmer but still nervous.

"You'll back me up on this, won't you?" Paulina says, when she pulls away. She gestures to the stove, where a pot of sauce bubbles. "My family has been making Bolognese for generations."

"Hello, Poppy," Mrs. McGregor says, smiling wide. "It's lovely to see you again."

"You too."

"Generations, ha," Mrs. McGregor snorts, rolling her eyes at Paulina. "Next you'll be saying you've been making Cullen Skink all your life."

Paulina looks flustered for a second and then straightens, her nose lifted. "I've made Cullen Skink a time or two."

"Right," Mrs. McGregor mutters.

I try to keep a straight face. "I'm sure it's going to be delicious," I say diplomatically. "It smells heavenly."

Bowie clears his throat. "Maybe the real secret ingredient is compromise?"

My lips twitch.

"Compromise?" Paulina echoes. "You mean cook the mirepoix first, then add the meat—"

"And then let it all simmer together until the flavors marry," Mrs. McGregor finishes, as if suddenly enlightened.

They both pause, eyeing each other warily, then simultaneously nod.

"I suppose that might result in a decent sauce," Paulina concedes. "Mrs. McGregor, would you like to be the one to add the wine?"

"Very well," she says. She gets the corkscrew out, tosses it in the air, catches it, and then grins at us.

I let out a loud laugh and Bowie starts laughing too. The women look at us in curiosity, like they have no idea the entertainment they're putting out there.

"Dinner here is never dull, I see," I whisper to Bowie.

"You have no idea."

Once the wine is added, I lean closer to the stove. "Smells perfect to me," I say softly.

Both women look pleased with the compliment.

"We'll see, dear," Paulina says, patting my arm. "Nothing

wrong with a bit of spirited debate in the name of good Bolognese."

"My Bolognese was fine without the debate, but I guess you're right," Mrs. McGregor says.

"Why settle with fine when you can have splendid?" Paulina tilts her head and Mrs. McGregor groans.

Bowie laughs. "Okay, ladies. Thank you."

Becca bursts through the kitchen with Martha on her heels and freezes when she sees me. And then she's rushing toward me. "Poppy!"

I love the way she always says my name with such joy.

"Hi, Becca!"

"Why are you here?" she asks happily.

"I'm…having dinner." I look at Bowie, uncertain what to say.

"I love dinner!" Becca throws her fist in the air.

"Me too." I laugh.

Bowie leans in to whisper. "Sorry, I thought this was going to be a quieter affair with maybe the three of us, but looks like there might be five or six."

"It's totally fine. I'm having fun," I tell him.

He grins at me and puts his hand on my cheek. For a second, I think he might kiss me, but he doesn't.

Becca looks at us and beams. "Poppy, you marry my dad like Tru and Henley?" she asks. "And Elle and Rhodes and Sadie and Weston?"

My mouth drops. "Uh. I—"

"First things first, Becca," Bowie says.

I expect him to be terrified by Becca trying to marry us off, but his look is teasing when he looks at me and scrunches up his face.

He leans in. "Well, we kind of already botched that, didn't we," he says, so only I can hear.

I nearly choke as I try to not burst out laughing.

"Yes, first you get Poppy a pretty ring," Becca says.

"Well, I have to convince her to like me," Bowie says.

I roll my eyes.

Becca's face brightens with understanding as she holds her fingers up and starts counting. She holds up her first finger and says, "My dad is very nice." Moving on, she counts off more reasons Bowie is the best. "My dad is tall and SO strong." She forgoes the counting to show me her big muscle pose.

I am so giddy with warm fuzzies that I can hardly contain it.

"He takes me to fun places," she continues. She points animatedly at Bowie like she just remembered something else. "He gives me presents. I love presents!" She gets more excited as she goes. "He reads me stories and plays dress up. I have a pink dress. I love pink!"

"He's a good dad, isn't he?" I say.

She nods, smiling happily. "My daddy is the best." Then she flings herself forward, wrapping her arms around my waist. "And my Poppy is the best. I am so happy," Becca says. "Can we take pictures?"

She lets me go and looks around, spotting Bowie's phone on the counter. She picks it up and hands it to him.

"We take pictures!" she says excitedly.

When he tries to take one of the two of us, she points at him.

"You too, Dad," she says. "Because we like you."

"Oh," he says, surprised.

He moves next to us and holds out his arm, taking a few selfies of us.

She turns to look at me. "You like my dad?"

"I do," I say, smiling at her and not looking at Bowie while my cheeks are burning.

"Then we get married like Tru and Henley," she says, nodding. "And Elle and Rhodes and Sadie and Weston."

Bowie groans and gives me an apologetic look.

"I see the pictures," Becca says.

Bowie shows her, and she claps her hands and says a loud, "Yes!" in approval.

"Join us for dinner, ladies?" Bowie says to his mom and Mrs. McGregor.

"Oh, we were just going to disappear." Mrs. McGregor looks at Paulina pointedly.

"Um, yes…you enjoy," Paulina says.

"You went to all this trouble," I say. "Join us." I look at Bowie and he looks amused but pleased.

"I'll just go tell Mr. McGregor to join us too." Mrs. McGregor goes off excitedly and we fill our plates before taking them to the table.

Later, after my stomach hurts from laughing and the delicious meal, Becca gets ready for bed. She comes out in her pajamas and looks at me, holding up a book. She hands it to me, looking shyer than usual.

"Would you like me to read you this story?" I ask.

"Yes."

I stand up and she takes my hand, leading me to her room. She crawls into bed and I sit on the edge and start to read in my best animated voice. When the story ends, she smiles drowsily up at me.

"You live with us too," she says.

"Uh," I shake my head, "I live at my house."

I hear something and turn back to see Bowie standing by the door, arms folded, and my heart twists in ways I can't describe.

"You live with us," Becca whispers.

"Night-night, sweet girl," I say as I lean down and press a gentle kiss to her forehead.

Bowie's eyes are heated as I walk past him. He goes over to tell Becca good night and then follows me out. When we're out in the hall, he takes my hand and tugs me toward his room. Once we're inside, he closes the door and then presses me against it.

"Poppy," he says huskily. "What are you doing to me?"

"What do you mean?"

"How are you doing this? You're burrowing into me like a persistent whisper I can't stop hearing," he breathes, his voice taut with emotion. "Your goodness is," his forehead rests against mine, the warmth of his breath fanning across my cheek, "consuming me. Your beauty. Your gentleness with Becca. The way you feel in my arms."

Sometimes when he speaks, I hear the slightest bit of an accent like his mom's.

I can feel the tremor in his chest, as if his heart's pounding as desperately as mine. His hands tighten at my waist.

"I can't think straight when I'm near you, and I can't think straight when I'm not."

I swallow, overcome by the honesty in his voice, the vulnerability in his eyes. "Bowie," I whisper.

I lift my hand to his cheek, uncertain of whether I should soothe him or kiss him.

"I'm terrified," he admits. His gaze drops to my mouth, then rises again, locking on my eyes. "And I don't want it to stop."

My breathing is shaky as I inhale and exhale. "Do you think you're feeling more because…I'm pregnant?" I whisper.

"I've thought of it nearly nonstop since you told me. I've had a whole slew of worries about the baby...except for tonight. All I've thought tonight is that I want to come up with more reasons for you to be here...because you're so fun, and a bright spot in this house that doesn't need another woman in it...but I'd do anything to have *you* in it..." His expression is shamed when he looks at me again. "I haven't thought of the baby once."

I giggle and he rears back to get a better look at my face.

"That's funny?"

"A little. You don't have to think about the baby nonstop. And I don't mind at *all* that you're thinking about me."

"If you knew how much I think about you, you'd probably run."

My brow creases and I try not to beam. "Um, no? Tell me more."

His lips lift and he leans in, his mouth brushing against mine.

"God, you taste so good," his voice is a low murmur, each word landing like a soft caress. "You *smell* so good."

He presses another slow, deliberate kiss to the corner of my mouth.

"Everything about you is so sweet. Your laugh, your smile..."

He moves to my cheek and then my ear. Between each press of his lips, his voice is low and intimate. A craving builds inside me until I'm trembling.

"You're so beautiful. So goddamn beautiful."

His lips trail back to mine, lingering there. I get lost in his kiss and then he trails back to my ear.

"I want to memorize every soft sound you make when I kiss you here—" he kisses just beneath my jaw "—and here—" another kiss at the base of my throat.

His smile turns wicked when I whimper. I tug him closer.

"Do you feel what you do to me?" he asks.

"Yes," I whisper.

"Every time your lips touch mine, I lose another piece of my restraint. And it's not just my body, Poppy."

He kisses me again, slower, deeper, his hands curling into my hair. I stand on my tiptoes to feel more of him and he lifts me, wrapping my legs around his waist. He takes me to his bed and lays me on top of it.

"We don't have to do anything more than you want. I can just kiss you for a while…"

I reach up and pull him down to kiss me again. "I don't know if I can relax to do more than that when your mom and Mrs. McGregor are here."

"Mrs. McGregor is in her cottage by now and my mom's on the opposite end of the house." His lips move to my ear and he whispers, "Can I taste you?"

"Oh…" I freeze. "I'm terrible at that," I say.

His lips lift and he laughs against my skin. "Not possible."

He leans back to look at me.

"I mean…I can't really relax when—" I pause, my cheeks heating.

"Do you not like it?" he asks.

"Usually, no," I say, crinkling my face. "But you have me curious now."

He looks so happy with that answer, I cover my face with my hand. His hand hovers over my jeans.

"May I?"

I nod, already anticipating how it'll feel, but nervous that I'll be too knotted up to enjoy it.

He undoes my jeans and slides them down my legs. I lift my hips, helping him get them off. When he sees my hot pink lacy panties, he takes me in for a few moments, sighing and then staring at me with his lust-filled eyes.

I'd say yes to anything he asks when he looks at me like this.

His hand cups my stomach and he places a soft kiss below my belly button.

"Hello, little one," he whispers. "Enjoy your sleep in there."

I die.

He slides the lace down my legs and then his mouth is on my bare torso as he lifts my shirt, and places open-mouth kisses that tease their way down my body. When he spreads me with his thumbs and bends to suck directly over my clit, I nearly convulse off the bed. His chuckle heats my skin and then his mouth is hungry, sucking and exploring me with that tongue. His fingers get in there too. Gentle at first, and then when I am so wet the sounds are filling his bedroom, it's no longer a teasing seduction but a full-on overwhelm of the senses. His fingers work deep and fast, his tongue flicking over me with such precision and perfection, everything in me feels achy and primed and so, so hungry. It's so intense and I let out a sharp cry before realizing I have to be quiet. I try to grab a pillow, but he tosses it aside.

So my cries come out like an anguished mewl, whimpering his name over and over again as I fall apart.

"Bowie, Bowie, Bowie, Bowie." It's a chant my heart keeps echoing after I stop saying it.

And then he presses one more kiss there, and I feel grounded to the earth, grounded to him, in a way I didn't know existed.

He crawls up my body, kissing his way up my skin, until he reaches my breasts. He lowers the cup of my bra and wraps his tongue around my nipple.

"Still not a fan?" he asks, looking up at me through half-lowered lids.

My arm is flung over my eyes and I start laughing and can't stop. He joins in and then lifts my arm, peering down at me.

"Well?"

"I'm your tongue and fingers' number one fan," I tell him sincerely.

CHAPTER TWENTY-NINE

REVVED UP

BOWIE

I move her panties back in place and move to her side, leaning up on my elbow to look at her. She stares up at me, her brow creasing.

"What are you doing?" she asks.

"I…what do you mean?"

"Why are you stopping?"

My mouth parts as I stare at her. "I was…trying to be a gentleman."

"That's never stopped you before."

A laugh bursts out of me. "It's stopped me many times, but with you, you're right…I haven't been a very good gentleman with you."

"Well, don't start being proper with me now," she huffs.

I can't stop smiling and it feels foreign on my face, foreign in my body to feel this good. "You want me, Poppy?"

"You did get me all revved up."

"I hoped I was satisfying you, but clearly I didn't do my job."

"Oh, you satisfied me. I'm just ready for more now."

I tug my shirt off and tilt my chin for her to take hers off. She grins at me, mischief and desire sparking in those eyes, and I am hers.

I don't let myself stay on that thought for too long, focusing instead on the way she looks, the way I'm going to make her feel.

Our clothes are tossed across the room and when there's nothing left between us, I pull her on top of me. My hands look huge splayed across her skin, and it's mesmerizing watching her body react to mine with every touch. She rocks against me and I see the chill bumps scatter across her skin.

"Are you cold?" I ask.

"No, it just feels so good, everywhere you touch."

"God, you're beautiful."

"You are too," she says, leaning down until her lips are on mine when she says it again. *"You are too."*

I reach for a condom and then pause. "We haven't really talked about tests, but I'm testing regularly with the team and all is clear."

"For me too," she says.

"We can still use condoms…if you want."

"I'd like to experience it without." Her cheeks are still flushed from her orgasm, but they heat to crimson again.

I twitch beneath her and her eyes flare. She leans down and kisses me, her long hair trailing against my chest. The lights are low from my bedside lamp, and I want to study every inch of her, learn the map of her freckles and memorize the contour of her skin. Our kiss starts out sweet but quickly boils over, her tongue feels like sex and I chase it, greedy for all of her. She sighs when her hands slide over my shoulders and down my chest, careful and reverent, like she's memorizing me too.

When she raises her hips and guides my tip inside, we both freeze for a second. I groan quietly with how good she feels. My palm slides down her side and around her back until I'm cupping her ass. She starts undulating over me and it's the most beautiful sight. I'm torn between never blinking and my eyes rolling back in my head because it's fucking heaven. I lean in and take her nipple in my mouth, twirling it around my tongue and nipping it with my teeth. I love the wet heat of her and the way she dances over me.

Her breathing gets erratic and I feel too close. I flip her onto her back and slide into her deep, so deep that we both lose our breath. Her sounds of pleasure threaten to make me lose it and I can't yet. I want this to last longer than two minutes. Her skin is heated under mine now, the only chill coming from the sheen of sweat on my forehead as I try to hold onto some restraint.

My strokes are slow and languid, and I watch as she takes me, feel the clench of her tightening and releasing as she tries to hold onto me inside.

"It's so good," she groans.

I swell at her words and give her a few deep, fast strokes.

When I pull out, flipping her onto her stomach, she cries out, "Come back."

"I'm not going anywhere," I tell her.

I tilt her hips and enter her in a single perfect slide. She screams into a pillow and I grin, bending down to kiss her shoulder.

"Told you," I say, laughing against her skin.

She laughs into the pillow and then cries out again when I bottom out inside of her, only to pull out and do it again, and again. She looks at me over her shoulder, her mouth parted before she bites down on her lip, her eyes squeezing shut as I fuck her relentlessly.

"Bowie," she pants. "This is—don't stop. Don't ever stop."

"I know, Angel. I know."

This isn't just sex. I'm going to have to work out what exactly this is later, but for now, I know this much: if Poppy Keane asked me for anything, I'd walk through coals of fire to give it to her.

"Come here," I say, sitting back on my heels and pulling her up into my lap.

I push into her as she grinds onto me, and my hand moves to her neck while the other moves between her legs, coaxing another orgasm out of her. I hold her up while she collapses, kissing her neck until my breath turns shaky, my own orgasm starting to barrel through me. I grip her hips then and move into her with solid strokes.

"Poppy," I rasp. "*Fuck*."

I shove into her deep and feel like I'll never stop coming, my body strung tight while she flutters and clenches around me. When the tremors eventually still between us, I lift her and spoon around her back, holding her close as we lie down.

She looks at me over her shoulder through half-lidded eyes and offers a small grin.

"That was…" she whispers.

"Yeah." My voice is rough. "It was."

She drifts off to sleep first and I'm not far behind her, and I have an unsettling dream. I don't see Poppy at all, but I know that she's about to have the baby, and I can't find her. I wake up gasping and only an hour and a half has passed since we fell asleep. I go into the bathroom and turn on the shower, hoping the water will clear my head. When I get out and I'm still a mess, I sit down on the floor and lean against the tub.

She stumbles in a few minutes later, her lips swollen and hair going everywhere. She's wearing her shirt and panties again and I want to strip them off.

Her beauty makes my heart catch in my throat.

"You okay?" she asks.

"I didn't want to wake you up," I say. When she doesn't say anything, I add, "Maybe having a little freakout. Bad dream."

"Do you want to talk about it?" she asks, sitting down next to me and taking my hand.

I take the first deep lungful of air since I woke up and look at her.

"I might have some abandonment issues," I say quietly. "It started with my father…when I'd do something he didn't approve of, he'd disappear. Sometimes for hours, sometimes for days, but it was usually in a strange city. When I was young, my dad and I traveled some with swimming, and when he'd leave, I wouldn't know what to do, where to go. I'd be in a hotel room too scared to even order room service because I knew if he did come back, I'd be in trouble for that too."

I meet her eyes reluctantly and her chin wobbles.

"That's heartbreaking," she says.

I look down at our feet. Her knees are tucked to her chest and her turquoise toenails are cute.

"Do you have any fears about having a baby…with me?" I ask after a long pause.

"I have fears about having a baby…yes. Normal fears, I think. Like, will I be a good mom, will our baby be healthy—"

My eyes meet hers. "You're worried our baby will have Down Syndrome?"

"No. I-I didn't mean that. I mean healthy in all the ways, mentally and physically. I think that's a normal fear to have… I just want to be prepared for all the things. Be capable of giving our child the best care possible." She frowns. "Down Syndrome isn't typically passed down from parents. You know that, right?"

I swallow and stare at the floor again. "Yeah, I know…but I thought you might be worried about that. And I guess…I just wonder what you'd do if…the baby weren't healthy in any way or…if you decided you didn't want to be a mom after all."

"Bowie," she whispers, turning to face me. "I've always wanted to be a mom. Is this the way I would've gone about having one? No. But I'm not going to abandon my child or you. No matter what. I don't know yet what you and I are going to be." She puts her hands on my cheeks and I meet her eyes. "Although, whatever that was in your bed…" Her lips lift and she shakes her head. "I don't know what that was."

"Me either," I admit. "Every time with you has felt…life-altering."

She nods. "Yes," she says softly. She takes a deep breath. "Wherever we land with one another, we're going to be parents together. You're kind of stuck with me."

I turn to face her and put my hands on her cheeks too. "You don't think you'll change your mind, once the baby comes?"

She leans into one of my hands. "I'm surrounded by kids all the time, Bowie. I chose a profession that deals with kids and disabilities. I'm not a runner." When my eyes lower, she dips her face until they meet again. "I promise."

I swallow and lean my forehead onto hers. "Okay," I whisper.

"Okay."

Her lips press softly against mine and then she stands up and holds out her hand.

"Come on, you should get back in bed. I'll head home and you can have it to yourself."

"I don't want the bed to myself," I say.

It's the most honest thing I've said in years.

She grins. "Well, maybe I can stay over another time. I've got work early tomorrow and didn't bring anything with me."

I curl up my face into a scowl and she laughs, leaning up to kiss me again.

"I promise I'm not going anywhere."

"Okay," I grumble.

I walk her to the door and she turns and hugs me. When we part, I smooth her hair back and kiss her.

"Next time, please bring your things," I say.

"Okay," she says, smiling up at me.

It suddenly falters and I'm back to nervous again. "What's wrong?"

"Easter's coming up. How would you feel about coming to meet my family?" Her nerves are back, and I feel bad that I've given her reason to be so hesitant. "You and Becca," she adds.

At those words, my chest expands. She's choosing me

and Becca, opening a door to a part of her life that matters. It might seem simple to her, but I haven't imagined that I could have this with someone.

I lean in and press a kiss to her forehead. "Thank you," I whisper, and in those two words I try to tell her everything—how grateful I am, how excited I could be if I only let myself be. "I'd love to meet your family."

"Really?"

"Really."

"Amazing," she says, her smile wide. "They're going to love you."

"Mmm, we'll see," I say, unable to resist smiling back at her.

I watch her walk to her car and stand there after she's driven away, the quiet night my only company.

I'm not sure what tomorrow holds, but tonight I've got something I thought I'd lost forever—hope.

CHAPTER THIRTY

I'LL BE HOME FOR EASTER

POPPY

The moment we step onto the porch of my parents' home, I get a wave of excitement and nerves. I'm so excited to see my family, to introduce them to Bowie and Becca, and so, *so* nervous to tell them about the baby. A wreath of spring flowers adorns the door and Becca leans in to touch them gently.

"Pretty," she says.

I can hear my mom singing through the open window.

Beside me, Bowie holds Becca's hand, and I think her excitement about being here is probably what has him anchored to the ground. Otherwise, he just might not be standing here. He has on his most stoic face and for a second, that wild, abandoned expression I only see on him when we've had sex comes to mind. I'd never know he was capable of that expression if I saw him right now.

We've seen each other every day since our date last week, but we haven't slept together again. Our schedules have been busy and I think we're both trying to pace ourselves. But that doesn't mean I'm not craving him like crazy. I don't know if pregnancy horniness can be a thing yet or if it's just because it's Bowie, but I think about him *all the time*.

I give him a reassuring smile. "You ready?"

He nods, and Becca says, "Ready!" in a bright chirp. She has no nerves about this whatsoever and her excitement is contagious. For me, anyway. Hopefully, Bowie will get there.

"They're going to love you guys," I tell them.

The door swings open before I can knock. Mom stands there, wearing a flour-dusted apron that's covered with bunnies. Her eyes crinkle at the corners as she beams at us.

"You're here!" she sings, pulling me into a quick hug before reaching out to greet Bowie and Becca.

Bowie clears his throat, but Mom doesn't waste any time with formalities. She tucks a stray curl behind her ear and then holds her arms wide.

"Welcome! I'm so glad you're here. Happy Easter!" she says.

Becca moves right into her arms, hugging her back. "I am Becca."

"It's lovely to meet you, Becca. I'm Jennifer, Poppy's mom."

"Wow," Becca breathes. "You are a pretty mom."

"Why, thank you. You're so sweet."

"You're so sweet," Becca repeats.

"And I'd recognize you anywhere, Bowie Fox," Mom says.

Bowie steps into her outstretched arms and pats her on the back, while I try not to get pregnant again over how cute he is when he's nervous. He smiles at me over her shoulder and already looks a little more relaxed. My mom has that effect on people.

We walk inside and Dad ambles out of the kitchen. His hair is graying at the temples, but otherwise he looks so young. My parents have more energy than I do.

He holds out his hand. "Bowie Fox," he says loudly.

He's always loud, while my mom's voice is light and airy. They're quite the pair.

"I've been looking forward to meeting you," Dad says.

"It's great to meet you, sir."

"Call me Joshua. I've followed your career since your rookie season. Should've won Defensive Player of the Year two years back, if you ask me."

"That's nice of you to say," Bowie says.

Dad winks at Becca, who's holding my hand now and staring at my dad with curiosity. "Hello there, Miss Becca. I sure am glad you're here. I heard you have a sweet little pup at home. Would you like to meet my dog in a little while?"

Becca's eyes widen. "Yes," she says, delighted. "First lunch, then meet your dog!"

"Excellent."

Bowie glances at me and gives me a relieved smile.

"There you are!" Marley cries, rushing toward me. We hug forever and I hear Eric introducing himself to Bowie and Becca before coming over and hugging me and Marley.

"I've missed you guys so much," I say, feeling my eyes

well up. I slowly let go of Marley's hand and look at my parents. "All of you."

"We've missed you too," Mom says. "Now that our traveling has slowed down and you're getting settled in Silver Hills, we need to get over there more often than a quick dinner here and there."

"Agreed. And I'll do better about coming home too," Marley says.

"Me too," I say.

Becca sees my dad's shadow, Alex, the Yorkie, and goes to pet him. Marley turns to Bowie and crosses her arms.

"So you're the guy," she says. "I hear you're some big NFL star." Her tone is casual like she's half-impressed, half-amused. "I guess you'll do." She doesn't wait for his reaction before leaning in, her hand dramatically slicing across her throat. "Don't be a dick to my sister or I'll end you," she whispers, eyes sparkling.

I cover my mouth with my hand when Bowie nods, completely serious.

"That's fair," he says. "I'm trying to amend my dickish ways."

That makes me crack up.

"Ignore my wife," Eric tells Bowie. "She's mostly bark, very little bite. I'm thrilled you're here. Huge fan."

Marley winks at me as she leans against Eric's chest, and Bowie relaxes another notch. We move into the family room and Becca sits next to my dad, studying his face. I think they're talking about dinosaurs, but I'm not positive. And then they're onto football because Dad pretends to be a quarterback, lifting an imaginary ball and calling, "Hut, hut!" which makes Becca laugh. Bowie looks on, a soft smile tugging at his mouth.

Our house has an open floor plan, so the family room

flows into the kitchen. My mom flits in and out, refusing my offer to help. I had told her very little about Bowie…until I got pregnant…and then I wasn't sure what to say. But now that we're spending time together, I've let her know I like him…a lot. And that we're…hanging out. Yeah, I've got some explaining to do.

She tilts her head toward Bowie and Becca as if to say, *Make sure they're having a good time*.

"*He's so handsome*," she mouths.

The house smells like ham and fresh bread, and I get a warm rush of love for my family.

"When are Grammy and Granddad getting here?" I ask.

"Did someone say Granddad?" My grandparents walk in and there's a whole new rush of hugs and introductions.

"What a wicked stellar day," Granddad says, mostly to make Marley and me laugh.

I exchange a look with Bowie and he's grinning wide.

"Told ya," I whisper.

"*You're* wicked stella," he whispers, saying it the way Granddad does, but the look he gives me makes me hot all over. He reaches out and threads his fingers through mine and my heart turns over.

When I look up, everyone is staring at us, but in the next second, they pretend not to be.

Bowie chuckles and leans closer. "Your family's pretty incredible too."

"Dinner is ready," Mom calls and we all move toward the long table.

Granddad says grace, thanking God for this wicked stellar spread, and then food gets passed around. My family is never short on opinions, and somehow, the hot topic becomes corn while we dollop corn casserole on our plates.

"Corn has its virtues," Dad says.

"Right," Marley snorts, and my mom hums softly, unconcerned.

"It's got fiber!" Dad says, gesturing with his fork. "We all need fiber."

"But it's also high in sugar. And doesn't digest well."

"TMI," Eric says, laughing.

Becca has been following the conversation like a tennis match and tugs on Bowie's sleeve. "Daddy, I eat corn?" she asks, as if wondering if it's okay.

He smiles at her and nods.

There's a flicker of tenderness when he glances at me and I can't wipe the smile off my face.

"It's really nice having you here, Bowie," Mom says. "I've heard Poppy's side of the story, but what did you think when you met our daughter?"

"Mom," I groan.

"What?" She laughs, pointing at the two of us. "A man that looks at you like that isn't afraid to answer the question. Are you, Bowie?"

I bury my face in my hands and Bowie tugs at my fingers, gently lowering them. He's smiling and my goodness, I don't know if my heart can take much more of this day.

"I thought she was beautiful, but Becca was the smart one. She was all in from the get-go. She wouldn't stop hassling me about taking her to Briar Hill."

Everyone laughs.

"*Aw*," my mom says, smiling at Becca.

"I love Poppy," Becca says proudly.

"I love *you*," I tell her.

Alex barks at something outside and it catches Becca's attention.

"I go play with Alex," she says, starting to get out of her chair.

"Eat a few more bites," Bowie says.

She crams a few more bites in quickly, which cracks everyone up, and then she rushes over to Alex.

"The yard is fenced in if she'd like to throw the ball to him outside," Dad tells Bowie.

He nods and tells Becca she can go outside if she wants. She loves that idea and they step outside.

Eric asks Bowie about the team and what it's like winning multiple Super Bowls.

"It's wicked stellar," he says, which earns him a huge laugh. "I highly recommend. Much better than what we went through this past season, but we're coming back. Cal has really stepped up since we lost Henley, and we're adjusting."

"I preferred hearing about how much you're into my sister," Marley says.

"You guys are killing me," I say, putting my iced glass up to my cheek to cool off.

"You put Eric through it the first time he came over for dinner," she says, laughing.

Eric groans. "I'd finally put that out of my mind."

"I wasn't that bad," I argue, but then I snort, laughing. "Yeah, I was."

"You asked what my intentions were, and I said I wanted to get to know your sister…and you said…'from what I've been told, you've already gotten to know her *very* well.'"

The table erupts and I laugh so hard, I have to fan my face.

"It loosened things up," I say, shrugging. "Sorry, not sorry."

"So, what are your intentions with my sister?" Marley asks Bowie, making us all laugh again.

I peek at Bowie through my hand and he looks happy.

The happiness hums in my veins, so full I can't keep it inside anymore.

"Bowie and I are having a baby," I blurt out.

The words come out louder than I meant them to. Instantly, everyone goes silent. Dad's fork hovers in the air, Marley's smug smile freezes, and Mom's jaw drops. Bowie tenses for a split second and then his hand squeezes mine under the table.

For a heartbeat, no one breathes.

Marley recovers first. "What?" she shrieks, nearly tipping her chair as she lunges around the table to wrap me in a hug. I told her to act like she didn't know yet so my mom wouldn't be hurt, but she's overdoing it just a bit. "Oh my God, Poppy! That's amazing!"

Eric whoops loudly. "Congratulations, you guys."

My dad grins so wide his face might split. My mom tears up, pressing a hand to her mouth as she stands and pulls me in a tight embrace.

"Oh, sweetheart," she whispers. "This is wonderful news."

Grammy pats my back. "A baby! We've needed a baby around here."

After my dad hugs me, he claps Bowie on the shoulder. "Welcome to the family."

Bowie gulps and tilts his head. "Thank you, sir. Thanks for being so kind. I'm honored to be here."

Our eyes meet and he reaches out and takes my hand again.

"Poppy makes me want a life I'd long given up hope on having for myself." He swallows and I squeeze his hand. "I feel really lucky to have met her."

My throat tightens. "I feel lucky too," I say, my voice barely above a whisper.

CHAPTER THIRTY-ONE

WE'RE DOING THIS

BOWIE

Poppy opens her door and smiles up at me. I've taken her on multiple dates now, but I still can't believe it. I wake up every day looking forward to seeing her, wishing she was in my bed every night, missing her when she's not. I step closer and kiss her.

"You ready for this?" she asks.

"So ready."

Once we're driving, her hand rests on my thigh, making

slow circles with her thumb that are probably innocent but are making me hard.

"After this, we can tell Becca," she says. "And your mom…and the McGregors…"

After Easter, we decided we'd wait to tell them until Poppy was twelve weeks along. Just to be sure everything is okay with the baby.

"I can't wait to see Becca's face when she finds out she's going to be a big sister," I say. "I can picture her face already. She's going to lose her mind with excitement." The thought makes me grin, some of the tension easing from my shoulders.

I'll feel better once this appointment is over…actually once that baby is in our arms, but I'm trying to not just be a downer with all my fears.

"I cannot wait," Poppy says, grinning at me.

Inside the clinic, we move through the halls hand in hand. I still have moments of *what the fuck am I doing in a relationship?* but Poppy makes it so easy. Honestly, she's the one forcing us to not just speed-walk into this relationship despite how we've gone about things backwards.

When her name is called, the nurse does a double take when she sees me next to Poppy, but fortunately, she recovers quickly.

"Oh, hello," she says warmly.

We're led back to the exam room and Dr. Talbot walks in and introduces herself to me. She asks Poppy a few questions and before I know it, Poppy is on the cushioned table, pulling up her shirt just enough for the ultrasound wand. I stand beside her, heart pounding so hard I'm sure the doctor can hear it. When there's a steady, quiet drumroll sound, Poppy gasps.

"That's your baby's heartbeat," Dr. Talbot says.

Poppy's eyes shine and I lean down, pressing my forehead lightly against hers. I'm not sure what to say, I'm too overwhelmed with relief, fear, wonder…it jumbles in my chest. Her hand finds mine and I exhale a shaky breath.

"Your baby is the size of a plum," Dr. Talbot says.

She talks about measurements and due dates, but all I can focus on is the warmth of Poppy's hand.

This is real. We're doing this.

We do CVS testing, a diagnostic test that identifies Down Syndrome. It's mostly to help alleviate my concerns. I know there's no way to know one hundred percent what you're dealing with when having a baby, but I want to be prepared as much as possible.

"We'll rush these results and let you know within the week," Dr. Talbot says.

"I appreciate that," I tell her gratefully.

When we leave, Poppy's still glowing, and I'm walking on a cloud. Mostly. There's a familiar knot that never fully goes away, the pile of fears I can't seem to shake. Sometimes after I've spent the evening with Poppy—we've cooked together or tangled ourselves in the sheets late into the night—I drive home and climb into bed thinking about the way Adriane left without a backwards glance. I don't miss Adriane. I don't want to ever see the woman again. But the fear grips me: what if Poppy does the same? What if I can't handle fatherhood again, with a newborn on top of being a good dad to Becca? What if I'm not enough?

"Hey, where did you go?" Poppy asks.

I look at her, see the softness in her eyes, remember the gentle press of her forehead against mine when we heard the heartbeat, and it's like the tension unravels. She's different. We're different. I'm…happy. Happy in a way I've never been.

"You make me happy, Wicked Stella," I say.

Her eyes crinkle when she laughs. I've been calling her that since Easter with her family and it never fails to crack her up.

"You make me happy too," she says.

"I texted Mom and Mrs. McGregor before we left the clinic, asking if we could all have dinner together tonight."

"Perfect," she says. "Should we head right there?"

She licks her lips and I stare at her mouth, squeezing her thigh. "How about we stop at your place first? Celebrate a little on our own first."

"I love this plan."

Her lips are on mine before I've even closed her front door. I clench her waist with both hands, and with her flush against me, I pivot us, pressing her against the wall. My mouth trails against her neck, hot and open, sucking where I feel her heartbeat against my lips. She slides her hands up my neck and into my hair. I love her hands in my hair, love her hands everywhere on me.

"Where do I start with you, little mama?"

She pulls my head down, kissing me. I groan at the contact, her sweet candy lips parting under my tongue. I bunch her shirt in my hands and tug it over her head, tossing it behind me. Her bra is next, my eyes feasting on her gorgeous tits.

I take a step back and just look at her.

"I can't believe you," I say in awe. "So fucking beautiful."

I slide her pants down her legs. She motions for me to get rid of my clothes and then stands demurely against the door, watching as I shuck my pants and shirt. When I stalk toward her again, she flicks her fingers for me to lose the boxer briefs too. I grin, taking them off and then reach out, tugging her pretty panties down her legs.

I pause and press a kiss on her stomach.

"Hey, little plum," I say, which makes Poppy laugh.

Then I straighten and brace one hand on the wall and with the other, I trace down her skin, down her breasts and along her stomach. Her nipples are hard and a blush crawls over her neck when I cup my hand over her breast. I can't resist tasting her and when I suck her nipple, my other hand cups around her ass. I love hearing the way her breath hitches when I do that.

"Where do you want me?" I ask, looking up at her with my tongue still swirling around her peak.

Her head falls back. "Everywhere."

I smile against her skin. "Why don't I take you to bed this time instead of desecrating this wall again?"

She laughs. More than once, we haven't made it to the bed. I stand and lift her by the thighs, wrapping her legs around me, another favorite position. She seems to love it as much as I do, whimpering when I rub against her core. She circles her hips against me and I love that she's already soaking wet.

"I can't wait," she says. "I want you too much to take our time…"

"I'm greedy for you too," I tell her.

When we reach her room, I lay her down and kiss my way up her body, my fingers moving between her legs. I dip one finger inside and then two, and when she's ready for it, three.

"Please," she whimpers, wiggling against me.

I move my fingers and slide into her in one long stroke.

"Bowie," she gasps.

I lose myself in her. Everything feels so right when we're together like this. All inhibitions and worries quiet down and all I think about is making her feel good. She's screaming my name within minutes. I love how loud she can be when we're here, but it's also fun when we're at my house and I'm quieting her cries with my mouth.

I flip her over and she rides me so hard, so perfect, that when I come, she comes again too.

When we get to my house, it smells like dinner is almost ready. My mom and Mrs. McGregor are mid-bicker over which napkins to use. Becca bursts into the room when we step inside, already launching into a story about her day. Martha looks exhausted from trying to keep up with Becca. She doesn't like Becca out of her sight, which makes me think pretty highly of the little beast. I watch Poppy laugh and reach out to touch Becca's hair fondly, and my heart twists.

I love her.

Holy shit. *I love her.*

I swallow hard and Poppy glances at me then, her eyes narrowing on me. She smiles quizzically and the knots loosen. She doesn't even know that she has my heart in her hands.

I'm in a bit of a fog as we sit down to eat and when Poppy leans over and asks if I'm okay, I take her hand and kiss her knuckles.

"Yes," I say, my voice low.

Her eyes crinkle with her smile.

I reluctantly tear my eyes from hers and look around the table.

"We have news," I say, glancing at Poppy again. She nods, beaming. "We're having a baby." I look at Becca. "You're going to be a big sister."

Her eyes widen. She sucks in a breath so fast she coughs. "A baby!" she squeaks, her voice high. "I'm a sister! Where is the baby?"

"In my stomach for now," Poppy says, laughing.

"Like Tru's belly," Becca says. She waves her fist in the air. "I'm a sister!"

My mom claps her hands, tears shimmering in her eyes. "This is the best news ever!"

Mrs. McGregor places a hand over her heart. "Congratulations. This household just keeps getting better and better."

Mr. McGregor proposes a toast. "To a healthy baby Fox!"

We all clank glasses, most of us with water, but it still takes, and the conversation is lively as Becca asks what the baby will look like. Mom does a little dance when she brings out the dessert. Mrs. McGregor fusses about portions, and Poppy rests her head on my shoulder, looking up at me with that soft look that makes me feel steady and like I'm falling harder, all at once.

"I hope our baby has your blue eyes," I tell her.

"I love your brown eyes so much," she whispers. "But Becca's blue eyes are beautiful, so maybe the baby *will* have blue…"

Later, when the plates are cleared and Becca is tucked in bed—a miracle because she was buzzing with excitement—Poppy lingers. She belongs here, now more than ever.

"Stay here tonight?" I ask. I've asked her to stay often, but she's never stayed the full night.

"I can stay a little longer," she says.

I lead her to my bedroom and close the door quietly. Poppy moves toward the window, looking out at the moonlit yard. I slip behind her, sliding my arms around her waist. She leans back into me.

I swallow hard. "What if you stayed…permanently?"

She stiffens and turns in my arms to face me.

"Move in with us?" I ask.

Her mouth parts and I reach up to cup her cheek. She leans into my hand.

"That wouldn't be taking things very slowly," she says.

"Think about it?" I ask.

She nods, her smile shy.

"Thank you," I say, my voice almost a whisper. "For being here. For fitting seamlessly into my life…for giving me the courage to hope again."

Her eyes get glassy.

"For everything," I continue. "For making me so happy."

"You make me so happy too," she whispers.

We kiss, slow and unhurried, savoring every touch. Holding her like this, my body boiling over with desire for her, my heart stays calm.

I didn't know when I met her that she'd be the antidote to my turmoil.

CHAPTER THIRTY-TWO

LULLABY PLAYLISTS

POPPY

The weather is perfect outside for our impromptu party. We're at Bowie's house—I still haven't agreed to move in with him. I don't know what I'm waiting for…I want to move in with him. I guess part of me just still needs to be sure he's all in this for *me* and not just because I'm having his baby. I think he is, but he hasn't exactly made any bold declarations about his feelings yet. Still…everything he does makes me feel like he's in this for me.

I know how I feel about him. I've gone and fallen in love with Bowie Fox.

I mean, who could blame me? It was basically a foregone conclusion, right?

But I'm trying so hard to maintain my wits. After all, I have pregnancy brain, so I've needed to be extra smart and mindful to combat that.

Yeah, there is no thinking smart when it comes to Bowie. I just love him, and I really hope he doesn't break my heart.

Henley and Tru are the first to arrive and I hug Tru. She's wearing a fitted dress and I can finally see the baby bump that she insists has been there for months.

"You look so gorgeous," I say.

"*You* do. Girl, you are radiant." She squeezes my arm when we pull apart and then the others arrive and there's a flurry of hugs.

"I'm so glad you decided to do this," Penn tells Bowie. "I've missed you guys. You've been a little quiet lately," he says, looking between the two of us.

Everyone's been so excited about the two of us dating, but we've hardly all been together at the same time since the funeral. Bowie's seen the guys and I've seen the girls, but everyone's been traveling a lot too, with it being the offseason. Now that Becca knows, not to mention that I'm starting to show a little bit, we can't keep the baby a secret any longer.

"She's kept me busy," Bowie says, glancing at me.

I laugh, feeling my cheeks heat, which makes everyone laugh.

We dig into the food and I'm taking a bite of salad when Bowie taps on his glass. Everyone turns to look at him, surprised that he's done something so noisy. He's zero decibels compared to everyone else in this group.

"I just wanted to say…the word is out. We've told our families, Becca knows…about the baby. We don't have to skirt around the topic anymore when she's around. We heard the heartbeat a few days ago and everything seems good."

"Becca got her wish," Weston says, sounding choked up. "She's gonna be a big sister."

"I still can't believe you're having a baby." Rhodes wipes his eyes and just holds his arms out to Bowie and me. We step forward and he hugs us both. "I can't wait to meet this little person," he says.

"Let me at 'em," Henley says, and Rhodes lets us go so Henley can hug us.

"There must be something in the water," Penn sings. He stops and points at Henley. "Your podcast is about to take a shocking twist...Baby 101 for Pro Athletes."

Henley laughs. "Despite the three kids and one on the way, I still don't feel qualified most days."

"That's crazy talk. Fatherhood tips. Newborn advice. Diaper-changing best practices. A lullaby playlist." Penn holds his arms out. "You're welcome."

We all laugh.

"I'd listen," I say.

"Hell, so would I," Rhodes says.

Henley sighs. "Right, and then listeners would expect me to rhyme 'onside kick' with 'onesie quick'."

That cracks me up and Elle's head falls back too. "I can see you guys dancing to that right now. Can Tru and I choreograph something for a newborn slash football rap?"

Tru snorts. "I am so here for this."

"This has to happen," Sadie says.

"And Bowie can guest-star demonstrating swaddling techniques," Weston says.

"That's your area of expertise," Bowie says.

When Becca walks over with the rest of the kids to see what everyone's laughing about, they all congratulate her.

"I'm a sister!" she yells. "My baby likes dinosaurs. Delightful!" She lets out a bubbly laugh and turns to give me a huge hug when she hears me laughing.

"Oh!" Bowie says, nodding sagely. "That is delightful."

Rhodes nudges Bowie. "Look at her go. She's ready to teach that baby everything."

Becca turns to Henley's girls and makes sure they heard about the baby. They congratulate her and come over to hug me and Bowie too.

After they've gone back to play across the yard, I lean my head against Bowie's shoulder.

"How are you, little mama?" he asks.

It melts my heart every time he calls me that.

"Everyone's so happy for us," I say softly. "I can't remember ever feeling so content."

He brushes a kiss against my hair. "I can't tell you how good it is to hear you say that."

I turn and put my hand on his face, leaning up to kiss him. When we reluctantly pull apart to the whoops and cheers of our friends, I stand on my tiptoes so he can hear me loud and clear.

"I'm not going anywhere, Bowie. You know that, right?"

His eyes flit between mine and his hands grip my waist tighter. "How soon can we clear everyone out of here so I can show you just how much that means to me?"

I press my lips together. "I'll hang around after they're gone, no matter how late they stay," I whisper.

His eyes are full of promise when I lower to the ground.

The music in the background shifts to a slower song, and everyone chatters, the sunshine hovering overhead making everyone glow. Tru and I share a smile when Henley pretends to groan about the guys' baby-related podcast episodes, as Penn looks over at us proudly.

Becca twirls around the yard with the girls, and Levi and Caleb run after them trying to keep up. Martha sits on the sidelines, keeping Becca in her sights. I watch them, wondering what our child will look like. They'll be surrounded with love, that's all I know.

CHAPTER THIRTY-THREE

THE BET

BOWIE

The clang of weights fills the gym as I finish my last set. Weston wipes his forehead, dropping onto the nearby bench, while Henley walks in looking far less sweaty than the rest of us.

"How's it hangin'?" he asks.

"Get in here and work out with us," Rhodes says. "Why are you still looking so good when you're not out there playing with us?"

Henley grins and slaps his hard abs. "I can't afford to go soft. Just fitting it in a lot earlier these days."

Penn cracks his neck loud enough to make us all wince.

I lean against the squat rack and think about the way Poppy kissed her way down my abs last night. She ended up getting on her knees, and holy shit, the sight of her mouth around me…it was—

"What's got you all smiley?" Penn asks. He steps closer and checks my forehead. "You feelin' okay?"

I mess his hair up, rolling my eyes. "I'm feeling just fine."

"You sure? Because you do look a little *love*sick," Rhodes says, laughing.

I shrug, catching sight of my reflection in the mirror. Shit, I am smiley. What the fuck? I run my fingers over my mouth, trying to sober up, and the guys laugh.

"Maybe I've been a little…brighter. Like the sun shines a little earlier these days," I say gruffly.

The guys freeze, mid-stretch, mid-breath. Rhodes drops the band he'd been toying with, and Weston's eyebrows shoot up. Even Henley's jaw slackens.

Penn blinks twice, clearing his throat. "That might have been the most romantic thing I've ever heard," he says. He points at me. "I never knew I'd be taking lessons from you too."

I toss a towel over my shoulder. "Really? Because I just made myself cringe."

"Whew. Until you said that, I thought someone might have body-swapped you," Henley teases.

I laugh and shake my head. "No, it's still me under here. I am having a good time though. Things are…good. Really good."

Rhodes whistles low. "You are wearing it well. I wouldn't believe what I'm hearing if I didn't see how happy you are."

"You act like I've never been happy," I say, mostly amused.

"You've never been happy like this before," Penn says, narrowing his eyes. "At least, not since we've known you."

"Not gonna lie, I love it," Weston says, grinning. "It's about time you got a little sunshine."

Henley claps me on the shoulder. "Poppy's good for you, man. We can all see that."

I exhale, a goofy smile popping out that I can't seem to stop.

Rhodes eyes me, a slow smirk forming. "Mark my words. You'll be married within six months, maybe even sooner."

My head snaps up, color creeping up my neck. "What? No. I mean, I—what?" I run my hand through my hair, sputtering at the sudden turn in conversation.

Rhodes crosses his arms. "I'm serious. If you aren't married within six months, I will cut this hair off," he says, tugging on his curls. "If you are, you have to cut your hair off."

I imagine Poppy pulling my hair when my head is between her legs and shift uncomfortably, turning so they don't notice. Poppy would be so pissed if I buzzed my hair.

"This just got interesting," Henley says, hardy-har-haring in the corner.

I glare at all of them.

Penn surveys my hair and then Rhodes'. "Your hair is your signature, both of you. You sure about this?"

Rhodes tilts his head and nods confidently. "Dead sure. That's how confident I am. Look at him." He waves his hand at me and I grumble when he says, "Dude's practically floating."

"I'm not marrying anyone in six months. That's insane," I pause, my cheeks still hot when I think of Poppy's laughter, the sounds she makes when she comes, the way her eyes light up every time she sees me and Becca, how she says my name… "Fuck," I whisper. "I mean, we just…we're happy, but that's—"

"Uh-huh," Weston says, patting my back. "Sure, buddy. Whatever you say."

Henley's still laughing. "You better brace yourself, Bowie. I say you cave sooner than later so your hair has time to grow out by the wedding."

"Do we need to get a contract? I can get a lawyer to draft something up," Penn, the shit-stirrer says.

I let out an aggrieved sigh, which only makes them laugh more. But deep down, I can't help the smile tugging at my lips. Part of me likes that they're razzing me, that they see what's happening between me and Poppy.

"We'll see who ends up bald," I say, tipping my chin at Rhodes.

"Harsh!" Penn cries.

"Hey, I didn't say bald," Rhodes holds up his hands. "I mean, you can if you want to, but I ain't doin' bald."

"I wouldn't complain if she moved in, but marriage?" I say with more bluster than I'm feeling. "Nah."

Can I see myself marrying Poppy? The idea of waking up to her every morning, of trusting that she's here for keeps…I never thought I'd even consider any of this.

There's a brief silence where they all exchange glances, each of them smirking like they know something I don't. Smug bastards.

Rhodes clasps my hand with a grin so self-assured it's infuriating. "We'll see, Fox. We'll see."

When I step through the door after hanging out with Poppy for a few hours, my house feels oddly quiet. Usually my mom and Mrs. McGregor create a constant low buzz of activity. They're getting along better, but I think they thrive on arguing. My mom has still made no move to find another place. I think it's going to take a major push for her to consider moving.

I drop my keys on the console and peek around the corner into the kitchen. My mom is perched on the barstool with a notebook in hand, and Mrs. McGregor is standing by the stovetop stirring her legendary plum jelly. The two of them stop talking the instant they see me, as if caught plotting. I would not put it past them for even a heartbeat.

"Good evening," my mom says, too chipper.

"You're home earlier than expected," Mrs. McGregor says, setting the spoon down. "Everything all right?"

My nerves suddenly make an appearance, pulling tight in my gut. I've faced down massive players and harsh coaches, walked into post-game press conferences with blood still trickling down my body. But somehow, telling these two women my latest plan has me on edge more than that. Not because of their reaction, but because I really want this.

"Everything's fine. Actually, I wanted to talk to you both about something."

Mom's notebook snaps shut and Mrs. McGregor folds her arms, as they give me their undivided attention.

I lean against the counter, trying to appear casual. "I'm hoping to convince Poppy to move in with me…with us."

Mom's eyes light up and Mrs. McGregor beams.

"This is wonderful news," Mom says. "We'll organize the guest room for her right away. New, softer linens…"

My head tilts. "Mmm, not exactly what I was thinking, Mom."

"For goodness sake, Paulina, they're having a baby together! Surely they'll be in the same bedroom," Mrs. McGregor says, tutting under her breath.

My mom looks at me, mouth forming in a tight line. "You should really make it official. She's having your baby."

"I'm not marrying anyone just because they're having my baby."

"Do you love her?" Mom asks.

My mouth parts and I swallow hard. "Yes," I say gruffly.

She looks so pleased I have to laugh.

"Okay then," she says like that settles that.

It isn't lost on me that this is the second time marriage has been brought up today.

"What can we do to help?" Mrs. McGregor asks. "We can have a dinner prepared, a nice dessert. Something special."

"Yes, a perfect evening. Flowers, the whole nine yards," my mom adds.

I try not to balk at their eagerness. "I'll figure it out," I say, holding up my hands in surrender. "It's not the first time I've mentioned it to her. She hasn't said yes yet, and she might not. I just wanted you to know what I'm thinking…that I'm trying to convince her. Let me do this my way. But I'll keep you posted, okay?"

They exchange a glowing look, probably the most peaceful they've been in weeks, and I can see the wheels turning behind their eyes.

"Just don't scare her off, okay?" I tease. "She's going to show up here and find casseroles and bouquets, isn't she?"

Mom tries to look innocent. "We would never," she says, failing to hide her grin.

"We'll keep it subtle, don't worry," Mrs. McGregor says, winking.

"Subtle. Right," I snort.

Now if Poppy will just say yes.

Who knew I'd be aching for a woman to move in with me?

Maybe if she moves in with me, I can get everyone off my back about marriage.

But even as I have the thought, I can picture Poppy walking down the aisle toward me in a white dress.

Fuck me.

I'm in this deeper than I realized.

I think maybe I'd do anything to make Poppy Keane my wife. The thought is too terrifying to untangle, so I go through Becca's nighttime routine with her and then swim until I'm too tired to think anymore.

CHAPTER THIRTY-FOUR

SO FAR GONE

POPPY

I do one last check in the mirror when I hear Bowie pull up. My hair is in two French braids that trail down my back. The weather has gotten a lot warmer and we'll be outside all day at a charity event, so I want my hair out of my way.

The bell rings and I grab my tote. When I open the door, Becca stands at Bowie's side, eyes going round.

"Your hair," she breathes.

"You like it?" I smile and touch one of the braids.

"I love it," she says. "I want it."

My heart squeezes. She wants to match me. "Would you like me to braid your hair?" I ask.

She nods emphatically.

"Do we have time?" I ask Bowie.

He glances at his watch. "Yeah, we've got a few extra minutes," he says. He leans down and kisses me, which makes Becca giggle. "You look extra cute today."

I flush and close the door behind them. "Thank you," I say, grinning at Becca.

"You my daddy's girlfriend!" she sings. "And you get married like—"

"Okay! Let's get those braids started," Bowie says.

I laugh and the tenderness in Bowie's eyes when I glance at him knocks the breath from my lungs.

I place a chair for Becca in front of the mirror. She bounces while I comb her hair.

"Okay, time to sit still," I say, smiling at her in the mirror.

She listens and watches as I start braiding her hair. I'm careful to not pull too hard and she sits patiently until I'm done.

Bowie snaps a picture of us when she stands up next to me.

"Thank you," he says.

"Thank you," Becca adds, her head bobbing.

Gah, my heart. Am I allowed to feel this strongly about this man? About his daughter? I've known for a while that what I'm feeling is big. The way he's letting me in, the way he looks at me now—it all spills over in my chest until I can barely hold it in. I want to believe he feels the same, but doubts still whisper to me now and then. He hasn't said he loves me, but I really hope he does.

Becca studies herself in the mirror and looks so proud. "I look like Poppy!" she cries.

I laugh, putting my arm around her shoulder. "You sure do."

The charity event is held in Denver, and there's an array of games out on the big grassy lawn. The crowd is buzzing, and I recognize a few reporters who've come to snap photos of Bowie Fox, NFL linebacker, here to raise money for Down Syndrome awareness.

Becca competes in several relays with other kids and Bowie and I stand on the sidelines, cheering her on. She does really well, and when she finishes, she beams like she's just won gold. Bowie and I whoop and clap.

Later, I'm signed up for a series of games for the adults—a bean bag toss, a hula hoop challenge, and some kind of plastic bowling pins set up on the grass. I'm typically good with this kind of thing…unless I'm nervous…and I'm extra jittery today. Maybe it's the crowd, or the cameras, or maybe it's the way I caught Bowie looking at me earlier, like I hung the moon.

Whatever the reason, I'm a disaster. I toss a beanbag and somehow manage to hurl it three feet to the left of the target, hitting a reporter square in the jaw. I'm still not showing a *ton*, but I guess I still don't know what to do with a pregnant belly because when I try the hula hoop, the hoop drops around my ankles and I trip, nearly going flying. If Bowie hadn't closed the distance and saved the day, I wouldn't have kept standing. Let's not even talk about the bowling. I swing my arm back and manage to fling the ball behind me, sending a group of people scattering. I rush to grab the ball and when I bend over, I feel my leggings split down the center of my rear end. Thankfully I'm wearing black underwear, so I hope that it's not noticeable to everyone watching.

I feel like a complete fool. My cheeks blaze and I resist the urge to run and hide behind the snack table.

But then I catch sight of Bowie.

He's laughing. Hard. He has one hand braced on his knee, the other covering his mouth, and he's laughing so hard, he can't breathe. I've never seen him laugh like this—an uncontrollable belly laugh, tears glistening in the corners of his eyes. It's so genuine and joyful that my embarrassment eases, and I soak in the accomplishment. I'm the one who made him laugh like this.

I grin, shrugging at him with mock helplessness, which just makes him laugh more.

I'd be a fool a thousand times over if it means coaxing this kind of laughter out of him.

When I finally give up on the games, I saunter over to him and he tugs me into a side-hug, his cheek pressing against my temple.

"That," he says, his voice still unsteady with laughter, "was priceless."

I pretend to pout. "Glad I could provide entertainment."

"You do more than that," he says, looking down at me. "You make everything brighter, Poppy." His voice dips, and the serious note there makes my heart squeeze.

He hands me a sweatshirt that he must have gone to get out of the car when I was finishing up the last race.

"Here's this if you need it, but I don't mind the hole showing your underwear at all. Gives me something to look forward to…if you let me come over tonight, I'll show you what I mean."

I fan my face. "I'd be happy to see what you mean."

Becca bounces over, grabbing our hands and pulling us toward the snack stand. As Becca and I eat our snacks, we watch Bowie sign footballs and get his picture taken with the fans who have come out to see him.

We take Becca home, exhausted from the sunshine and all the activity. She falls asleep as I'm reading her a story, and Bowie drives me home.

When we step inside, dusk is turning the windows golden. I'm so happy to have the longer, warmer days. I set down my bag, still grinning over what a mess I made of everything I tried. I'm about to ask Bowie if he wants something to drink, but then he's there, behind me, so close that the heat of him chases a shiver down my spine.

His arms slip around my waist, and he fits perfectly against my back, his fingers splaying across the curve of my stomach. I sigh contentedly. I haven't gotten used to this feeling, how right it feels every time he touches me.

"I love the way you're showing," he whispers.

I inhale softly, my hands coming up to rest over his.

"You look more beautiful than ever, Poppy."

I tilt my head, closing my eyes when his lips find the side of my neck. My heart aches in the best way. He steps back just enough that his fingers dip to the waistband of my leggings. There's playful tension in the air now, and I don't need to see his face to imagine the wicked grin there.

He gives the material a tug, pausing just a moment before he abruptly tears it, the rest of the fabric ripping with a dramatic sound. I gasp, startled, but when I twist to look at him over my shoulder, he's the picture of innocence…except for the gleam in his eyes.

"That hole has been tempting me all day," he says.

I burst into laughter, my cheeks warm.

"If you still want me after the way I managed to make a complete fool of myself all day long, then…well, I don't know what that says about you," I tease, reaching back to swat him.

He just catches my hand and presses a kiss to my knuckles.

"I do…want you. More and more all the time," he says. "I blame you…for being so irresistible."

I turn in his arms, sliding my arms up the broad planes of his chest. And I lean up and kiss him, too afraid that if I don't, I'll end up telling him I'm so far gone, so madly in love with him.

CHAPTER THIRTY-FIVE

BUZZ CUT SEASON

BOWIE

The morning sun filters through the old blinds at Men are from Mars Barber Shop, casting lines across the worn leather chairs. I stare at my reflection. I've gone through so many rough NFL seasons, thousands of stressful nights as a single dad, and countless days assuming that my life would never have a woman I love in it.

I woke up with a whim this morning and I'm here to go for it.

Jeffrey, my barber, hovers behind me, clippers in hand. He looks sick. "You're sure you want to do this?" he asks for the third time.

I exhale slowly. "It'll grow back."

Something is shifting inside me, an acceptance that I'm changing…I want something I haven't allowed myself to want.

Jeffrey sighs, shoulders drooping. "All right. But I'm blaming you if your fans riot."

I offer a small grin. "I'll handle it."

There's a buzz and my hair falls in piles to the floor. By the end, I'm left with stubble so short it barely registers as hair. The change is drastic, and in the mirror, I hardly recognize myself.

I've officially lost that bet.

When I step into Luminary Coffeehouse, Clara doesn't even ask me to dance because she's stunned speechless.

"Mornin', Clara," I say, as if nothing is out of the ordinary.

When I walk back to our room, the guys are already there waiting. The reaction is immediate. They all yell in shock, staring at me.

"Holy shit!" Penn blurts, nearly knocking over his coffee.

Rhodes grips the edge of the table and then stands, slowly coming over to slide his hand over my head. "You…you buzzed it all off. Does this mean what I think it does?"

Weston shakes his head as he comes over to feel it too, his eyes shining bright. "Congratulations, motherfucker."

Henley comes over and we share a bro-clasp and hug.

"Settle down," I say, when I back up. "I haven't asked her to marry me," I pause, knowing how badly I want her in my life permanently. "Yet. Hell, I still haven't gotten her to agree to moving in with me…although I hope to tonight. Again." I shrug, smiling sheepishly. "But I've still lost the bet, because I am so far gone on this girl."

They erupt in whistles and dramatic pounding on the table. Rhodes looks personally vindicated and the rest of them are grinning like they've won too.

"I knew it," Rhodes says.

I laugh, shaking my head. "I never thought I'd be here, guys."

"You deserve it more than anyone," Weston says, and the rest of them add their agreement.

Penn taps The Single Dad Playbook that's lying on the table, and I sit down, opening it up.

I can hardly believe I'm going to be a dad again.
In a way, it feels like starting over
because I've been past the baby phase
for such a long time.
And maybe because I'm older now too,
I'm appreciating it all the more.
I'm soaking up every moment.
With Tru. With the girls. With you guys.
Because I know now how fast the time goes.
So read the extra bedtime story,
Linger at the dinner table,
Take all the pictures…
Time is a vapor.
~Henley

I nod at Henley. "You're not wrong, man."

I look back at the book and keep reading.

. . .

Two things I'm learning about little boys…
1. Never underestimate their commitment to chaos.
2. Always have an extra pair of clothes handy.
~Weston

I laugh, looking at Weston. "What's the story here?"

"There are too many stories there," Weston says, laughing. "It doesn't matter what we're doing, he finds a way to make a mess and will inevitably need to change his clothes." He lifts a shoulder. "Maybe little girls are like that too."

Henley nods, grinning. "Pretty much. Except their clothing changes are more about wanting to put on something cuter…"

Everyone laughs at that.

I glance at my watch and wince. "I'm sorry to cut this short, but I've gotta go. I have to get some things ready for tonight."

"Yeah, what's this you're planning for tonight?" Rhodes asks.

"Project Woo," I say, pointing at Rhodes. "I'm going to woo the fuck out of this girl."

They all laugh. It's the advice Penn gave Rhodes about Elle…advice Henley and Weston adhered with Tru and Sadie too actually.

"I figure it's worth a go since it worked for the three of you," I say.

"Something tells me she's already wooed, but you do this," Weston says, laughing. "I can't wait to hear what happens."

"Best advice I ever gave," Penn says.

I snort. "Mm-hmm. I think you were heavily influenced by these jokers," I point to Henley and Weston, "but it did work. Elle married the guy."

Rhodes smiles proudly. "Damn straight she did." He looks at me and his expression turns serious. "Make us proud, man. You've got this."

"I'll let you know how it goes."

I leave and get to work, wanting everything to be perfect. Later that afternoon, I pick Poppy up and she gasps, her eyes going wide when she sees my haircut.

"What did you *do*?" She laughs. She reaches forward to smooth a hand over my scalp. Her touch sets off sparks.

"Lost a bet with the guys. Still want to go out with me?"

I can tell she's curious about the bet, but she doesn't push for me to tell her.

"Absolutely," she says. "You look different. Good different though."

"It'll grow back." That's going to be my line for the next month at least, I think.

We drive to the marina and I lead her to the boat I've rented. It's a small, classic vessel adorned with an insane amount of flowers. They spill out over the edges of the boat, a flurry of white and pink and lavender that nearly fills the whole boat.

I might have overdone it with the flowers, but when she sees it, she lets out a gasp, her hand flying to her mouth.

"Bowie!" She turns to look at me, her eyes shining. "This is...*wow*."

I grin, feeling a blush climb my neck. "I wanted it to be special."

We step onto the boat and I help her sit. I sit across from her and the gentle sway of the water calms me, helping me focus on what I want to say. For now, we glide out onto the lake, sunlight dancing on the surface. I have a picnic basket filled with her favorite foods—fruit, cheese, her favorite bread, and desserts from Serendipity. We settle in, cushions and blankets softening the seats.

As we drift, my nerves pick up. But Poppy talks about her day at work, and I tell her about the way Becca's been collecting funny-shaped leaves lately, even finding one that looks like a helicopter. Every moment feels like a step closer to what I need to say. I wait until after we've eaten to take her hand in mine.

"Poppy," I begin, my throat tightening slightly. "These past few months have…changed everything for me. I don't know if you realize just how opposed I was to a relationship, but you've changed all of that. I love spending time with you. I love everything about you. I'm in love with you."

I hear the hitch in her breath, and the tremulous way her mouth gets when her eyes water.

"I'm in love with you too," she whispers.

My heart thumps in response to that.

"When I drop you off at night, I'm sad to leave you. When I wake up in the morning, I miss you. I can't stand to spend another day waking up without you. Would you please move in with me?" My eyes get big and I clasp my hands together. "*Please*?"

I haven't forgotten how much she likes it when I say *please*.

Her lips part, a small "oh" escaping. Her eyes shine brighter than the water's reflection.

"I'm so gone on you, Poppy," I say, leaning in so we're close, foreheads touching.

Her hands land on my face and we kiss. It's the sweetest kiss, as if the whole world is holding its breath. The flowers sway in the breeze, the boat gently rocks, and a bird cries softly overhead.

Then Poppy pulls back and smiles, and her face is mesmerizing, it's so radiant.

"Yes," she says simply. "I'll move in with you."

"I love you," I tell her again, relief flooding through me.

"I love you," she says, and the words have never sounded better.

CHAPTER THIRTY-SIX

HEART RUSH

POPPY

It's been a few weeks since Bowie told me he loved me. I've been floating on cloud nine during that time and have slowly moved out of my condo. It's taken time to sell some of my furniture and to get everything situated into his place, but we brought the last load over last night. I didn't want to take over Becca and Bowie's space the way Bowie's mom did and yet, Bowie hasn't seemed to mind anything I've brought into his house. Our house. It's going to take a while to get used to saying that.

I've slept in his bed every night since his lake declaration though, and I have zero regrets. Morning and night he makes love to me and while that part has always been mind-blowing between us, now it's next level. Maybe because he trusts me now...or that we know how the other feels, but each day just gets sweeter. Bowie's heart opens more all the time. I feel like I see more of his guard dropping nearly by the minute.

Becca is so happy I'm living with them, it's a constant rush of heartwarming butterflies. And Paulina and Mrs. McGregor are never-ending entertainment. It's a good thing the house is huge though because it's a lot of opinionated women under one roof.

But I didn't think I could be this happy, ever.

I've tried not to pay too much attention to it, but the news of us has gotten out. I've even seen myself in some of the BHOTD posts. And while he didn't say too much about it, when he was asked by a reporter after a game recently if it was true he had a baby on the way, he confirmed that he and his girlfriend are having a baby.

Girlfriend! That's me!

Today, we're standing in the aisle of a massive baby store in Denver, staring blankly at the shelves. I turn to look at him, at a loss...but as usual, I get distracted by staring at him. His hair has grown out some since he first cut it. It's long enough to tug again, but just barely. I miss his hair, but he looks so delicious with it like this too, I'm not complaining. I will enjoy every look because there are no bad ones when it comes to Bowie Fox.

"What?" he asks, smiling.

"I just like looking at you."

He leans down and kisses me. "I like looking at you too."

I cut it short, giving him a slight shove back. "Okay, over there. I'm already horny all the time," I whisper.

His eyes light up. "Is that because of pregnancy or…"

I wave my hand in his direction. "Pretty sure it's just you…but pregnancy could be contributing to me wanting it every single second of the day."

"You will not find me complaining about this…ever," he says, adjusting himself.

My mouth goes dry and he laughs when I gape at him.

"Let's get through this so I can give you what you want before our appointment this afternoon," he teases.

"Oh, you're doing me a solid?" I narrow my eyes.

"I want you every single second of the day too, Wicked Stella."

I giggle and then sigh. "Not sure it's possible to hurry through this. I'm not sure what I expected from baby registry shopping, but being overwhelmed by a million baby bottles was not high on the list."

Our friends and family want to have a baby shower for us before the baby comes. Marley and Eric will even be flying out for it. Marley instructed us to register on the earlier side…just in case we think of more things we want in the meantime. I can't imagine that we'll need all that much, but now, I realize I must be wrong. There are bottles to mimic breastfeeding, bottles with anti-colic systems, bottles that reduce air intake, and on and on…and that's just bottles!

Bowie shifts his weight and exhales. "There are so many more choices now than when Becca was born. I didn't know we needed a PhD to pick out a bottle."

I groan and laugh, pressing my lips together. "Should we just close our eyes and pick one? It might be the only way."

I move toward the breastfeeding options, close my eyes, and pick one. He scans it and we move on to the pacifiers and diaper pails with grim determination. It's hilarious and bizarre, and more than once, it makes me feel inadequately prepared for what life with a baby will really entail.

"Miracle swaddle?" Bowie says, raising his eyebrows. "Does that mean it makes a baby sleep a solid eight hours?"

We end up with a random assortment of things—some for style, some for function, and some purely because we're too tired to figure out which is better. I have no idea if we did well or not, but we have fun in the process. Bowie keeps grinning at me like we're in this together, and I live for that look from him.

"Oh!" I freeze as we're walking out. "Wow, the baby is moving a ton."

Bowie reaches out and puts his hand on my stomach. I position his hands where I feel the baby moving. He stares at me as he waits and then his eyes light up when he feels a kick.

"I love that so much," he whispers.

He leans down and kisses my stomach right there in the parking lot.

"Hey, little banana," he says. "I can't wait to see you today."

I drink a ton of water and snooze as we go back to Silver Hills and pick up Becca from school. From there, we head to the clinic for our ultrasound. I'm about to burst when we're taken back to the room to get the ultrasound. Becca sits perched on the chair, legs swinging, her excitement contagious. She's been talking about this appointment for days, asking if the baby will see her on the screen too.

I lie back as the technician moves the wand over my belly.

"Actually, I need you to go empty your bladder because you're too full," the technician says.

"Oh thank God," I say.

Bowie laughs at me and I hold up my hand.

"No laughing. I can't laugh right now," I say, hurrying to the bathroom.

I can hear his laughter from down the hall and it makes me smile so hard.

When I get back in place, he holds my hand, his thumb rubbing gentle circles over my knuckles. We're having a 4D ultrasound done, so when the screen flickers and shows the little world our baby is living in right now, my breath catches.

This is *our* baby, Bowie's and mine, and Becca's too. My lip trembles and a tear runs down my cheek when I see the features of our baby.

"Hi, baby!" Becca says in awe.

"This is amazing," Bowie says, his own voice catching. "I can't believe how clear it is. I can actually see what our baby will look like."

A little fist goes up in the air and the baby's feet move back and forth.

"Can see how wiggly…" I say, smiling through my tears.

Bowie's grip on my hand tightens when the technician says, "Do you want to know the sex?"

We both nod, glancing at each other. We'd already decided we wanted to know. My pulse flutters in anticipation. I can't wait to know.

"It's a boy," she says warmly, and then she points out exactly how she knows.

A boy.

Bowie exhales a shaky laugh, resting his forehead on mine for a second and I see the tears in his eyes too.

We're having a son.

"A little boy," Bowie says hoarsely. "Becca, you're going to have a little brother."

"My baby a brother!" Becca says happily. She points toward the screen and looks so proud. "He a dinosaur! Rawr!"

"You think he looks like a dinosaur?" Bowie laughs.

She nods and we all laugh.

Bowie puts his arms around her and squeezes and then he's back, kissing my temple.

"This is happening, isn't it?" he whispers.

I meet his eyes. "It really is."

"We're so lucky," he whispers.

I nod, more tears spilling over.

He kisses me and then we go back to watching as the technician points out that the baby has the hiccups.

My heart is so full of love I can barely contain it.

And that feeling carries over into the rest of our day. We head to Starlight Cafe after our appointment, sliding into a booth. Becca demands to sit by me, and Bowie pouts when I say yes. He's grinning as he takes the opposite side though.

We order burgers and shakes, and Becca swings her feet under the table, announcing every detail about the baby to Bowie as if he wasn't there.

"My brother loves dinosaurs, Daddy. We read my books. I teach him about dinosaurs." She looks at me. "I be the best big sister."

"You'll be the best big sister ever," I tell her.

Bowie nods. "I have no doubt he'll be a dinosaur expert because of you, Becca."

"Daddy, what is expert?"

"Someone who knows a lot about something…the way you know a lot about dinosaurs."

"Oh, yes. I know a lot. I an expert," she says.

When our shakes arrive, Bowie lifts his glass and I lift

mine too. Becca carefully picks up her glass and we gently tap hers so she doesn't have to lift it very high.

"To our baby boy, to Becca's little brother," Bowie says. "To our family," he adds.

My heart gallops under his gaze, the intent promise in that look.

"To our family," I repeat, eyes welling again. I laugh and shake my head when a tear spills over. "No more tears today."

"Why you sad, Poppy?" Becca asks.

"I'm crying because I'm so happy," I say.

She still reaches over to hug me, rubbing my back the way we do when she's upset.

"You're the sweetest, Becca," I say when I pull back.

She grins bigger when she sees me smiling, reassured that I'm okay.

Bowie is staring at us, and I swear, there are hearts in his eyes. I love the way he looks at me now. "You're beautiful," he says.

"You're the *best*," Becca adds.

"You guys are the best," I cry.

When we get home, we show the sonogram pictures to Paulina and the McGregors.

And then Bowie takes me to bed and makes sure I fall asleep feeling completely loved and satiated.

CHAPTER THIRTY-SEVEN

GHOSTS ON THE FIELD

BOWIE

The locker room always smells the same—sweat and the faint tang of antiseptic from the trainers' area. I'm back in the fray of football season, taping my wrists, pulling on gear, running through plays in my head. The Mustangs are off to a great start this season. The defense is clicking, and the coaches are pleased. By all accounts, I should be riding high on the excitement of the turnaround this season.

And I am. But it's different now. Every time I say

goodbye to Poppy and Becca, I feel a tug in my chest. Becca's happier than ever, having Poppy with her when I can't be, but I miss them so much. When I'm suiting up before a game, I think about how Becca might be playing with her new dinosaur figurines or playing in the yard with Poppy. Staying in yet another hotel room with cookie-cutter art on the walls is a glaring contrast to Poppy's laughter ringing from the kitchen, or the sound of Becca's voice.

It's a new kind of homesickness, one I haven't experienced to this level. I've always been a bit detached, my heart with Becca, but now, no matter how much I try to focus on the next opponent, part of me is back home.

We do what we can to stay connected. After I've done all the interviews and showered up, I find a quiet corner and FaceTime Poppy. She picks up and there's Becca's face, too close to the camera at first, so all I see is a swirl of her hair. Then she adjusts the angle and I get the full picture. Poppy's leaning against a pillow, her baby bump more pronounced now, and there's a look in her eyes that says she misses me too.

"Great game," she says, smiling wide.

"It was a tough matchup, but we did it."

Becca pokes her head back in view, waving a tiny T-Rex. "This is Bobo."

"Bobo, huh? Good choice. You taking good care of him?"

Becca nods solemnly. "He thinks broccoli is yucky."

Poppy laughs. "He takes after Becca that way."

Becca makes a blech sound and I laugh. "Broccoli's not that bad. You should keep trying it." I stare at them for a second. It's small moments like these that I crave. I get snapshots when I'm gone and it just doesn't feel like enough. "I miss you guys," I say.

"We miss you," Poppy says, her voice wistful.

"I'll call you when I get to the hotel." We typically fly back after a game, but since we're in New York, we're leaving in the morning.

They blow kisses and I hang up feeling that ache, counting the hours until I'm back home, wrapping an arm around Poppy's waist and crouching down so Becca can jump on my back.

I walk out and try to shake the melancholy before I get on the bus. The guys are having a heyday with my lovesick self. When we get to the hotel, I think about taking a walk. Sometimes I need to wind down after a game and just regroup.

"Bowie." It's a voice I thought I'd never hear again.

I turn, and there she is. Adriane. She's standing near the entrance of the hotel. Her hair's shorter than I remember, her face fuller. She smiles and my gut twists. I wouldn't expect to still know her at all, but I recognize the look on her face instantly. The look that says she thinks she can walk back into my life and pick up where we left off. My stomach knots tighter.

"What are you doing here?" My voice comes out rougher than I intended.

The last time we spoke was a lifetime ago. She left me without a backward glance, leaving me to raise Becca alone, leaving me to grieve the loss of what I thought we had.

She steps forward, hands spread as if to show she's harmless. "When I heard you were playing here, I had to see you," she says, as if she didn't turn my world upside down.

Before I can back away, she's hugging me. My arms stay at my sides, refusing to return the embrace. The scent of her perfume is cloying and I back away. She stumbles a little and looks up at me, looking slightly hurt.

"You look good," she says, her voice low. "Really good." Her hand tries to settle on my chest, but I step out of reach.

She lost access to me a long time ago and I'm not giving her the satisfaction of pretending like everything's okay. She doesn't miss it, but I see desire in her eyes anyway…like old habits can just resume if she pushes hard enough.

My teeth grind. "What were you hoping to accomplish by coming tonight, Adriane?" I ask bluntly, cutting through the bullshit.

Her lips twist into a hurt expression. "Just time with you. I miss you, Bowie." Her voice dips to something smoother, softer, and there was a time when I would've caved.

Those days are long gone.

"I've never found anything close to what we had. I follow you enough online to know you've never married anyone either…" She takes a step closer. "I'd love to catch up, spend a little time—"

Her audacity shocks me. She has no right to speak as if she knows my heart or my life, and she certainly has no right to want access to any of it.

"I am far from single," I tell her, each word precise. "I have found love, Adriane. True love. Beyond anything you and I ever experienced."

There. I said it, and I mean it. Poppy and Becca's faces smiling at me through the phone screen comes to mind and I feel another rush of love for the woman who has accepted my daughter with open arms.

Adriane's eyes widen, and I'm stunned to see pain there. As if she can't fathom that I've moved on. As if I should've been waiting around for the day she suddenly decided she missed me.

"Bowie—"

"I find it ironic that you haven't said a single word about Becca. That you'd want to, what—go down memory lane with me? Have sex with me tonight to get another fix? When you have a chance to ask me how our daughter's doing, what she's into these days." I shake my head, hands falling to my hips. "Unbelievable."

Her mouth parts.

"You don't get to do this. You made your choices. And there is no part of me that wants anything to do with you."

"Bowie?" Rhodes calls behind me. "There you are. We're having a nightcap, man. Everyone's—" He pauses when he sees who I'm talking to.

I glance back at Adriane. Her lips tremble and it doesn't pull me in even a little bit.

"Don't ever contact me again, Adriane." I turn and walk toward Rhodes, leaving Adriane behind for good.

"You okay?" he asks.

"I could probably play another game right now, with all this adrenaline inside me," I say. "She's got some fucking nerve."

"What did she want?"

"Me."

"*Fuck.* You're not…you're not tempted by that, are you?" He sounds worried and I pause, turning toward him.

"Fuck, no. What I felt for Adriane, even during our best times…there's no comparison to what I feel for Poppy. I am so in love with that woman," I trail off.

He grips my shoulder and beams. "Thank fuck. That's what I wanted to hear," he says, shaking me slightly. "Put a ring on her finger, man."

"I just might do that," I say.

His eyes light up and he smirks. "See, when someone else says that, I'd think maybe…maybe not. But when you say that, I know that you're thinking about it…a lot."

Like every hour of every day.

But I just smirk right back at him. "Maybe, maybe not."

He groans and tries to pull me into a headlock, but I'm too fast for him.

"I wish we were flying out tonight," I say.

More than ever, I want Poppy to know that she is it for me. I can't wait to get home to her and spend the rest of our lives proving it.

"Me too." He sighs. "Me too."

I talk to Poppy briefly when I get back to the room, but she's so sleepy that we don't stay on long. I don't tell her about Adriane. I'll wait and tell her about it in person. It's really a non-issue, and I never thought I'd be able to say that.

But I'm not the man Adriane left behind.

I don't even still wish for Becca to have a relationship with her. Now that I know how adored Becca is from the other people in her life, Poppy being at the top of that list, my daughter is taken care of. She's accepted, she's loved, and that has all been no thanks to Adriane. She will never dim our light again.

CHAPTER THIRTY-EIGHT

REUNITED AND IT FEELS SO GOOD

POPPY

The morning starts out normal…I go to work, dragging slightly because I don't sleep great when Bowie's gone. But as the morning continues, something feels off. There's a hush when I walk into the room. I catch a few staff members whispering behind their clipboards, glancing my way with pitying looks.

"What is going on?" I mutter under my breath, forcing a

smile at the next person I pass and getting a tight-lipped grin in return.

By the time lunch rolls around, I'm on edge.

I lean against my desk and pull out my lunch, scrolling on my phone. And then I see it, a picture posted online of Bowie hugging a woman—a beautiful woman with perfect hair and a body that won't quit.

The headline says: ***Has Bowie Fox reunited with Adriane Fletcher?***

Oh my God. Adriane? My appetite vanishes. I'm grateful I didn't take a bite of my sandwich yet, because I'm pretty sure I'd choke. The image sends my mind spinning. Why is she there? Why is he hugging her like that? Is she back? Oh, God, *is she back?* And how does everyone here know about it before me?

I try to get a grip. Have they been talking again? I thought he hadn't spoken to her in years. I thought they didn't leave it on friendly terms when they talked last. Who am I kidding? This woman's body language doesn't scream anything close to friends. One of her hands is up in his hair, and I see red.

I hear my name and look up. Bowie stands in the doorway, grinning at me. The relief in his eyes drops and his brow furrows when he sees my face. Normally, I'd melt at how glad he seems to see me, but right now, everything feels shaky.

"Hey," he says softly, leaning in to kiss me. I turn slightly, just enough to make him pause. Confusion flickers in his eyes. "Poppy, what's wrong?"

I draw a tremulous breath, which is just so annoying—I wish I could keep my cool, but I can't. I unlock my phone, turning the screen so he can see the photo.

"This. Everyone's been acting weird this morning, so I went searching online and found this. What happened?"

His jaw clenches. "Damn it," he mutters under his breath. "Adriane was at the hotel when we got back after the game last night." He drags a hand over his head, frustration radiating off him. "I'm so sorry. I was going to tell you about this last night, but you were so tired, I thought it could wait until I told you in person."

"Did you know she was going to be there?" I ask, feeling myself go numb.

"No," he says, setting his hands on my shoulders. "I had no idea. She caught me completely off guard and just showed up, acting like she expected us to just ease back into what we were." He grimaces, shaking his head. "She tried to hug me. I stepped out of it right after this was taken."

I bite my lip, searching his face. He looks upset and sincere, but would he really have told me if this hadn't been taken?

"So she's back," I say carefully, my voice cracking. "Why now? Are you…I mean, do you still…?"

He stiffens before his expression softens. "No," he says firmly. "Absolutely not. Seeing her again just reminded me of everything I don't want. She tried to convince me that what we had was something special. And I told her what we had doesn't come close to what you and I have. That I've found true love."

The words should comfort me, but doubt still gnaws at my mind. I drop my gaze and try to move away, but he lowers his head and forces me to make eye contact with him.

"Poppy," he says softly.

"Were you just saying that to hurt her back?" I ask quietly. "Or because we have a baby on the way and you feel…I don't know…obligated?"

His eyes widen and he looks wounded. "Poppy, no." He reaches for my hands, holding them firmly in his. "I'm happy about the baby, but this feeling, what I feel for you, it was there before I knew about him. I haven't been able to get you out of my mind since Becca tried to force us together in Twinkle Tales." His eyes crinkle as he smiles, trying to shoot levity into our conversation, but it drops when he sees that I'm still close to tears. "It's not duty or confusion. It's love. Pure and simple. I'm not in love with you because I have to be. In fact, I tried really hard not to fall for you, if you'll remember what an ass I was."

That finally makes me smile. "An enormous ass," I add softly.

He tilts his head. "Right. An enormous ass." His forehead leans on mine for a second. "You're everything to me, Poppy. I'm in love with you because I can't help but be, and I never want to stop."

I press my lips together when they go wobbly. "Bowie, I just…" I lift my eyes to his and see no hesitation, no lie, no guard put up between us. I let out a shaky breath. "Everyone was looking at me like they felt sorry for me. I didn't know what to think."

"I'm so sorry. I should've told you as soon as it happened. I couldn't wait to get home to you. I don't want you to doubt how I feel. There's no part of me that wants Adriane back. I hope you know that."

"I don't want to lose what we have. This is real for me too."

His arms slide around me, pulling me close. "You're not going to lose me," he says against my hair. "Seeing her changed nothing except solidifying that what I have with you is the best thing to ever happen to me…which I already knew."

He pulls back and puts his hands on my cheeks.

"Do you trust me?" he asks.

I stare up at him for a long moment and then nod. "I do."

I see the relief in his eyes and the ache in my chest dulls. Our lips meet so softly at first, it's just the faintest brush, a quiet question. My hands climb up his shoulders, my fingers curling into his shirt, and he answers by leaning in, his fingers grazing lightly down my arm.

For a moment, it's gentle, but then the sparks rush in. My heart thuds against his chest and he angles his head, deepening the kiss. His mouth becomes more insistent, coaxing me open, and our kiss changes from careful and sweet to a heat that makes my toes curl. His hands slip to my waist, pulling me closer, and I make an urgent sound in his mouth. His body is taut, hard planes against my soft, and I stand on my tiptoes, trying to get as close as I can.

A noise outside my office reminds me where I am and I pull away, breathless. He stares back at me with hunger.

"I better get back to work," I tell him.

"Are we good?" he asks.

"We're good," I say. "As long as we keep talking to each other…and kissing like that."

His lips lift. He presses a kiss to my forehead and I exhale. The rest of the world can think what they want, but we know where we stand.

"I'll see you at home in a few hours?" he asks.

I nod. "Yes," I say softly.

He walks out and I get a swift kick from the baby that makes me smile. I feel a little wrung out from the roller coaster of emotions, but I do trust Bowie. We've come a long way.

CHAPTER THIRTY-NINE

HEAVY BOXES

BOWIE

As soon as I leave Poppy, I pull out my phone and start texting.

> Remember how I mentioned before I went out of town that I needed your help? I'd like to move forward with our plan.

SADIE

Say less. When and where?

TRU

I'm in.

ELLE

Me too.

Half an hour later, we're assembled in Treasure Trove, the local jewelry store. The guys might give me shit when they hear about this, but I trust the girls to keep this secret a helluva lot more than I do the guys. And I need the help desperately.

On my right, Tru is tapping her chin thoughtfully, and on my left, Elle and Sadie stifle laughs when I so much as glance at a ring that's not Poppy's style.

When I hover near a giant, princess-cut rock that I figure looks nice, they shake their heads.

"Poppy's not a princess-cut kind of girl," Tru says. "Think oval or round."

"It really matters that much?" I ask, sweating under my collar. I've faced down crucial playoff games with far more confidence than I have right now.

"This ring will be on her hand every day. People will study it on social media. It represents your eternal love. It's good that you have us here," Sadie says.

"People will study it?" I echo.

Elle pats my arm. "Don't worry, Bowie. We've got you." She directs my attention to a stunner.

Ed, the owner, perks up when he sees our interest.

"This is a 3-carat Art Deco piece. See the filigree flowers and scrolls?" he says, holding the diamond up. There's a large round diamond in the center and the way it sparkles is out of this world. "The diamond lies flush so it doesn't catch on things."

"Perfect for Poppy when she's at work," Sadie says, sounding giddy next to me.

"It's beautiful," I agree. I nod, staring at the ring. "That's the one."

The girls squeal and squeeze my arm, hugging me as I pay for the ring.

"Thanks for the help," I say when we're standing outside the store.

"Anytime," Tru says.

"Let us know what else we can do to help," Sadie says.

"I'm so proud of you, Bowie," Elle says sincerely. "You picked a good one." She pauses. "And I'm proud of you for having the sense to realize it." She smirks and I laugh sheepishly.

"I don't know if she'll say yes, but I have to let her know that I hope with all my heart that she will."

They all *Awwww,* and I head home, eager to get things ready.

I gave Mrs. McGregor the night off and asked Mom to take Becca out for a while. I know they'll be eager to celebrate with us later, but for this, I want it to just be the two of us.

I prepared an easy meal that I know Poppy likes. I rarely cook with the ladies around, but I'm capable, and I just needed to do this for her.

When Poppy steps through the door, I almost forget the little speech I rehearsed. She looks tired but happy to be home, and when she sees me, she gives me a warm smile.

"Hey," she says softly, leaning in for a kiss. I linger there, inhaling the scent of her hair, memorizing this moment. "You okay? You look…intense."

"I'm good," I smile, trying to chill the fuck out. The last

thing I want to do is scare her. "I made dinner for us. Do you want to get comfortable and meet me on the deck?"

Her smile lights up the room. "That sounds perfect. I'll be right back."

When she comes back a few minutes later, I'm waiting for her at the small round table lit with candles and a vase of hydrangeas and roses from the yard. We sit and I pass her the pasta dish.

"This looks so good, Bowie. Thank you. It's just us tonight?"

"Just us."

She grins and I try to relax and ease into conversation, but I'm nervous. And she notices.

"You're okay?" she asks when there's a lull in conversation.

"I'm so good," I say, wanting to snap myself out of the nerves but failing. "And you?"

"Still good," she says, starting to look concerned.

I hop up and return with a small platter of chocolate-dipped strawberries. Her eyes widen.

"You're spoiling me," she says. She reaches for one, and I watch her savor it, my own mouth watering.

And then I remember the music. "Shit," I say under my breath, hopping up again and rushing to turn on the music. My playlist, with everyone from James Arthur to Rihanna, is primed to set the mood.

When Calum Scott starts singing, "You are the Reason," the timing is perfect.

She looks concerned when I sit back down. I lace my fingers with hers and inhale deeply, trying to gather courage.

"I know it's been a whirlwind, you and me," I say. "When I look at you, I see the woman who holds my heart. You have taken the empty spaces inside of me and filled them with light. I was living before you came into my life, but I wasn't truly *alive*."

Her eyes shimmer, her lips parting. When I rise from the chair and kneel in front of her, her breath catches. I reach into my pocket, pulling out the small velvet box, and open it to reveal the ring.

"I started putting this in motion before the weekend," I tell her, wanting her to know this proposal has nothing to do with proving myself but everything to do with wanting her to be my wife. "I love you. I want to spend every day making you feel as cherished as you make me feel. You don't have to say yes now," I say, voice slightly unsteady, "but I'd marry you today if I could. I want you to know that my heart belongs to you, and I want our forever to start as soon as you say the word. Will you marry me, Poppy?"

"Bowie," she whispers, her hand flying to cover her heart.

Her lips tremble and tears slip down her cheeks. She's quiet for a moment, and I realize I'm holding my breath.

She reaches out, taking my face in her hands. "You've given me everything I've ever wanted," she says. "I love you so much. I knew the moment I saw you with Becca that I was in trouble." She smiles and heat thrums through me. "I want to be your wife more than anything."

"You do?" I rasp.

She doesn't hesitate. "Yes."

I slip the ring onto her finger, my hands shaking slightly. Then I stand and gather her against me. I kiss her forehead, her cheeks, and her lips, as we laugh.

"How long do we have before everyone gets home?" she asks.

"Not long enough," I say, grinning against her skin.

She takes my hand and leads me upstairs to our room. "I can't wait to tell Becca, but first I need to show you how much I missed you."

We peel away our clothing as fast as we can. When we reach the edge of the bed, she gives me a soft shove and laughs when I pretend like she's knocked me out.

"Wow, I didn't realize my strength," she says, laughing.

I lean up and put my hands on her stomach, leaning in to kiss it. "Hey there, little coconut," I say softly.

I kiss her belly, my hands going up to her tits. They're so sensitive lately that sometimes she comes from me playing with her nipples alone.

I swirl my tongue around them one at a time, and her legs buckle. I steady her and lean back, guiding her over me. She looks like a goddess with her hair falling over her breasts and grazing her baby bump. I tug her forward.

"I need you up here, Wicked Stella." I tilt my head back. "On my face."

She gasps. "I'll suffocate you."

"Please suffocate me." I point to the headboard. "You can hold on there or here." I point to my hair. "Growing it out just because I miss you pulling it," I say roughly. "And that bet I lost was with Rhodes. He bet that I'd be married within six months—not that you have to marry me that soon," I hurry to add, "but I conceded when I realized how much I hoped that would come true."

Her eyes get all melty and I grin.

She shifts so her tits are at eye level and I lavish them. I can feel how wet she is on my chest and when she starts rubbing against me, I lift her so she's on my mouth. Her head falls back with her moan and I savagely suck on her clit until her thighs are shaking. Her pussy is greedy and I give her everything she wants. When I twist her nipple as she's starting to flutter against my tongue, she screams my name. Her hands fist my hair as she bucks against me, riding it out until she's limp.

Then I lower her and her head falls into the crook of my neck. I let her catch her breath for a second, my tip bumping her impatiently, as I try to tell my lower half to behave and have some manners.

"Yes, please," she says when my cock bobs again, and that's all the invitation I need.

I glide into her and she's so ready, so eager. She lifts off of me and then slams back into me, pulling a hoarse cry out of me.

"So good, Poppy," I rumble. "Do whatever you want with me. I'm yours."

She goes faster, her breath rasping as she chases her pleasure, and I fucking love it. I love seeing her wild and hungry for me. It's the best feeling in the whole fucking world. I pump up into her and her head falls back. I take a fist full of her hair and hold on for dear life as I fill her as deep as I can go. Her orgasm creates a call and response. She calls and I follow, spasms shooting through me as I spill into her. My lips find hers and we kiss and kiss and kiss as I keep pulsing inside of her.

"Daddy, Poppy! You wrestle now?" Becca says, sticking her head in the door.

Poppy squeaks and I yank the comforter over us faster than lightning.

"I'm giving your dad a massage," Poppy says under the covers.

"I…pulled a muscle…lifting boxes for the nursery. We'll be right out, Becca. Go get a snack and Poppy and I will come out soon. My massage is almost done," I finish weakly.

"Okay," Becca says happily, closing the door.

Poppy's head pops out of the comforter and she looks mortified.

"What just *happened*?" she whispers.

I press my lips together. "I'm glad if she saw an ass at all that it was yours and not mine. But hopefully she didn't see anything." My fingers rub my eyes and I try to scrub the image away of my daughter walking in on us. "She didn't, right?"

My lips twitch.

"You pulled a muscle?" Poppy says, voice cracking. And then her shoulders shake in silent laughter. "I am so embarrassed," she wheezes. "God, please give her temporary amnesia over anything she might've seen," she prays, and then I'm laughing too.

We clutch each other as I laugh into her shoulder. As soon as I think I'm past it, I get hit with another round of hysteria.

"Definitely got to lock the door next time," I barely manage to get out.

When we finally get our bearings and put our clothes back on, we go downstairs. I half expect to be chewed out by my mom, but she acts like nothing out of the ordinary has happened. Mrs. McGregor is here despite having the night off, and for a second, I wonder if she'll scold me too. Becca is eating a banana and holds out one for me and Poppy.

Poppy looks at me tentatively and I lift my shoulder. Maybe we're in the clear.

And then Becca puts her hand on her chest and says, "When we wrestle, I wear clothes!"

I can't look at Poppy. I can't. My eyes are round with the effort to not burst out laughing again. When I do look at Poppy, her face burns as she presses her lips together.

"Clothes, got it," I manage, voice strangled, while Poppy coughs to cover a snort.

Becca smiles, pleased with her suggestion.

"Oh!" Poppy yelps. "We have news."

"Oh my God, only being caught giving massages could sidetrack me from the news," I say under my breath, sending Poppy into another round of giggles.

She elbows my side and I put my arms around her, pulling her back against my chest.

I hold up her hand and wave it, ring out, to Becca and my mom and Mrs. McGregor. It takes a minute for them to all notice and when they do, they rush toward us.

"Poppy's going to be my wife," I say, feeling elated all over again. "She said yes."

"You get married like Tru and Henley and Elle and Rhodes and Sadie and Weston!" Becca yells. "I wear a pretty pink dress!"

"We might actually beat Henley and Tru down the aisle, who knows?" I say, lifting my shoulder. "But yes. We're getting married and you'll wear a pretty pink dress."

"Yay!" Becca says, pumping her fist in the air.

I lean in and kiss Poppy's head and then we all hug each other.

I think maybe all I've gone through in my life, the pain, the feeling of rejection…all of it has been worth it to know how to appreciate this now. It's why I'd marry her today if I could. Now that I know what it's like to feel this complete, I want to bask in it forever and never let it go.

Poppy and I celebrate again when we get to our room, this time with the door locked. And then I text the guys before we fall asleep.

> Poppy Keane said she'll marry me.

"Watch this," I tell Poppy, holding up my phone. Her eyes widen when it goes crazy with notifications.

> **PENN**
>
> WHAT THE FUCK. WHAT IS HAPPENING? WE ARE THE SINGLE DAD PLAYERS.

> **RHODES**
>
> Holy shit, I am the happiest motherfucker who ever lived. And Penn, let's not start, okay? We all know how you've hassled us over that name from the beginning. Get with the times, man. We are growing up.

> **PENN**
>
> Anyone who says get with the times has a foot in the grave.

> **WESTON**
>
> LMAO. Ahhh, this is the best news. Sadie just came to see why I was yelling in the kitchen and I told her. She said she helped you pick out the ring with Elle and Tru. What the hell? If I weren't so happy for you, I'd be offended.

> Ask the professionals or ask you dumb asses, you do the math.

> **RHODES**
>
> Whatever. I'll have you know Elle is obsessed with what I picked out for her.

> **HENLEY**
>
> Bowie, this is the BEST! I am so fucking happy and proud of us right now. You'll get there, Penn.

PENN

How many times do I have to say I DON'T WANT TO GET THERE. But I love you guys. Happy for you, Bow.

We laugh about Penn and I close my eyes, feeling happier than I can ever remember feeling.

CHAPTER FORTY

SWIFT KICK

POPPY

I tug Bowie's oversized jersey over my head, the fabric comforting as it drapes over my fully popped belly. Once I crossed the seventh-month mark, baby boy fully took over my body. Bowie's number—23—stretches across my midsection, but I don't mind. I like my pregnant body. It probably helps that Bowie is obsessed with it too. I swear sometimes he sets up a little shrine there and worships. I am oiled up, lotioned up, and loved up at all times.

I like the visible reminder that we're connected. Me, Bowie, Becca, and our very own champ punter.

Speaking of, the little guy gives me a swift kick and I'm back in the bathroom one more time before I head to Elle's to ride with the girls to the stadium.

Tru and I commiserate in the backseat. She's about to pop. Due any day. In fact, Henley tried to talk her out of coming tonight, but she didn't want to miss out. He was only appeased if Chelle, the wife of one of the defensive tackles who's also a nurse, would be nearby. Fortunately, Chelle's great and she happily agreed to hang out with us in a suite tonight.

When we arrive at the stadium, the energy is electric. The crowd is already roaring, and the smell of popcorn and hot dogs drifts through the air despite our spread of chicken wings and fruit trays. Becca is next to me eating a pretzel when she yelps, pointing at the big screen.

"Look, Poppy! We on TV!" she says as the camera pans over us, showing us both proudly wearing Bowie's jerseys.

Tru has the audio cranked so she can hear Henley commentating while we watch the game, and when the camera focuses on me alone, Henley's playful drawl makes me snort.

"And here we go, ladies and gentlemen, Bowie Fox's number one fan is cheering him on tonight. No wonder Bowie's in fine form, looking like a lumberjack ready to tackle a grizzly."

Daniel, another commentator, chimes in dryly. "I'd pay good money to see that—Fox versus a grizzly."

Melanie, the third voice, laughs. "I'm just glad his hair is growing back. You don't think he'll buzz it again, do you? I like to think he plays better with it longer…but maybe that's just me."

"Oh, I don't think it's just you," Henley says, laughing. "I was worried we'd have to call him Cueball Fox all season. Now that it's coming in again, we can all breathe easier…that was too much shine under the stadium lights."

The girls and I crack up.

Henley snaps back to the play. "And he's a powerhouse tonight," he says, his voice rising in excitement. "Knocking that running back into next week and forcing a fourth down."

When Bowie runs back to the sidelines, he looks up and I can tell, even from a distance, he's looking for me. My heart swells. I hold my fist up high and when he spots me, he does the same.

"Flattened him like a pancake," Melanie says. "Someone pass the syrup."

I'm still laughing when the Mustangs' offense takes the field again and makes a touchdown on the first play.

The Mustangs dominate and when they win, the sound is deafening. Becca and I cheer our heads off.

When we get home, the house is warm and quiet. I go through the bedtime routine with Becca and by the time Bowie is home, the lights are low. Bowie finds me in the kitchen, and his arms slide around me from behind.

"You're stunning," he murmurs, kissing my neck. "Seeing you in my jersey…I think it gave me superhuman strength."

"Is that right?" I tease, turning in his arms. "Feels like that superhuman strength is still pulsing through you." I grin when he bends his knees to slide his hardness over my core. "Ahh, proof that I'm right." I slide out from his grasp and throw out over my shoulder, "Race you upstairs."

He lets out a playful growl, easily catching me. "Should we leave this on or strip you bare?" His grabby hands are all over me, and I laugh as I turn and face him, walking backwards.

"How about both? You should know by now that I'm up for it."

"My greedy little fiancée," he says, smirking. "You should know by now that I'm up for it too." He strokes his long, thick length slowly and deliberately, and my mouth waters.

I hustle to our bedroom and we prove that, by now, we know each other very well.

"You're insatiable and I fucking love it," Bowie says, driving into me as deep as he can go.

The first time was on the bathroom counter. He set me up there and I leaned my head against the mirror, tilted back enough to give him easy access. This time, his chest is draped over my back as he takes me from behind in the shower. I've already had three orgasms tonight.

He's right, I am insatiable. I want him all the time.

He thinks it's pregnancy and I think it's him. We have to work around my basketball belly a little bit, but it's not been a problem. AT ALL.

The next morning, both our phones are lit with notifications. I look at my text messages as Bowie looks at his, and I gasp.

"Tru and Henley had a girl!" I cry. "Avery Claire Ward. I love that."

> TRU
>
> Don't tell Henley, but he was right…the excitement of the game DID send me into labor! Okay, okay, the sex afterward probably also contributed. 😊 Sorry, TMI. Avery Claire was born at 3 this morning and she's healthy and the absolute sweetest thing. I'm so in love.

A picture of the little angel is attached and she's gorgeous. Dark hair and full lips, she is a dream.

> **SADIE**
>
> Oh my God, I can't believe it. She's finally here! She is gorgeous. I'm so happy for you guys and cannot WAIT to meet her!

> **ELLE**
>
> Such a beautiful name, such a beautiful baby. I'm not crying. How are you, Mama?

> **CALISTA**
>
> Way to go out with a bang. 😉 She's stunning, Tru. 🩶

I shoot off a text next.

> She is a dream. Just perfection. I'm so excited to meet her!!

Bowie's chuckling next to me and I show him my text thread. He grins and shows me his.

> **HENLEY**
>
> Welp, I've got another little girl to dote on! She has already wrapped her tiny fingers around my heart. Meet your newest Ward, Avery Claire.

The picture is similar to the one Tru sent, but in this one it looks like she's smirking. I smile at the phone.

> **RHODES**
>
> Holy shit, she's perfect.

> **WESTON**
>
> I'm so happy for you guys! Say the word and we're there.

HENLEY

She really is perfect. I'll let you know when we get home. I'm going to force my girl to sleep as long as we're in the hospital. She's my hero. You'd never know she just had a baby. She's too busy staring at our girl to rest.

I hand it back to Bowie and he types something, a smile playing on his lips.

I get up and go to the bathroom and as I'm brushing my teeth, Bowie comes in and starts brushing his. When we're done, he slides his arms around my waist, looking at me in the mirror.

"I'm so happy for them," I say. "I can't believe our baby will be here before we know it."

He nuzzles my neck. His hair is not quite to his chin yet, but it's wavy and flopping in his eyes and tickling my skin. It's going in every direction from me tugging on it last night.

"I can't wait to meet him." He leans his chin on my head. "Should we talk about a date for the wedding? I haven't wanted to rush you, but—" He grins at me.

It still makes my heart stutter that he's so quick with his smiles these days.

"I haven't wanted to rush *you*," I admit.

"Today then?" he says, and I laugh.

I point at my stomach. "I'm a house."

"You are not. I'm going to miss this little basketball belly," he says, rubbing my belly.

We laugh when my stomach rolls under his hands.

"Maybe once your season is over?" I stare at his hands in the mirror, getting lost in thought.

"Where'd you go?" he teases.

"Oh," I grin, leaning my head back against his chest. "I

was imagining us getting married on a beach somewhere tropical."

"Is that your dream wedding? On a beach?"

I sigh. "It sounds nice, doesn't it?"

"Well, if that's what you want, that's what we'll do."

My eyebrows lift. "I…we don't have to do that. I was just—"

"I want you to just…" He teases. "It should be exactly what you want."

"What do you want?"

"I want you to be my wife. The sooner, the better."

I turn and lace my fingers around his neck. "I love you."

"I love you," he says, leaning in to kiss my temple. "So we'll get married after the baby comes?" His lips poke out in a slight pout.

I laugh. "I mean, it'd be *nice* to be married before, but that's so soon."

"Yeah, and you can't fly anywhere now anyway…"

I grin. "You'd really want to marry me right away?"

He makes a face. "Are you really in doubt?"

I laugh. "Oh, how the mighty have fallen…"

He tickles my side and I jerk out of the way, cracking up. He chases me out of the bathroom and when the backs of my knees hit the bed, he wraps his arms around me, hands landing on my backside.

"You make me fall deeper every single day," he says.

CHAPTER FORTY-ONE

MOMOSAS

BOWIE

The moment we get to Rhodes' house, I know this baby shower is going to be legendary. There's a huge floral display hanging between the trees that we drive through, and then a balloon arch leading to the area behind their house. Their property is stunning, with the lake glistening not too far away. We debated on whether we should have the shower inside, but the weather has been too perfect to miss out on this beautiful October day.

"Everything looks so beautiful," Poppy gasps.

The girls surround her, hugging her and then me. I'm grateful all over again that these women, who are married to my best friends and have become family to me too, have welcomed Poppy so completely. Our framily.

"Bree helped a ton," Elle says, her smile wide. "I couldn't have pulled it off without her."

Henley's ex-wife Bree hears her name and comes over to hug us too. She's great. Henley lucked out, having a peaceful relationship with his ex.

"Thanks, Bree," I say when I hug her. "Everything looks beautiful."

"I'm just so happy for you guys," she says, squeezing my arm. "It's wonderful to see you like this."

I smile at her and when she walks over to straighten something, I take it all in. There's a cute "Baby Fox" banner fluttering in the breeze, and it matches the woodland fox theme that's everywhere I look. The grill is going, the music is cranked at the perfect level, and everyone is happy to be together. My hodge-podge family…don't know what I'd do without them.

Mr. and Mrs. McGregor are here. My mom is too, flitting about. I see her laughing with Stephanie, Tru's mom, nodding and gesturing like she's in her element. She's already hit it off with Poppy's parents, and they're here too, sipping hot cider nearby. It's good to see Mom making friends. God knows she needs someone to focus on besides me.

Marley and Eric are even here for the weekend and a few of Poppy's friends from work.

Poppy's eyes are sparkling as she greets everyone and we're led to the table with all the food.

"Oh my goodness, a momosa bar," Poppy says. "You've thought of everything!"

"I was excited about this too," Tru says. She points at another table set up with alcohol. "Bowie, you might like to visit that mimosa bar, but help yourself to the momosas too."

I chuckle and help Becca with her plate.

"Hey, Bowie."

I turn and see Coach Evans. I set my things down and shake his hand.

"Thanks for coming," I tell him.

"I'm glad it worked out," he says. "When I got my invitation and heard the whole team was coming, I knew I couldn't miss it."

"Means a lot that you're here."

He squeezes my shoulder and we find a seat. After we eat, I get my turn holding Avery. She's so cute, it makes my heart ache. I look at Henley and shake my head.

"I can't believe how tiny," I say.

"Right? And she's already grown so much," he says proudly.

"I know. The last time I held her, she was even lighter."

"Okay, it's present time," Elle sings out a little later. She motions for us to move to the chairs set up for us, also bedecked with flowers and balloons, so we do.

"You sure we can't just sit over there with everyone else?" I ask, and everyone laughs.

"You don't get to hide while you open presents," Rhodes says. "No, sir."

We start opening. Some gifts are practical…soft blankets, tiny socks, a monitor that Henley claims is so thorough, it doubles as a spy gadget. Others are funny…a baby rattle with Penn's face on it, a bib from Rhodes that says "Uncle Rhodes is boss," and from Sadie and Weston, a set of onesies with football puns.

Becca is having the time of her life. She loves presents and the girls were looking out for her too, giving her a shirt that says, "Best Big Sister Ever," and a few new frames so she'll have some for her collection when her baby brother comes.

Poppy and I can't stop laughing as we open each gift. And then we move into the ones that have me shaking my head in awe that I have such amazing friends. The stroller we registered for, a high chair...we get all the necessities and then some.

"You guys, this is just...I'm blown away," Poppy says, her voice cracking. "Thank you so much. You've made this so special." She turns to Elle, Tru, Sadie, and Calista. "Sometimes I can't believe that I've known you such a short time. You've welcomed me in and made me feel so loved. I love you all so much. I love all of you," she says to everyone. And then she turns to me and gives me a wobbly smile. "I love you," she says.

"Awwww," everyone cries.

"I love you," I tell her. "And what she said. This has been an incredible day...an incredible ride. You guys warned me that when I'd find love, I'd get the hype, and you were so right."

"Could you repeat that a little louder for the people in the back?" Rhodes yells.

I snort. "You were right," I yell.

"That's more like it," he says, laughing.

Henley steps forward, holding a microphone. Penn, Rhodes, and Weston surround him on either side.

"We've prepared a little something," Henley announces, eyes twinkling. "A rap, in honor of Baby Fox."

Poppy laughs and I groan.

"This should be good," I say. "Bring it."

A beat starts thumping from the speakers. They all bob their heads and Penn rolls his shoulders.

Henley holds his hand up as he takes off.

"Yo, step up to the nursery,
Join the baby daddy tribe,
We got big, bad beats and a baby talk vibe.
Here's the play, Mom and Papa,
It's about to get rad,
I'ma callin' an audible, I'm a football dad."

I wipe my eyes, I'm laughing so hard, watching Henley go. When Henley hands the mic to Rhodes, we cheer for Henley.

"Hut, hut! Hike! Let's go!" the guys all yell.

Rhodes gives me a cocky smirk as he starts his verse.

"Get cha onesies and ya diapers and ya pacis in a row
Keep your voice up high
And your powder down low
Put a cloth over-the-shoulder,
'Cause the spit-up gonna fly,
Then you work your tight end
While you sing a lullaby.
Work your tight end while you sing a lullaby."

He winks when he says tight end and I lose my shit. And lose it even more when they all yell that last line before starting the chorus.

. . .

"Touchdown, do the rock-and-sway,
  Do the rock-and-sway, rock-and-sway all night.
  Touchdown, do the rock-and-sway,
  Do the rock-and-sway, rock-and-sway all night."

Weston is next and he looks the most nervous, but he delivers.

"Get them arms tucked in
  When you swaddle 'em tight,
  Ya better cover the end zone or be up all night
  Gotta wrap that ass crack up like a tailback
  Lay 'em in the crib like
  You're sackin' a quarterback.
  Lay 'em in the crib like
  You're sackin' a quarterback."

They do a hilarious dance that I didn't know they had in them and I've seen them dance a lot. And then they all sing the chorus again.

"Touchdown, do the rock-and-sway,
  Do the rock-and-sway, rock-and-sway all night.
  Touchdown, do the rock-and-sway,
  Do the rock-and-sway, rock-and-sway all night."

Penn motions for Sam to join him and they breakdance

together. Everyone's clapping and cheering and then Penn takes the mic.

"Huddle up, little buddy,
  You're the star of this game.
  Gonna rock ya, baby Fox,
  Gonna whisper ya name.
  Gonna hold you like a football,
  Kiss you when you scream,
  No fumbles, only cuddles
  Till you're sleeping like a dream.
  No fumbles, only cuddles
  Till you're sleeping like a dream!"

He points to all of us. "Everyone now!"
  And we all sing the chorus.

"Touchdown, do the rock-and-sway,
  Do the rock-and-sway, rock-and-sway all night.
  Touchdown, do the rock-and-sway,
  Do the rock-and-sway, rock-and-sway all night."

By the end we're all on our feet, swaying and singing. My mom and Stephanie hip-bump each other, and when the rap ends, everyone cheers and lets out loud catcalls.

Poppy wipes her eyes, leaning into me. "That was… something else." She laughs. "That was too good," she says louder. "I can't believe you did that. If football doesn't work out for you…"

"Stick to football," I fill in, making everyone laugh harder. I go over and hug them. "I'm gonna be singing that song when I'm half asleep, rocking the baby…and thinking about you guys. That was great."

"We're happy to make fools of ourselves for you," Weston says, laughing.

"Hell yeah, we are," Rhodes says. "Wouldn't have it any other way."

"Neither would I," I say.

CHAPTER FORTY-TWO

SURPRISES

POPPY

A few weeks later, I'm deep into nesting mode. It's the beginning of November and the weather has turned cold. The nesting urge has hit me full force. My due date is not for another week and my doctor keeps reminding me that first-time moms are often later than their due date, so I'm trying not to rush the process…but I am so ready to have this baby. I've spent the past week rearranging the nursery, folding and refolding tiny shirts, and obsessively checking the hospital bag. Everything is as ready as it can be.

When Henley and Tru invite everyone to Rose & Thorn for a night out, I'm eager for a break. I'm still not on maternity leave and don't *really* feel like leaving the house, but I need a distraction.

I realize immediately it's not just a casual gathering when we step inside the restaurant.

"What is going on?" I ask Bowie.

"Beats me," he says.

There are only high-top tables surrounding a huge cake. There are flowers and music, and the whole crew is here. Henley and Tru beam at us when we walk in. Once everyone has a drink (sparkling juice for me, obvs), Henley clears his throat, and Tru loops her arm through his.

"So," Henley begins, a grin lighting up his face, "we have something to tell you all…"

He glances at Tru, and she nods, grinning. "We got married!" she announces.

The room explodes in shrieks and whoops and laughter. My jaw drops.

"What? When?" I ask, along with everyone else.

"Two nights ago," Henley says. "We flew to Vegas, just us and the kids, and had a quiet ceremony in a pretty little chapel."

Tru smiles, leaning into him. "We just didn't want a big event. Too much fuss. And we were tired of waiting for the right time, so we kept it quiet and took off after Bree dropped off the kids. We're putting off the honeymoon until the season's over, and wanted to spend more time and money on that than the actual ceremony."

"I can't believe you got married without us," Penn groans dramatically.

"At least we're here for the after-party!" Sadie says, lifting her glass.

Henley launches into a funny story about an Elvis officiant trying to marry them and they had to ask for the *more subdued minister, please*. He's so animated in his delivery that I find myself laughing harder than I have in weeks. And then I feel it—a strange, low sensation, like the baby suddenly shifting downward.

I stop laughing abruptly, placing a hand under my belly, almost like I'm trying to hold it up. "Oh," I say quietly.

Bowie's eyes dart to me instantly. He's learned to read every subtle change in my expression since he watches me like a *hawk* these days. A paranoid hawk at that.

"Something just happened," I say, blinking in surprise.

His hand goes around my waist and another on my stomach. "Happened how? Are you okay?" he asks, worry filling his eyes.

"I think the baby just…dropped," I manage, swallowing nervously. It's different from all the other movements I've felt before—heavier, a more forceful press on my bladder. "Bowie…I think I need to go to the hospital."

His eyes go wide, and the entire group falls silent, hearing me. I thought I was being quiet, but the urgency must have come through. There's a rush of hugs and well-wishes, and we say quick goodbyes.

"I don't even have my bag," I say.

"We'll bring it to you," Elle says. "Don't worry about a thing. See how things are going and we can bring Becca when you're ready too."

Becca hovers near me, concerned.

"I'm fine," I tell her. "Stay here and have fun for a while with everyone. We'll let you know what the doctor says. It might not even be time for baby brother yet, but we'll find out."

"I go too," she says, stomping her foot.

I'm too nervous to have her there during the delivery, uncertain of how she'd react to all of that, but I know I want her there the minute our baby boy arrives.

"I promise we'll make sure you're there as soon as he gets here, okay?" Bowie tells her.

"Don't worry, one of us will make sure you get there quickly," Sadie says.

"I want to see him," Becca says excitedly.

I hug her. "Me too."

Bowie hugs her next and then the guys, and we're led toward the exit.

"I wish we were married already too," Bowie blurts out suddenly.

Henley pats him on the shoulder, grinning.

"Me too," I tell him, smiling.

There's no time to delve deeper into the sentiment than that because I feel an urgency to get to the hospital, but knowing he's thinking this way settles into my heart like a warm promise.

Bowie tries to exit out the wrong door.

"Bowie, other way, buddy!" Weston calls after him.

Everyone chuckles softly, but I can see the concern on their faces too.

"You'll be okay getting there?" Rhodes asks.

"Yes," Bowie says.

But then we get in the car and my normally stoic man stammers, talking nonsense about traffic routes and shortcuts that don't exist…and I wonder if we should've had someone else drive.

"We'll take the highway—no, wait, the side street might

be faster…I mean, I'll just fly the car. Uh, no, not what I meant."

I place a hand on his arm and give him a reassuring squeeze. "I'm okay," I tell him softly. "I'm scared, but we'll be okay."

"Yes." He nods and takes a deep breath. "I love you, Poppy."

"I love you."

The words seem to steady him, but it's a miracle that we end up at the hospital. We arrive, shaky but ready. For all the preparing I've done, I wasn't ready to have a baby *tonight*, but I'm not complaining.

I'm wheeled back and the wait isn't too long before they come back to check my progress.

"We've put in a call to Dr. Talbot, just letting her know you're here, and after we find out whether you're in labor or not, we'll update her."

"Okay," I say.

A few minutes later, they announce that I'm dilated to a two and that I'm staying overnight. It's a little bit of a wait before I'm moved to my room and Bowie updates my family and everyone on our group text.

The hospital room is quiet compared to the steady hum in the hallway. I'm propped up against floppy white pillows and hooked up to a machine monitoring all the things, a band around my stomach to monitor contractions, which have picked up. Bowie hasn't left my side. He has our delivery playlist going, hospital ice within close reach, and is holding my hand, looking slightly panicked.

"Are you hurting?" he asks.

"I'm okay. It hasn't been too bad yet. Mostly just like bad cramps, although that last contraction wasn't great." I wrinkle my nose.

He shakes his head. "I don't want you to hurt. That's the worst part of this."

"I'll be all right…I think. The unknown is the scariest."

"You're—"

There's a knock and Rhodes sticks his head in the door. "Hey…feel free to send us away, but we have a little surprise."

"Oh…okay," Bowie says, looking at me. "Who is us?" he asks Rhodes.

"All of us."

Bowie's eyes are wide when he looks at me again.

"I'm curious," I say and he nods, his lips quirking up.

"Okay, come in. You let me know the second you need them out," he tells me.

I nod. Everyone files into the room and the mood is charged. Becca hugs Bowie and looks worried when she sees me. I reach out and take her hand.

"I'm okay," I tell her.

Penn steps in last with a woman I don't recognize, and my eyes narrow.

"Penn," Bowie says slowly, "what are you wearing?"

Penn looks crazy proud as he straightens his black shirt and taps the white strip peeking out at his neck. "Oh, this?" he says, nonchalantly. "I got ordained for you. Online. I'm a man of the cloth now. Always wanted to say that. Not really, but it sounded good." He shrugs, grinning. "And this is Dorene. Not sure if you've met her yet, Poppy."

"I don't think so," I say.

Dorene smiles warmly. She's holding a file and says hello.

"Dorene is Joseph Collins' cousin—our center, remember? Anyway…she works for the county clerk's office and can get you set up with a marriage license."

I stare at Penn and then Dorene. "No way," I breathe. I glance at Bowie, who looks as shocked as I feel. And then he starts laughing, *hard*. It catches everyone so off guard that they're quiet for a full thirty seconds before they crack up too.

"Let's have a wedding!" Bowie says. And just as quickly, he puts his hand on my face. "If you want to."

I nod, grinning.

"Are you sure?" he asks. "I'll still take you somewhere tropical for a full ceremony."

"Yes, please. There won't be much of a honeymoon though." I make a face and he laughs.

"There will be plenty of time for that later," he says.

Elle lifts our hospital bag. "We have your bag here if you need anything out of here before you say I do."

"I'd like to at least get out of this hospital gown and into my cute pajamas," I say.

"Okay, take five, everyone," Bowie says.

They leave the room and I have a contraction as I'm getting up to change. I pause and breathe through it and then Bowie helps me change. Once I'm settled again, I sigh.

"Not exactly how I imagined looking on my wedding day."

He tips my chin to look up at him. "You've never looked more beautiful to me than you do right now."

"Remember this then because I'm about to scar your retinas when I give birth."

He bursts out laughing and kisses me and then goes to tell everyone that I'm ready. As he turns back around, I'm having another contraction, and he's by my side in the next second.

"It needs to be quick because her contractions are picking up," he tells Penn.

Everyone gathers around the bed. Becca leans against Bowie and smiles at me.

"Dearly beloved," Penn starts, and there's more than one snort. "We are gathered around this hospital bed to celebrate the love of Bowie Fox and Poppy Keane."

I get the giggles and then take a deep breath when my stomach starts tightening. Penn's eyes grow round when he sees the machine tracking my contractions leaving a high peak.

"Are you having one right now?" he asks in a high voice.

I nod and squeeze Bowie's hand hard.

"Keep going," I say between my teeth.

"Do you, Bowie Fox, take Poppy Keane to be your husband? I mean, wife?"

More titters.

"I do," Bowie says.

"Do you, Poppy Keane, take Bowie Fox to be your husband?"

The contraction starts to ease and I let out a shaky breath. "I do."

"Do you have any words you'd like to share?" Penn says, looking between the two of us.

"I love you more than I ever thought possible," Bowie says. "You have made me the happiest man, which is a miracle in itself. Sharing a life with you is all I want. And I'll work on better vows when we get married on the beach."

I smile at him. "Sounds like perfect vows to me already. I love you so much, Bowie. Being your wife is..." I breathe out through my mouth. "Everything," I rush out. I try to focus on him, but it's getting harder to talk through this one. I nod at Bowie, biting down on my lip as I try to work through the pain.

Bowie motions for Penn to wrap it up.

"By the power vested in me through the state of Colorado, I pronounce you husband and wife," Penn says, so fast it sounds like a song being fast-forwarded. *"You may kiss the bride."* His shoulders drop as he loses his breath, just as I'm catching mine.

I laugh and Bowie kisses me. Everyone cheers and congratulates us.

"Best wedding ever," Penn says proudly.

"Thank you. That was the best surprise ever," I say. "We're married!"

"Are you my mommy now?" Becca asks.

"If you want me to be," I tell her, eyes welling with tears.

"Yes," she says simply.

"Yes," I agree. "I love you, my sweet Tater Tot," I say, and she beams.

"And we make Mommy and Becca pictures?"

"Of course, we will."

Another contraction hits and Sadie ushers Becca out of the room, saying, "Let us know when the baby gets here!"

"Love you," Tru says.

"I love you all," I tell them.

When the room is quiet again, Bowie leans in and kisses me. This one is slow and so sweet.

"Hello, Mrs. Fox," he says.

I tug on his hair and kiss him again, my *husband*.

CHAPTER FORTY-THREE

WELCOME TO THE WORLD

BOWIE

It's the wee hours of the next morning. The hospital room feels like a furnace, and unfortunately, nothing I do cools the room. One of the nurses said they're having issues with the HVAC. My shirt sticks to my back, and there's a fine sheen of sweat on my forehead. Poppy's cheeks are flushed, her hair damp at the temples. She's exhausted. I lean over her, trying to blow cool air in her face, desperate to do something—anything to help.

"Your breath is hot," she mumbles, eyes squeezed shut, and I jerk back.

Right. Of course it's not helping. I feel useless, my heart hammering against my ribs. How do I fix this for her? I'm supposed to be her rock right now, and I'm floundering.

What if I can't do this? I've been a good dad to Becca, but I started from a place of fear and uncertainty, and now here I am again, starting over with a brand-new baby. I'll have two kids, just like my dad. Two souls depending on me. And Poppy, the love of my life, counting on me to be steady.

I stare at her face. Her beautiful, angelic face. She's breathing through a contraction, her jaw set as she stares at me with resilience in her gaze. She's so much stronger than me. She's the champion here, the rock. And she's looking at me with so much trust and love, it's humbling.

Before I know it, her grip on my hand tightens, and the room moves into a blur of instructions and encouragement from the nurse. And then Dr. Talbot is there, smiling warmly.

"Are we ready to have this baby?" she asks.

"So ready," Poppy grits out. She lets out a sound that's both pain and determination, and my heart aches with how much I love her.

"You're doing so amazing, Poppy. You're incredible. I love you so much," I tell her as she pushes.

When I see that little guy's head for the first time, I start to cry, and then his shoulders slide out. I cut the cord and a tiny cry slices through the air.

He's here. My son. Our little boy.

Dr. Talbot places him in Poppy's arms and I'm torn between which one to stare at. My emotions are on overload. I kiss Poppy's forehead.

"You did it," I whisper.

We stare at him, his scrunched-up nose settling as he's

next to his mama, his tiny fists flailing. All earlier panic dissolves, and it's replaced by something vast and quiet and warm. A knowing that sits deep in my chest. This is exactly where I'm supposed to be. All I have to do is love them the way I've wanted to be loved, and that's already been established. I love them with all my heart.

Poppy and I exchange a trembling smile, tears in our eyes.

"He's perfect," she whispers.

"Yes, he is."

"Jonas Everett Fox, welcome to the world," she says.

We chose this name to honor our grandfathers. Jonas was my mom's dad and my favorite grandpa, and Everett is Poppy's.

"It fits him," I say.

The next few hours are like living in a dream bubble. Poppy nurses the baby, and we stare at him and each other. Later, I hold Jonas while Poppy drifts in and out of sleep. I doze myself and when I'm awake, I'm surprised by my earlier panic, because this just feels like heaven.

It's late afternoon when Mom brings Becca to meet Jonas. Poppy has washed up and looks peaceful as she holds Jonas bundled in her arms, his tiny face peeking out from the blanket. I can't resist stroking his downy hair. He has a full head of hair—*just like his dad*, according to the nurses.

Becca steps forward slowly, her eyes wide and bright, as if she's crossing into sacred territory.

"She's been waiting for this moment all morning," Mom says, "asking every five minutes if it's time yet."

Now that she's here, she takes her time, each step smaller than the last until she's close enough to see her baby brother.

I lean down and whisper, "Becca, this is Jonas, your baby brother."

She tilts her head, studying him like he's the most fascinating creature. She tries to whisper too, but it's more of a whisper-shout, "He so little." She looks up at me and then Poppy, as if needing confirmation.

Poppy smiles, shifting slightly so Becca can see better. "Isn't he? He's your brother. You can say hi, if you want."

Becca's hand hovers near Jonas's blanket. "Hi, baby Jonas," she says gently. She glances up at me, eyes shining, and I nod, squeezing her shoulder.

"You're a big sister now," I remind her. "He's going to love you so much. You can show him all your favorite things."

At that, Becca's face lights up. She leans in and whispers to Jonas, "I show you all my favorite things!"

Poppy lifts a corner of the blanket so Becca can see more of Jonas's tiny fingers. One of them twitches and Becca gasps, turning to look at me in amazement.

"He moves!" she says, as if his small stretch is the best performance she's ever seen.

I chuckle, pressing a kiss to her temple. "He's going to move a lot, and he'll grow really fast too."

Becca beams at me and then at Poppy. "I like him," she says proudly. "He's perfect."

We laugh. I have to admit I'm relieved. I was certain she'd learn to like him but not sure how she'd feel to have our attention divided. We'll see how it goes when we're home and he's more demanding, but this is such a great start.

"He's perfect just like you, Becca," I tell her.

She can't possibly smile any wider at that, and my heart quadruples in size.

We take him home the next day and it's surreal. I'm still in disbelief that I'm living this life. The McGregors greet us at the door, voices hushed as if the baby might wake with the slightest sound. So far, he seems to be able to sleep through anything. Mrs. McGregor, usually so brisk and no-nonsense, gazes at Jonas with melty eyes.

"Just look at those fingers," she murmurs, completely charmed, and Mr. McGregor grunts his agreement.

Martha reluctantly comes over and sniffs the baby and then nuzzles my hand when I pet her.

Becca waits impatiently, bouncing on her toes. "I show him my pictures!"

I smile at her excitement. "Lead the way," I tell her.

We follow her to her room and she points to the new one: a small silver frame holding a photo taken just yesterday of Becca and Jonas.

"Me and my baby brother," she says proudly.

"It's perfect," Poppy says, blinking back tears. She points at her eyes. "Happy tears," she tells Becca.

After a nap, the crew arrives. Rhodes, Elle, and Levi sweep in carrying food and flowers. Weston, Sadie, and Caleb follow, whispering praises about Jonas's hair and discussing who he resembles most—my hair and eyes, and Poppy's lips. Henley and Tru with baby Avery peek over Poppy's shoulder and coo. Penn lurks at the edge, looking nervous.

"All right, Penn, come on, your turn to hold the baby," I say.

"What? No…that's okay."

I ease Jonas into his arms and he holds him like a precious artifact, eyes wide, mouth slightly open.

"He's so tiny," Penn whispers. "Oh my God. How do you not break him?" He looks over at Weston, then at me, panic flaring. "I mean…I kind of want one now, but I see what you mean about needing a playbook, Weston. Where to even begin?"

We all laugh.

"You'll be fine when the time comes, Penn," Poppy says. "You learn as you go. At least, that's what I'm telling myself." She laughs.

Our friends only stay long enough to leave their gifts and to stare at Jonas for a few minutes.

"Call us when you need to sleep and want an extra set of hands," Rhodes says as he hugs me.

Things get a little stressful for Poppy when she tries to feed the baby and he fusses, rooting but not quite latching. Terms I never thought I'd know or be using, but hello, fatherhood up close and personal.

Poppy's forehead furrows and she gets more and more concerned when it's not working. I hover uselessly near her, adjusting the pillow where she wants it but feeling generally helpless.

My mom steps forward, and before Poppy or I can say anything, she reaches down and actually repositions Poppy's boob, lining it up for Jonas like a football being placed for a field goal.

"There," she says matter-of-factly. "He should latch better like that."

For a moment, Poppy and I are stunned speechless. Poppy's eyes are round and her cheeks are pink. Then Jonas latches on, and Poppy breathes out a sigh of relief.

Helpful, yes, but also the kind of boundary crossing that's just a little too much. Poppy smiles weakly at my mom, a mix of gratitude and shock.

"Thank you," Poppy says.

My mom steps back, folding her arms with a satisfied nod.

There's a beat of silence and then my mom clears her throat. "Yep, it's probably time that I get my own place, isn't it?"

I catch Poppy's eye. She looks relieved and is biting back a laugh.

"You said it, not me," I tell Mom, raising my hands in mock surrender.

Mom grins. There's no argument this time—no guilt, no pushback—and I'm grateful. Maybe we've grown beyond those old patterns. She's proven she can be helpful, despite it being mortifying at times, and now she knows when it's time to step back.

"Maybe after Thanksgiving," she adds.

"Okay, Mom. Thanks. That sounds good. Somewhere close, though, so we can see you often."

She pats my arm. "I like the sound of that."

When we crawl into bed that night, Jonas asleep in the little bassinet on Poppy's side, I turn and face Poppy.

"I'm in awe of you," I tell her. "And I feel like the luckiest man alive."

She turns and smiles at me. "I'm so glad you opened your heart to me, Bowie. I love our life. I know we're just getting started, but I love it so much."

I lean in and kiss her.

"Me too, little mama. Me too. Life is beyond good."

CHAPTER FORTY-FOUR

HERBS AND SPICY

POPPY

The house smells like sage and rosemary, with a hint of cinnamon lingering from the apple cider simmering on the stove. We've pushed together extra tables and borrowed chairs so everyone can sit around the long makeshift dining arrangement. Friendsgiving at our place has turned into an extravaganza. It's not just our friends; it's our families too, all mingling as if they've known each other forever.

Rhodes' parents are even here and I absolutely love them.

I confess to being more than a little starstruck by both of them. I've watched Troy Archer's movies from the time I was a little girl, and I've followed Amara in magazines and on social media for almost as long. My mom always loved them too and she and Amara hit it off right away.

Jonas dozes in a sling against my chest, his breathing rising and falling in a rhythm that calms me. I'm absolutely obsessed with him. We all are. Becca adores him. She's flitting around, greeting everyone, and then comes back to check on her baby brother every few minutes. She shows off her frame collection to anyone who will look, now featuring multiple pictures of Jonas.

Mrs. McGregor fusses in the kitchen, making sure all the dishes have a serving spoon. My mom chats with Bowie's mom near the fireplace, the two of them looking over my way every now and then with proud looks. Marley and Eric stand by the dessert table, laughing with Tru, as they watch Caleb and Levi cooing over Avery. Tobias—yes, Tobias actually came—is sitting in the living room with Rhodes and Weston, trading quiet jokes and stories, and I can see Bowie chuckling from across the room.

I catch Bowie's eye and he gives me the slow, contented smile that makes his eyes crinkle at the corners. In that moment, I can feel all the effort, all the love…all the changes in him that have led us here. He comes over, slipping an arm around my waist and pressing a kiss to Jonas's head.

After everyone's settled with plates heaped high, the room fills with a buzz as everyone talks and eats.

"Just putting it out there, I volunteer to taste-test every dessert," Penn says.

"One bite per pie," Sadie says then laughs. "Kidding!" she sings.

Bowie clears his throat. It's subtle, but everyone knows to

stop and listen when he decides to speak. "So," he starts, glancing around the table. "We've been thinking about doing something special in February…"

Everyone perks up, curious.

Bowie takes a breath. "We're considering a trip. A family vacation…a friend-family vacation," he adds, smiling around the table. "Everyone who can come, really. The season will be over by then, and we'd like to go to the Bahamas."

"Ooo," Elle squeals. "I'm in."

She smiles at Rhodes, who nods. "If she's in, you know I am too."

"And," Bowie says, squeezing my hand, "we'd like to have a tropical wedding there. I know we're already married…" He glances at me with a grin, letting me know he's not discounting our spontaneous hospital wedding. "But I want to give Poppy the day she deserves. Something relaxed, fun, and about celebrating all of you…all of us. Nothing stressful at all, just us, exchanging vows in the sunshine and having a good time together."

"It's a good month for a honeymoon," Weston says, grinning. "And for celebrating an anniversary."

"You'll have two anniversaries!" Sadie says, turning to me.

I love the way we got married in the hospital, love having Poppy *Fox* on our baby's birth certificate, love knowing I'm his wife…but I love this too, the thought of us doing something special to celebrate when I'm not in the throes of labor.

Penn taps a dramatic hand to his chest. "Do I get to perform the ceremony again?" he asks.

There's a ripple of laughter and Penn looks around indignantly.

"I take my duties seriously!" he says.

"Absolutely," Bowie says without missing a beat. "You're our official man of the cloth now."

Henley snorts, pulling The Single Dad Playbook out of his bag, and he pretends to write in it. "Big news: Penn is now the permanent officiant of all Mustangs weddings."

Penn waves a hand, as if overwhelmed by the honor. "It's a good thing the rest of you are married already…my schedule's booking up fast."

Elle's phone buzzes on the coffee table. "Sorry," she says, standing up. "I meant to turn that off." Her smile falters when she sees the number and she snatches it up quickly.

The room's chatter dips for a moment, but resumes when she slips into the hallway, pressing the phone to her ear. When she comes back a few minutes later, she's practically glowing. "Guys," she says, voice breathless, "that was my agent. There's a movie deal in the works for *It Was Always You*…like it's *happening*, happening. No more maybes."

Tru nearly chokes on her cider. Rhodes is on his feet, hugging Elle so tightly, she squeaks. The rest of us surround her, huddling together to congratulate her.

"You've poured your heart into this story. I'm so excited for you, Elle," I say.

She wipes her eyes. "I can't believe this is happening."

"I can't wait to see who they get to play Ryder and Eliza," Tru says, sighing wistfully.

Elle turns and hugs Rhodes' parents. "Thank you for whatever strings you pulled," she says.

"This was all you, my dear," Troy Archer says in his rich British accent. "I didn't have to say a word," he says, winking at her.

"Hmm, I don't know if I believe you, but either way, I'm thrilled." Elle laughs.

Later, after we've cleared the dishes, too full for dessert

just yet, the girls and I are huddled in the living room, looking at Pinterest and talking about dresses. Elle perches on the arm of the couch as she looks over Tru's shoulder at the laptop screen.

"Linen dresses?" she asks.

"I vote for knockout gowns," Sadie says.

"Or full tropical glam with flower crowns," Tru says.

"Let's not forget we'll be near the ocean," Marley says, always the practical one. "Wind plus flowers equals a potential fashion disaster." She grins, shrugging. "You want all that drama?"

I laugh, leaning back and smiling down at Jonas, who's just opening his eyes. "You guys, remember—low-key. I got married in a hospital wearing pajamas. I'm not exactly a diva. I promise not to turn into Bridezilla once we get there either."

Elle exchanges a look with Tru. "We hear ya. We went low-key too. And this one didn't even invite us," she says, pointing at Tru.

Tru makes a face. "Guilty. We figured there was always time for a good party together," she says, laughing.

"Your wedding was still gorgeous, Elle. And I'm sure yours was too, Tru," Sadie says, teasing Tru with a pointed look. "I can't believe I'm the only one who went the whole nine yards."

"It was classy and elegant," Tru says.

"The most beautiful wedding," Elle agrees.

"Whatever you want, Poppy. Whether it's elaborate mermaid tails or color-coordinated outfits or barefoot in sundresses, that's what we'll do," Sadie says.

I motion for Tru to hand me the laptop and I pull up a picture. "It's funny you say mermaid because that's in the description of this dress…although I don't know why." They ooh and ahh over the plunging boho lace dress I show them.

"I can just slide that strap down when Jonas wants to nurse—"

"And still look like a freaking goddess," Elle finishes. "That is stunning, Poppy."

Everyone else agrees.

"And Bowie will be sliding that strap down the first chance he gets," Calista says under her breath.

We all laugh.

"I was *thrilled* to be in the clear for sex again," Tru whispers. "We didn't make it to the six-week mark." She makes a face.

"Do most people?" Sadie asks. "It's hard to imagine going that long without."

"It's hard for me to imagine wanting to have sex after a baby's come out of there," Calista says, shuddering. She's late from being at her family's event and takes her shoes off, getting comfortable.

"I'm with you," Marley says.

My face heats as I think about last night with Bowie. He told me not to when I surprised him in the shower and took his hot, hard length into my mouth. He didn't want me to feel like I had to do anything while I'm still recovering. I ignored him, and later, when he was chanting my name in reverent gasps, I was glad I had.

The worship in his eyes, watching him fall apart because of me…it's such a powerful feeling.

"You filthy little minx," Marley says, nudging me. "You've already had sex, haven't you?"

"What? No, it's not been four weeks yet," I say adamantly, like she's crazy. "But there's no way I can wait until six," I add, blushing a deeper red.

We all laugh.

Martha comes over and sidles up next to me and Jonas,

plopping down with a thunk. The girls lose it, laughing harder, and it's only then that I look down to see that the little hair Martha has is splayed out in every direction with a severe case of static cling.

"Oh my goodness, Martha," I crack up. "Wow. You make every day feel like a good hair day for me…not for you unfortunately, but I love you anyway."

CHAPTER FORTY-FIVE

ZING

BOWIE

A few months later, February

"This is definitely the loudest plane I've ever been on," Poppy says, laughing.

I nod, smiling as I look around the packed cabin full of family and friends. Even Bogey, Rhodes and Elle's bulldog, is snoring quietly next to them. A few others will be arriving later than us, but we managed to fill this plane.

We didn't make it to the Super Bowl—we lost in the play-offs. But compared to last year's rocky season, we finished strong, and there's a sense of pride and gratitude in the air. Instead of dwelling on what might've been, we're all just excited and ready for this vacation. The mood is infectious.

Poppy is beside me, Jonas cradled in her arms. He's gotten so big in the past three months. It's going way too fast. Becca is on the other side of Poppy, next to the window, and exclaiming about everything she sees below. I rest my hand on Poppy's knee and she gives me a sweet smile that zings directly to my chest. I've got it so fucking bad for this woman.

Rhodes strolls down the aisle and pauses by my seat.

"Hey…got any Bogey tricks planned for my wedding like you did for yours?" I ask.

He shrugs, but there's a mischievous glint in his eye. "He can always bring the ring down the aisle if you want him to," he says. "Or maybe he knows a few other tricks he can pull out." He winks.

I laugh. "Somehow I knew you would."

By the time we land in the Bahamas and step outside the airport, I can already feel the tension of the season melting away. The resort is breathtaking. Palm trees swaying, crystalline waves rolling onto white sand. Sunlight bounces off the water, and everyone looks more relaxed already as we cheese-smile at each other.

"This is heaven," Poppy sighs.

We enjoy an amazing dinner out on the sand and then leave Becca and Jonas in the capable hands of their grandparents for the night. Jonas is just starting to sleep through the night, but Poppy's dad says he'll bring him to our hut for

Poppy to nurse him if he wakes up before morning. Poppy and I settle into our romantic getaway, the sound of the ocean like a lullaby. But who wants to sleep when we have all night to love each other?

If it had been even a month ago, we would've.

But after a couple weeks of sleeping better, I love the eager way Poppy eyes my body like she's been craving me as much as I'm craving her. I missed her body in the weeks after Jonas was born, but I have not suffered. I feel closer to her than ever. But now, kissing my way down her body and taking my time with her without worrying about the baby waking up or anyone hearing, is a luxury. I can't get enough of her, the way she arches into my mouth, her wet core coating my fingers and then sinking into her like I'm a man coming home.

"Ohhh," she moans. "You feel so good. Can we do this all night?"

"I want to more than anything." I try to stay still, every muscle clenched in anticipation, but the need to move is too strong.

A hundred expressions cross her face as I drag in and out of her. Tension, relief, ecstasy, lust…it's intoxicating to watch her. She's warm and so wet and her hands find my ass, pulling me so deep I bottom out. She rocks with me to get me deeper, whispering, "More."

I give her everything. All of me. Once I gave her my heart, I don't do anything half-assed. I tell her how I feel, I tell her what I want, I show her how much I love her, need her…

I groan. "I'm so close and I don't want it to be over."

"I'm close too," she says.

Her tits bounce and one of them leaks on me, which makes me grin. I love every fucking thing about her. I flip us over so she's on top of me, and she grinds against me, her head falling back as she chases her orgasm.

"That's it," I tell her.

"So good," she cries.

Her orgasm comes hard and fast, and it nearly squeezes the life out of me, but I'm determined to prolong this. I squeeze my eyes closed and she rolls her hips, riding me to the edge again. Right before she nearly falls, I flip her on her back again, and drive into her, hitting that spot that makes her see stars.

"Bowie," she yells.

And when she comes again, I'm right there with her.

It's otherworldly good.

"I love you," I say when we go still, nothing moving but where I'm joined to her, tiny pulses and her answering squeezes.

"I love you too," she says softly.

And despite our wishes to go all night, we fall asleep and sleep like the dead…like the parents of a three-month-old.

I wake up feeling more rested than I have in months.

Poppy looks over at me and grins. "So much for our sexual renaissance," she says. "But our honeymoon is just beginning."

"There's hope for us yet," I say, pressing a kiss on her stomach. "Good morning, Mrs. Fox. Are you ready to marry me again?"

"So ready."

We get ready and Poppy feeds Jonas. We enjoy a late, leisurely breakfast and then I head over to Rhodes' hut to get ready with the guys. I pass the girls on their way to get ready with Poppy.

"Your hair is the perfect length for the wedding, Bowie,"

Elle says. "Don't let Rhodes talk you into a bet involving your hair ever again."

"You wearing a man bun today?" Tru asks, grinning.

"You think it's long enough for that?" I ask, running my hand through it. "My girl likes it down best, I think."

"Then definitely go with that," Sadie says.

"You can't really go wrong," Calista adds. She looks around. "There's not any paparazzi around snapping pictures of today's hair, is there?" she teases.

"God, I hope not," I say.

In Rhodes' hut, the party has already started. Rhodes adjusts my collar and Weston pretends to fluff my hair.

"Where's Penn?" Henley asks.

"I haven't seen him today," Rhodes says. He frowns. "You know, he was acting weird last night, super evasive and shit."

"Wonder what's going on with him," Weston says.

"I guess it's a good thing we're already married," I say, chuckling. "He'll show up, I'm sure."

By the time the ceremony rolls around, I can't believe how many people showed up for this. Coach Evans is even here, nodding at me with a small smile after I seat my mother and then turn to face the audience.

The guys stand next to me, Penn in his place just in the nick of time, and the girls walk down the aisle, each in a different color dress. I couldn't tell you what the colors are... some kind of green and a pink and a light brown. I'm sure there are fancier names for all of it, but it's lost on me.

I know Becca's dress is pink and I start grinning in anticipation, knowing she's coming out next. The swell of music quietens and a recording with Becca's voice starts playing. My eyes widen in surprise as she says, "Hi, Daddy, I walk down to see you now. Happy wedding."

Oh God. I shake my head and look around at the guys, my eyes blurring. Rhodes blows out through his mouth like he's trying not to sob.

"I love you lots and I love Poppy lots," Becca says. "She looks beautiful, like me. Bye!"

Everyone laughs and I wipe my face with the tissue Weston hands me.

Becca moves into place and grins at me as she drops flower petals by the handful on the sand. She looks *so* beautiful.

"I love you so much," I tell her when she reaches me. I kiss her cheek and she hugs me before going to sit down by my mom.

My heart is thudding out of my chest when Poppy appears.

She comes into view, walking toward me in a dress that's elegant and sexy, hugging her body in a way that makes me swallow hard. Her hair is down, and it catches in the sunlight. I've never seen anyone so beautiful. I can't wait to peel that dress off of her later, but for now, I just want to memorize every detail. She smiles at a few people, but then her eyes find mine and she walks toward me with purpose.

"I love you," I whisper when she reaches me.

"I love you," she whispers back.

Penn is in a nice suit, wearing a more official clerical collar just for fun.

"I've teased Bowie mercilessly about being the last man standing with me. Everyone's getting married and now I'm the lone wolf," he says, smiling at the crowd. "But when I met Poppy and saw her with Bowie, I knew she was worth going down for the count. The two of you have something special," he says to us. "A love that will stand the test of time. And I'm just glad that I have the privilege of witnessing it, proud that I can give my stamp of approval…I mean, I got ordained for this,"—everyone laughs—"so I think it's safe to say, I am behind you one hundred percent. And I'm not the only one. You're surrounded today by so many people who love you. You're both the kind of people who would do anything for anyone, and we want you to know that you're not alone. We've got your back, and we will support you through whatever life brings."

My throat tightens and I swallow hard, blinking back unshed tears.

"Bowie and Poppy have prepared vows," Penn says, and I get a burst of pride over how official he sounds. He nods at us and I look at Poppy. Her hands are already in mine and I squeeze them.

"You look beautiful," I tell her.

"Thank you," she whispers. "So do you." Her lips lift and the audience laughs.

"Before I met you, I never allowed myself to dream too large or hope too brightly. I built walls around my heart, convinced I had all I needed. Then you walked into my world, quietly and unexpectedly, yet with such a powerful impact. Becca knew you were right for me before I did."

The audience laughs again.

"Yes!" Becca agrees.

"Your kindness softened me, your laughter steadied me, and your love made me believe in possibilities. You've made me a better man, a better father, a better human than I thought possible.

"Today, I promise you that I will never stop showing up for you. I will celebrate all the wins and hold you through all the losses. I will listen and learn and grow beside you. I will protect our family and love you without limits. I vow to honor the trust you've placed in me, every day, for all the days to come.

"I have been unsure of so much in the past, but when I look at you, I know with absolute certainty: I am where I am meant to be, by your side, forever. I love you, Poppy."

Poppy presses her trembling lips together and dabs her eyes with a lacy cloth.

"I love *you*, Bowie. I never imagined that love could feel so honest, so gentle and strong all at once. You saw the person I was—clumsy, blunt, and always hopeful—and you never asked me to be anyone else. You've shown me that love is not only about holding on when it's easy, but it's about standing together when life is messy and unpredictable. Your patience, your quiet strength, and the way you love my heart and our children have filled me up with more joy than I thought possible. Your hair is also really amazing."

Everyone cracks up and there are a few whistles and catcalls.

"Today, I promise to cherish the man you are and the man you strive to be. You're perfect to me, and I can't wait to laugh and cry with you for the rest of our lives. I love you so much, today and forever."

I put my hand on her cheek, thumbing away the tear, and lean in to kiss her softly.

"Ahh…I guess I'll allow that," Penn says, laughing.

When it's time for the rings, Poppy turns to get hers and I turn to Rhodes. He makes a clicking sound with his mouth and Bogey runs up, dressed in a bowtie. He twirls around twice and Rhodes bends down and retrieves the ring that's connected to his tie. Once the ring is in Rhodes' hand, confetti shoots out of Bogey's bowtie as he runs back to his spot.

There's applause and I turn to Rhodes.

"How in the hell—" I ask.

"Dog whisperer," he says smugly.

We exchange rings and before we're pronounced husband and wife, Poppy turns and looks at Becca. Marley hands Poppy a beautiful frame, and my eyes water when I see what it is. I didn't realize Poppy wanted to do this in front of everyone, and once I do, the waterworks start flowing. *This woman.*

"Becca, can you come up here, please?" she says, smiling at Becca.

Becca jumps up, always ecstatic to do what Poppy asks of her.

Poppy takes Becca's hand.

"You have a picture for me," Becca says, excited.

"Yes, and I want to tell you what it says," Poppy says, holding the frame up for Becca to see. "It says that I'm officially your mom now." She points at their names. "See, right there? Becca Fox has officially been adopted by Poppy Fox. That means I'm your mom forever and forever."

"You are?" Becca gasps.

"Yes," Poppy says. She puts her arms around Becca and they hug. "You can call me whatever you want, Poppy or Mom or Mommy…"

"I call you my mom," she says, sounding like a teenager all of a sudden. She beams at me. "Daddy, I have a mom!"

"Yes, my sweet girl. You do."

She turns to the crowd and yells, "I have a mom!"

Everyone cheers and the three of us huddle into a hug.

"Perfect," Poppy says, laughing through her tears.

I am a fucking puddle. When Poppy asked about adopting Becca, I was also a puddle. I've never considered asking Adriane to sign over her rights before, because I've always hoped she'd eventually want to have some part in Becca's life. For Becca's sake, I've wanted that door to always be open, but Adriane has proven she has no intention of ever being in Becca's life. When Adriane didn't have any objection to relinquishing her rights, I knew even more that this was the right thing.

Poppy isn't going anywhere. She's loved Becca from day one and the bond they have gets stronger every day.

Everyone keeps clapping and cheering. I look back and the guys are wiping their eyes. Softies, the whole lot of them.

"It's official," Penn says. "Introducing…the Fox family. Bowie, you may kiss your bride now."

I dip Poppy back and kiss her. Long after the music starts playing and we're supposed to be walking down the aisle, I'm still kissing her. I don't plan on ever stopping.

EPILOGUE
BEACH VIBES

BOWIE

I walk into Luminary with Jonas cradled in one arm, a diaper bag slung over my shoulder. The bells jingle overhead and before Clara can even clear her throat and point toward the makeshift dance zone, I launch into a ridiculous little jig. Sort of a two-step shuffle combined with a wiggly shoulder move. Jonas bounces gently in my arm, eyes wide, and then he lets out a high-pitched squeal that echoes through the shop.

Clara's jaw drops and I think she might collapse from surprise.

Instead, her eyes get misty, and she claps a hand to her heart. "I just love seeing you like this," she says, her voice thick.

I grin at her. She's not the first person I've heard this from, and I'm more aware than ever that I must have been a real barrel of laughs before Poppy turned my life around.

"You're looking awfully happy for a man who didn't win the Super Bowl," Walter grumps.

"Yes, I am," I say, and he rears back in surprise.

"Harumph," Marv says.

"I just got back from my honeymoon and it was incredible," I tell them, walking past their table. I lift Jonas's hand and have him wave, and they stare at me in shock.

The guys are waiting for me. It's been a struggle to get anywhere on time since having Jonas. I think I'm only five minutes late, so I'm counting it as a win. Everyone greets us happily, still looking like they're riding the good vibe waves from our vacation.

"How's everyone doing?" I ask, settling Jonas onto my lap.

Everyone goes on over him and he laughs at them. He laughs at everything, it's the absolute best.

Penn leans forward, clearing his throat. He looks oddly bashful. "So…I sort of met someone."

We all perk up instantly, sitting up straighter.

"What?" Rhodes demands.

Penn drums his fingers on the table. "It was actually at the wedding…like, the night before the ceremony. I was making sure everything was right for you, Bowie, and I ran into this woman, Addy. We hit it off, talked for a long time, had a drink…other things happened. It was, I don't know. Different."

"Is that why you kept disappearing during that weekend?" Weston says, giving Penn a slight shrug.

Penn is sheepish as he nods. "Not my finest hour, I know, but fuck me, she was beautiful."

"Who was she?" I ask, intrigued. "I don't know anyone named Addy. One of our guests? A friend of someone?"

Penn shakes his head, frustration in his eyes. "I'm not sure. I think she must have been a guest at the resort because I told her I was there for a wedding and she didn't say she was. I was so busy running around, making sure I had everything down for the ceremony, and then…I never saw her again after that night."

Henley tilts his head. "You're telling me you had a night like that and you didn't get a number, a last name, a social media handle?"

"I don't typically!" Penn throws his hands up in the air. "And I was so shaken up over how good it was, I wasn't thinking! We were just so in the moment, and I thought I'd see her again."

Rhodes chuckles. "And you're still thinking about her. We need to figure out who she is. If you're still thinking about her, that's…shit…you know what that means."

"Don't say it." Penn exhales heavily, shoulders slumping. "Forget about it. The wedding, the re-wedding, whatever we're calling it…it was spectacular. It was probably just the romance in the air that had me making more out of it than it was." He runs his hands through his hair, looking genuinely perplexed. "Just a lingering aftereffect of a perfect night. And I mean, was that not the most spectacular wedding?" he says, sitting up straighter. His chest puffs with pride, as if he personally orchestrated not only the ceremony, but the perfect ocean breeze and sunset as well.

Henley raises his coffee cup. "It was indeed spectacular. I'll give you that, Reverend Penn."

Weston laughs in his mug, and Rhodes smirks as he nods. Jonas slams the Penn rattle on the table and Penn flinches.

"I didn't really think through that gift," he says. "It's jarring, seeing my face slammed like that."

We all laugh. I press a light kiss to Jonas's forehead before taking a sip of my coffee. I grin at Penn. "So, what's the plan? Gonna track her down?"

Penn shrugs. "Maybe. Or maybe I'll just chalk it up to being a magical moment and leave it at that." But he doesn't sound convinced. Whoever this girl was really got to him.

He pulls out The Single Dad Playbook and sets it on the table.

I tug it toward me.

I've been told that I have a knack for seeing patterns.
It was regarding football,
but I like to think I've carried that over
into my life as well.
So much is changing for all of us,
and here are the patterns I'm seeing in us.
I've seen you guys become
the best husbands and fathers.
I already knew you were the best friends.
But seeing you open your hearts to love...
It's been so inspiring.
I love that we laugh more now.
Trust more.

*Let more people in.
We've become men who wear
our hearts on our sleeves,
and I'm so fucking proud of us.
~Henley*

"I'm really fucking proud of us too," I say thickly.

"Are you crying?" Rhodes asks, shocked. "Let me read that."

"No, I'm not crying!" I say, laughing because clearly, I am talking through blurry eyes. "What the fuck has happened to me? How did falling in love turn me into such a sap?"

Weston reads the entry and clears his throat, blinking up at the ceiling.

"Hell no, I'm not doing it," Penn says, shaking his head. "You can keep your love crap to yourselves and I will remain sap-free, thank you very much."

Rhodes points at Henley's entry, his eyes shining. "I dare you to read that and not weep," he says to Penn.

Sighing, Penn pulls the book over and reads. When he's done, he presses his palms into his eyes. *"Goddammit."*

We laugh and tease Penn mercilessly, still the same motherfuckers even while we're evolving.

Life is full of surprises. Good ones, mostly. I happened to hit a gold mine with Poppy, and I'll never stop being grateful for it.

Want more Bowie and Poppy? Click here!
https://bookhip.com/XAKDGSL

. . .

**For Penns' story
pre order Crazy Love Here!**
https://geni.us/Crazylove

CRAZY LOVE COMING SOON!

Prologue
Screeching Halt

PENN

February

The sun is just starting to set over the turquoise waters of the Bahamas and I'm trying not to freak out over this ceremony. I'm officiating the wedding of one of my best friends tomorrow—Bowie Fox. I technically married him and Poppy in their hospital room while they were giving birth to their baby, but this is the polished-up, beautiful version. The pressure is on. I've gotta get this right.

I try out a few lines under my breath as I stare out at the water, willing it to calm me. "Marriage is like the ocean—vast, mysterious, and full of surprises." I wince. "Nope. Too deep. Literally."

"You might want to avoid ocean metaphors unless you're

comparing love to a hurricane…which *has* been done, I suppose."

My thoughts halt like a record scratch when I look over and see an impossibly gorgeous woman staring out pensively at the ocean. Her long, black hair cascades down her back and her skin looks bronzed in this light. She's wearing a white tank top and *short* white shorts and she is wearing them *well*.

When her eyes meet mine, she gives me an amused smirk and I get this weird ping in my gut. Like I just went skydiving and lost my stomach.

"Caught me practicing," I say sheepishly. "I'm marrying my friends tomorrow."

Her eyebrows lift. "You're marrying your friends…"

"I mean, I'm officiating…" I tug on my shirt, feeling hot all of a sudden.

"And you're nervous?" Her gaze drifts over my face and I swallow hard but then try to play it off.

"I-no. Not really. I—" I run my hands through my hair and laugh. "Well, yeah. I am. Words matter, you know? I love my friends and they're trusting me to set the tone for their wedding…and the rest of their lives. No pressure or anything."

Her smirk widens into a smile and I'm done. Sign me up. I'm in.

"Well, preacher man, I think you'll be just fine."

"Preacher man?" I volley, a grin taking over my entire face.

Damn, she's pretty.

"Sounds like it fits." She gives a slight shrug and my eyes drop to her delicate shoulder. Her skin looks so soft and it takes effort to drag my eyes away from her body, but her big brown eyes and pouty lips are oh so alluring, so the payoff is still huge when I do.

"Trust me, I am not...holy."

There's a beat where we stare at each other. My eyes drop to her mouth and stay fixated there for a few seconds. God, I've never wanted to kiss someone so badly in all my life. Not after just meeting, for Christ's sake, and honestly...kissing isn't really my thing. I find kissing way more intimate than sex.

"I have just the thing to help you relax," she says.

"Oh...*really*." I have to say I'm surprised that she's going there so soon, but you won't find me complaining.

"Yes, follow me." She turns and walks toward the resort, turning once to look at me over her shoulder. She smiles when she sees that I'm following, and my stomach does that free-fall again...it's the weirdest thing.

I'm not sure where this girl is leading me, but I'm beyond caring. I take her hand and let her guide me through the sandy paths of the resort.

"Where are you taking me?" I ask.

"Patience is a virtue," she teases.

"Virtue is overrated."

"Says the preacher man."

I laugh. "Right. Preacher man. Name's actually Penn. What's yours?"

"Addy."

The path opens up and there's a secluded section of the beach that wasn't visible before, and a group of people are stretching.

"What—" I gasp when a group of flamingos move between the people. Some might think they're beautiful, and I guess they are in an odd, gangly, *terrifying* way.

"Yoga with flamingos," Addy announces, like it's a perfectly normal thing to do...ever. "This will help you relax for sure."

"I assure you it will not," I say under my breath. Louder, I say, "Yoga with that?" I point to a flamingo that has locked eyes with me, its head tilted as if to say, *You lookin' at me?*

She laughs, and fuck me, if my dick doesn't respond in spite of the flamingo staring me down like a mob boss.

"You're not scared of flamingos, are you?" she asks.

"Are you sure this is a good idea?" I back up a step. "That one is looking at me funny."

She glances at the bird, her grin widening. "You'll be fine. Look, they're used to people." She points at another bird being petted by a guest. That one does look sweeter, far less Al Capone. "Besides, don't you want to try something new? Live a little?"

"I was thinking more along the lines of a cocktail I haven't tried before…with a gorgeous woman…whose name starts with an A."

One of her shoulders lifts and she bats her eyelashes. "Aw, thank you." Her smile deepens and she gives me a pointed look. "Maybe we can have that cocktail after the yoga."

"Fine," I mutter. "But if I get pecked to death, I'm haunting you."

She laughs and I'd appreciate that it sounds like music if I wasn't worried for my life.

We join the group and I do my best to focus on the instructor's overly serene voice instead of Capone the flamingo, who seems *very* interested in my mat. It begins innocently enough—stretching, deep breaths, the usual yoga stuff. But then, as I'm bent into what the instructor calls Warrior II, Capone decides to move in closer. As in, absolutely no respect for my personal boundaries whatsoever.

"Hey, dude. Back off," I say between my teeth.

He waddles closer and pecks at my foot.

"Hey!" I yelp.

The bastard stands on my mat, staring me down like I owe him something.

"What do you want from me?" I ask, trying to give it the evil eye.

Addy bursts out laughing. "I think she likes you!"

"There's no way this one is a female. He's sizing me up for dinner," I mutter. When it steps closer, I try to shoo it away. The flamingo responds by flapping its wings and letting out an ear-splitting squawk that startles me so much, I trip over my own feet and fall flat on my back.

The instructor gasps and hurries over when the flamingo's face dips closer to mine. I hear a camera click from a person nearby and cover my face to avoid being pecked to death. It's not fun to be under a pileup on the football field by a three-hundred-pound freight train, but this flamingo right now with that sharp, hooked beak that's deceptively precise and those beady little eyes that scream chaos? That's a fucking horror show.

Instead of the peck of death, I feel a soft hand on my arm and peek between my hands. Addy is laughing so hard, she's clutching her side, but with the other hand, she tries to pull me up.

"Okay," she says between laughing. "Maybe yoga with flamingos isn't your thing."

"It's so not," I tell her, scrambling to my feet. "Let's get out of here before he calls for backup."

We bolt from the beach, and now that I have some distance from the claws of Satan, I can see a little bit of the humor in the situation. We end up at the tiki bar. Addy leans into me, still laughing, her eyes sparkling in the sunset.

I put my arms around her, leaning in to whisper, "We survived. Barely."

"I'll buy you a drink to make up for it," she says softly.

"Oh no. I'm buying you a drink. I need to make sure you stick around long enough for me to recover my dignity."

She giggles. "It will be hard to get that image of you dominated by the flamingo out of my head, preacher man."

I turn to face her, my hands going to either side of her face, as I dip down, eyes level with hers. "Tell me what I have to do," I say huskily.

She bites her lower lip to keep from laughing and I struggle to keep from laughing myself, but this close to her, barely a breath between us…it's intoxicating.

"Give me a new memory," she whispers.

The air between us is charged. I feel her warmth, her breath mingling with mine, the faintest scent of her perfume. She isn't just beautiful, she's magnetic—a force pulling me in until the distance becomes unbearable.

There's nothing left to do but close the distance between us. It's a *need*.

My thumb trails the curve of her jaw and her eyes are steady and unflinching, like she can see straight into the part of me I don't show anyone.

And just like that, I give in.

When our lips meet, it isn't fireworks—it's a detonation. A deep, bone-shaking, soul-rattling detonation that shatters me into pieces and rebuilds me in the same instant. Her lips are so soft, but the kiss isn't. It's raw, consuming. It's a thousand unspoken words all pouring out at once.

Time stops. The noise in the bar falls away. There's no past, no future, only this moment with her.

She kisses me back with the same abandon I feel. It's intense, the way we crash into each other with everything in us.

When we finally break apart, my forehead rests against hers, both of us breathing hard.

"That was…the best thing I've ever felt," I say.

"Yeah," she says breathlessly.

Just then an annoying sound erupts from my phone. Dammit. My alarm. I'd forgotten I'd even set it, but it's a good thing or I think I would've remained in this stunned stupor for a while.

"I can't believe this. I've gotta go. The rehearsal dinner. Come with me? My friends won't mind."

She wrinkles her nose. "Oh, no. I couldn't."

"Really, it'll be okay." My face falls when she shakes her head. "Okay, meet me afterward? Right here? I'll be back by nine."

She lifts her chin, eyes dancing with amusement. "You sure you can pull that off?"

I smile. "I'm determined."

She studies me for a second before nodding. "Okay, I'll be here."

***

The second I walk in, I spot her. I'm conflicted about leaving Bowie's rehearsal dinner until I see Addy sitting in a dark corner, twisting the stem of her martini glass between her fingers. She's the kind of girl who owns the room without even trying.

I walk over, slipping onto the stool next to her. "Told you I'd be here, beautiful."

She doesn't look at me right away, just takes a slow sip of her drink. "Right on time too."

"You thought I wouldn't show?"

She tilts her head toward me, her lips curving up. "I considered it."

"You wound me."

"Do I?" she asks, playfully.

"Deeply." I place a hand over my heart and lean in. "Tell me what's on your mind."

I never ask women this because that's a minefield waiting to explode, but I genuinely want to know with her.

Her eyes narrow.

"Uh-oh." I laugh when she doesn't say anything, just studies me. "You're plotting something. Based on previous experience when you get that look, it means trouble. No more flamingos tonight." I lift my hands up.

She exhales dramatically. "Damn it. You catch on way too fast."

I smirk. "What are you scheming?"

"Not so fast. How was the rehearsal dinner?"

"It was great. Good food. Everyone's so happy to be here, happy to be together…"

Her nose crinkles up. "I feel bad for taking you away from your friends."

I shake my head. "We have fun whenever we're together. You should meet them. Tomorrow?" I ask hopefully.

She grins and gets that mischievous look again.

"So, what were you thinking about when I got here?" I take her hand and thread my fingers in hers.

She turns in her seat, facing me. "Whether or not I should kiss you again."

Heat licks up my spine. "And?"

"I mean, the first kiss was good…"

"Good?" I scoff. "Addy, that kiss deserved a standing O."

She lifts a shoulder. "Eh. Seven out of ten."

"Seven? Why does that crush my ego into dust?"

She bites her lip to keep from laughing. "Okay, eight."

"Unbelievable," I mutter. "You *loved* it."

She leans in, close enough that I smell the soft vanilla and coconut scent of her skin. "Maybe you should remind me," she whispers.

That's all the invitation I need.

I kiss her, slow and deep, letting it build. And holy hell, it's even better than the first time. The way she melts into me after luring me in with her sexy mouth—I'm gone.

She lets out a small, satisfied hum against my lips, and I smile against her mouth. "Still an eight?"

"Nine," she says, breathless. "But if we keep going, I *might* consider a ten."

"Let's test that theory."

I stand up and hold out my hand, and she takes it, smiling up at me. I lead her to the elevators, both of us buzzing with anticipation. By the time we reach my room, we barely make it inside before my hands are on her waist, her fingers threading through my hair. It's ridiculous how fucking good this feels with her.

She presses against me, her breath warm against my jaw. "You always move this fast?"

I chuckle, brushing my lips against her ear. "I could kiss you all night long and die happy…and no, I do *not* always work like that."

Her breath hitches. "You like kissing me?"

"More than I should," I admit, my voice rough.

She pulls me down for another kiss, and I swear, I could get lost in her mouth forever.

And then—

My phone rings.

I groan against her lips and consider ignoring the call, but when I see Rhodes' name on the screen, I exhale sharply. "I have to take this.

She steps back and nods. "It's okay. Go ahead."

I answer. "Rhodes?"

"Hey, man. I haven't seen you in a while and need a favor. Some of Poppy's friends had a little too much to drink and Elle and I are going to take them to their rooms. Any chance you could help us handle them? We're still at the restaurant. It's like herding cats over here."

I crinkle up my face, giving Addy an apologetic look. "Yeah, I'll be right there."

When I hang up, I turn to Addy, brushing my fingers along her jaw before kissing her softly. I just can't resist those lips. She is a taste that leaves me feeling both sated and hungry. I drag myself away and stare at her.

"You're so beautiful, Addy."

Her cheeks flame and I can't stop smiling.

"Don't move," I tell her. "I'll be right back. I need to help wrangle some people back to their hotel rooms."

She smiles, giving me one more quick kiss. "Hurry back."

I walk backwards, still staring at her like I've been struck by lightning because that's how I feel. "I promise you, I will be so fast."

"Go, go." She laughs.

I grin and bolt out of the door, already desperate to get back to her.

Of course it takes longer than expected. Poppy's friends are nice and so happy to be on a tropical getaway, but they are hard to finagle drunk. Fifteen minutes stretches into thirty and I'm sweating by the time I reach my door.

When I walk into my hotel room…she's gone.

For Penns' story
pre order Crazy Love Here!
https://geni.us/Crazylove

ACKNOWLEDGMENTS

This book was a joy to write, but I had so much help! To the following people, I love you all SO MUCH.

To my husband, Nate, and kids, Greyley & Kira, and Indigo, thank you for supporting my dreams and being so excited with me about this whole thing. You have my whole heart and then some. Nate, thank you for taking the rap to the next level. :) Love you so.

Georgie Grinstead, thank you from the bottom of my heart for believing in me.

Christine Estevez, thank you for being a constant in my life.

Natalie Burtner, thank you for always saying yes…you can say no too. :)

Kelly Yates, thank you for your help with this book. Your input was invaluable and so much fun!

Katie Friend, thank you for loving Bowie from the get-go.

Kira Sabin, your watercolor artwork is magical. YOU are magical.

Kess Fennell, thank you for indulging me. I love every bit of artwork you've ever made for me.

Emily Wittig, thank you for being so lovely and for the beautiful covers.

Laura Pavlov and Catherine Cowles, the love chain, there are no words to express how grateful I am for you both.

To the VPR team, thank you, thank you, thank you! Nina, Kim, Valentine, Charlie, Christine, Sarah, Josette, Meagan,

Kelley, Ratula, Tiffany, Stephanie, Jaime, Amy, Jill, Megan, Emma, and Jess, thank you for EVERYTHING!

To the Lyric team, Kim Gilmour and Katie Robinson, you're so great!

J.F. Harding and Samantha Brentmoor, thank you for bringing these characters to life in audio. And Lily D. Moore, I am so honored to have your voice on this book—thank you!

Thank you to The Seymour Agency!

And huge thanks and love and hugs to Christine Bowden, Tosha Khoury, Courtney Nunness, Gracelyn Szynal, Kalie Phillips, Steve & Jill Erickson, Savita Naik, Claire Contreras, Tarryn Fisher, Troi Atkinson, Phyllis Atkinson, David Atkinson, Destini Simmons, Terrijo Montgomery, and Jesse Nava. Anthony Colletti, that goes for you too. And Winston, my sidekick who makes me smile every day.

Thank you to every reader, bookstagrammer, booktoker, fill-in-the-blank for whoever gives my books a try! Thanks for the reviews, the sweet messages, the beautiful collages, and for spreading the word about my books. I couldn't do it without you!

XO,
Willow

ALSO BY WILLOW ASTER

The Single Dad Playbook Series

Mad Love

Secret Love

Reckless Love

Wicked Love

Crazy Love

Landmark Mountain Series

Unforgettable

Someday

Irresistible

Falling

Stay

Standalones with Interconnected Characters

Summertime

Autumn Nights

Kingdoms of Sin Series

Downfall

Exposed

Ruin

Pride

Standalones

True Love Story

Fade to Red

In the Fields

Maybe Maby (also available on all retailer sites)

Lilith (also available on all retailer sites)

Miles Apart (also available on all retailer sites)

Falling in Eden

The G.D. Taylors Series with Laura Pavlov

Wanted Wed or Alive

The Bold and the Bullheaded

Another Motherfaker

Don't Cry Over Spilled MILF

Friends with Benefactors

The End of Men Series with Tarryn Fisher

Folsom

Jackal

FOLLOW ME

JOIN MY MASTER LIST…
https://bit.ly/3CMKz5y

Website willowaster.com
Facebook @willowasterauthor
Instagram @willowaster
Amazon @willowaster
Bookbub @willow-aster
TikTok @willowaster1
Goodreads @willow_aster
Asters group @Astersgroup
Pinterest@willowaster

www.ingramcontent.com/pod-product-compliance
Ingram Content Group UK Ltd.
Pitfield, Milton Keynes, MK11 3LW, UK
UKHW040630040425
456976UK00002B/149